PETER VANSITTART was born in 1920 and educated at Haileybury and Worcester College, Oxford. He has taught and lectured on English and History, and he reviews for various leading newspapers and periodicals. He is the author of more than twenty-one novels, three books for children and he has also written or compiled seven books of non-fiction, including *Voices from the Great War*, a narrative anthology which was adapted for the stage. His autobiographical book, *Paths from a White Horse*, subtitled *A Writer's Memoir* and published in 1985, received high praise from critics. In 1969 he won the Society of Authors Travelling Scholarship, and in 1981 he was one of six recipients of the first Writers' Bursaries awarded by the Arts Council.

Peter Owen have published eight of Peter Vansittart's novels: *The Story Teller* (1968); *Pastimes of a Red Summer* (1969); *Landlord* (1970); *Quintet* (1976); *Lancelot* (1978); *The Death of Robin Hood* (1981); *Three Six Seven* (1983); *The Tournament* (1984); and a work of non-fiction, *Worlds and Underworlds: Anglo-European History through the Centuries* (1974).

ASPECTS OF FEELING

BY THE SAME AUTHOR
(published by Peter Owen)

FICTION
The Story Teller
Pastimes of a Red Summer
Landlord
Quintet
Lancelot
The Death of Robin Hood
Three Six Seven
The Tournament

NON-FICTION
Worlds and Underworlds: Anglo-European History
through the Centuries

PETER VANSITTART

ASPECTS OF FEELING

A Novel

United States distributor
DUFOUR EDITIONS, INC.
Booksellers and Publishers
Chester Springs, PA 19425
215-458-5005

PETER OWEN · LONDON

ISBN 0 7206 0637 3

All Rights Reserved. No part of this publication may be reproduced in any form or by any means without the prior permission of the publishers.

PETER OWEN PUBLISHERS
73 Kenway Road London SW5 0RE

First published in Great Britain 1986
© Peter Vansittart 1986

Photoset and printed in Great Britain by
Redwood Burn Limited Trowbridge Wiltshire

To Freddie

and in loving memory of Vanessa

ACKNOWLEDGEMENTS

For some material I am indebted to Nicholas Bethell for his book *The Last Secret* (New York: Basic Books, 1974); to Nikolai Tolstoy for *Victims of Yalta* (London: Hodder & Stoughton, 1977); and to Mark R. Elliott for *Pawns of Yalta* (Champaign, Ill.: University of Illinois Press, 1982). The lines quoted on page 12 are from 'Mud' by Richard Church.

One section of this novel was published in *Firebird*, edited by Robin Robertson (Penguin, 1985).

P.V.

PROLOGUE

*

But man can never plumb the depths of his own being; his image is not to be discovered in the extent of the knowledge he acquires but in the questions he asks.

André Malraux

You can't enter into an extreme situation.... No one has much capacity for feeling. It could be something we're all losing. There are times that it frightens me. I'd choose for us to have bad feeling than not to feel at all. I'd choose for us to be cruel with feeling than to be cruel without. The evidence is that's how the maximum horrors have been done.

C. P. Snow

Usually after dark, Bryce, who liked to call herself the Staff, with a sudden, not always understandable wink, would talk with the children, sometimes telling the future with cherrystones. Della had the prospect of becoming a bishop or engineer. She and Graham heard from Bryce what Bayard claimed to have long known, that adults, Bluebeard, Bing Crosby, Cleopatra, even Laurel and Hardy, have extraordinary secrets.

'That Mr Costard, down in the village ...' – Bryce lowered her voice, as if over a disreputable tribe buried in some hole – 'knows more than he should. His own daughter!' Her wink was fat, then stubbed out on a face Bayard called a mess of paste. 'You hear such things,' he now said, bored, though the others did not. Bayard obviously heard nothing else. He sometimes mentioned that he was five centuries old, an unsatisfactory tale, though just possibly not an absolute fib. Uncle Roger had said that when five people say the same thing, only one is telling the truth. As for Mr Costard, few grown-ups knew anything of children, or they had forgotten. The Kirklands, Uncle Roger and Aunt Janet, very sensibly, did not have any.

'Evil,' Bryce ended. Always in rat black, she had tiny, repellent hands moving so quickly that Della could never prove what she sometimes suspected, that a finger or two were sometimes missing. The others never noticed, or seemed not to. You did not discuss such matters, but suspicions remained, breeding like money in the bank. Bryce's brother had been in the Great War, shot to pieces for all to see. Perhaps, at night, he took off her fingers and could forget to put them back.

Bryce also knew why Margaret in the kitchen was lost for ever. 'Some aren't careful.' Also that when one star flared brighter than others, hell was unusually full. Bayard, however, with his thin, disobliging smile, afterwards declared that this was superstitious rot. Hell had long been closed, absolutely full up, because of the popes' sins. One pope indeed ... he sighed, but said no more.

Bayard could smile but never laughed, and perhaps couldn't. He would repeat, rather importantly, bits from the wireless. 'The dollar has fallen sharply in New York.' There seemed only one dollar, as if dropped from a skyscraper and bouncing about the streets chased by fat men falling over each other's hats.

Once, after Bryce had spoken, he looked puzzled. 'Did you speak? Or did your nose waggle?' Actually, he revealed afterwards, she had laid an egg.

Graham and Della, distantly related, spent holidays at Dragon House because their parents helped govern India, where violent suns and horrid water destroyed children, and 'The Mutiny' hovered like an indistinct crucifixion. Bayard's origins were undisclosed; he himself, with recollections of those five centuries, was what many would call an unreliable witness.

In England, you feared not mutiny but having to go on the

panel, presumably laid flat on a coffin lid.

Bayard moved confidently between adults like a packet-boat between fleets. Like them, he used expressions like Australian Common Law Wife, someone who lived on the Fat of the Land, yet they never seemed greatly pleased. He could be an heir without a realm, or virgin born, like so many used to be, or an orphan found on Plynlimon, a mountain in Wales. He was also a type of spy, speaking confidently about Moscow Trials, mysteriously different from Badminton Trials, where Aunt Janet rode. He was amused by Mr Baldwin, Mr Ramsay Mac, and knew that Mr Joe Louis would knock over Mr James L. Braddock, who wanted to stop him. He might well become a Private Secretary, or even Consultant.

Graham agreed that interesting names came from Moscow. Radek, Bukharin, Stalin, Suvorov, they sounded like planets but were more likely to resemble poor Margaret or Mr Costard, knowing what they should not.

Bayard was mischievous but seldom proved really mistaken. He used words like illegitimate, explaining that it meant an illegal operation.

'Is Mr Clavering illegitimate?'

Graham's blue, unsteady eyes, not very level, under massed, yellowy hair, on square, high-cheeked face soiled as a pirate's even after washing, always wanted a simple answer, though only from Janet did he often get it, and very seldom from Bayard, whose shrug was copied from, or exchanged with, the great actor Leslie Howard. Bayard's own eyes moved more than his shoulders, and his shoulders usually more than anything else. He was thin, without much eyebrow, and with light hair and eyes of no very obvious colour, a droop from the mouth making him look slightly disapproving. His know-all chilliness could anger Graham, but also dismay him. Graham's strength was useless against Bayard, who never fought and, if consenting to tennis, refused to play for points, leaving himself somehow unbeatable.

'That remains undecided,' Bayard said. 'You must wait until you see Mr Clavering in his bath.'

They had not yet done so and might have to consult Uncle Roger.

Roger Knowles Kirkland was a high *sans peur*; were he to turn his ring, there might float up a twinkling pagoda, troubled cavern, moonlit isle carved from a gigantic acorn, which Della had occasionally observed, without precisely seeing. He knew people like Sir Charles Kingsford-Smith, the airman, who flew even faster than those winged Greeks, themselves so swift that they never had time to dress.

Between sundown and dawn losers could win, the meek turn terrible before inheriting the earth, and ghastly riders be silently abroad. But the morning could promise marvels. A Della can lie in bed, hearing birds and trees. Slowly the buds of light unfold, the room blinks as the birds fly past. Swallows, swallows. The fields squared out on Hackpen Hill will be picking up their separate greens and yellows, softs and hards, red soil glinting beneath.

Watching the light free itself, making the air sparkle, Della thought of Graham. He was fiercely excited by the coin he had found and which had made him dream. He had seen a monster, porpoise-snouted, with a tail like an S. Then a snake, crawling over a Z. Breaking in two, the snake made twin circles which quickly became squares, under two suns. What did it mean? Nothing very much, Bayard said, only Picts, in his own experience not much good.

Uncle Roger said that Picts had indeed reached these parts, though indeed with no very generous intentions.

She herself probably dreamed better than Graham or Bayard. Sleep was the start of a green pit scratched with important signs that soon faded: at the bottom lay a frightful gleam, like a dentist's chair or sleeping cobra. This she could share only with Graham and Janet, for Bayard had the knack of making ordinary things atrocious. Why need he say that, in the lavatory, everyone sheds more microbes than the population of the entire world?

No microbe was now in sight. All was orderly as a triangle. Dew glittered on leaves in blue air while the house eased itself into a lovely day. The mirror caught her greenish eyes, she touched her black straight hair. A pretty girl, Bayard said, can always make a packet, but was she pretty? Mirror, mirror on the wall gave many smiling replies but too often whispered 'others are better'.

The Claverings and others were coming to lunch. Rather

Prologue

boring. Mr Clavering always called his grown-up daughters 'You fellows' because he had hoped for sons. There was also to be a children's treasure-hunt, and this too might be tiresome. 'They want us out of the way.' Bayard might be less casual than he sounded, knowing one more secret.

Dragon House had chestnut-brown panels, black beams, grainy floors, and very few doors. Arches were everywhere, not always curtained, for, in these times, people lay in wait for important men who kept all rooms as open as they decently could. In school plays too, someone was always crouching behind the arras, then wishing he hadn't. Under each arch the light was different. Arches displayed half-seen paintings, fragments of tables and books, bright slices of carpets, flowers, Chinese screens, windows. Beyond them, the lake, meadows, woods. Even in stillness much was happening. The woods slowly let loose their shadows, gold shone from long grass, pigeons darted up like a puff of smoke and the moon waited to be lit. Paths, hillsides, opened like books. Strangers seated in the graveyard must be the dead, who, for special purposes, could be more than they sometimes pretended.

The study did have a door, but the long, shining lines of desk, the three red telephones, strict rows of books, thin sharp knife beside a heap of letters, presented hard angles of defence. The narrow, black-rimmed windows made pictures: of tiled, mossy, slanted roofs, like the creepers changing tints with the seasons; tall, knobbed chimneys, a white bridge, a courtyard with clambering vines and small green grapes hard as marbles, a pool, a bronze boy with a fish, naked. A furtive shape, mostly shadow, was known to hover there, but Janet said the presence was kindly.

Della and Graham, after breakfast, went to the study. 'You can find useful things there,' Bayard admitted, though, oddly, going only when Roger was absent. For him, people, animals, things, were either useful or useless. Roger, of course, was far from useless, but, though Bayard preferred adults to children, you seldom saw him and Roger talking together. Strange, for the others agreed that he often seemed the favourite, and he himself would speak of Roger with unusual respect, or caution, though without calling him 'Uncle'.

Graham sprawled, reading *The Times History of the War*, while Roger worked, writing between the telephones that reached to Moscow, Paris, Hollywood, Saffron Walden, even Buckingham Palace, filled with uniforms and lumbago. Earlier, Della had called him dirty, and it was true that he always looked rather smudged, as if he had brooded too long on a poem he had found in Janet's sitting-room:

> Twenty years ago
> My generation learnt
> To be afraid of mud.

We can't afford that, ever again, Roger had pronounced. So much couldn't be afforded. Yachts, Florida, a box at Covent Garden, though that could scarcely be expensive, even if it had silk butterflies and Japanese ribbons.

Flanders fields could show things worse than mud. In this very book was the photo of a man strapped to a chair, Bryce's brother perhaps, gas mask over his head like a huge frog's mask, soldiers digging. They would remain frozen for ever, like the people clinging to the mast of the *Titanic*, which they said even God couldn't sink, and the Guy screaming from the fire, and the Duke of Norfolk spattered with stars and medals and as if preserved in jelly. It was generally known that, in the Great War, armies shot as many of their own men as possible, to avoid paying pensions. Austria had been left only with generals, the Emperor left shivering in winds sweeping from Red Russia. In peacetime England, it was said at school that King George attended each hanging in person, then gave himself another medal.

Graham turned to another book, then looked up. 'Did you know, Uncle, from our village a weaver called Perrot and a saddler called Mauder went to join the Duke of Monmouth.'

Roger Kirkland smiled gravely. 'They would have ended as slaves in the Caribbean. They wouldn't have come back.' You knew from him that smiles had various purposes.

Della listened. She ventured here mostly to be with Roger. Like Merlin at the crossroads, he understood her. Last week, returning from London, he had brought a John Buchan for Graham, glass pen for Bayard, and, for herself, a red red rose. She now gazed past his trim, absorbed head, the hand travelling across paper, and enjoyed the paintings. Corot's trees, darkening around water glimmer, Van Gogh's flaring petals.

Nearby, on a small, dark table, were delphiniums Graham had chosen for Janet's birthday.

Of the books slabbed between glass and pewter, model ships, stuffed, plumed birds, golden candlesticks, she preferred atlases, finding enchantment in the mighty olive hunk of the USA wedged between crimson Canada and yellow Mexico: by Greenland, actually white, Iceland, where gods had died, improbably blue. She wanted to transform such calm colours to her own pictures. Miss Needham, ARA, assured her that they had style without discipline, and certainly the unexpected might upset her intentions. A bloodshot hole split open a cool green prairie, summer trees turned black, a river curved from lips dry and rusty. Like words that came uninvited. She had once astonished herself by declaring 'I will be changed to deadly stone'. Graham, cross because no one had laughed at his new joke, said the change might not be noticed.

Roger continued to write his important missives, Graham read on, about the Duke of Monmouth, killed only after six red chops on his white neck. The guests would be driving down green lanes, silver roads, greedy for lunch and secrets. Aunt Janet had promised her that three favourite wishes might be fulfilled, though she might have to wait.

I want to be rescued in a forest, to see the matchless, and have a boy who dazzles.

'Lentil soup,' Bryce whispered, handing the plates. The gleaming refectory table was crowded with silver, fruits, candlesticks, with Mr Clavering talking, talking, always so jolly, Mrs Clavering, painted too bright, very narrow, all tweed and pearl, looking as if anxious to jump into her soup. She always ate ferociously, her hand darting out for an extra potato, another wallop of sauce, like an animal which, her face implied, did not belong to her. Mr Clavering ate little, and was fat, but she remained like a string. 'You fellows' had not come but Sir Hartley Clegg was seated in state. He always seemed to have returned from somewhere important, without actually having been away. Farther off, in white next to Billy Fisher, the agent, was nervous Lady Clegg, who always visited the dentist in her best clothes and jewels, all colours flying, to give herself confidence, though, as everyone said, this probably terrified the man, or tempted him to steal. She still had what was called the remains of beauty though these were irregular, stuck on like stamps, rather carelessly. Such folk were useless, and, as if confirming it, Bayard was late for lunch.

Roger's grey eyes seldom blinked, and now looked at the empty chair as if professionally admiring it. 'Bayard, we can suppose, is still about his own concerns.' His laugh was amused, though, from the other end, Janet's gentle eye was almost worried. She was the younger, almost a girl, Della thought, less useful but beautiful in browns and golds, always happy to see you, though often grave even on laughing occasions. She was now very grave indeed, listening to Mrs Clavering's complaints of a hen which seemed to have persecuted her.

Roger, with hair black and smooth, in pale, slim trousers, dark jacket, silvery scarf, was an admiral on leave, or Black Prince with Honey Princess. They were obviously but not sloppily in love.

Aunt Janet was a Carole Lombard, name from underground waters flowing through crystal caverns measureless to man.

A short silence followed Roger's words. Mrs Clavering laid aside the anarchist hen. Then Janet spoke, low but distinct: 'He will come.' Words like those of the vicar.

A very small stir rippled through the ladies and gentlemen, perhaps uneasily, but was at once dammed by a cough from Lady Clegg. Apologetically, her rough cheeks crinkled into a smile. Billy Fisher waited for it to disappear, then mentioned the Coronation. 'You'll be going, Roger. You're invited, of course?'

'We've decided not to. Historical occasions, wouldn't you say, are only interesting when the outcome's uncertain. This scarcely applies. I'd certainly have watched poor silly David's performance. We can welcome his successor as a defence against fashion. For different reasons, the same can be said of Winston.'

He made staying away the more thrilling. Della and Graham both knew each other's thoughts. Poor silly King Edward had joined other Edwards, kings who hadn't come off.

'Roast lamb,' Bryce was saying. Nice crispy skin. Mrs Clavering, stranded between courses, seemed to be chewing her glass. Sunlight streamed into hair, flowers, silver, lay like shillings on Sir Hartley's specs. Talk was easy – investments, liners, racing, until finally Bayard entered, grey flannels, linen jacket, very neat, very posh, a club member, so unlike dirty Graham munching too many roast potatoes, watched enviously by Mrs Clavering.

'Ah, Bayard!' Roger's tone suggested that all the others had arrived too early.

Bayard only looked around like someone owed quiet applause. Seating himself beside Della he touched a wine bottle, as if to reassure himself of its vintage.

Again the talk resumed. The men's voices lay on top of their wives'. Bombs were banging Spain, the Government retreating to Barcelona, the Minister of the Interior fleeing to the interior. Mr Clavering was delighted. Despite his shape, he never ceased running for Parliament and never ceased to be pleased. He would have rejoiced at Jesus' cruel death or The Mutiny, or demanded his money back.

'In Moscow, I gather that our friend Suvorov is likely to be released. Well, they may yet have need of him. But that name of his ... his ancestor irritated the eighteenth century. He could have walloped Napoleon. It may not stand his descendant in very good stead.'

Sir Hartley drank too noisily, like an unstopped drain. His eyes, reddish under white hairs, looked sharply at sunlight on silver, which might expose its trade mark. 'You expect the worst, Clavering?'

'No, no. The best. Stalin's pulling our chestnuts out of the fire. I happen to know ... though Roger's the man to ask, of course.' But Clavering did not ask, and rumbled on: 'In fact, Hit and Muss are doing precisely the same, without knowing it.'

Uncle Roger seemed very interested, but perhaps wasn't. Aunt Janet gazed towards flower, butterfly, grass. The great Mussolini was about to meet Herr Hitler.

'It is difficult', Mr Clavering made it sound easy, 'to exaggerate the Duce's importance. Yet he remains the servant of his lord. The Italian King. The King Emperor of Italy. He'll keep the Huns in their place. And even if he doesn't, we've still got a rock. I don't mean Gib, I don't mean the Rock of Ages, of course. No.' He lifted one hand, 'No. The French Army.'

Sir Hartley nodded. 'Yes. Whoever loses, it won't be the Empire, though a few years ago I had my doubts. Our Mr Lansbury wants to abolish the Air Force. God Almighty, it chills the blood. But, if war does come, you know where you'll find me.'

'In church, darling?'

'No, no, of course not. In the front line.'

Mr Clavering's pig face moistened. 'There you have it. That Socialist, Stafford Cripps ... telling us that a British defeat by Germany wouldn't harm the working man! What about that, Roger?'

Roger Kirkland had finished his dish without seeming to use his hands. 'Did not the Israelites ...' – his eyes questioned them all, halted at Bayard – 'use an expression, "walking through raindrops"? It might, I suppose, describe our foreign policy.'

'I say ...' – Billy Fisher's voice waved like a flag – 'you saw the German Ambassador give the King the Hitler salute? Bounder!'

'Herr von Brickendrop, as the saying goes.'

'It's said well,' Roger considered it, 'another prisoner of the dream. The answer is that we must coax the best from an unfeeling and humourless universe which thrives on stupidity and men of wrath.' His smile included them all.

'Wasn't it you, Roger, who told us that Mr Eden was very impressed by Stalin's manners?'

Roger's reply could not be heard, save, apparently, by Bayard, who suddenly looked as if he'd forgotten something very important. But in an instant Roger was very distinct. 'There's a remark in Thucydides, isn't there....' He always spoke as if others knew more than he did, just as his dark, full hair, finely curved smile, made him younger than he probably was. 'He says that in the instant of triumph, when Fortune appears, without warning, beside him, the victor is in most deadly danger.'

'You know best, Roger. You know best.'

By manipulating her tumbler, Della could mirror them all, giving them not different but further identities. Trapped in glass, Sir Hartley became huge-nosed on body first tiny, then thin and pointed like a zeppelin, Mr Clavering absolutely round, Lady Gregg a squashy mass, Roger abnormally tall, very hard at the edges.

She hastily put it down and Bryce refilled it, as if to extinguish the visions.

'Children think they know better.' Mrs Clavering glanced at Bayard. She did not seem glad of it.

'Perhaps.' Roger Kirkland used that word when he meant something quite different.

About thirty children gathered at the treasure-hunt. Loudest was the Lloyd family: Susan, who sang hymns to the flowers, Rosamund, who read to them, Henry always rude to them, especially hollyhocks, and Nancy, who ate them. All were being marshalled by the curate, rugger-playing Mr Blakely Pyke, rather a hanger-on, Bayard said. Janet called him Blake, Roger, Mr Blow-me-Tight, and he had a small hole in his chin. Perhaps worms were at it. In his house was a picture of Jesus, pale olive, walking on waves in an offhand way. He organized picnics on Dartmoor, drives to sad Sedgemoor, to cricket matches. Too hot in the golden heat, his dog-collar like a slave's collar-ring, he called for silence, in the imbecile voice reserved for animals, children and foreigners.

'Now, everyone, listen carefully. There are twenty clues written plain for all to see, hidden between the lake and the rose garden. They lead to the treasure, which is easy to find, provided, of course, you know how to read.'

Bayard looked disapproving, a few tittered, the broad, veined face grinned. 'When the bell rings, at five, we'll all come back for tea on the lawn, very generously allowed us by Mr and Mrs Kirkland. If the treasure hasn't been found, a prize will go to whoever's nearest.'

A cheer, some claps. Graham was eager, he had crazes, and was now an emperor, ranging the veldt, the sierra, the prairie.

Mr Pyke waved a paper, like news of victory or reprieve. 'I'll now read out the first clue which will lead you to the second, and so on. Now. *Where my shadow falls you need wonder no more.*'

Who couldn't know that? After an instant of good-mannered hesitation, the coloured mob rushed towards the sundial behind the summer-house, Graham in the lead.

Della disliked running, save alone at night, but had started to follow. She rather liked the thought of treasure, and imagined doubloons in a ditch, guarded by a pretty snake. Almost at once she was halted by Bayard. He swiftly pulled her behind a yew hedge, his narrow face, pale, haughty eyes inveigling her into conspiracy. Certainly his dapper clothes were unsuited to children's games.

They leaned against the hedge. The gleeful children fled away. View halloo, they were hounds, on a short-cut to the ends of the earth. Already leaders were snatching the second clue, voices adrift, bits of confusion, then complaints, cries for Mr Pyke.

She did not ask Bayard, who seemed curtly satisfied. 'They won't be getting far.' He peered through a gap at distant flurried treasure-seekers. 'Meanwhile, we'd better lie low. Down there. Into the trees.'

Bayards never get lost, they are gamekeepers, stalking to exact destinations, pushing through bramble, branch, shadow, sometimes laying traps, prepared to injure. He had led her to the little wood to the left of the lake. Now near, now far, the hunters plunged and darted, sounding more and more distracted. Something was awry, an angry shout made them leap away on another scent, but still with whines and frets, their voices mad.

'But it doesn't make sense.'

'This number's all wrong.'

'Someone's been playing the giddy goat.'

Bayard nodded now, the judge finding all things well, then, moving farther into the trees, murmured about idiot laughter. She suddenly understood his lateness for lunch.

'You've muddled the clues.'

It was very funny, it was very sad: Graham, burning and glaring, galloping round circle after circle, each smaller than the next, everyone collapsing from heat and distress and one by one dropping into the lake.

Bayard slowly considered it, frowning importantly. 'Someone had to.'

Della was uncertain. She looked about her, ready to return home. Generally she preferred to think about Bayard than to be alone with him.

Indifferent, he pointed to a small clearing, across which lay a fallen tree, grey and cracked as an elephant. 'Yes. That might do.' Daintily, he moved some moss and thistle. 'We need a rest.'

She did not, but sat down, leaning against a leafless branch. Around were bracken, spiteful toadstools, dry, brown roots, and, very close, the encircling trees.

Suddenly she saw a hole, freshly dug. In it was treasure, a large fruit-cake, a bottle of cider. Gosh! No snake.

Munching, sipping, they heard uproar. Graham was shouting, the great captain frantic for a mislaid battlefield, troops helter-skelter, baffled by orders issued from the unseen and treacherous, sustained only by hopes of plundering the tea so generously allowed them.

Here, beneath leaves and insects, all was *luxuriant*, a new word to play with. The most beautiful word on earth was, of course, *ballerina*, making you free of the ground, going up and up, falling long after the word was silent.

Bayard, for once, was content to say nothing, to let the wood speak for itself. The heat pressed through the trees but left him dry, untouched. Ribbons of light streamed over them, to be lost in undergrowth. She drank more cider and forgot Bayard, Graham, all else save the wood. It was never as large as she imagined, so that she could not get lost, as sometimes she desired. Messages, riddles, life itself, came from trees and water. Here, the snobbish, elegant unicorn was always on the way, and the one-eyed poacher in broad hat, and the word *fear*, invented from dark groves. Merlin's tower, Robin's bower, and what Miss Measures called the dappled fools of the forest. Here, a tall man with horse's head could offer her the three wishes. At this moment she wanted tangerines in snow, another bottle of cider, and, yes, Graham to find treasure.

All was hushed, still, they sat in green fathoms of light. The hunters might have surrendered. Bayard, beside her, had his eyes closed, though this could mean he was exceptionally watchful.

Della knew that like, she supposed, many girls, she always had more time to use than had Grahams and Bayards. A moment, during which Graham rushed towards nowhere and Bayard lingered behind hedges, was for her prolonged, like elastic. In it she saw cracks lengthen on walls, on the air, within silence: dragonflies live their brief lives: treaties being swapped between grown-ups by a glance, smile, whisper, and sometimes broken, in a stillness cold as keys.

Once, during men's talk of guns and politics, Janet had given her a glance, very quiet, very long, probably in just such a moment. Presumably you lost childhood when such moments ceased to happen, so that Janet was even younger than she looked. This explained their closeness.

Sunlight dropped over Della and Bayard like a tent until shouts and stamps revived. Bayard sat up, listening thoughtfully. 'Where are they? Where's Della?' Graham was clamouring, angry, seeking vengeance, the disappointed pack at his heels. Their breath was nearer. Sun ribbons had swiftly changed to slanting spears, shadows were live and tense. Defenceless, she was Monmouth running from battle, hiding, betrayed by his eye, bright with terror amongst the ferns. Closing her own eyes she saw dense blood-reds, sun-yellows, butcher's boy blues. She was in red cap, hideously alone, sniffed by the wolf. Hunted, she might claim her earlier first wish, to be rescued from the forest. Yet wishes so often got twisted: princes could glitter in the dark, but too far away, beyond reach, and now her long moment was hurtful, allowing time for her to be changed to deadly stone.

Gently coughing, to remind her of his presence, Bayard rose, and her fears dissolved. If in his five centuries he had known Picts, in the land of sky-blue pink, he could withstand a lot of silly children.

Graham choked back tears. 'I suppose you think you're clever!'

'I am clever.' Bayard sighed, dismissing cleverness as fit only for monkeys and Claverings.

'You spoilt everything! The whole afternoon mucked up. Everyone hated you.'

'Yes, it was very bad.' He made it appear very good. 'The trouble was, I wanted a different sort of day. So really did most of them.'

'You shouldn't sneer at what you don't understand.'

'I don't. Only at what I do understand. If I knew how to spit at old Pyke, I would.'

'You love spoiling things.'

'You need a drying wind.'

Mr Pyke addressed them after tea. The worms in his chin were almost visible, his footballer's beefiness wasted. He was grieved at the irresponsibility, bad manners, ingratitude, of some cowardly miscreant towards his host and hostess, whose kindness could not possibly be exaggerated. Nevertheless, some prizes could be awarded after all.

Filled with cake and cream, the children said hooray. Later, Aunt Janet, bare-armed, bracelets shining, stood some way between smiles and concern. 'Poor Blake. He takes so much trouble.'

'Yes. Old Blow-me-Tight could only watch the feeding of the five thousand. But they ate well, don't you think?'

Roger was certainly smiling, with no concern whatsoever, though obviously knowing the culprit, who was gazing keenly at nothing in particular.

Graham refused to be comforted. His anger smarted. Could he do so, he would make his veins stand out like knotted cords. How puzzling that almost all boys could have broken Bayard in two, torn him apart like wild horses, yet none ever did. Bayard had leper's safety; from an unpleasant circle he watched races in which the fastest got left behind, cricket matches where the splendid hitter was often run out.

Life played tricks. There had been a beautiful summer, during which an important man had written that he felt every step in his plan had been taken with God's help. General Sir Douglas Haig, planning the Battle of the Somme.

'Shouldn't we go to the pub?' Always master of circumstances, Roger Kirkland, dark and supple in late afternoon sunlight, was rearranging the day, as if suddenly making the apt, happy suggestion which he had, in fact, long ago decided.

After supper, with Hackpen dusky above dark blue woods, they listened to the wireless, Kathleen Long playing Beethoven. Later on, Bayard remarked that actually she was rather short but did know her E flats. No one bothered to reply, not even Roger. The funny man was funny no longer, the hour was not his. Slightly shrugging, he withdrew, Della imagined him locking his door, then becoming unimaginable, even communing with Bluebeard. He said he remembered the Pied Piper. Listen to what actually happened. Inside the mountain, the Piper changed the children into rats, then sent them home, back to small, pretty houses where parents, still scared, waited with axe and knife.

She could hear him even when he was away. He was always talking.

'I'm thinking of doing something very simple. I'm going up the Thames with a large cork. It gets narrower and narrower. Up in the hills it flows out of a hole. I'll stuff in my cork. It's never been done before. The river will dry up. No more Thames. Ships perched on the mud, fishes getting away, very angry. Just a bit of sea barging in from the other end.'

He had looked unspeakably bored.

Graham was soon in bed, curled up under the lamp, reading. He was happy. The day had periodically turned traitor, darkened as if by the dull shape of the block, but here all was good, tomorrow would be well. He loved these late hours alone, in this small circle of light. General Hannay was at hand. *I had just finished breakfast and was filling my pipe when I got Bullivant's telegram.* A very few words could swing life into the extraordinary. *I was fairly certain that the meeting had not been accidental.* In a few pages Colonel Arbuthnot would say that it was time for him to take a hand in the game. And Baker Street was astir. *He gave a shrill whistle, on which a street arab led a four-wheeler, and opened the door. The man who addressed us mounted to the box, while we took our places inside. We had hardly done so before the driver whipped up his horse, and we plunged away at a furious pace through the foggy streets. The situation was a curious one. We were driving to an unknown place, on an unknown errand.*

Bayard was forgiven, he was like medicine, bitter but somehow necessary. You could imagine him drowning, you plunge in, haul him out, kiss him back to life. Then he starts to quarrel, he was only pretending and hates being kissed, even by Janet.

Much was unexplained, or explained too easily. Fingernails were pink at bedtime, black by morning. When Hitler bellowed, the world shook but no one could tell why he looked so lonely. The fat man beside him was a time bomb. In Germany, covered with iron, people were beheaded by an executioner in evening dress, wearing white gloves. And suppose, just suppose, the headsman set up a tent, down in the village, promising free executions, how long would be the queue?

Della was at her window, contemplating the moonlit garden, deep sumptuous blacks, elfin greens lustred with silver, the glimmer picking out a rose, pool, wall.

Earlier, with the Cleggs and Claverings, they had sat in the garden of the Star and Garter. Wines and *Spirits*. She had once seen spirits, slim Byrons and floating ladies, and now thought of a mocking, gartered king keeping a star in a black box.

She shivered, for once she had been to a party, or thought she had, and at tea sat next to a black bag tied with thin silver string, and suddenly, inside it, something moved, as if struggling to uncoil.

They had sat at rough, wooden tables, smooth, coloured hills rising from the end of the garden. The women were quiet, with sherry or gin, while still the men talked, talked.

'What are our chances in Australia this winter, Clavering?'

Wet teeth gleamed above a tankard. 'A battle. Friend Bradman, eh!'

Uncle Roger nodded agreeably, but probably was not listening.

Battle Field. Battle *Meadow* did not fit: meadows were lush, dotted with cows, cricketers, occasionally monks. Fields were neuter, often gritty. After old battles, bishops under heavy banners had slowly paced the fields in parallel lines, counting the sliced arms, slashed necks, the bodies, to decide who'd won.

Aunt Janet, gazing into the orchard, mentioned swimming at Lyme, and Roger, still more agreeable, said that she had shown him the waves doing their best to confirm what Mrs Woolf had written of them. Yet though he smiled, Janet did not. Della was anxious, imagining Mrs *Wolf*, until Sir Hartley offered her a chocolate. She would have liked music to start, perhaps 'The Earl of Essex's Galliard', probably very slow, very stately, lords and ladies in separate circles, moving in opposite ways, on tiptoe, as if the floor were slightly too hot.

The bright air struck all the faces, for a little they were silent, perhaps dreaming. A few more of Lady Clegg's remains had been scratched off by the sun. She looked discontented, dried out. In the orchard Graham and Bayard, friends again, were tossing a ball, the ball of pleasure. Butterflies wavered amongst tumbling roses, she counted the daisies at her feet. All was exact, visible, yet could it be complete? She had once seen a happy valley, the fox had fled, the birds were safe, then it vanished, as if abruptly snatched from a wall, leaving only a threatening figure in green cloak, blue cap. Her feet seemed tied to the earth, she was dumb, he moved, then slumped, becoming only part of a story.

'Well, one more round, Roger, then me and mine must depart. What are the kiddies drinking? You've given us a good day. Both of you, of course,' the voice added in afterthought.

They all sat up. 'Most of us would agree...' Roger Kirkland began, as he very often did. Most of us would agree that Mr Roosevelt showed the limitations of newspaper power, that Madagascar might do for the Jews, that people love their defeated generals, that the structural underpinning of Poland was unsound.

'Most of us would agree, Hartley, that the old girl's a mite crankish, bringing them up only on salads. I wouldn't risk much on their chances in a high wind.'

They had returned through cornfields reddening as the sun over Hackpen drooped like a wounded firebird. All was peaceful, glad, until, as if in one of her paintings, a black, jagged streak ripped open the harvest.

Everyone pretended not to notice, save Janet who, in one more stretched, peculiar movement, gave an understanding nod.

Now, watching the moonlit night, she was alert for the surreptitious stir, slither, or croak. A golden day could, sudden as a partridge, turn terrible, like the tent in merry, singing Kentisbeare Fair, which you entered very happily, then saw a child with two small ears like potatoes on one side of his head and none on the other. With knowledge of the Great War and the Piper's deadly stare, even of love for defeated generals, did boys also see raw, sliced feet dancing in red shoes.

Up in the attics, Bryce's brother might be adding or subtracting another finger, very possibly dividing by three.

At last, the night could safely be left to itself and, comfortable between cool sheets, she began counting favourite words, from *Noble Thoughts in Noble Language*, very likely the best book ever written. She was superior. Graham read only of war and adventure, thinking himself a bulldog, and Bayard never read at all, though quoting from books surely imaginary.

Ballerina, Tryst, Solace, Crystal, Dalliance, Emerald, Melancholy, Wan. They could be piled like a tower of cards, dissolved at a breath, yet leave a shape on the air.

Signs lay waiting, fragments of the riddles left in classrooms, overheard on the wireless, seen on the faces of strangers and in favourite stories, often, like accidents, offering new chances, painful choices. 'The silence of the mad,' someone had said, perhaps about Bayard. But that silence might be roaring. More probably, rather spooky.

Riddles dropped like promises; shrouded, they were ghosts lurking in a ravine. Today, she had, in a manner, been hunted, then been rescued from a forest.

Janet and Roger would soon be making love, an ugly expression, as if love were carpentry.

Again, she listened in darkness for what did not come, or might already have come, unseen. But no, and another day had perfected itself, and she was very likely to survive the traps and hazards of the night.

What, though, was a prisoner of the dream?

BOOK ONE

*

I saw several men commit suicide. Two rammed their heads through windows sawing their necks on the broken glass until they cut their jugular veins. Another took his leather bootstraps, tied a loop through the noose and did a back flip over the edge which broke his neck.

William Sloane Coffin, jr,
Chief US Interlocutor, Plattling, Germany (1946)

It is evil things we fight.

Winston S. Churchill

A prisoner captured alive by the enemy is *ipso facto* a traitor.

Russian Decree 270 (1942)

Crusade in Europe.

Dwight D. Eisenhower

1

'Well, Graham love, have you heard?'

'Do any of us hear a thing before you do?'

'Pax. Bass Banes is leaving. Grace's heart ... they can't carry on.'

'Sounds as if the heart can't either.'

Sheila watched him. To pupils he was the Viking, tough, scarred strider through seas, his corsair face smudged, slightly pitted, at odds with light, massed hair and blue, candid eyes, untidily set.

'You're next in line, Graham. Next into the mangle.'

'There's Kelly.'

'Rubbish! I can't see the HM daring to disappoint you, of all people.'

They relapsed into their different silence. The HM, Eric Waterfield, Dr Whisky Meadow, diffident, with a war wound used more as a refuge than a trophy and achieved, people said, by holding a gun upside-down, hated to disappoint.

Playing fields slanted through trees into the vast East Anglian sky worn thin by sea-winds, now swarthy, now bright with tumbling clouds. At this range, the school was an untidy jumble of rich-red Tudor brick, strict classicism, ornate Victorian afterthoughts. Behind bells, slamming doors, surging voices, beyond pillar and dome, was this austere, secretive countryside, the ancient barns and churches, the beamed hamlets, lonely shores, small, dark creeks, the estuary where wooden hulks still rotted, half-buried in mud.

Sheila was tall, well-boned, her vigorous eyes moving under a litter of fresh, brown hair as if to keep pace with the thoughts hurrying behind them. Rigged out more trimly than most, she was enthusiastic in class, and perhaps bed, though here he doubted whether anyone yet knew. Like many young teachers she could sometimes look spoilt by something not yet quite traceable, like a hint of damp in a bright house. She was popular, reliable, humorous, sometimes caustic, the best of the common-room pack, though, still barely perceptible, tiny creases could droop from her mouth, a threat of dismay ahead. Meanwhile, on court, she rushed to volley his strongest drives, and elsewhere, briskly contradicted any flounderings from Eric Waterfield.

At the gates she halted. 'How was the last rehearsal? Sorry I couldn't come. Any explosions?'

'I kept my temper, most of the time. Quite often ... well, sometimes!'

2

Effective teaching demanded powerful memories. In common-room too many had forgotten their childhoods, their mainsprings. Time made even monotony bizarre. In memory, as in desire, the sea was always alluring, reaching Tripoli, Corfu, Casablanca: sleek and blue, lapping Troy, Carthage, Syracuse. It was black, high and curling where Steerforth lay dead on the sand and Bayard was threatened by roaring tides, and lay, a tempting mirage, as young Ralegh watched a brown old hand pointing westwards.

Stories, secrets random and strange, needed to be shared. He would read aloud, the smooth, unfinished faces absorbed, apathetic, dreamy, unknowable, but always challenging his eagerness to arouse, convince, excite.

'In Paris, under the Empire, thirteen men came together.'

The tumultuous past flowed into a present heaving with the movement, choice, anger of cannibal Europe. Sources of legend and unrest, the reliving of adventures imaginary or still possible. Picts had swarmed, dark blurs always watching the bright city. 'He was lost in Spain.' Charlemagne's eyes went vast and dim and tragic.

Graham told Janet that he loved his pupils: more truthfully, he loved a minority. Did not, Kelly had inquired, in his hearing, Admiral Fisher, world famous though dotty, maintain that favouritism was the secret of success? But Kelly was negligible, his head too small, perched on a narrow neck and wide shoulders.

The pupils were unpredictable, refuting Herbert Clavering's belief that education was a matter of breeding, he himself, Bayard had reflected, possessing neither of these. A lout, spotty, like a diseased tart, had wept at Gandhi's murder. Following Roger Kirkland's address to the VIth, describing Emperor Hirohito travelling with sacred sword and jewel to the Ise Temple, to report defeat to the Sun Goddess, a girl, hitherto almost dumb, had written a poem, very short, very malicious, very funny, which might have affronted Roger in his glory.

All had lived amongst permanent images of taking aim, taking cover. Cinema screens throughout Britain showed Belsen figures, skeletal as if gnawed, still wincing from a twinge of life: then de Gaulle, the towering impossible, stalking a Paris street unconcerned with Nazi snipers. Today the Berlin crisis threatened an atomic downpour, and several pupils had been flown to Canada by scared parents. Rumours, bat-like, batty, flitted by, of Alexis Suvorov, tsarist Cossack general, a link with ancient Hetmen and forgotten rebels, then hero of revolution and civil war, of desperate break-outs from overpowering encirclements, reckless cavalry forays, vanishing in thirties' show trials that swathed the officer élite, resurrected to save Stalin's throne in the Great Patriotic War, regaining a halo that must have been too bright for his morose employer, dipping gauntleted hands into wild ferocities at Stalingrad, then again vanishing, now probably dead as a doornail, though doornails can be less dead than they seem. He that sitteth on a nail, a familiar voice had said, long ago, will surely rise.

Beyond crisis and Bomb waited the Mediterranean: villas, ruins, tinted promontories, sunlit beaches and vines, Moorish terraces, grottoes, siren rocks and classical headlands, broken columns sheltering immemorial goats, antique trade routes supporting history, each pool, tree, grove, demanding a nymph and sometimes getting one. The South. In English winters he warmed himself on recollections of vacations, the glitter of dawn waters, parties on yachts, patios, roofs, drives to Cartagena, Grosseto, Syracuse, through air scented and silky as Bourbons, through wine, through webs of deft, unhurried jazz, within reach of tired, walled villages, slumped citadels, mountain caves, an aurochs' cemetery, all packed within a single motion, a magician's beckon. A Banes, a Kelly, taught by the book, were licensed by exams and reports, scared of admitting the fairground realities of history which, by some rigged tribunal, spectacular overthrow, evil confrontation, could occasionally collide with stolid, classroom faces, and make grief, astonishment, wonder.

Another past lurked in ambush. Beyond the idyllic South, the serene summers of Dragon House and loves, was what he had told no one and might never tell. He had almost certainly killed, not in warrior pride, Suvorov craziness, Montgomery éclat, but shabbily, in a campaign scarcely explicable, never officially divulged by Cabinet or War Office. To pupils, it might have rung like a Viking boast, a saga turmoil, but, kept private, it was only an unhealed scab, bleeding when picked.

The past never remained still, was restless and nervy as a comedian. Overnight, heroes and villains exchanged places, a beloved tale was pronounced untrue, a god tumbled with his own temple. When, just before the war, Della discovered that, despite appearances so solidly presented, the Kirklands were not formally married, laughs, pauses, undertones, had to be reassessed. Vintage occasions shifted, premise and perspective wavered, though Bayard, of course, displayed unconcern.

'What made you both so convinced of the marriage lines? It was all perfectly obvious.'

'Is anything perfectly obvious?'

'Far too much.'

In post-war Britain such formalities mattered less, save at Ascot and the Palace, themselves lapped by protest, denunciation, Labour austerity. Throughout, Roger had been at the Foreign Office, the coming man who had quickly arrived. The prima donna and the actor-manager, clubland murmured. He had also sat on a committee connected with radar, and been praised by Mountbatten as ambassador between politics and technology. Later he had helped prepare briefs for the

Nuremberg trials. Retaining political interests without party commitment he had lately returned to the Bar which, Della said, made him sound like Dylan Thomas.

Roger remained tolerant, benevolent, very slightly amused by evidence of human, even divine incapacity. 'Judge not that ye be not judged always seemed to me deplorable teaching. A surrender of self-respect, even self-interest. Useless, unless, as many do, you prefer the Stone Age. Stone Age art does have excitements, which our contemporaries notice a trifle too avidly.'

He said later, 'I admit, Graham, I was a bit startled by the Hitler–Stalin pact. Unlike the former, I overlooked Joe's desire for the Baltic states, both for defence and, as we now see, for expansionism. They were, in fact, crucial. I should also have remembered that dictators are fascinated by each other, smothering the ideological and self-critical. I was astonished by Stalin's eagerness to meet Hitler's terms, sending manganese, petrol, phosphates, a million tons of grain, like a superior grocer, getting back guns, planes, tools, a cruiser. The same Stalin and Molotov who now denounce Marshall Aid as a device to enslave Europe! Marxism omits human terms even more drastically than Fascism, which hasn't any real terms at all. Well, even the best of us can learn. You yourself are not ashamed of a disposition to teach. With active war service, you're well fitted to disabuse that vain old Stalinist showman, GBS, who once said in my hearing that the vilest abortionist is whoever attempts to mould a child's character. I was tempted, though not for long, to address him as Bernie. Still, he's had a considerable day, and we've not yet had ours.' The smile was offhand, that of a millionaire crumpling a cheque. 'In my *ci-devant* capacity as your guardian, I can risk reminding you that wisdom does not end in Saint-Germain-des-Prés, as Della seemed once to imagine, if not precisely think, mercifully not for long. It does not even begin. More important, she's coming to dine. She's upstairs with Janet, bless them both. We may not actually bleat ourselves silly with starvation.'

At the Kirklands' London home in Montpelier Square shortages were only hearsay, obliterated by servants, opulent meats, sauces, wines. The Dragon House mostly remained unoccupied, though Janet sometimes stayed there. Wandering lawns and rose gardens, she had remembered Della's young speculations about the Women's Institute, uncharitable, loftily obscene, unconfirmed by the externals of its members.

Della herself camped alone in an unwholesome Clapham flatlet, very at odds with her needs and personality, where she wrote poems as yet unpublished. With the scrapping of the Raj, her father had returned to England but, momentarily back in jungle and plain, had seen a taxi on the far side of the road, then fatally forgot the traffic. Her mother sulked in Buxton. Della herself listened fervently to the inaudible, which apparently too often remained inaudible. 'I'm tangled in extremes,' she would say, 'like Anne Boleyn. In Spain she's become a witch.'

Her current lover was an Australian rugby star whom she called Beast, with several intonations of disgust. He was amiable, rich, clumsy and inarticulate, a type which mysteriously, though inconclusively, attracted her. At the Dragon House she would stand long moments before a stone satyr with cruel eyes and thick, lolling cock, heavy as a coconut.

Graham's own parents remained strangers from abroad. Instead of love, he dispatched them presents he could not always afford.

Bayard had vanished. He might have been crushed in the Blitz, drowned off Murmansk, absented himself without leave in Ethiopia, entered, with some condescension, a Nepalese monastery, or, on his sixth hundredth birthday, collapsed into dust. One envisaged him, as always, the thin boy strolling towards a football he lacked urgent desire to possess; courteously but firmly declining to let the school barber rub his hair with nameless oils. He had never conformed to the simple, not always to the explicable. Natural saboteur, he had enjoyed others' toy trains, contriving elaborate crashes. Misbehaving at cards, he explained that he had been distracted by the Scarlet Pimpernel. Rejecting intimacies, he had always been elusive, returning less than he received, never keeping the score, and, if dead, would have died without caring that he had been loved, and perhaps still believing his own stories.

Janet was reticent, Roger spoke of him as he might a wilful pet or domestic jester too often on irregular holiday. To Della, he was a displaced person destroyed by some bizarre emergency of his own designing.

A Viking, however, loves and hates full-bloodedly, despises

and worships, without bothering to explain, not always knowing how to. To him, weedy, disengaged Bayard had displayed particular gleams but no real friendship. Enough.

Meanwhile, from Clapham fastness, Della signalled. Please write. In this dust and rain letters are spells. She was sometimes beautiful, sharp-eyed Anne emerging from a river, running over grass, brooding in a summer-house, like the doomed queen laughing unexpectedly or cruelly joking. He liked remembering her childhood belief that at county boundaries air and colour changed texture.

Conscripted in 1944, Graham was eventually stationed far from the front, in a conquered North German landscape of small, silent towns, farms darkened and despoiled, gritty heaths. This was boarding-school at grosser remove, residue of catapults in unsupervised break, venomous promises and unpleasant deals after dark, punishments for enormities often unexplained. He sustained himself with hopes of leave, of peacetime adventure, and with bright recollections. In a mislaid antipodes the Dragon House was always lit with blossom, with Janet in a richly brown robe awaiting Roger who crossed towards her under a sky of unshakeable blue.

Daily he was engulfed in petty swindles, listless black marketing, with watches, cigarettes, fountain-pens exchanged for unwilling flesh, the subterfuges engrossing conqueror and conquered alike. Two cigarettes for rights of a breast, journey's end for ten. Despite *No Fratting*, the sly traffic was led by officers greedy for spoils due to earlier, braver men. Between them and their subordinates was barely expressed complicity, a dully shared mart of German needs, resources, limits, offers.

With no particular friend or ally, Graham settled to endure a winter term exceptionally noxious. Annoyed at missing action in the final Allied victories, he was simultaneously glad of survival. He would have relished a whirligig blow at the Nazis but hankered for no Somme, was not a Charlie seeking a moor at Culloden, though curious about his battle nerve. Would he quail? Probably less than most. Meanwhile, the glum day released few abnormal appetites; he could be roused by the accidental and small: a sunlit leaf, a swim, a plate of eatable chips, a bottle of wine, a hymn. He had always, as Della put it, been helpless against tunes, and continuous Forces Music relayed from London wrapped him in a warm, communal fug in which he joined in sudden, rowdy choruses, half-remembered lilts, lewd parodies. There's a hot time up the old girl tonight.

Boredom forced one into postures more excruciating than those of Houdini. Men had religious fantasies, bouts of tearful generosity, maudlin intimacies, and had, with joyless, erratic mirth, sawn off the beak of a looted parrot, 'Kraut bloke', stolen from a cottage.

While Montgomery drove inexorably towards Lüneburg, they drank in canteens, brooding, swearing, quarrelling, starting abrupt, vicious fights. 'Tart, Tart, Tart.' Voices were strained, weird, as Ron Cohn defended his loins at strip ping-pong. Pert buttocks, dark wide eyes flat as if painted on skin pale and soft. 'Bloody cake,' muttered Foxwell who, next week, was inexplicably carted away, head down, screaming like a stuck pig, never seen again. Graham himself staring at tearful, hapless Cohn, felt a muffled desire, then awaited a real spasm, a marvellous wave, which dissolved at the raucous yell, 'Yiddish cock ... tuppence a suck.' Lance-Corporal Rosen was foremost in jeering.

The surrounding Germans were the least dangerous. Savagery to the bird, the beak hacked, feathers wrenched out, provoked a brawl in which Graham assaulted a lumberjack grouser, probably innocent, in berserk mindlessness that later made him shiver, though it increased his standing if not his popularity. Disembarking from a troop train, marshalled for two hours, unsheltered in wind and rain, they were resentful, almost mutinous, until an Irish voice broke ranks. 'Anyone here the Chosen? The cattle-trucks are coming!' Even the platoon commanders smiled, the tensions melted.

He listened to random, jerked-out confidences. 'Death isn't easy, mate. Not fuckin' easy. They plug your holes before you're quite done. Don't trust the medicos. They can box you alive.'

Discipline wavered between ludicrous bull and the slovenly. Off-duty, men slouched morose, unlit streets, watched by secretive townsfolk, the men maimed, misshapen, the women, as if deliberately, looking older than they probably were. Children were seldom seen, as if in hiding. All were existing on salted spinach, acorn coffee.

How much had they known? Mass exterminations were now being uncovered by Allied advance troops. Here, the wind blew squalor from a valley quite close, *Verboten* to villagers for seven years, stricken by the methodical, infamous, the very quiet, until dismantled by a bewildered, then uncontrollable Scots battalion. The Kraut commandant, neat, cultivated, desirous to please, was said to have been stamped to death by the Jocks, amid the starving and typhus-ridden.

Against orders, Graham trudged grey holts, through winter pall, reaching low, dirty houses, silent, but within which eyes must be watching. Small, tight gardens had disciplined grass but no flowers, as if these too had been conscripted. Flashy with lust, he would have bidden much for the dirty, even the gruesome, and occasionally did so.

The officers, games-hating amateurs, were uneasy outside their mess, visibly glad of security, but resentful at being debarred from the looting enjoyed by those embattled in the South. One was court-martialled on a vice charge, some joyless seduction in a rat-festered barn. Acquitted, he was transferred, his name becoming an adjective, lingering like a stain which attempts to rub off only expose more clearly.

'You Turks!' Between routine obscenities, Sergeant Cosgrave made his overgrown joke. 'Turks in Constantinoseful.' He was trained like a police dog to pounce on trifling errors, minor omissions, was a machine of hide, gristle, with a flair for mediocrity. Contemptuously servile to officers, he could pummel without lifting an arm. His stare, unblinking on the lined, crudely hewn head, was not lordly but powerful, inescapable in these dirty yards, fuggy rooms, on plains flayed by Polish winds.

Large and careless, Graham sought no intimacies. Amongst these small, gregarious South Londoners the public-school voice, though suspect, was not damnable unless laced with condescension. He could join bargainers, card-players, grumblers, swillers, never quite sharing but never fastidiously aloof. Most of them he liked without relishing. Gumboil Frank, scared that the others would discover his real name, Francis, yet confiding it to each in turn. Vince, who thought circumcision denoted both disease and immense wealth. Toddy, posted for desertion, found stabbed, but alive, in a scrappy wood, smuggled away before he could reveal more, joining Foxwell in camp legend.

Because of his fair, woolly hair, Graham was called Baa Baa. It could have been worse. So could this life, within sound of momentous events farther east. He could find a home almost anywhere. No talent need be buried deep in this stony ground, talents could be reserved only for what chance offered, or could be made to offer. Even in this drab outpost in enemy land, flatness and monotony concealed crevices, ravines, bridges to the unexpected. In Della's poems, bridges were always paths to underworlds and changes of fortune.

Odd twists of self, of make-believe, were extracted in this temporary scrap-heap ingloriously becalmed in a Germany ostensibly cowed, but bloodshot and still fighting. Graham had joined a raid on a peasant widow's isolated cottage. Beginning as caprice, dull hope of a fuck, a cache of beer, all changed to anger when they found the wretched place empty. Frustrated search for drink ended in wild smashing of windows and furniture, the fouling of walls and beds, theft of humble toys, tools, dishes. One man walked on his hands, cock-crowing, urinating; another, goaded by gibbering applause, drove a nail through his own hand, then took a bow. Then all was swiftly effaced, as if at a signal, leaving nervous silence, the unspoken search for a scapegoat.

Graham pondered his lack of self-disgust. In Devon a car had flattened a row of ducklings; at once the parent birds began devouring the sodden innards. Bayard remarked that this reminded him of death, Della was unexpectedly dry-eyed. The most concerned was Janet, who had not seen it. Graham himself had felt little, until, a year later, in a dream, he had been overtaken by horror.

The episode might have been reduced to a dirty joke save for Cosgrave. A half-leer, an unfinished jibe, conveyed that he knew of it, was the blackmailer staying his hand to enjoy their fear.

'You chums ... seen action at last! Bleedin' medals on the way. Just wait ... just keep waitin'.' A hectoring stump of gun-metal greyness, he once softened, untrustworthily. 'You owe me more than you know. Each one of you. Bastards! Even soddin' Jesus never said thanks to his own prick. Are ye telling me 'e 'adn't one?'

On a low, dark afternoon Graham encountered a stranger in the changing-room, a youth, no stripes on his crumpled, shoddy battledress, slender, clear-eyed, smooth skin minutely tinged with blue as though from early parade. 'Hullo!' His voice, not quite English, not identifiably foreign, seemed resuming a talk earlier interrupted.

They sat together surrounded by damp, drying fatigue kits, muddied boots and shirts. Always lacking small talk, Graham backed into a friendly grin, listening perplexedly, but with sensations of affection, even hopes of love. The newcome seemed anxious to talk, his words were precise, easy, yet added up to the unaccountable, as if read from an unknown book opened at random.

'Once a year, in the first week of spring, piles of winter clothes were strewn on the grass. Fur coats, evening gowns, shawls, scarves, cloaks, opera hats, woollen suits, shoes. Each servant in turn, by seniority, was allowed to select one garment, however valuable. A hunting outfit, a crimson sash.'

Graham heard it as he might a bedtime story, then, at approaching voices, the other jumped up and vanished. He was not seen again, no one else knew of him. Some tiny clue was offered some weeks later, in an official warning against 'unorthodox enemies'. German partisans, wild, starving men and children escaping POW and slave camps where cannibalism had begun, even Allied deserters.

In early summer, 1945, some dozen jeeps swerved aside from the main road and new, hardened officers, very tabbed, very professional, descended, followed by a flotilla of lorries. The barracks emptied, men clambered aboard, and for two days, two nights, a grinding cavalcade bumped south along broken routes, through smashed towns, shattered hills, pausing only to repair bridges. Little was vouchsafed, but evidently they were at last to partake in battle, the final tug. They began talking big, suppressing all doubts and terrors. The new command imposed a discipline, a morale, though some agreed that battle might give a chance, such things were heard, to plug Cosgrave.

Graham welcomed action. He believed he would hold out and survive. He was right, though not as he supposed. In recollection, the adventure, like a dream, cut corners, leapt gaps, dissolved solids.

Arriving at wooded hills, vine-dressed valleys, they were soon facing a silent, unidentifiable crowd gathered at a small railway station hung with pots of gaudy flowers. A line of dirty, empty trucks was visible behind an old-fashioned, tall-funnelled engine, even dirtier. Many were civilians: women shawled and booted despite the heat, scarves hiding most of their faces, but looking bowed and sexless; men mostly bearded, all unshaven, in bulging but dilapidated civvies, or in uniforms faded and miscellaneous, some apparently German, with ragged forage-caps amongst them. Trousered children were crying half-heartedly, while their elders, several hundreds, stood waiting, very still, intent, hunched as if against wind, though the day was utterly calm.

Armed partisans? Refugees? Nothing was said until suddenly a banner rippled out. *Free Ukraine*. At this an officer spoke. Very formal, very composed. 'Personnel will entrain these people, without exception, tolerating no resistance, listening to no excuse.'

Cosgrave's order to fix bayonets was obeyed without question, the officer commanded advance. As if tilted by earthquake they were advancing, instantaneously met with club, knife, the occasional gun. Graham, a corporal, led his section at the double into a yelling, gesticulating mass, to struggle, swing rifle-butts, and, on some yelled order, lunge with bayonets. He wrenched a woman's hand from his throat, instinctively dodging an aimed pistol, trapped in shots, confused appeals, screams. A sharp-toothed, vagabond child was at his leg and, bitten, he kicked her back into the scrimmage. Flying dust drenched the tumult, all was incoherent, a long delirium of each for himself. The Pict flared in the blood, eyes were redder, wilder, gashes and moans more agonized, more savage. Another small girl, with long, dirty hair and in cut-down grey breeches and military shirt, seemed charging all ways at once like a crazed dog, fisting, kicking, in uncanny silence, spinning towards bayonets until knocked dead or senseless from behind. Sky and hill had vanished utterly, the world shrivelling to this packed, fanged uproar. Graham, struggling with irregular, dreamlike slowness, sensed rather than saw a young, sallow face jeering at him, a blow from a log stung his mouth, he stumbled, then, recovering, frantic with anger, he fired, the face dropped away, wiped off by another swarm, and clearing a space, he felt exultant, super-sized, in charge.

Throughout that week officers and drivers were constantly replaced as, in jeeps and armoured cars, once in tanks, the man-hunt ranged between horizons, over hills, through vineyards and postcard Austrian villages, into farms, hospitals, monasteries, rounding up with threats, promises, entreaties through military interpreters in Slavonic dialects, sometimes with shots at the head. Several couples, after a promise of safety which, judging by the interpreter's expression, was unconvincing even to him, dived from a bridge, head-down on to dry boulders. Escaping his escort, a youth smashed his head against a wall, leaving brains dripping like dark tears. Stories were told, retold, of Russian slaves, displaced persons, prisoners of war, struggling with furious despair against repatriation, a welcome from Uncle Joe. Stories assembled a sickening jigsaw of ambush, disembowelling, shootings through the mouth, a child cut down still living, clutching a doll, her dead parents hanging from a gatepost. By some hurried irregularity, all three were dumped in a truck. One would not forget the bearded cripple tearing his grandchildren's wrists with a broken tin-opener before inexpertly but calmly gashing his throat, or the girls collapsing on a litter of bloodied teeth and lifeless hands, or the families, fleeing an armoured car, rushing headlong into a steep quarry. An outpost of hell coloured by the Union Jack.

Flayed by Cosgrave, leashed by the competent, deadly officers, the men were puzzled, sullen, ashamed, but obedient, until revived, not by human blood and gristle but the fall of Berlin.

Graham's brief exhilaration at his puny fighting moments in the Second World War, his gesture for Western freedom, had evaporated. Like others he had obeyed, turned a blind eye when possible, felt nausea, distress, guilt, then exhaustion and apathy. When all was done, the mission completed to HQ's satisfaction, 'foreign personnel dispatched home in reasonable comfort', incredulity grew in him like intimations of cancer. Had he really witnessed, quite passively, the infant bouncing down a stony defile? Certainly he could not forget those groups, finally disarmed and shackled, some praying, some cringing, others upright, expressionless, fatalistic, stricken as if by curse, above wretched bundles, kettles, baskets, the children still pretending to play, occasionally smiling at the foreign soldiers. Scrawny, abject, degraded, the women went first, pushed at bayonet-point on to trains and lorries facing east, their splitting wails receding on the summer breeze. He would never know whether his was the bullet that struck the girl who, blood spurting, crumpled at Cosgrave's feet, and had then been turned over, face down, by that implacable boot. As if in the dock under a cold judge he felt once more the whooping delight, now spoilt by sardonic dreams, sober reflections, when his fist met the youth's bone and, like Hercules, he clubbed a head surprisingly soft. Evil summer secrets.

Once, amongst screams, frantic appeals, defiance, an English voice had drawled, 'Have you noticed how quiet it really is, underneath? Strategy's working well. God arrived at 1200 hours, probably at 200 m.p.h.'

On a mound, gathering all ranks, gesturing towards prisoners, men still in German battledress, many with small, rather tinny medals of unknown armies, huddled in an improvised cage, some kneeling, one, with a broken knee, scrambling crabwise, for scraps of cigarettes thrown by passing troops, against orders, not quarrelling, always sharing the meagre finds, Colonel FitzMaurice frowned. 'A thoroughly annoying matter, in which you all played your part well. I'm grateful to each one of you. It wasn't precisely your favourite cup of tea. Those fellows, mostly anti-Stalin, volunteered for the bloody Wehrmacht. Why? To escape rotting in camps, or mines, to hit the Reds, or merely to do something. Traitors, I suppose, but, poor devils, who can blame them! The women seem to have worked in factories, for the Hun war effort. Well, they all know what to expect. Loser's rights! None of our business, of course. But I don't myself feel like crowing, you needn't quote me, but ... a thoroughly un-British undertaking. I don't yet know how the Yanks are seeing it. Still, it's over. Winston and Eden know their business, even if the business can sometimes be rotten. That's war.'

One wondered if they did know their business, or had even heard of it. Only a Cosgrave had any inclination to crow. A Roger, even a Bayard, would have dissented, not by sensational courage or spectacular mutiny, but with adroit and successful manipulation, the detection of ambiguity in orders, demands for telephone instructions to be repeated in writing.

Muscle, self-assurance, pleasing intentions, above-average intelligence were insufficient: a cast-iron cause was not general absolution for the Britain which one respected, and, in careless, unuttered ways, loved.

In Naafi the men swapped experiences, daily less reliable, achieving sudden maturity, a disposition to serious, unsteady argument about treason, politics, punishment. They awaited a newspaper follow-up, a general's pronouncement, Downing Street communiqué, but received silence.

One might ask Roger and all might be clear, proven, justified. Yet Roger did not always give the answers desired. The questions would not be asked. To confess the vile, and be handed inside knowledge of immaculate diplomacy, military pledges, gentlemen's agreements, would be hateful. Only the healing grin of Time must rub away the outcast cries won by the thoroughly un-British undertaking.

Muted unease was dispersed by the general election. Labour victory was cheered by almost all Other Ranks, the officers perplexed, angered, suspicious at the jubilation over Churchill's defeat. We don't need the Big Cigar, Gumboil said, and we never did. He might be mistaken, but a New Britain promised fairer incomes, squarer meals, a sort of sharing, a taller, cleaner population, better eyes and teeth, a more generous voice in the world. Oh, to be in England now that Winston's out, an American voice sang, though from military prison, in expectation of treason trial or the asylum.

Only Sergeant Cosgrave remained unmoved. 'You fuckers may 'ave a Red Parliament but ye don't 'ave no fuckin' union.'

3

Demobilized, ignoring Roger Kirkland's advice, Graham snatched the first job offered. Teaching was sharing, sparring at secrets. He was striding, controversial, with florid shirt, aggressive tie, but with war service and good degree. His blue, restless eyes had quicksilver changes, now fierce, now enthusiastic, at times unexpectedly shy. His laugh was too frequent, too noisy, his face, pitted, rough as if badly shaven, made some admire him as a commando, others call him Othello and mutter that he was a disciple of George Bernard Cocksure who insisted that soap was harmful. Pupils nicknamed him the Viking and joked about his beer intake. He was, the common-room admitted, a born teacher, though Bass Banes grumbled that birth did not axiomatically entail maturity. Someone said he was very dry timber. There was concern about his carelessness, not in university preparation but the fortnightly form marks.

'Marks!' He glowered. 'Christ, Sheila, we're not salesmen.'

Now he was in promotion stakes, though with hurdles ahead. That no one mentioned Gail meant that none had forgotten her. With sooty hair, dark brown eyes sometimes fervid, sometimes sullen, she had been a disturbing, even baleful presence in class. She had an unstable mother, absentee father, precocious physical awareness and a disdainful manner. Graham liked her, and insisted, against general scepticism, that she had talent.

In class he would present finely bound notebooks in which to embalm exceptional work, and Gail had collected perhaps too many. She seldom addressed him, save to ask irrelevant, drily insolent questions, 'Was Bismarck left-handed?', as if playing for more than giggles. Then she began waylaying him in town, saying little but familiarly taking his arm. At first he enjoyed it, thoughtlessly, would have liked more, but finally scented danger and avoided her. One morning in class she stood up, shouting about cruelties, betrayals, payments, incoherently but accusingly between wild tears. The porter had to remove her, she never returned, was rumoured to have been pregnant. It was agreed that Graham had carelessly overplayed his Viking style.

'You misread her fine eyes.'

'Forget it. Her eyes were bog-pools. She'll drown in them....'

But he knew he had escaped a more drastic verdict, one that he had partly willed. Puny enemies always lurked, assiduously taking notes. In a nearby grammar school a teacher had recently been arrested on a sexual charge, legally dubious but hard to refute absolutely.

With Banes retiring, his successor must be chosen very soon. One need fear only Kelly. He himself had procured more university scholarships, Kelly was more patient with the less gifted, though classes complained of his 'tons of sarcasm'. You never saw him in a bait; the Viking was easy to set alight and, with the wind behind him, could have outblasted Mussolini.

To rely on the HM was dangerous. On meeting him, Roger Kirkland had remarked that Britain had won two world wars but her professional classes cherished timidity like a houseplant. Meanwhile one need not brood over Kelly, who could win medals for petty grievance and rank ambition, and the school itself was not the sum of the world. When thunder filled the sky and planes headed for Berlin, he wanted a place in crisis and action, while apt to be halted by recollections of those hapless White Russians, still to be mentioned to no one, certainly not to Sheila, though secrets were never wholly kept from women. 'You are thinking', Sheila teased, 'of all the *Fräuleins* you seduced. Five for a tin of bully beef. My, you must have left Germany in a shambles!'

Chuckling, he did not deny it.

Janet, quiet, circumspect, observant, sometimes seemed awaiting a confidence that she did not expect to receive. Della called him Captain Cartridge, packed with energies liable to explode in directions unexpected, sometimes unnecessary: a war hero dreading too easy a target.

He continued to search memoirs and histories, unable wholly to credit the orders he had been given, but found nothing. On chance encounters with fellow conscripts he heard vague reports of American humanity and lukewarmness, individual but notable British refusals, but nothing was substantial. The short, brutal episode was officially closed, barely indeed opened, was a dusty heap in a locked archive. The Katyn Murders periodically resurfaced, with volunteer committees, unofficial inquiries, proposals for a memorial opposed by Conservative and Labour front benches, but elicited no counter-accusations. Yet the screams had been real, and the frantic, grasping hands, the bespattered face and savaged children.

If only Bayard ... but, though Bayard too might have delicately disobeyed orders, he might also have officiously counted the dead, calculated the cost of burial, and dispatched the bill to some inappropriate quarter, perhaps even to Roger.

4

College suffered an annual Shakespeare play, on behalf of Eng. Lit. examinations. Last year Kelly had produced a well-drilled, conventional *Macbeth*, at which Graham heedlessly gibed, they wished he had not, for Waterfield at once requested him to follow up with the examiners' next choice, *Twelfth Night*. He groaned frequently and at length. In much pain is much retribution.

Sheila volunteered to help, other colleagues joined them, but production developed waywardly, on more than a tiresome effort to downgrade Kelly. The play offered many problems.

'Disguise, I see, thou art a wickedness.' Having, too hastily, envisaged it as fairy-tale, Graham was deflected by the information from the chaplain, Martin Emery, that *fairy-tale* was a late medieval corruption of *fate-tale*, itself revealing not butterfly enchantments but the hard process of self-discovery and fulfilment through trials and initiations.

'Damn you, Martin, you've wrecked my bugger-all play.'

'Don't be such a defeatist Philistine! You can see it all perfectly. The Tartar King rides through each of us, even that prig Orsino, dragging us to our appointed ends. You yourself may well snatch the princess, but also get landed with the unproductive part of the kingdom. More likely, of course, as an eager beaver, you'll get crucified, and cause an earthquake by your grumbles about arrangements for resurrection. As for me,' he spread dainty hands in artful simplicity, rolled eyes in his act of stage parson, 'I may penetrate the Rose of the World, but I fear me not. But don't get afflicted with too many fairies. Fate's a quieter matter of purposeful wandering. There's your Shakespeare, and for that matter the Gospels. For good measure. Very good measure. Jesus, or somebody very much like him, taught just that. What else?'

'Plenty, I'd say. *Twelfth Night*! More like All Fools' Day.'

Nevertheless, this provided useful revisions. He would now have preferred help not from Sheila but Della. Her paintings and stories were dense with quests, initiations, transformations.

The first performance was approaching. He groaned, he cursed, he despaired, through rowdy rehearsals. Nothing would transform these coltish girls and oafish boys; their fates, like their commonplace limbs, wooden voices, dreary sniggers, had been settled at birth. He was almost tempted to consult Kelly, who would impose order, though a tedious one, on this incomprehension and chaos. With Sheila he argued, pleaded, quarrelled, he slapped her, she slapped him back.

How did Shakespeare's folk walk, speak, use swords, wear clothes? How induce the cunning of passion or suggest a mind like an opal? How best use music? He saw bright phantoms already vanishing, heard a song only before it was uttered, a grove rustling with the invisible. Was Toby Belch anything more than Cosgrave in ludicrous dress, was Maria a Bryce with all fingers intact? Bayard certainly hovered behind the play, but, as always, was of small help. Perhaps a glimpse of Olivia could be won from Janet, and Della's caprices give hints to Viola. Wildly, he envisaged stealing the HM's familiar tweeds, filling them with Aguecheek, and earning uproarious dismissal.

No good. The stuff had no heroes, perhaps no issues. But something. Personal truths, disillusions, pothouse horseplay, exquisite winks, bawdy faith in nothing very much. Colours laden with lost meanings, music the only art allowed in Paradise, loneliness rampant amid uproarious, posturing crowds.

Groping for advice to which he never listened, he envisaged not evanescent Illyria with comedy heedless as moonlight but England, half-pagan, with effulgent goddess always off-stage yet never wholly absent, pain-wracked and nervous, yet dancing, hunting, jesting, a living refinement of golds and blacks. Nothing, he insisted irritably to the stolid, puzzled or rebellious, must be either strange or familiar. The scented, gemmed hand reaching for wine or rapier had once been a claw, might be so again. Orsino, a second-eleven Leicester or Essex, governed a realm which was at once mood and brute substance, with clowns thrown adrift in midwinter. Behind languid resplendants and jovial swillers hung withered leaves and frost. Rare song and high conceits could not disperse bearpit and madhouse. An atmosphere ambiguous as goddess and ruler, to be touched with archaic remnants: sexes exchanging clothes to confuse demons, a forgotten echo of blood sacrifice, a reminder of hell. Without knowing why, he impulsively ordered that Feste must wear a feathered cloak.

'Would it not be simpler', Sheila looked up from fake satins and painted swords, 'to deliver a lecture?'

'Yes.'

Rehearsals were shouting contests, almost brawls, the boys sullen, the girls tearful, and at last he began enjoying himself. A visiting parent complained that not only did the master look like a street arab but spoke like one. Routine spun off into loud questions, sudden impasses, the unexpected improvisation, the adventure in colour. Pupils became players, calling him Graham without seeming aware of it.

Sheila now insisted that they were adapting with extraordinary speed. Blunt hearties, busy prefects, heavy prudes as if instinctively merged into pretence, trickery, malicious jokes and lyrical tenderness. The dumpy contrived litheness, a hearty prankster became a gaunt Feste, caustic, with frost-bound wit and, masked, often gliding unnoticed through revellers, toadies, lovers. As Malvolio, golden-haired Nigel sported a head bald, yellow, soured by interior failures, and with the tiny, suspicious eyes of a Holbein monarch. Antonio, clumsy, improvident, doggy, was undertaken, very competently, by a bullying, extrovert goalkeeper.

Big School, wide and vaulted, where Mary Tudor had once heard forbidden mass, and Kett's rebels pleaded for bread and straw, displayed long, ornate balconies, a giant, handless Gothic clock surmounted by squatting crows, arches pointed and rounded, a fountain sometimes visible through one of them, Ali Baba jars of rose and myrtle, a criss-cross of golden wires, a wall tapestried with a mythical hunt above a silver table strewn with guitars and lutes. Geoffrey Wilder, art beak, used lights to blur the frontiers between danger and pleasure, the seen and unseen, man and woman. The grotesque, the banal, the wretched joined in brilliant grouping, then parted, exposing a figure haggard in isolation, not hearing the chatter, frivolity, the plucked strings, then dissolving into twilight. Spangled rich as a fuchsia, Olivia begged escape from callous solitude, broke a wineglass, stood appalled. Geoffrey drew gasps, perhaps shudders, as he flooded a garden with mist, eerily green. Orsino's folk were beautiful but incomplete, casting too small shadows, yawning, and etiolated, yo-yo adepts with insufficient to do. Shimmering, opalescent, neatly coupled, few would bear children. Mockery and phrases were easier than intimacy. A child in wraithish blue, a last-minute invention, wandered amongst them, sometimes inveigled dangerously near candles, holding a balloon, unwelcome, passing from one glittering form to another, seeking a smile, an embrace, from all but Aguecheek who, to his own distress, scared him. Of them all, the child preferred Antonio, who did not realize it. Salutes and vows, smiles and inclinations, were too often parodies, teasing, false. Against protests, Graham kept laughter subdued. Beneath his antics, Belch was inescapably ravaged, Malvolio's sincerity embarrassed. 'None can be called deformed but the unkind' harked back to Janet Kirkland, very pale, absolutely still, rebuking a farmer for cruelty to a horse. Viola, with exquisite play of identities, could have hankered to set up house with Bayard, and soon regretted it.

Lapses occurred, a critical line was forgotten, cues were missed, the balloon, very tactlessly, finally burst, giving Viola at her most appealing a resonant guffaw. Malvolio, stepping grandly into an arch which immediately collapsed, uttered a word counter to the text. Yet much of it succeeded, owing, Graham reflected, morose, triumphant, furious, very much to the emergent personalities of the actors. 'Denied me my own purse.' Chunky-nosed Antonio was realizing a pathos that might one day damage him. He stood, young but charmless, brooding amongst beauty, casually disregarded like a muffled report of pain, though he might be the longest remembered of these figures lent precarious grace by powder, tints, satins, and heightened not by language, which they uttered badly and barely understood, but by novice ardour.

'But that's all one, our play is done.'

Backstage was a laughing, disarranged inquest: spendthrift faces streaked with cracking paint, falling powder, tossed wigs, rowdy self-congratulations. 'Yes, yes,' Toby Belch tugged off whiskers, 'I did pretty well. The trouble is ... such a bloody bad play!' Near Sheila, piling clothes, collecting jewels, was a clerkish intruder amongst elves and mignons, Kelly, kindly nodding goodwill and praise, himself part of a further drama. Flushed with acclaim, Graham recalled last year's snow fight, staff and pupils at hilarious grips, yet revealing other, truer selves – lovers and haters, favourites and victims, scared, blustering leaders and obdurate losers, an indelible stain of opposites.

'I say, sir...'

'Graham, over here...'

Beer was thrust at him, embraces were being swapped, eyes and cheeks, hair and lips glowed hideously raw in fierce lights, and in shadow went abnormally sombre. Boys were still rouged and earringed, a girl, masquerading as an ostler, still bearded. Hands touched his arm, from a stage-dream not quite ended.

'Graham!'

Another laminated face, under black wig, pouting with epicine insolence, not yet identifiable. Slender, cloaked, sly Valentine or attendant lady, out of an hour of reversals and sea-change. He heard an indistinct whisper, carelessly, brusquely kissed the upturned face, and pushed on, already slumping into boredom, wanting to be rid of them all.

5

Flambeaux and pearls, doublets and brooches were bundled away, and in common-room attention returned to Bass

Banes's successor. Headship of department was essential for promotion. *Twelfth Night* had fortified Graham's rating, though Kelly, subdued, had been heard to mention pretentious goings-on in Big School.

'Ah, Graham! Have you too heard...?'

Judd, ageing classics chief, presiding over dwindling classes, the subject itself reduced to an option, drew him aside. His fumbling tones were more than usually disagreeable, his gown the torn wings of an indicted angel.

'This may or may not gratify you young men. There's a move to abolish my department when I go. Perhaps even before. I wouldn't put that past the Vandals. Dead languages, they call it. Centuries of effort to be sent to pot. A nation cutting its own roots. That new broom on the governing body, chattering about the shortage of industrial technology. Wanting to exchange wisdom for gadgets. Well,' the reddened, drinker's eyes blinked unhappily, 'the HM's had a word with me. Calls it "rescheduling". Prated about accommodating majority needs. Bah! Majority hogwash. I did my bounden best to convince him of heresy, outrageous betrayal. He quivered like a scared horse when I mentioned the Visitor. An appeal to Caesar, you follow. Even he might still acknowledge the reference. Ah me!' Briefly, the depleted face recovered, the eyes gleamed. 'Most of us are doomed. More than is realized.'

'But Waterfield's a classics man. Can't he stand up for himself?'

'My dear young friend, we both know that our Whisky Meadow doesn't stand, he lies down.'

He smiled mirthlessly, was a front-line bore, but he left an obvious warning. After classics, scripture, music, history itself might follow, shoved aside by civics, accountancy, advanced physics, and obsession with the rights of turbulent minorities.

Sheila had been absent sick. On return, she was apparently unchanged, ready for a random kiss under a tree, a quick embrace on an evening path. If she wanted extras, her brown, lively face did not show it. He himself could be tempted further, but somehow desisted. There was, about her, that sensation of standstill. She was jollier than most girls he had bedded, but jolliness also reminded him of his relief at losing them. He flinched at loving Della. Della's quick, captious voice, never admiring, never quite accusing, enjoyed teasing.

'You're incapable of irony, darling Graham, one of those stalwarts who nail their colours to the mast and are so busy saluting that they forget to swim.'

Della wrote letters only in what she called, ambiguously, her periodic low. The childish handwriting seemed coping with thoughts that moved too fast.

> Last month I wrote several poems and sent them out, doves from the Ark, they fluttered a bit but alighted nowhere and returned to Momma. Beast laughs, of course. I thought of him when I saw a Zola novel in a dirty bookshop and bought it, not to read but to rescue it from revolting company. I tore off the obscene cover, Beast of course thought it rather splendid. Last week we were driving to Aldeburgh quarrelling about whether Stalin will fight for Berlin. Beast says he hopes so, and we saw a *terrible accident*, five cars piled up, the first two utterly smashed, and smoking. Bodies everywhere, covered with blood-drenched newspapers, one had a headline Why Waste Paper? I can't forget two hands crusted with jewels, stretched as if for display. We heard later it was caused by a family row about how much was to be spent on somebody's wreath! People are venial. As for Beast, he keeps breaking **his leg**. Not on me. He's a heroic affliction and I'm glad to **see that** he bores you. Yet he admires *you*, says he could do **with you** in the scrum. How horrid! I'd hate to be in the scrum and very likely never will be. At the very best I'd like to follow the pack, at some distance, on one of Bayard's false scents. Did I tell you, I asked Uncle Roger whether Bayard had possibly done war work so secret that he's still not allowed to reappear. More probably, he ran a black market from the Zoo. Giraffe's feet! But I only got that small, playful smile which says that girls should avoid toys too big for them! Anyway, I'm feeling petulant. I'm twenty-three and all I've published is very dry land sub-Masefield and damp Housman in the school mag. Editors, useful people, make an iron ring I can't smash. So I'm changed to stone, petrified, am stupidly lost in a forest, and am being worried by an impossible girl, actually rather enticing, who

goes on and on about Keats's use of the vocative.

I sometimes think that I don't yet know my own name. We all have a secret name. What's yours? Beau Geste? The Man Who Broke the Bank at Monte Carlo? Beast is, well, Beast, with no proper jungle and heading for no good, like King Agamemnon. At school they called me the Sleeping Beauty, but only because I was lazy and had a big bust, which Beast doesn't let me forget. Yeats, I've read, knew of a Japanese painter so realistic that his horses, painted on a temple wall, would slip away at night and trample the rice fields. An early worshipper saw them returning, still wet from dew, and, back on the wall, trembling into stillness. That's like the moment before starting a poem, when I'm a bird hovering about that marvellous yet threatening white strip, half-afraid to descend.

You, Graham, don't try hard enough, you go where you want to, but not where you must. I invent the name of a place before I've discovered it, and the name creates the place. Anyway, I'm never going to perch a golf-club on the Matterhorn or run a mile even in half an hour, let alone join the scrum, but I can see Yeats's horses. I can see blue cows and the stones that have been known to speak. Even you must see the cloud that's dragonish, but would spoil it by teaching me the origins of dragons. I do think of you, darling Graham, as the airman who notes a cloud only as a factor for consideration in periods of renewed stress! But bless you always, never be just a face scarred by grief, journeys and football pools.

She was immoderate, he could see her green eyes widening, voice hoarsening, small determined chin lifting, as she tossed aside a flap of hair, was very serious, the blackbird above the pale, glistening field, a moon lady in a hurry.

What else, Graham? I've read *Ape and Essence*, or most of it, hoping for analysis of Beast, but even Huxley would jib at that. I'm looking for Mahaux's *Psychology of Art*, which I won't understand and won't need to. That's arrogance, but arrogance has made me a poet, Roger a great man, and will always pull you out of the pits which it makes you dig for yourself. In Uncle Roger's study I'd read what I couldn't quite understand yet knew that it didn't matter, that words have meanings for me alone. When I worked out what the writer really meant, I'd find I'd drained myself empty. 'Dead words smell badly.' I tend to fall very deeply out of love. With people, books, landscapes. Old Wells so thrilled me, but then wanted to teach me answers to fairly small questions. I prefer impossible answers without the questions. It makes life difficult. Roger, of course, keeps an eye on me, he's marvellous at knowing when to ring, to invite, or keep aloof. I suppose I could ask him to pull strings, lobby publishers, etc., but I won't, yet. The begging-bowl can be kept in hock. Really, I want to drive away with Janet, but who knows what she wants? She may be seeking what Job calls the treasures of the snow. I wrote a good poem about snow, but what nasty stuff it really is! We both gave up drink, for Lent, but she was calm, and I got bad tempered. If you ask me, my soul's going to be hard to find. I've also given up painting – not for Lent, but for ever. I can only dream or write pictures now and anyway something always wrecked them, a perversity or unlucky charm. A demon jogging my arm. Lately I dreamed of a pavilion green as Glastonbury, latticed, frescoed. I was both inside and outside. It was bolted within, so that I couldn't enter without spoiling a fresco. I was dragging my eyes through myself – the frescoes, all monsters, curling waves, plants becoming people, rather spooky. I tried to paint them, later, but they escaped, crumbled, and I was left, locked in the pavilion, haunted by animals and human plants. I was small and shrill and woebegone, a scream from a snail.

He kept her letters; they would, she said, one day make a very bad book. Never knowing how much to believe, he resented her entanglement with Beast, though 'Beast' might be only a title, worn by youngsters hulking but transient.

Almost siblings, never quite lovers, Della and he would always banter, quarrel, confide. Defiantly offhand, they both made friends easily, and easily disposed of them. She might go the further. The transparent forests, empty streets, bare courtyards and indeterminate labyrinths, the victims skulking or pursued in her poems and in early paintings suggested spaces waiting to be filled, perhaps powerfully, perhaps by shadows, though, like a Devon villager, like Bryce, she saw more in shadows than mere shadow. But she was also the more vulnerable, like a child enriched by a promise, given, not dishonestly but carelessly. 'Do you *promise*?' Small and insistent, she would accost Roger, grab Janet's hand.

'But it's not exactly an occasion for summary execution, only for a decent measure of taming. Have the lad beaten, the little miss scolded out of her wits. Carefully, mind, she's precious few.'

Sardonic Kelly awoke the staff discussion of two truants detected at a roadside café. Arguments were irritable, late-termy, always about to explode without quite doing so. Waterfield's pale, clear, sheep's eyes were worried as he strove to reconcile incompatibles. The referee who periodically swallows his whistle.

Graham ostentatiously said nothing. Colleagues interested him more than minor delinquents. Bass Banes, already sunk in the miseries of retirement, Judd clutching the remnants of his department, Miss Heppenstall who had failed so many applications, Waterfield, knowing himself appointed not for his talents but for his war wound.

'The trouble is,' Martin Emery seemed pleasantly untroubled, 'that, for sexual lapses, the big stick is rather too close to whatever it penalizes.' This worried the HM further, his face, like a cracked mirror, sporting several expressions at once.

Emery published articles in weeklies of large horizons and small circulations. They were sketches for a creed at odds with the bland, comradely sermons he cooked for chapel, suggesting notions of divine weakness and sceptical of a literal hereafter. God is possibility, he wrote, more than once. Christ is movement or he is nothing. Emery sometimes appeared to prefer the latter notion.

Challenged to the contest by Sheila's wink, Graham interrupted Miss Heppenstall, too brusquely. 'Dammit, nobody's actually been raped.'

'My dear Graham, don't sound so disappointed! With your Byronic tendencies, that's exactly what you would say.'

Well-scrubbed, needing a girl, Kelly was candidly malicious, presumably exhuming Gail. The atmosphere tautened, Waterfield's smile was inappropriate, Sheila started up indignantly, the others were silent for slightly too long. Kelly had scored, though from offside. Then Judd intoned, 'Omnis festinatio ex parti diaboli est.' He translated as if for slum dwellers, 'All haste is from the Devil.' Graham had sensed the unease, the droning occasion held a threat – the marks on snow of an animal not readily identifiable. He shook it aside. Sappy kids seething in a café, good luck to them, they would need it. He himself fretted at rules, had been something of a bully, more than something of a seducer, exorbitantly demanding other boys' bodies, then lapsing into disgust, anger, absurd accusations of betrayal. Twice, Roger Kirkland had saved him from expulsion. Omitted, he considered, unjustly from an eleven, he had fired a pavilion roof. Accused of theft, he defended himself with noisy panache, received apologies, then tearfully, abjectly, confessed guilt, was thrashed, and boastfully displayed his stripes.

Waterfield finally agreed to administer quiet reproof and the younger set departed to the pub, Kelly buying the first pints and doubles, very contented. 'Graham, you deserve extra. You remind us of durabilities.'

'Don't you mean Durex?' His affability was genuine. Kelly's head remained too small for serious consideration.

They sat at fireside tables over baked herrings, pale grey-gold ovals on green platters. 'I adore silence,' Miss Heppenstall said, then briskly dispersed it, resuming debate with Emery. 'How are we to regard angels?'

'Actually, angels are out. Pagan ritual disguise, bird gods, images of the soul in transit. A bit of unseemliness at times.'

'And miracles?'

'I fear they're out too. Our Lord wouldn't have noticed most of them and, when he did, he was usually embarrassed. They contradict the whole point of the Kingdom, the hard labour in the vineyard. Jesus, mind, can be opaque, which gives him news value.'

'I wish I knew when you're serious. What about the Second Coming?'

'Ah, haven't you heard? It's happened! Matthew 16. Incidentally, I like Huxley's belief that Man is capable of God.

But', he was mock-severe, 'you should all keep your eye on the Holy Ghost.'

'I bet you never pray.' Graham enjoyed the grinning warfare and truces of taproom debate, and saw Emery scrutinizing his empty tankard as if miracles, though superannuated, would yet be welcome and, unexpectedly responding, La Heppenstall suddenly bought a round.

'Well, Graham, though mistaken, you're not wholly wrong. Prayer I do indeed find a mite difficult. The kids probably cherish it more than I can. They take it for granted, whereas I tend to regard it as damp dynamite.'

He was pliant as a boudoir monsignor temporarily stranded in quarters congenial but scarcely boastworthy. Agile, dry, with mock self-depreciation, the Revd Emery, like his nominal master, was engaged in movement. The College regarded him with tolerant affection, believing, in his favour, that he had once been a jockey. Applause had started on a hot day when, carefully removing his jacket, he displayed a pullover, selected even more carefully and stitched with a large white rabbit.

Kelly, with suspect friendliness, tapped Graham's knee with woodpecker determination. 'No hard feelings, man!'

Sheila watched, her manner suggesting hard feelings in plenty.

6

Sir Roger Kirkland had left the Foreign Office in 1947, after brief intervention at Nuremberg. Hermann Goering, at long last roused and powerful, had been silenced by a single question, misleadingly casual. Occasionally seen in the Law Courts, he was now more prominent as legal adviser to one of the pushing property complexes soaring on post-war reconstruction with its appropriations, take-overs, threats, confusions. Admired and discussed, he would know of unfriendly voices. He survived from times discredited. Over Munich, he had accused Labour of withstanding Hitler only with pomposity, had agreed with Lord Halifax that, in 1940, Winston was apt to talk the most frightful rot: had urged military support for Finland against Russia as a pretext for capturing or neutralizing Swedish ore. He had been a wartime assistant to Eden. When Labour rejected the European Coal and Steel Pool, Kirkland, Boothby, Maxwell Fyfe and Macmillan had joined Churchill, urging the necessity of victorious Britain to establish, ahead of France and West Germany, a United Europe, undeterred by the Foreign Secretary, Ernest Bevin. 'I don't like it,' Bevin said. 'I don't like it. When you open that Pandora's box, you'll find it full of Trojan horses.' Kirkland had vainly liaised with Jean Monnet, head of the French Planning Commissariat, in efforts towards European economic unity. At Strasbourg he had demanded British promotion and largely financing of a European army, though Eden and Butler were apathetic, Attlee and Bevin hostile. 'Continentals don't play cricket,' Attlee remarked. France rejected it. British Socialism, Kirkland said on radio, had the vision enjoyed by newts, Mr Eden rather less.

London clubs remained, rare nests perched on a lofty, fissured cliff. Paintings, libraries, silver plate, fine wines were back, household gods once borne away by patricians fleeing a siege. The citadel had been reoccupied, palace and cathedral, law court and the noose were intact, danger now squatted in Berlin where relief planes descended and threats from Moscow loudened.

At the Gridiron Club ornate mirrors reflected an ambassador's profile, an ex-premier's shoulder, a glistening chandelier. No food rationing here. One did not envisage these jowled, mottled personages queueing for one egg a week and thirteen ounces of meat. We do not, Roger had just said, as yet demand you share your tankard with the club porter.

The Decimus Burton dining-room glimmered with classical busts, portraits of dead members – Gladstone, Balfour, Allenby, Smuts, Kipling, Galsworthy, Gosse. Under a ceiling sprawling with wanton gods and lolling, grateful goddesses, backed by ovalled, dark-red panels, the arched Chatillon windows and Le Blasseur mouldings, heads nodded, voices conferred, courteous restraint glossing the momentum of those in the know, at ease with unimpeachable sources in the right quarters. Off-centre, Sir Herbert Clavering, knighted for a sojourn in the Ministry of Information, from which only a memo from Downing Street succeeded in ejecting him, was breathing good news into a whiskered ear elaborately cupped.

'Very much between ourselves, of course, this Berlin rumpus, if it does nothing else, will reconcile us to Germany, whose best qualities are now as plain as Dr Adenauer himself, I should say manifest.'

'That East African scandal. Socialism in this very nutshell! A ground-nutshell. The fellow lost us forty million...'

'These ventures benefit a few, I suppose.'

'A very few, and I'd be grateful to know whom.'

Graham was thinking not of Kipling or Gosse but of Buchan. There, a Sea Lord departing, there the former Chancellor, the French Ambassador shaking out smiles with Astaire delicacy, the intricacies of powers not wholly fictional. A dour ex-England cricket captain was leaning towards a banker with more millions than inches. The useful people. Since childhood, to accompany Roger into a club was an initiation into social and political mystery, and he particularly revered the Gridiron, its silver, wines, aura, supplemented by pride in Roger himself, at home with the mighty.

'Ah, Roger....' The name rang like a title, fitting the smooth, ever-interested face, the polished hair still very black, the grey, examiner's eyes reflected in a mass of cutlery. Strong head, strong teeth. The wide, silvery tie decorated with black Picasso centaurs, the pale yellow jacket and faintly blue trousers challenged the prim Whitehall suits and recalled Roger's velvet waistcoat at Oxford, embroidered with nursery rhymes. In current biographies he appeared as a dandy at Sligger's gatherings, at Ronnie's luncheons, in roof-climbings and railway parties, amongst high-pitched connoisseurs and practical jokers with solemn poses and elaborate diction. Like others here, weighted by mastery, bulky with achievement, he was not imaginable soaring into inordinate passions, wild surmises. Instead, he was lifting a hand to one craggy face, raising a glass to another, with his usual punctilious attention.

'Now, Graham, it's time to tuck in. What do you see on this small menu of ours.'

'Your small menu looks like a Trollope novel. What about steak and kidney?'

With Roger, one begged for the least and was granted the best.

'Oh, nonsense! Good heavens, we're being offered salmon fresh from Iain's private loch, four times the market price and eight times better. You'll need a double portion after pigging the atrocities of school meals. Even pre-war house joints compared unfavourably with football boots. Now, to begin with ... yes, just so. But do glance down the wine list. Now you're in your proper quarters, you'll need something a bit special.'

There followed solemn conference with the wine steward. Roger's treating of domestic staff as slightly superior colleagues could be agreeable, provocative, or unnerving. Word perfect, he finally gave a nod, grateful for what he had from the first decided, then uncaged his most intimate smile.

'You may want filling in with some of these household names which so few households actually recognize. By the window, rather pleased with himself, is a chap with some right to be so. He himself is questionable, his role is not. Auditor-General. Keeps an eye on the financial bureaucracy. Not exactly the equivalent of bringing in the scene-shifters' beer at Covent Garden – assuming, of course, they don't demand champagne. In my limited experience, the Treasury can exploit, hoodwink or simply ignore most chancellors and cabinets after an administration's first year. Charles could control absolutely, I'm not saying he actually does so, the departments, super-departments, pseudo-departments which engorge so much of our cash. Governments seldom control expenditure, dictatorships least of all, onwards from friend Nero. It may, of course, be that Parliament has always existed to thwart public opinion. Probably very rightly. As for Charles, he sits on so many boards that he's been known to refer to his wife as the last speaker.'

'Roger, you don't make a first-class case for the democracy you helped rescue!'

'I may have done as much as anyone else, save, on a rapid count, seventeen others. Incidentally, like you, I welcomed Labour's win in '45. They did attempt, rather manfully, to cure the worst excesses of the body politic, but their attitude to Europe and the Empire was pitiful. The opportunities we've missed, in our concern to gratify India, the miners, the sick, even the degenerate. We've been watching suggestive ideas harden into clannish dogma. Yet the coming change of government will not, inevitably, induce sensational change. As for dictatorship, I must confess some initial sympathy for Mussolini as a remedy for pure Woggishness, though he himself didn't improve on acquaintance. I could never exactly think of him as Ben. He once told me that he ranked himself with Dante, and above Verdi and Michelangelo. I suppose I kept a straight face. I left it to another to tell him that a ruler's worst danger is incense. Dictatorship does have merits, as Díaz showed in awful Mexico. You might agree that it can be justified only if it promptly starts preparing better conditions for its own abdication. Sadly, it never does. Mind, during the war, by strictly controlling food, we ourselves made people fitter, leaner, more balanced, without them knowing it. As for Hitler, as Hugh says, he had a court but no government. Those earnest folk who find crime caused by bad drains and domestic tyrannies neglect the role of greed, vanity and the irredeemably vulgar.'

'What's your chief fault? Assuming you have one!'

'Vanity, of course.'

The supple smile, from a humour seldom more than half-disclosed and never that of stand-up comics, and now mock-rueful, defused the admission, almost transferring vanity to the commendable, even inspiring. Roger's sharp smiles, which, without insincerity, never became a whole-hearted grin, flattered, but Graham, as often before, had to suppress an instinct to rebel, to twist the lion's tail. He distrusted the Auditor-General, and Balfour, framed above, looked a dead fish, little better than old Clavering now displaying his breeding on the soft, resplendent carpet, and doubtless convinced that those good chaps his daughters were qualified for the club. And add a peruke, a cloak, to these fleshy patricians and you'd see long-dead cabals enjoying first fruits, guzzling spoils, soothing the grieved and bereft with plausible reasons of policy, and pittances offered with fine discrimination of rank.

'Who's Bertie's chum?'

Kirkland had a habit of leaning forward as if to gather the exceptional, yet was apt to relax abruptly, as if disappointed, though now he was looking pleased, the great coach applauding his star player.

'He doesn't look much, does he! He hasn't changed that suit for eleven years. Yet he worked with Alan Turing. Who does that mean to the gentleman in the street? Nobody! Yet he's one of the greatest electronic pioneers in the world. His, and the American cryptographic computers, cracked German Intelligence and finished Italy. What rather worries me, Graham, in your choice of profession is that our most civilized academies seem very stylishly applying themselves to a world rapidly ceasing to exist.'

Judd's classics rusting on the bough, Shakespeare obsolete in a glitter of tubes, retorts and switches, one's own classes condemned as irredeemably trivial, though there was the saving inference that Roger, always the guardian, elder brother, pathfinder, had further plans for him, not gallant but high-flying.

Roger, at this instant, was more concerned with the bottle slanted in its silver ice-bucket, then inspected juicy slivers of salmon. 'During the Normandy landings, when I visited the decoding service HQ at Bletchley, I realized that it was there, rather than with the brave lads in France wielding musket and pike, that victory was being assured. I actually witnessed the breaking of Runstedt's ciphers, by the last word in maths, mechanics, electronic engineering.'

Something, however, was due to the brave lads in France, though there was no chance to say so. 'I don't envy you your field. Too many swanking young go Bolshie, then whine that they're scared of the Bomb. Do you meet any who actually are? It sometimes seems an easy device to smother thought. Get them to try to imagine Stalingrad, even Pearl Harbor, and you might split their tender bowels and give red meat to their consciences. I myself tend to agree with Einstein that the Bomb may intimidate the human race into bringing order into its international affairs, which, without the pressure of fear, it would not do. Bertrand Russell has said much the same.'

His expression denied any hope of Graham's refuting Einstein, Russell and, not least, himself. Further savouring the wine, the salmon, he shrugged, still watching not only his guest but his fellow members, as if they were pawns on his board. 'I suppose it's now common knowledge that when Attlee took over government no minister knew a scrap about the atomic project. We still lack a coherent atomic strategy. Cabinet had no say in establishing the plutonium research base. Indeed, our Clem spent some hundred millions to make us an atomic power without reference to the Commons, taxpayers, most of his senior colleagues. I myself had some part in the problem of gaseous diffusion dividing up Uranium 235, and can claim more familiarity with our nuclear dealing abroad than did Premier and Monarch.'

The words, uttered negligently, were those of a tyro seldom needing full strength. The intimacy was inviting, and had they been alone, Graham might have exorcized that stillborn, tortuous, perplexed guilt left by the scalding time when Winston, Eden and, presumably, Ike, had known their business. Roger could be trusted to know the truth, the reasons of policy echoing for so long through lustred apartments. Some of these men here, so visibly enjoying their fruits of labour, so jovial within their dignity, ennobled by the past, glad of the future, might have issued the orders. At this instant a direct question would be maladroit, answered too readily, too reasonably, appeasing the membership.

The instant passed, dissolved into sorbet and booze. Kirkland ordered another bottle, sipped, rejected it, demanded replacement with apologetic movement of eyebrow. Again the glasses foamed, faces beyond lost some distinctness, voices went fuzzy, until a lately dismissed Permanent Under-Secretary restored focus, pausing at their table, his wide smile addressed to them both. After he had gone, Roger slightly lowered his voice. 'We'll be getting you to meet him in due course. I doubt if the general gender quite appreciated the limitations of his authority. Bevin let him down badly. He at least managed to sabotage a dotty proposal for all UK and Empire citizens, indeed citizens of all countries, having rights of appeal to the Secretary-General of the United Nations. Imagine how many appeals would be likely to emanate from Moscow! It did show that the real dangers are less east of the Elbe than within ourselves. Meanwhile, and for the nonce more important, where have our excellent Hebes parked the brandy?'

He looked about him as if expecting to find it afloat beside him. Then an impatience drifted across him, making him more easily imaginable at Nuremberg, demanding more than brandy. 'Did you see a letter in *The Times*, gabbling about something calling itself Crystal Knot? Accusing it of collecting money for nefarious purposes, from sources unknown and probably equally subversive.'

He did not expect an answer, though Graham reflected the name, vaguely overheard, quickly forgotten. He was soon asking about Janet.

'I've seen her lately.' Kirkland's response was unexpected, but he and Janet had their own ways. 'She frets for flowers and home-made silence. London can get too strenuous. But I'm worried about Della.' He spoke so fluently that the change of subject was barely discernible. 'That dreary little flat! She's never very easy to keep track of, though she sends me a poem occasionally. Poetry, I admit, is one of many areas where my judgement's risky. She's chosen hard roads, and when a roadside inn turns out to be a pigsty, she's inclined to be rash. That young swain of hers, to put it kindly, is an outsize pig, a living dirge. You did once remind me that Celts worshipped pigs, but she's not a Celt. She knows, and enjoys it. She's never said one word of common politeness about him, seems to recoil from men of substance, prefers her grimy entourage of mountainous hair and pretentious idleness. Like certain of our theatrical luminaries who purposefully surround themselves with the mediocre. The dear girl has so many assets. That lopsided smile of hers wins her many hearts, she has brains and capacity for hard work, but she carries her moods and wounds like a flagellant. She can be a child on a birthday of disappointments. Anyway, she's hoping to get a book ready. I'm not a crony of any publishers of standing, though I can see to it that she doesn't get fleeced. I won't recommend her to Rufus over there, falling asleep, or dying. He's reviewed that new biography of Ramsay MacDonald as "a masterpiece of tact", evidently considering this a compliment.'

The brandy was starting to slosh about inside him, with a reminder of Bayard saying that whenever Roger said he was worried, one could be certain that he was not.

'No news of Bayard?'

Though it was a ritual question, Roger very minutely hesitated. 'No.' He seemed about to continue, but only summoned a waitress. 'Do you think, Sarah, we could possibly be allowed some additional brandy?' His politeness, mannered friendliness, air of giving others slightly more than their due, expressed both some doubt about the availability of brandy and no doubt of an ability to fetch it for himself if necessary.

Whatever he might have divulged about Bayard was abandoned. 'I'm afraid he may have rejected us, though I can't help thinking that he's biding his time.'

A Bayard, existing through centuries, should contrive to do that. His defection must have hurt the Kirklands but in different degrees.

Roger was satisfied with the brandy. They smiled, very pleased with each other, the guiding elder, the younger man trusting, admiring, but now, like a stage solicitor, a steward was handing Roger a note.

'Damn! Sorry, Graham, I thought we might have gone off together to look at a few paintings, but I'm summoned. Finish your drink, take your time.' And he was already departing, dispensing brisk farewells to observant men of substance.

Graham was incapable of leaving a glass or bottle unemptied. Afterwards, slightly unsteady, he spoke to gruff, bleary Clavering, who promised that next month would bring wonderful news. Aloft, the painted illustrious, all high-nosed sneers, furs and satins, were fleetingly seen through trickly streaks of sunlight and fumes of the best cigars in London. A Devon magnate advanced, then receded, one who had, in fact, died years ago. Notables stood before the fire as if for a square dance. What would they say if a steward courteously offered them, on the revered Montanus plate, a still moist parrot's beak?

He managed to reach the hot, empty street. He felt sick, the spring air barred by swollen, quivering doors, thickening curtains and pillars. He saw, or thought he saw, a tousled youth extending a raw, scratched hand, faintly bleeding. At once it was replaced by a red and black placard: *We voted Labour and got it. Hard.* Wanting to vomit, in clubman's uniform, college tie, he felt grotesquely outsize. Sickly, overheated traffic trailed past, through air travestied by fumes. A gull flew up, lurid and dangerous; dodging, he almost fell, but it was only white paper freakishly stirred by a dusty puff. He was fumbling with a locked gate that withheld cool grass, smooth aloof trees starting to lurch. A woman's scarlet mouth stared, a hideous wound, a man's cry thudded from a window, a girl's nose was demoniacally long. Pavements were steps, he was Nijinsky in gumboots, blundering eastwards under a raucous sky. The heavy dome smouldered, a brain smeared with hefty, consistent brightness. He sought the bomb ruins, soon lying in heady vetch, thistle, fireweed, unnaturally tall, almost human, suckled by the flesh beneath.

7

Berlin remained beleaguered, Europe survived on sufferance, on others' oil. Mr Masaryk lay dead under his window. Graffiti, tilted lines around a circle, enscribed 'Crystal Knot', drawn with unusual competence, appeared on London walls and were mentioned in an Emery article as an image of God, very properly lacking gender.

The College appointment was almost due. Waterfield smiled in all directions, governors flicked through Quad, the Visitor had visited. Richly unperturbed, summer unfolded and Kelly dwindled, submerged in blues, greens and the foams of Queen Anne's Lace.

Sheila showed worry. 'You aren't over-confident?'

'But I've got you on my side.'

She began a wry smile. 'You use me like a cricket bat. Guaranteed to make ninety-nine.' She left him to complete the smile.

'Ninety-nine, hit wicket.'

'Probably run out.'

The bell rang. He made for the classroom with renewed zest. Life was a matter of rough balances, unexpected checks. Existence requires the difficult, even a hideous command.

Summer term. We take pride, Mr Waterfield assured parents, in our family atmosphere; a recommendation, Kelly said, that only adults assumed was praise.

Graham strode through cool cloisters on his way to nets. A shadow sidled towards him, some boy, blurred, soft-faced, with eyes darkish and indeterminate.

'Sir!'

In a hurry, always in a hurry, Graham halted. He had never seen him before.

'I'm terribly disappointed, sir.'

Then he was gone, reclaimed by thick, yellow light. Graham stood motionless, suddenly stricken with depression, chilled in the hot afternoon.

For that week, he was puzzled, beginning to see the boy more clearly. Pale skin, dark hair, the concerned voice, not callow but oddly knowing. He described him to Emery, who did not recall him. Then to Sheila, and was surprised by her quick, backward glance, precaution against the gowned and prying.

'What was so wrong about him?'

'I haven't said anything was wrong.'

The irritability, the ill-banked-down impatience made him overgrown and coarse, the Viking surly from an improvident voyage.

'Tell me...' – she had hardened, the brightness giving her fair head a sharp halo, as she questioned him like a doctor – 'what happened after the play? Immediately it finished?'

He stared. The sun was battering too many minds.

She was too casual. 'Did you kiss one of the boys?'

'I kissed something not particularly nice. What about it?'

'Don't you think it was rather dangerous?'

Chill descended again as she brought her hands together in a plea strangely urgent. 'There was talk. There always is. I think there still is, but people go quiet when they see me. Priceless tact! They say he was Langdon. James Langdon. Who was he? Curio, I think, I wound his sash.'

'Acne and wet eyes. Too wet and packed too bloody neatly. Christ, can they make dirt from that!'

Remembering Gail, he said more slowly, 'Well, the fellow in Cloisters certainly wasn't Langdon. I don't think he was anyone. Perhaps Martin's holy ghost. They say corpses sometimes gleam. But you're really suggesting blackmail?'

'Kelly was there too. Backstage.'

'And I dare say in sniper's pose. Still, we're told that microbes enrich the body.'

Much would remain unexplained. Life sometimes threw out one notion too many.

8

Draw a window, peer through it, gaze into faces, tired, saucered pools that have stood too long before gas fires. Watching them, Della reflected that the prolonged childhood summers had always foretold happiness. Elms, rivers, meadows slid safe through darkness, through dawn, colours mounting, like Bavarian princes who summon midnight retainers. Butterflies had scattered above zinnia and tansy, marigold and delphinium, and along hedges ripe with the crimson and speckled, the mauves and yellows which, on canvas, solidified in points and angles, rectangles and circles of light. In this oblong of sunlight quivering before her were other shapes, the tiny, particled masses which make worlds.

In his head-on, embattled way, Graham, the brigand, Captain Cartridge, shared her sense of life, its traps and joys, shared it perhaps too completely. When a boy, he would unexpectedly start running, had inexplicable fits of laughter and weeping. He lived in a western, was temperamentally violent, but of his war service, presumably valiant, he never boasted, did not even speak. Like her, he demanded space, independence, shying from domesticity and expectation of pensions. He saw himself not as a prince with transforming kiss, deliverer to awaken a season, though it was to him she so often turned, without his being aware of it.

She needed deliverance, was the painter who sees a forest as the green, columned citadel in a dream Poznan but has ceased to examine root, bark, leaf. She would await the curtain to rise, without realizing that it had done so, or that there might be no curtain, not even a theatre. She watched the common, but it appeared winter-bound despite lovers and cricketers, lifeless as her poem about dwarfs, all absent, in five stanzas, none started, and the voyager who now angrily, now slyly, refused to appear. At times very hot, at times very cold, as if submitting to ambiguous healers, she could not break out, she fumbled for shapes and sounds that abjured an author. Inner veins and bones and song eluded her, discoveries failed to reach paper or, doing so, degenerated into idle comment, or died. Imagination folded inexpert wings, then lay still. Editors turned away: Mortimer, Lehmann, Connolly. She could only reach back to the Dragon House where she had imagined that a ceiling, intricately enscrolled, was wedding-cake, always beyond reach. Janet's bedroom had glamour imaginable only through music.

She also recalled a queer conviction that bowls of flowers had often stood on the very rims of tables, so that she feared to breathe an air too taut.

Here, in Clapham, her pen was blighted, voices within her had sickened on rubbish, her face had frozen. A verdict was being prepared, like fire smouldering beneath the nursery floor, soon to flaunt the atrocious. No sage waited at crossroads, no clues lay on forest paths, treasure was as improbable as *arse* in a Henry James novel or a dirty shirt on M. Swann. Like a Victorian governess, she was fondling impossibles.

Mornings quickly sagged into desert on which, stark as cacti, waited Clare with her troubles, Jo with insufficient troubles, Jeff his own trouble, with talk of high-rise subculture. She would start writing, soon desist, stare hopefully, apprehensively, at wall or tree, then depart. A dog had trotted towards her, then collapsed, dead. An Irishman gestured like a terrorist, 'We'll be coming to get you.' One bright summer noon London darkened, the sun was extinguished, people were suddenly kneeling on pavements enclosed in foggy night. Once, fear had sped through houses at a rumour of tinkers with goats, occupying back gardens. On all sides, madmen babbled of world conquest, cherished their oddity. To risk solitude could be extinction, or greater being, on the frontier between living and dead, the distinction not always visible. But too often the moment lost its spine, she relapsed into café moods, boulevard instincts, in which to watch with Beast a Whitechapel stripper, tight skin and too much rib, moaning of pauper's love, while a blotched art critic, sacked for preferring Turner to de Staël, his painted lip and black-ringed eye twitching in creepy duet, banged the table, 'Traitors ... upper-class traitors', then screamed that the beer had scalded him. Upstairs, Beast said, rather wistfully, veterans would be floundering on naked kids, some crippled, under ceiling mirrors. Here, a prudish, intellectual voice remarked, 'We are in Alexandria', and Beast mumbled that toothpaste spread on biscuit assisted sexual performance. He showed no inclination to prove it: he fulfilled few wants, no necessities, he demanded too little, revered her, was a useful provider and butt, but too often like a noseless gardener offering geraniums for their smell alone. A languorous smile from Susie, light embrace from Rose, an oath from Graham or invitation from Roger stirred her more. Yet, obscurely, she craved to love the unlovable, and accept the unpleasant chalice. Much love, nevertheless, was a search for much grievance. The Kirklands knew sufficient of love to avoid marriage, itself military terrain, a space not for comedy but in which to broadcast threats, raise troops, entice allies, manoeuvre, deploy, skirmish, feign retreat, signal for offshore support, then mount the attack.

Chekhov had written: 'I promise to be a marvellous husband, but give me a wife who is like the moon and won't appear in my sky every day.'

Yet men, however gross, could surprise. She had once shown Beast her manuscript, cautiously, as if feeding a rhino. He held it for a time, upside-down, then at last began reading, laboriously, then uttered approvingly, 'A warmth of misunderstandings'. She was puzzled, the line was surely not hers, certainly not his. He grinned as if at a changing-room witticism, returned the papers and at once she saw the line but remembering neither it nor the poem, as though the page itself had written it. And nail-biting, tantrumy Graham at times showed symptoms of a would-be mystic, wallowing in seas and skies of unlikely blue.

Life withheld much, but dropped sleight-of-hand prizes. A spell of depression, when she daily expected her hair to fall out, her skin to wither and eyes lose all message, was dispersed when an attractive student photographed her from an angle tellingly dramatic – perhaps, like the mysterious poem, prophetic: it bespoke a flair of insight through which she could welcome herself anew. The unexplained, inexplicable poem suggested, more than its companions, that she might possess talent, like a speck of glass buried in a dirty carpet but occasionally flashing. She still possessed those elastic moments, to prise secrets from the common street. Who else noticed the iron Victorian lids on pavements, their scrolls, letterings, fancies, entry to coal-holes, entry to poems? She alone had described the London square where, last year, a man and woman, all smiles, had offered poisoned chocolates to strangers, and left several adults and children dying on the grass. At the Goat and Compasses opposite sat the mackintoshed ghost, apprehended through senses almost lost. Everywhere hovered infinite pressures, delicate exchanges.

Parties were an escape, people complained of them but always went. Sometimes there seemed but a single party, flowing continuously, in which to dip, swim a few strokes, or strike out, get rescued, win a race. Roaring parties where you screamed for silence, parties where fireside poets praised winter, the strict tree and the solid sky, and critics like auctioneers compared Betjeman to Bartok; publishers' parties at which, still only a hanger-on, like jolly Mr Blow-me-Tight, she might speak to Mr Spender, smile at Mr MacNeice.

Prayers align to fate, the psychic groove, which ensure they get answered, though obliquely, ironically, sardonically, or too late. Returning home, she found her door open, though surely she had locked it, and a stranger standing at the window. Outlined against bright air, he was thin rather than lean, vague hair, eyes blocked by dark glasses, a drooping mouth. He moved, the brightness parted, she saw dark blue coat, whitish trousers, a tie patterned with small pale squiggles, like knots.

'Do come in.'

Behind the glasses he was impersonal, like a scientist, not quite a stranger but unfamiliar, his presence at once making her ashamed of the stained kettle and gas-ring, tired rugs and stale Cubist reproductions. He gave her a nod of pronounced condescension.

'Bayard!'

Actually, he had changed little, and was now opening a

bottle she did not recall buying.

'Bayard, it's you!'

He was more concerned with the wine, and began dusting two glasses, more fussily than she considered necessary. Weakly, she asked him how he was.

'I've agreed to call it a bad cold. You'll be glad, though, that I've just been delivered a largish cheque for a job I haven't agreed to undertake.'

Useless to ask what the job was, or question the cheque.

'But where've you been? All these years! We've missed you. Missed you terribly.'

He seated himself, at once rose, found a cushion, tried again, looked around for something else, which he failed to find, like an actor who's spoken a witty line inadequately heard, then inspected her.

'I was dead for some time.' He was modest, deprecatory, 'One can only put it so. I rose again. One always does.'

'I suppose so. But what was it like?'

She too could play games, and watched the long, colourless face consider the question as it might a text of secondary importance.

'Not, as you might suppose, a complete nothingness. Sounds occasionally came through. Shadows sometimes moved, as if seen through dark tissue. No change to bright colour, no feeling of waiting, expectation, belief. Not silence, but a continuous rustling like dry leaves or papers. Some sense of identity but no memories whatsoever. Just as well. My memories rot the soul, like old Bryce's home-made jam. In the Islamic paradise, you may know, bananas are provided. Despite our present gluttony, very understandable, more than forgivable, that's scarcely an inducement to convert.'

'It sounds like school.'

'Very like school. Not, I'd say, the highest praise. Now, what about your writing?'

'Not good.'

'You may need adventures. Sherlock Holmes still maintains that the example of patient suffering is the most precious lesson in an impatient world. Scarcely advice for a new and ambitious scribbler and not, in all aspects, for me. But I suppose you've a clutch of poems ready for showing?'

'Nobody's interested. Sometimes, not even me!'

'The world may have to get used to you. There's no pressing reason to obstruct it. Well then, publishers buzz around like bluebottles, and they're now allowed more paper. I'm not going to recommend Julian. I know he publishes your friend Rosemary, rather torrid stuff, you might say and have probably done so, but at his dinner-table he offers the choice of hearing Seven Serious Songs, by Brahms, or most of Churchill's war speeches. Should you prefer honest conversation, he recounts in some detail the plots of Laurel and Hardy movies. He paints a red spot on his wife's forehead. Not even the wife cares to inquire why. No, we'll exclude Julian. That leaves Reggie. But, dealing with poetry, he's always reaching for a ball which the batsman has, very sensibly, covered with grease. Also, he does rather hate books. His ideal production would be a best-seller with wide margins, huge print, and seventeen pages, marketing at fifteen pounds. He enjoys killing snails. An unequal contest, you might think.'

'I used to imagine that in every book was a devil or faceless fairy, so that it had to be opened gingerly, or not at all.'

'You may not have been far wrong, but let me get this settled. Ronnie has started a new firm. I've known him seventy years and am still uncertain whether he knows how to read. But, more important, he's got flair, and we'll keep him in mind. He's a friend of the famous Stravinsky – not the composer, but the more useful one. At present, he's displeased with me, for reminding him that we only have the Jews' word for it that they actually were chosen.'

Yes, he was Bayard, the empty light behind him outlined him like a kiosk. He was masked, always joking yet affronted by laughter, the stranger from the East, Dionysos turned puritan.

He had not touched his own glass but refilled hers. He was pleased, in his stiff manner.

'We'll let Rick publish you. Rick Allweather, you must know him. He's rather in need of youth. With his backing, people find themselves inventing talents they weren't born with, providing they really want to. Actually, the born writer often throws it away, like Mr Belloc, who needs a very serious talking to. Do you think you ... no, perhaps not. Rick will badger you into paying money to hear Stella, his wife or something very much like it, six hands high, showing her paintings in a draughty church hall in Islington or an open-end tent in Croydon. Dryness is all.'

She had wanted to hurry into talk of Graham, the Kirklands, the war, even the Clavering mess-room where the fellows must be due for promotion, but she could think only of Mr Allweather. At school, wild-eyed Miss Ashby, 'You must all now meet dear Emily Dickinson', had lent her *The London Forum*, in which Allweather published Huxley, Forster, Waugh, Sitwells, Norman Douglas, Lawrence. Stories about him revolved like planets. He had charged the Arts Council for his taxi to Wales, for Dylan Thomas's funeral, invited Harold Acton to dinner, then locked him in the study to write a longish article, and, for a Benjamin Britten essay, paid with a promise to include a drawing of Britten at Mrs Allweather's next exhibition. At the birth of her baby Rick had flared into a hand rash, the baby itself soon dying, apparently from Stella's showing works by Klee and forgetting to stop.

Bayard was gently self-satisfied, evidently expecting her to drink all the wine. His own physique did suggest kinship with some lord of air and darkness, or Keats's gipsy who ''stead of supper would gaze full hard against the moon'.

'Is that a club tie, Bayard?'

A Bayard is never astonished, seldom surprised, but a faint ridge of perplexity lifted above the dark glasses.

'It is, of course, the Crystal Knot.'

'I've heard of that. Only just. What is it?'

His mouth, his eyebrows, remained severe, slightly put out.

'Even you, Della, should know of the Saratoga League. It could become your hope of salvation, if indeed it hasn't already done so. If you don't know, you deserve censure. But yes, it's a club, of sorts, and the Knot is its emblem.'

He was patient, he was reasonable, he was almost convincing, his tone quietly monotonous, reciting like a guide, peeling off facts staled by repetition.

'It began in pre-revolutionary Paris, with an Orleanist banquet to celebrate the British surrender in America. At Saratoga. We held out for moderate radicalism. Lafayette, rather a bore, had a hand in it, so did Beaumarchais, when sparing time from arms profiteering. Likewise, when Minister in Paris, Benjamin Franklin. Very prudently he hedged his bets and traded French naval secrets both to Pitt and Washington. I gave him a word of warning. An early member was Laudet, of whom you won't have heard. Graham would have heard, but forgotten. One hot night in the Convention he nerved himself to demand Robespierre's arrest. And won. Saratoga proved more important in resisting Terror, red and white, than many historians have allowed. We wanted not wild victory but reasonable compromises. This meant spirited opposition assisted by sly cunning, against high-minded asses and careerist thugs. I really do agree with Roger that revolutionaries always misunderstand the nature of life. So, of course, does he. You don't readily imagine Uncle Roger in a morality, depicting Charity.'

'Uncle' was uttered as if it were an award, resonant, romantic, but unacknowledged in polite places. Bayard had been Roger's favourite, but Bayard's manner always implied some grudge, and he disliked being alone with Roger. She had seen them as magicians with rival prophecies, and now wondered whether, during these missing years, he had been secretly visiting Janet, who had said nothing. The thought was disturbing.

Removing the dark glasses, he regarded her severely. The eyes were unchanged, bland, still, set slightly too close. A face pared, charmless, of scant feature, yet part of Bayard whom they had loved. Already chairs, tables, shelves, even the horrid carpet had brightened.

'The League's outside political parties, which at best are organized prejudice. Adlai Stevenson goes about saying that in order to obtain office a candidate has to render himself unfit for it. I can't very often put it better. Like Roger, I disdain the hurly-burly. Like you, I'm a detective, interested in certain people, certain hints, with an end in view.'

Another plane of life was beginning, where parallel lines meet.

'After 1939 the League revived, reinforced by recruits from underground Resistance conferences in 1944 from fifteen different countries. We enrolled the Gestapo boss of Occupied Holland, who risked his own fairly thick neck to release a German refugee, condemned to hang, after reading his book *The Rebirth of Europe*. Stauffenberg applied too late. Not so Wallenberg, Rauel Wallenberg. An amateurish Swedish diplomat in wartime Hungary, he rescued thousands of Jews by boarding the Auschwitz train, dishing out Swedish passports and marching them off, having frozen the SS gents with an unfriendly stare. He later blackmailed the Gestapo into cancelling the blowing-up of the entire Budapest ghetto. He's still alive', Bayard's glasses seemed to hollow, sockets in a bleached skull, 'in a Russian gaol, and it's been largely left to us to try and extract him. The League exists to note those unforgettable enormities which, like Stella Allweather's daubs, are forgotten very easily. In May '45 our Russian allies, having arrested Wallenberg on charges never made public, shot fifteen Poles who'd returned to Warsaw on a safe conduct. Our foremost Socialist journal called it of secondary importance, the Tories were too busy toadying to a country where the Torture Squad is called the Service for Intensified Investigation. The poetry of mother tongues! Mind, much of the League has to be fairly low-key. You may have noticed our bulletin exposing the Government's confiscating a naval officer's farm and then not using it.'

Bayard had always been least trustworthy when most plausible. She wanted to giggle and perhaps did so, imagining him cross-legged for years behind an arras designed by Disney and imagining himself rolling up the world, then looking for somewhere to stack it. He himself, never deterred by acknowledgements of absurdity, looked like a B movie character, so over-evidently a terrorist that the police erroneously search elsewhere.

An instant later, standing up, elongated, motionless, he was no terrorist but a drab apostle spoon unable to bend.

'Bayard, you've treated us badly. Graham's always missed you, he's been unhappy. And have you seen Roger and Janet?'

'I understand he keeps her tucked away like a talisman. Rather sensible, in the circumstances.'

'What circumstances?'

'I used to believe that a love relationship was best fostered by never keeping quite enough blankets on the bed. They're devoted, but I dare say each has spoilsport tendencies. I rather enjoy being reminded of my own faults, when they can be detected. Roger, we can agree, does not.'

'What matters is that you must see them, and Graham. Tomorrow Roger's giving a party, and you'll come.'

'I shall, of course, have to clear it with the Air Vice Marshal.'

'Who?'

Again, that joky, maddening incredulity. If you handed Bayard a sugar-stick he'd feign ignorance of its purpose. Then he resumed the dark glasses and spoke like a prosecutor ill-favoured by the Saratoga League.

'You know perfectly well, and it's sheer snobbery to pretend you do not. Meanwhile, you must nail Rick Allweather to the mast. You'll find him a virtuoso, rather exhausting display of catholic taste and goodwill.'

9

June had cloyed, the blue days clouded, east wind blew litter through Quad. Annoyed by Bayard's secrecies, Graham was sceptical of Crystal Knots, Saratago Leagues, which, if more than a gravely conducted and expensive prank, could be compared only to such small-scale groups as Empire Loyalists, Anarchist League of Freedom, Anti-Nazi Movement, Men of the Trees, Save the Whale. Bayard could qualify for a Chair of Hypothetical History, lecturing minuscule audiences on Shakespeare's autobiography, William's defeat at Hastings, Hitler's acquisition of the A Bomb. From Della's reports, he might have spent long years in an asylum. To demand a serious answer from him had never been rewarding. He affected to exist in metaphor, surely to conceal deficiencies common enough. It allowed him a certain presence.

When at last they met, at Montpelier Square, he had talked his customary, mystifying patter within which probably Janet would discern another, more intimate language.

Change of weather, change of mood. Younger beaks tried to rally him. 'Graham, your light's out. Where's your life structure?' Martin Emery was particularly concerned and encouraging. But authority, bright ribbons, popularity, could be won too easily. Challenges from children were puny, ridiculed by the late siege of Berlin, by East European take-overs and Chinese mass executions, crisis in Malaya, threats in Korea; by post-war Britain and Empire with generous chances and chances of generosity, for better bodies and higher spirit, and Roger's talk of fortunes wrapped in the unfamiliar – petro-chemical conversions and stabilizations, capital intrusive ventures, transmission pipe consorts. He was corrupted by merry-go-round routine, was Antonio getting nowhere.

Waterfield summoned him, uneasy behind a chin-up manner. 'My dear fellow, do come in.' He hesitated, 'I don't want to beat about the bush.'

He at once did so. Kelly had said that he had beaten for so long that the bush was invisible.

'Graham, I count on you. I've an imposition to impose on your broad shoulders. I don't have to tell you what a success you've proved with us. Nevertheless....' Further hesitations, the scratch, the cough, the whole repertoire of well-intentioned, self-indulgent junk. 'It's this very dim matter. The History Department is still, so to speak, one hopes temporarily, in declension, ah decline. I'm going to have to ask you, beg you, to take on an extra subject.'

Afterwards Sheila, the decent sort, arrived too promptly, urged by planted news.

'You're not getting the Department?'

'If there's still to be a department, I'll probably stay where I bloody well am, with extra French chucked in, to lighten some-body else's load. I'd like to have been born a land-mine.'

'So Kelly gets it!'

'The old fool didn't actually nerve himself to say so.' He went very quiet. 'Well, I'm no fool generalissimo, swaggering through fears of the future. Stupid Waterfields and dreary Kellys who've got no spunk for a new life.'

He was startled by the pink anger, scraped from a face suddenly schoolmarmish, then slamming down as if to conceal tears.

'You're the blessed, for whom everything turns out well. To do you justice, if it doesn't, you make it so. But you look over all our heads, always looking for something better, someone better. You've thrown away the job, it's the excuse you've wanted. Others abide our question, but you're fucking well free.'

10

From a night of beldam clouds and hectic moon Sunday was being opened by sunlight brilliantly fresh, while broken pictures from her dream remained scattered like the segments of carpet, flower, sky, glimpsed through Dragon House arches, each disclosing ciphers which so swiftly vanished into an infinite pool of chances. Leaves, though past midsummer, looked deeply green, very gentle. Discoveries fell into her, she netted images, overheard hints. A raindrop hung from a twig: white, it trembled, reddened, winked into green, shook back into pale transparency, then dissolved as if shaken by a swallow's shadow.

Five poems had been accepted by *The London Forum*. Mr Allweather had replied at once, writing that despite the clatter of the Festival of Britain, his own festival, the discovery of new talent, had never ceased. Would she not present herself, for Sunday lunch, a humble repast but graced by fellow artists. He enclosed an announcement of his dear wife's exhibition at Slough Temperance Hall.

Graham, in hoity-toity pique, had resigned his job, would require flattery, reassurance, consolation surprising for so hefty a man. What tempests and madcap raids Graham imagined he suffered and how small they actually were! Soon he would be roaming not desolate, beauty-spun Antarctica or Patagonian wilderness but Mediterranean sunlands before, rather too grandly, accepting new employment, jumping a queue without knowing it.

She herself had no time for pique or ravagement. New skies had slid open, oceans of light were sweeping broken, wargnawed London. 'Your poems excite me greatly ... your mastery of spacing ... your bruising imagery.' Through Mr Allweather the fine meshes of words coiled within her would

unwind like a shimmering turban, then solidify into poetry.
    She felt herself sparkle in green linen jacket, green slacks, blue scarf, Graham's gift: golden bracelet. Her hair, like the raven in ballads, was fresh, her skin tangy, as she strode over bounds closed to Steve and Jo, unheard of by Beast. Members Only.

Château Allweather, high, pillared, shabby. *No War over Berlin* still stuck on a window, probably replacing *Arms for Spain*. A man and a girl politely – too politely? – talking on the pavement, swiftly melted into a story, becoming Bob and Hélène, Bob never stamping envelopes so that girls would better remember him, riding a naked typist in an office ashine with red telephone, black desk, matt olive carpet, polar white shelves, a girl's portrait on the wall. Hélène's? No, she was vaguer, sillier, scarcely assembled, though apt to call herself orphaned, once to a sympathetic cluster that included her mother.
    Rick's bell did not ring, she pushed into a hall cluttered with boots and cycles, making for the voices beyond.
    A long room was lazy with sunlight revoked by lively, chattering guests, none of whom had yet seen her as she waited, not nervous but like a child pausing before a favourite meal: sausages, ice-cream, bramble jelly, crumpets, chocolate gâteau. One wall was crammed with *The London Forum*, standard classics, proof copies, paperbacks. On another a messy, thickly worked painting, a reminder of Bomberg, was a confluence of blunt reds, trickling blues and yellows, through which an orange girl was just visible, reading at a window above a densely flowered garden. Stella's perhaps.
    'Della! How kind! How very, very kind!'
    Holding, like a stage prop, an unlit pipe, Mr Allweather, in crumpled brown tweeds, pink, hairy tie, was advancing as though leading a regiment. He spoke with the exaggerated gravity too often adopted for girls and dogs. He would not have used it on Huxley or Mr Shaw. Florid, bald, large, he was a chunk of countryside long tamed. A moist, beefy face, grooved with purples, patched with discolours of age and drink, smiling generously, opened on stained, irregular teeth, closing as he gripped her arm, then her hand. His breath was steamy and like the badly shaved chin, coarse. High on each

sleeve was a small pocket, each holding cigarettes which, at a distance, had suggested additions to a uniform. His blue eyes, about to overflow, under grey hedges, encased in tiny tricks of fat, were affectionate, a kiss hovered, then changed course and dissolved. Following him like a tough dinghy, grey, stout, in long, red, rustling skirt, was a serious lady, equine beneath grey, untidy fringe, her skin, despite heavy powder, seeming to retain the light imprint of a veil. Their progress made some dozen heads at last turn, more or less surreptitiously, to inspect the latest recruit, the nursing lass or drummer boy, and nick off points of interest or worse.

Mr Allweather's voice crushed all murmurs, was rasping, strained from so many conferences, congresses, exhibitions of cultural vivacity, platform oratory.

'Della, this is Stella ...' – the rhyme almost induced her laughter but the voice was stern, as if declaring an emergency – 'the companion of my labours. I expect you know everyone else. I particularly wanted to rope in our friend Bayard. What a resourceful fellow he is! Someone called him a wisecrack insulated by brackets. But he had to be in Paris by noon today.'

She smiled, feeling she was expected to curtsy. Paris at once merged into fantasy, a medley of crystal knots engulfing the Louvre, Montmartre, the Eiffel Tower. Stella had grunted, the sound suggesting, not wholly absurdly, that she had mistaken herself for a bassoon.

Momentarily, flanked by Allweathers, she gazed at the others, identifying several writers arguing about Mao, Russia, Mr Max Adrian, Princess Margaret, as though reading aloud from menus, each providing a favourite dish. All were older than herself, slanting back to foxtrots, zeppelins, Edward Windsor and his lady. Easily recognized, as advertised, in pale blue shirt, creamy linen jacket, blue and green check trousers, jazzy silk scarf and powerful tan, was the actor, Martin Montag, hero of war movies – swerving his Spitfire through exploding skies, lifting spyglass to identify the *Bismarck*, slogging through Norman minefields, and now listening with ornate lack of interest to the novelist, Majid Readymoney, whose musical-box voice was complaining, probably justifiably, of publishers.

'I had the damned heck of a blow-up with that rascal, take it from me. He's a very bad record for the course.'

Mr Allweather at last released her on circuit. 'Martin, Theo, Verity, here at last is Della, I was remarking on those splendid poems of hers.' The rasping tone then ground down, lowered for her alone. 'A personage who should as yet be nameless but who sits not far from that luminous cultural establishment presided over by Great Tom, is very interested. There may be considerable *accruements*.'

The word pleased him as if he had invented it, he seemed disposed to repeat it, but instead pretended alarm at Stella's bluff gaze. 'Swipe me, if only I was allowed more than a wee dram. One isn't a scribe for nothing, though that's what one usually gets.'

This promised non-payment for poems, or at best a ticket for Slough. 'The appetite grows on what is not.' Mr Allweather was jovial, then stumped towards the drink trolley, past Vermilion Verity, her dark eyes fiercely ringed on blank white face. A rose by any other name, swaying gently as if dancing with her glass, all petals drooping.

'Della!' Smiles enclosed her, graciousness dazzled, notably from Martin Montag. Out of uniform he was older, with heavy cheek-bones pulling up the brown, lined skin, firmly preventing it slipping. With their trained capacity to weep at will, the quiet eyes must have extracted him from many critical encounters, and plunged him into as many more.

His voice lapped over her. 'Old Rick's very excited by your new work. I'm enormously looking forward to reading it. Who are your favourite poets? Chesterton?'

But Rick was back, like a tourist guide. 'Here is Della's drink. My dear, get a skinful on board.' It tasted like meek fruit juice yet might conceal a bang. Montag receded, Stella's smile, still hanging close by, had a vagueness at odds with her officer's profile, though her voice was unexpectedly sharp. 'We're so glad of your nice face.'

Perhaps this suggested Stella was more glad of her face than respectful of her talent.

Rick raised a hand, traffic cop or umpire. Voices clattered around Montag, agog for the latest. Ralphie had refused, Johnny was in New York, Larry too busy, but perhaps Alec....

The smiles, she decided, were deceptive. These people were

professionals, probably resenting her intrusion. Like most others, they contained summit and abyss, perilous marsh, sunken roads down which dragoons sped to capture a salient, meadows very smooth but sheltering mines. The very drink, with its sparkle, its nursery flavours, could be a ruse to extract confidences and pledges.

'He was incarcerated for many months.' Mr Readymoney's brown eyes were very round, as if from an infant's drawing. 'It confirms', an older man was addressing her, 'what's really behind these strikes. That awful orchestra boycotting a composer for omitting a harp! So they say. I could tell Attlee a thing or two.' He glanced at his watch as if pondering the moment to do so. 'Though at least he's had the guts to use the troops against those cocky dockers.'

But his cracked smile was uncertain, he must be calculating her status, her possibilities. His snowy hair, dark, double-breasted jacket with gold naval buttons, suggested a hoary senator in a Hollywood musical unwisely backing the Broadway show. Silver tinged, sagging wrinkles, well-dusted moustache. 'Irish labourers,' he was very clear, as if reading the news, which, in a way, he actually was, 'they're working on a deep, underground railway, and getting a very foul disease. It'll kill them within fifteen years. No great loss perhaps. On railways, canals, they terrorized the citizenry. A century ago, of course.'

Riots, he assured her, were occurring, skulls shattered, down in deep, atrocious air. He coughed, regarded her more closely, then nodded in relief. 'I hear you're a friend of the great Sir Roger. A man we're all going to need. Meanwhile you have your own triumph, and more to come, I'll be bound.'

This entitled him to pat her hand before he moved on. A grey woman in a long mauve gown, with painted, wooden necklace, Olive Product, critic, gripping a large canvas bag doubtless containing review copies, inspected her like a horse trainer. Thin black brows curled upwards, rhyming with those at her mouth, suggesting continuous, rather mournful laughter. She did not speak, eventually looked away.

'Should be hanged,' a voice was saying, 'but almost certainly won't be.'

'Lalage does not observe the bloody proprieties,' Mr Readymoney's little mouth dropped, then opened, like a shutter, 'up to the neck. Thought, word, and very likely, deed.' His giggle rustled, subsided, as Stella appeared and Rick clapped, dispensing expectations of plenty. 'Lunch, gentles, lunch!'

'Miss Della...' – the senator's expensive voice was kindly as he escorted her – 'I'm afraid I don't read highbrow stuff any more. Biographies only. Haig ... Marie Corelli.... But I trust the critics will be kind to you.'

What could he be? Impresario, viscount, Churchill's cigar-purveyor, groundnuts investor with vast cars, vast overdraft? She risked saying that, in his position, he himself could disregard critics. The penalty was a squeeze on her arm, then a shy grin. 'Bless you, my dear, bless you. Soon...' – another squeeze promised more than what came – 'soon you'll have us all in your pocket.'

The long refectory table, badly polished, was lit by glass, silver, roses, fruit, arranged less clumsily than she would have expected, absorbing in subtle degrees the soft falls of sunlight. Under the appreciative flutters, Montag, with unearned intimacy, murmured that Stella was renowned, if not for the perfection of her brush, at least for her board.

She smiled, she felt better, glad of her youth, her body, the future. She could hold her own.

'Della ... over here.' She was quickly seated between a ginger-bearded, morose man, and Martin Montag. 'Your neighbour's got abstracts hanging about in that Leicester Gallery exhibition which so few are talking about.'

At once she recalled that gallery's poster, of a magnolia tortured into tubular spikes, purple, as if disease-smitten. She said, in cool tones filched from Bayard, 'It's legitimate, isn't it, to prefer one's conception of objects to the objects themselves?'

'Lovely comment, Della.'

But he was aggrieved, by more than the over-chilled avocados. Girls, evidently, were unentitled to rights of reply. Now, however, the painter was turning to her, his eyes, bright blue, slitty, on parched, indoor face, the beard dry, very flammable. He was covered, rather than dressed, in baggy, bluish, silky Italian suit, without a tie. Drawing in lips, he was about to speak, then desisted, staring at her chunky Todd-Arbin ring, Janet's present, reviled by Beast, who called it a glacier mint. Then Rick leant between them, jolly uncle at the children's feast. 'Try this vintage, Della. Not a bad year, not a bad year at all.'

The avenue of faces made small, unseen bridges across which words flowed with pleasures unstinted.

'Martin, how's Geoff taking it?'

The hubbub abruptly stilled, Montag's cough was ostentatiously deliberate. 'Dear Geoff!' He savoured it like a title, or as if he were Bayard's mythical Air Vice Marshal about to issue a gazette. 'He gave so many of us our first chance.'

Rick's granite head jerked up, as if guarding its own position. With elbow firm on the table he was holding, some way above it, his fork impaling a potato, to which he periodically, regally, lowered his mouth.

Ignoring him, Stella cleared plates, the rest still intent upon Geoff, manifestly the famous producer, Geoffrey Grex, 'G.G.' to his friends. 'Gee Gee' to others.

'Poor darling G.G. I'm dashing round tomorrow.'

'Naturally, I'm writing.'

'His creative make-up, though not quite T'ai Chi...'

Montag glistened. 'You know about this, Della?'

'Not quite everything.'

'Ah! Geoff's wife, Jilly, was a sleepwalker. Yesterday she was found dead on the pavement. Oozing, like a bunch of hares after coursing.'

'A very trim model, Jilly,' Rick declaimed. 'Edition de luxe. Anyone would have wished to keep her in print.'

'Scuppered!' Mr Readymoney was judicial. 'But a nice woman. A kind woman. Clean as a whistle.'

'Geoff too, he always had sympathy, as well as talent.'

Glasses were raised, but as if Geoff too had been scuppered.

The painter's face was back. He was like a nodding duck, which Roger foretold would force electricity from waves. His voice was soft without being gentle, like a salesman's.

'During the war, after a raid, I found on my doorstep a woman's shoe with a foot in it. I've kept the shoe.'

It was as if a book, hitherto forbidden, had broken regulations and opened itself. The friendly, Sunday faces were transformed to the angry hunters, strange captains, of childhood. The men must have bombed, shot, set kids on fire, knifed, or fled howling, and, like Graham, revealed nothing. Those neat fingers stroking a goblet might have strangler's strength, the quiet gentleman discussing Virginia Woolf might have dived through scalding air to strafe the dam, cruiser, hospital. And how had Jill really died?

The painter continued, mouth twisted over some wry joke, but she was thinking of Dr Meridew, very hearty, with stories of Africa and deserts, generous to children but who had, Bayard said, killed his wife. Bayard's usual make-up, of course, but one day, after laughter, Aunt Janet had said, very gently, that Dr Meridew, despite his cheery stories, lived in aching and permanent distress.

'Jolly good tuck-in, Stella.'

Sprinkled with mint and cumin, the lamb was soft, the salad crisp. The wine almost as tasty as Rick, red as a Sioux, periodically proclaimed it.

The painter was still talking: 'Napoleon's little palace at Porto Ferraio, filled with things he'd actually handled. Small leather books, with his seal. Old prints and maps. Green and gold ceilings. I drew a fishing-smack perched on bright, curling water, and old women selling octopus under that ugly, whitewashed church, little boats filled with grapes and wine. Genre scenes.'

Mr Readymoney leant across and chuckled. 'That's the ticket!'

Martin Montag's fine summer skin had very minutely slackened, then, at her glance, tautened again. He showed impeccable teeth, eyes at full strength as he told Geoff's tale of dear old Donald's impersonation of blind Oedipus, at the Lyric, suddenly impaired by his furious glare at two girls departing in mid-scene.

'You must know Geoffrey Grex very well, Mr Montag.'

'To call me Martin is just about the one thing we don't have to beg permission for from bloody Mr Truman and General Santa Claus Marshall. As for Geoff, yes, we've shaken paws, I've had the run of his lair, drunk at his water-hole. His car is as long as *The Tempest*. Working together, we've had rounds of, how shall I put it. . . .' He thought, then said with an ease that suggested he'd put it very often before, 'Well, of antipathetic friendship which never actually achieved a knock-out.'

Boyish, pleased, he contemplated a silver candlestick as if testing its authenticity. 'One meets people, Della. Yet must move on. O my Fairbanks and my Barrymore long ago.'

'She was well past it,' Mr Readymoney brought his hands

together, and Vermilion Verity's broad, sunset face smiled as she drew breath, then said, 'Good!'

Coffee was served upstairs, where blinds now refined the sunlight, laying thin yellow parallels along the carpet, fragmenting them on piano, chair, tables. A mirror, almost wholly relapsed into shadow, was pulling fiery roses deeper within it.

On a high floor, seeking the loo, she was ambushed by a gust of sunlight from an uncurtained window. A clock was ticking, close but unseen, very slowly, above the distant hum of voices. The insistent tap of a lame, blind child. Time moving inexorably yet, in monotony of sound, remaining still. A crack lengthened down a wall, on the sky a bird seemed gradually dying; she heard a rustle as though from imaginary curtains. Momentarily she was engulfed, in cool heat, in silence that spoke. The voices ceased, perhaps at an order from Stella, more probably from a remark about herself. Uneasily, she tried a door. Locked. Then another, also locked. She was in Bluebeard's castle. All doors were of thin, identical grey, receding into the brightness, and behind one she fancied something had moved. An animal, a critic? Perhaps fooled by too much wine, by surreptitious drug, she imagined Bob and Hélène naked behind the woodwork, Bob, between spasms, drooling that she was the poem, he was only the lines. His eyes gave an illusion of blushing. Could this couple be traced to Roger and Janet in an earlier, more foolish time, the milkmaid beautiful but penniless, the deft, all-purpose Man of the Future? Bob and Hélène, though, would not be happy, would be spoilt by too much freedom, too much ardour for what they imperfectly defined, or had defined too exactly what should not be uttered, though bravely sought.

She recovered from a slight blur, an instant of faintness, and the nearest door opened almost before she touched it. On descent, she felt the voices rougher, edgier.

'I'll be whizzing over to dispute that. To say ye nay.'

The armoury of heads, indistinct in the subdued light, ignored her. She had survived inspection, was one of them, however junior the rank they granted her. The only empty seat was now on a divan between a new couple, tall, very straight, like Bayard: straight limbs, straight features. They acknowledged her kindly, then talked across her, as if she were a tennis net.

'This foul country, Tim! What will you do when they've ruined everything?'

'Exactly.'

Farther off, Stella stood like a dry mop, staring down, as if at a musical score on the rug, and a man's voice strutted toward Miss Product. 'Olive, I was born in May, which gives physical advantages and several psychic ones. You remember Arthur, royal Arthur, killing all May-born children, because of some busybody oracle!'

'I do not remember it.'

Very fair, flinty, very Prussian, in bed Tim would be a machine: glum, soundless, set too exactly.

Rick loomed, the big-chinned field-marshal re-entering his salient. 'Della, my dear, just a spot of brandy?'

Caressing the glass, she unexpectedly had an intimation of Bayard's cheerless gaze penetrating this shrouded, unsteady room. Hurriedly she sipped, the sharpness giving signal to disengage. Bayard shrugged disapprovingly and filtered away into the sunlight which must be piling up outside the blinds, lying in barely supportable weight against blistered walls, dirty windows. An ovalled jug had joined the charred roses in the mirror. Cups and glasses were outlined more clearly than the hands and faces behind them. Martin Montag's eyes were open but dull, almost empty, as he drank with staged ostentation, camouflaging his thoughts. The sibilant hush became emphatic when the Allweathers, transferred as though by stealth, began arguing in another room.

Dance, a bleep of jazz, a bugle call, might release them all, tear off their famous names, disclose appetites raw but felt. Some might even belong in secret to the Saratoga League – but no, they wouldn't, there wasn't any League, and the treadmill of talk was resuming.

'I remember Geoff liking to quote Flaubert, Gustave Flaubert, one doesn't altogether care to address him as Gus ... that with cheek one can always get on in the world.'

'Geoff knew something about cheek. Even in Jill's presence he would say monogamy was a form of insolence.'

'Poor old Jill! She wanted to raise a family and she's ended up raising a scene. She could never quite grow the necessary wings.'

Hands flapped over vague, crossed legs, blurred heads lifted with difficulty. 'I suppose', Tim spoke, 'she couldn't have left him much?'

'Quite enough.'

Martin Montag stirred, sat up, refreshed as if from a successful audition. 'He'll be needing all he can find, Verity. It's two years since he's gained a real credit. I never cease to congratulate myself, or rather, my agent, for scrapping that pernicious contract. For once, I didn't jib when he bayed for his percentage. As for Geoff, to put it kindly, he's parsimonious. Backstage we call him the Golden Mean.'

Some poor, broken mind and a stain on the pavement.

Tim and his lady had melted, and the senator was back, courtly old fumble-fingers, once, apparently, a very commercial publisher – warily intimate, picking through brandy fumes, glass held like a begging-bowl which Rick, straddling a thick stool, seemed to be deliberately ignoring. From a shadowy corner a stranger's voice was saying 'She'd child's legs on a square, rank body. They told me that kindness was due to her because of her unhappy life, but personally I'd have sent her by parcel post to the knackers. I trust, sir, my frankness does not shock!'

Rick seemed barely aware of them, deep in some larger discontent, giving only an occasional, disparaging grunt, but, for her, the words had peeled off memories of first day at school. She was pretty, had eyes, Janet said, like green fireflies, she was loved, but at once met a drooling face, dragged-down, hopeless eyes, a voice dribbling from a lumpy, disordered body. 'I can't be your best friend but I'll go for a walk with you. They're sending me to a bat's place.'

The senator was complaining of his son. Drugs, girls, car smashes. She was bored, then impatient, remembering sons who dazzled. 'I suppose the test of parenthood is the confidence of one's children!'

'Of course, of course.'

But stricken, very old, his refulgent face withering, he was silent. The party's flame was shaky. Mr Readymoney, prone on cushions, was drowsy, or dead. Stella, restless, out of range by the door, muttered, as though bargaining, with a mannish, trousered woman who then vanished without a word. In the glare outside, grass, flower, tree, would be secure in their empery but, in this false twilight, minds were groping, voices fragmenting, and someone, from the piano, could be heard saying that Jill Grex might have been pushed to her death.

Draped in long, chaffinch-pink ovals, one woman heard nothing. A fly buzzed, settled on her cheek, explored its broad acres, avoiding its cracks with spy's care, but still she did not move. She might have been non-existent, more fatal than being imaginary.

The guests slumped, none risked being the first to desert the company to be followed by immediate bad reports, dark charge-sheets. Only Mr Montag remained active, even mutinous, redistributing, as if to casualties, the brandy which Rick, still spread on his stool in nominal command, might strategically have overlooked. Stella, now speechless, looked flabby, though with eyes unexpectedly cynical. Unpacking a walnut, Verity dreamily scattered chips over the carpet. Other eyes were stamped flat on tired faces, in light monitored by the lattice dropping prison bars in unexpected places. People were images: a giant towering over a fairground, bored with his monstrous strength; a teacher throwing coins, superciliously watching children scramble and root; ducks gobbling their smashed offspring; sad, jettisoned movie stars who still dance, love, aspire, in cinemas ever more slummy in Lagos, Tunis, Bangkok, while, in flesh warped and hardened, they seek the sleep they dread.

At this impasse, even Beast would acquire grandeur, demolishing them all with his football yell. Graham's face, coarse and square, could have routed them, but might have desisted. It had trembled, then moistened, as he read to her of the son of the False Dmitri, publicly hanged, aged four. Yet, seeing Mr Allweather, he might have envisaged a punctured Alp, then ground out a song of their childhood, 'Horsey, Keep Tail Up.'

She had only to uncover the windows and, in surging light, the casualties would revive. But of course she did not do so. She must depart, mission accomplished; she had encountered the magnificent general, one of the useful people. Henceforward she could talk of 'my publisher'. She was grateful, feeling the first flicker of a new poem, a glimmer, like light on a moth's wing. She could invent the invisible. In the painting the orange girl still read and, were she to raise her head, she would see the mottled garden, the smooth, sweet greengages hanging in leaves still greener.

Rick startled her, back in pounding authority, crying havoc. 'I'd refer him to the more specialized literature available in public privies. Reputations, bah! Wrung from false rumour. Most of history's a matter of mistaken identity.'

As if abashed, the blinds rose, the apartment swam in light, and ladies and gentlemen of reputation began expecting tea, replenishing themselves against the moment when, like Jill, they would be inexorably out of print.

BOOK TWO

*

It is not true that love makes all things easy: it makes us choose what is difficult.
George Eliot

How small of all that human hearts endure,
That part which laws or kings can cause or cure.
Dr Johnson

1

The Dragon House, for the first time since the war, glittered across freezing woods and flood-meadows in the December night. Carol singers and hand-bellsmen had come, now less musical, more chatty. The Christmas tree on a lawn was a pyramid of lights in the clean darkness. Nightly, gusts of laughter and music muffled the hoot of distant trams and the call of owl and fox. Fireworks had sprayed dazzling splinters across the sky. Rooms swarmed with guests from London, with old friends from neighbouring clans and those whom Roger termed the better-disposed tenantry. Everywhere, fierce squires with chipped, pebble-dash faces, tottering, ironic widows, once magnificent officers now found at the kitchen sink, handed dirty plates by wives in rubber gloves: streaked huntsmen with tally-ho, give-away laughs, porcelain girls still eager for fun. Bryce, the Staff, had reappeared, hands slower but complete, herself still bossy: 'Now, Miss Della ... oh, Master Graham.... Thank you, Mr Bayard.'

'He trained fifteen parachutists to jump with the gold over Germany. Fourteen bodies were found, more or less human, and are buried near Cologne, the western side. The other we saw a few months ago, heading a group of bakeries, in Hamburg.'

A Feste with bitter wit, scalding comments, exists only in public. To imagine Bayard with a private life of midnight tears, masturbation, doomed, passionate assignments, taxi queues, was impossible. He spoke of most life as he might of a minor disease inherited from careless parents. Of himself, the more he spoke, the less he revealed. In inventive patter, he spoke of in a single day assisting in a slum youth club, advising the National Gallery about a Titian of dubious provenance, and attending in menial capacity a League conference at Bruges. In the London of studios and coffee bars he had quickly acquired a modish gloss, as of a droll left over from an indefinite past. Not obviously popular, he was rated a social asset, though few could say why, and none did so. A travelling rumour told of people like supers leaving his flat with right hands bandaged, left arms seemingly the smaller, another had him living free during the war in the vacated German Embassy, having bought a chisel and a chauffeur's uniform, then, not from the Zoo but Ribbentrop's study, supervising a black market. He had not hastened to deny it. He might envisage himself as a dandy from romance who stills a lynch mob with a fatigued glance, halts the concrete-jawed leader while he is still drawing breath, and, with a bored yawn, announces in afterthought that he has inherited five estates. Without beauty, without discernible talent or the epigrammatic wit that once dislodged ministers, he survived by his eyebrows, themselves virtually colourless. In a rare instance of impatience, Roger had once called him a gap in nature.

Yesterday, at church, Bayard had unexpectedly read a lesson, very monotonously, and detected a bottle of Veuve du Vernay amongst the choir, nodding, but as if not quite convinced as the congregation sang, 'Ransomed, healed, restored, forgiven', though recovering a superior, private satisfaction at 'A few more years shall roll'.

Very recently, a columnist wrote that Bayard had tramped post-war Sweden in clerical garb, off-handedly baptizing infants and marrying awkward villagers.

Most importantly, the Crystal Knot probably signified a tiresome hoax, but this was no absolute certainty. Graham found two ambiguous references in the British Library, not to any Crystal Knot but to Saratogans, one in Risorgimento Italy, one in 1911 in Spain. But, during Churchill's second premiership, several articles suggesting considerable, if erratic scholarship, had appeared, tentatively listing the Saratoga League alongside the French Calgoulards of the thirties, the Orange Orders, Broederbond, and a few Slavonic political dissenters. It had been dismissed as a financial fraud, planned by a West German *flâneur*, a political pressure group in Rome, a cosmopolitan syndicate blackmailing the ex-Nazis, who, in both Germanies, had filtered back into public life.

Graham had ability in research, unsystematic, easily distracted into vivid irrelevancies, yet thorough. To cross-examine Bayard himself would be futile, and he returned to the Library with further results, disappointing but not negligible. A scrawled, scarcely legible signature on Swiss notepaper seemed traceable to the ex-Carbonari, Louis Napoleon, who had added, perhaps facetiously, an ill-drawn pattern which might represent a knot. The young Disraeli, in a letter from Egypt, had gibed at 'a reckless, absurd Saratogan', but the remainder of the page was missing. In Dresden, Bakunin had been rebuffed by a group whose name was inked out, with Sa ... just possibly discernible. In 1917 'Saratogans', left unexplained, were reported in the *Frankfurter Allegemeine Zeitung* as libelling German officers' behaviour in Belgium and Poland: the Paris *Matin*, in 1916, reported 'Sarits' naming three French generals who had shot suspected deserters without trial. As late as 1950 *Figaro* alleged that wartime funds sent to Sweden to assist Rauel Wallenberg succour Hungarian Jews, had been sponsored by a society with the code name 'Crystal Knot'. The League was now prodding the UN to demand Wallenberg's release from Russia, following his obscure arrest, in 1945, and hinting at his murder. From Lisbon a radio commentator had quoted Saratoga's riposte to the Russian Ambassador over the 1940 rape of the Baltic states, conveniently forgotten by the West.

In no capital was the League's address formally listed. London journalists spoke of a North Kensington flat, permanently locked, curtained, and without a telephone.

At dinner, commanding the gowns and dinner-jackets, Roger Kirkland was attentive to all. A few dabs of grey empathized his continuous, incisive youthfulness. Opposite, at the far end, Janet too had changed little, her hair massed in browns into which candlelight dropped splashes, then pools, of old gold. The finely groomed gentlemen, well-powdered ladies, were deferential, as they had always been, with only Bryce, serving vegetables, showing any disposition to contradict.

Roger was describing a new university, on whose planning committee he had sat. Difficulties still multiplied like herrings.

'In appointing the Vice-Chancellor, my colleagues were seeking not only talent for leadership, itself suspect in these our times, but, more surprisingly, qualities that one can only call gentlemanly.'

The smiles were obedient, a little self-conscious. Della glanced at Janet, apparently listening but almost certainly not fully considering vice-chancellors. Bayard, on her right, was politely regarding Roger, but, in formal clothes, cap and bells foregone, he looked inconspicuous, undernourished, dull.

'It's disputable whether James, with all his charm, good sense, moral worth, would be one's first pick as a gentleman, while old Clavering, whom we'll be seeing tomorrow, with no charm, not much sense, and no talent whatsoever, together with capacities for leadership far less detectable than those of the nearest gander, is a gentleman or a buffoon.' His pause allowed room for speculation. 'To attempt formal definition, you may tell me, destroys the question. The concept of a gentleman will anyway very soon concern only etymologists and antiquarians.'

No one of course told him, and Graham grinned to himself, happy with the talk, the shimmer of fruits and wine, silver on black wood, white on gold, flash of jewel and eye, the lure of days ahead, here where so much feeling and curiosity had begun, spells of pleasure, the pull of old times. In soft radiance faces were younger, back in tea-time England with Mr Blow-me-Tight in the pulpit, Bryce in the kitchen, dance-tunes from the Embassy, the Savoy, Ramsay Mac and Stan Baldwin in their clodding minuet.

Confident, he fed Roger a question about new spies defaulting from the Foreign Office. Murmurs faded, heads turned, and Bayard inspected his claret as if, at very long last, he might allow himself a delicate sip.

'I confess that I'm sometimes unfortunate in my professional associates. Sometimes I've felt myself a Horthy, admiral of a land-locked country. In its middle and some of its higher reaches the Foreign Office was pretty malodorous. Ageing nancies, hunchbacked with debts to pimps and dram-shops, loathing themselves, their class, most of their friends, and immoderate in their love of abstractions, they forgot that mankind may survive by bed alone, but men themselves do not. Bevin, for all his bull energy, couldn't really envisage such types, Winston left them to Eden, Clem was too busy. Dear old Ernie,' Roger was amiably resolved to entertain, 'we gave him a Gridiron dinner, he pecked at the caviare, then announced that the jam tasted fishy.'

The clever grey eyes were glad of them all, on his own terms. Conversation again became general. Old Tom down the road had swallowed a pin, the Test bowlers in Australia were bowling mighty fast. Della was talking very spiritedly, in greeny, low-cut sheath, bare shoulders, emerald eyes shining. One noticed that, as he had years ago, Roger at times looked at Bayard as if for assent, but Bayard, perhaps cannily, was concerned only with Janet, occasionally with some aside, probably disrespectful, for twice she affectionately slapped his hand. To Roger's disclosures, he remained like a tennis player disdaining to intercept volleys.

Over dessert, Roger, theatrically rueful, sent Janet down a smile. 'In London I don't always see people warts and all, too often only the warts. Drastic contrasts between the visible and the potential. Down here, people are less tabloid. Even my own atrocious forbears gleam more singularly. That old ruffian hanging above Julia's head thrashed his children almost into their graves, but he did help pioneer the Eight-Hour Bill. In London, a Chelsea fireman told me that when he enters a burning homestead the first thing he does is to rescue the baby.'

'But Roger, my dear, it would be wicked if he didn't.'

'Ah yes, Ella, but think further. He swore that Londoners' first instinct is to save themselves, then the furniture, then, if there's time, the children. It did ring rather too true for comfort.'

No one spoke, though Janet very slowly lowered her head. When they all rose, Roger waited for Bayard, and they momentarily stood together. Roger spoke, Bayard replied, but the exchange was inaudible. 'I'd forgotten that,' Roger said as they departed, not quite together. Della and Graham smiled at each other, recalling that Bayard had once complained that Roger would sometimes forget but never confess that he had not known, his tone contriving to make superior the forgetting.

Graham and Della had driven from London together. Bayard,

insisting that he had his own transport, arrived very late, soundlessly, as though by balloon.

'Graham, let's explore!' She was extraordinarily animated. Look! The whist table engraved with whorls and lilies, the mallards and misty hills on Chinese screens, the Peyton grandfather clock with its moon dial, which at once struck seventeen after Hartley Clegg had repaired it, a great Coxon chest in which by legend a child had been mislaid for two centuries – scarcely *crème brûlée* by the end, Bayard considered – the silver ornamented powder-flask under the Malplaquet musket, prints of Regency cricketers, portly and top-hatted in trim, pale-green meadows, and, throughout, Della's delighted exclamations at the oblique, the scarcely seen, the half-promises of arches.

On Christmas Eve they again motored together, leaving Bayard immersed in the unimaginable, very possibly with Janet. With her he was always scrupulously attentive and, one guessed, confiding, without that air of forbearance which he reserved for others, for Roger himself. Lady Debney said that when Bayard looked at her she felt that a moth had touched her face, and that she herself was a wilful delinquent.

Drives in Graham's ramshackle car were usually longer than was planned. He despised maps, quarrelled with garage attendants, would drive for miles into the wrong horizon to avoid asking directions. Now they sped through fretful wind and drizzle, low, random gleams briefly alighting on branch, roof, pool. Under this bare, rippling line of hills, little trains had once chugged through fields, on one occasion driven by Graham himself. They were comfortable, complete as a bandstand, swapping memories – trouble with gipsies, Kentisbeare Fair, Bayard dismantling a boring picnic by announcing 'perfect adder country'. Then she sobered, mentioning Geoffrey Grex, found six months dead in a canal.

She touched his arm as he blindly turned at a forgotten crossroads.

'Last winter I was in Herts for a literary do, a woman read trash aloud for hours, and when it was over, we clapped very loudly to restore our circulations, and, mistaking, she began all over again. But the countryside's getting built up. Bits of suburb strewn over ancient fields. Yet with slices of forest still left between new roads, factories, bungalows, motels. Some deer had been breaking into gardens. They rather haunted me. Terribly sad. Janet understood perfectly. Those animals, in a world of concrete and barbed wire, surviving, year after year, staying on, though trees are cut down and grass vanishes.'

'Have you written of them?'

'Not yet. But I've completed the book.'

His one-armed embrace almost skidded them into a hedge. 'Will Allweather want to publish it?'

'Of course. He's been wonderful. Always encouraging. He's had faith, he moves mountains like toys. Thanks to the *Forum*, I'm getting invitations to send poems to fine places.'

She spoke as if very young, though in loose furs, brilliant Veltman scarf, a brilliance reflected in brooch and rings, she was far from innocence.

They drove deeper into small, glassy hills and crumpled valleys, towards Dartmoor. Her excitement remained. 'Do you remember, Janet liked us to collect tin foil from chocolate wrappings? To help the cottage hospital, which had that transparent box hanging outside stuffed with the soft, shiny stuff. I imagined the wards sheeted with it, the poor imagining themselves already in heaven before they died. Yeats would have spoilt it, when he said that heaven is an improvement of the spirit.'

'I don't remember the poor reading Yeats. But at the Golden Wall, at Smolensk Cathedral even Napoleon removed his hat. Nobody cared to ask why he was actually there.'

'You know so much.' Her sigh was ostentatious, making his remark sound indecent.

On return, having mistaken *No Road* for *By-Road*, they at last halted at a pub, and found old Hicks, a gardener long retired from the Dragon House. He greeted them cautiously, Della asked whether he ever revisited but, although he accepted a pint, he muttered, 'We don't speak much of Mr Kirkland round here', went silent, then stumped out, leaving them alone in the small, stuffy bar.

Subdued, she said nothing, then recovered, opened her bag, pulled out a press-cutting. Graham took it. 'This Crystal Knot again. Do you know much about it by now.'

'Bayard only says that particular types in the world recognize and support each other. E. M. Forster said something like it, years ago: "The aristocracy of the sensitive, the considerate, and the plucky". I don't think of Bayard as exactly that. And he always strikes me as knowing how to write, without having learnt to read. Mind, I don't see much of him. It's impossible to phone him, don't you find? Either one gets the engaged signal, or a man's voice, always a different voice, says "Wrong number" before you've spoken.'

'He may have once earned his keep at Delphi, inventing slippery answers. A literal godsend.'

He too saw little of Bayard, who would call uninvited, at an hour usually inconvenient, sometimes embarrassing, for no stated reason. Why? He never displayed affection, when he spoke of old times he referred to Richelieu, the Duchesse de Chevreux, and unengaging popes.

Della gazed wonderingly at the smoky fire. 'Yes. But didn't the oracle's answers often turn out less absurd than they first sounded? He told me about having tea with Lord Alfred Douglas, knowing he was expected to pay five shillings, and he didn't hear anything old Bosie said because of wondering whether to blatantly hand over the cash, or leave it on a chair or on the chimney-piece. I didn't believe this, but then I met a friend of Rick's who'd been charged five bob as well. Bayard also speaks of an actor taking him to tea with two ladies descended from Dickens. He was warned not to eat much, because they were to dine well, at the Garrick. One lady was pretty, the other plain. The actor began on the pretty one, all about Shakespeare's use of music. The plain one was looking worried, Bayard asked why. Very timidly, she asked whether his friend enjoyed cake. Rather, Bayard said, more than anything, except Shakespeare. She was terribly glad, had spent hours making one. When she produced it, the actor was still in full flow, but she managed to interrupt, asking if he'd like a slice. He said crossly that he wouldn't, and carried on talking, so Bayard had to wreck the great dinner by eating all the cake himself.'

She was dreamy. 'We both care for him, we don't know why, he'll never know, and wouldn't be much interested. How very unsatisfactory it is. You'd get so angry at tennis, when he referred to the court as "the floor".'

Bayard, no teddy bear, could not be associated with forms of love, even pronounced aspects of feeling. Ask him to select the loveliest of three divine nudes, he would set himself to eat the apple, having carefully examined it for quality.

The fire drowsed, shadows seemed solid. 'Della, did you notice that when Clavering asked Roger whether he'd ever heard of the Saratoga League, Roger didn't like it.'

'He was angry. He didn't show it, but I can tell.'

'Could he possibly have been afraid?'

'Afraid? *Roger!*'

They laughed, not quite in unison. She touched her hair. 'It's beginning to tingle. Snow's coming. It always tells me.'

In bed, Graham wondered about her dreams. She had said that night was hangman's habitat, and he remembered the headsman with white gloves. Her joys were precarious, her vivacity always about to slump. She would praise some writer, then attack him with absurd vehemence, defend some palpable untruth with flashy ill-temper or the joyless Boleyn mirth. She collected not husbands but funsters. Broadmuzzled Beast had been ditched, but her London was dense with parties which, evaporating, left her clutching some hulking, bad-mannered bruiser or grubby, assertive girl, and the poems suggested that she found a rank Cosgrave more 'real' than those now recharging the Dragon House, and the house itself was the most real of all. It was said that she had told one youngster that he was gentle in bed. 'I try to be.' His eyes brimmed with dog-love, and she ejected him forthwith, then wrote 'Late Summer', sadly comic.

'And you, Graham,' she once retorted, 'where are your wives? All those Sallys and Miriams!' They both, she said, drifted from lovers on a mild breeze, fleeing the agony of repose. Not very seriously, they had discussed living together, even marrying, as a sort of serum, but then, abruptly, she went silent, and they relapsed into bad, nervous jokes.

During this week, Week of the Tree braided and decorated as a giant archduke, of bottles uncorking, of veterans and bobby-soxers, carols and jazz, greetings thrown like confetti, she too was often alone with Janet, discussing he knew not what, presumably not experimenting with mescalin, as recommended by several of her chosen authors.

No young children came, and this, from Janet's love of them, was surprising, though, for Graham, a pleasure. In an ideal dispensation, children would be born aged fifteen.

At meals, Bayard was on view, though still eating very little, drinking not at all. 'Mr Bayard', Bryce was reproachful, 'will die of too much air.'

The sky lifted, drizzle turned to snow, curtaining them with white, drifting flurries that made unfinished statues, ramparts, dolmens, scrawled glistening tangles on trees. Is there a poet in the house? Yes, but dancing, talking, without eyes for snow, for windows.

When it cleared, the air, perforated by innumerable sparkles, revealed the frozen lake, and swiftly the skaters gathered, the lithe, the bulky, the preposterous, cutting through, darting past, loudly tumbling, barging, recovering from frantic collisions. Inset, Della, boyish in slacks, glided through pale ovals of light towards a sun red and exorbitant above woods striped black and white, with Orsinos and Olivias, Geralds and Susans around her, rapt in cutting air and mindless physical exultation.

Graham, useless at skating, watched with envious irritation. The Claverings arrived, the ageing fellows, clad like jockeys, hooting that they could race till kingdom come. 'That's the ticket,' Bertie Clavering, in a scarf hanging like a gigantic horseshoe, was proud, 'all hands on deck.'

Amongst the skaters was a thin figure, darkly luminous, sun-glassed, swift, dexterous, seemingly unaware of others as he circled and swerved, struck patterns, changed course, in assured, continuous movement – a hiss, a glitter, a twist, the half-seen – and now in firm, professional zeal, aloof, so that the others slowly withdrew, to applaud a performance that, with no grand manner yet had a whisper of passion, a timely elegance, with a glint of the uncanny, as if from the East. Perhaps a hired, seasonal extravagance, presented by immaculate Kirkhood hospitality.

But no. A hand touched Graham, a weathered, bootish face opened. 'Graham, my lad ... that chap, dark goggles, foreign isn't he? I almost said, isn't *it*! But he moves well enough. Yet, good gracious, it's only young Bayard.'

With cut-glass magnificence, the tree outshone the revellers, gleaming without heat, a mass of green patched with fractured blues, golds, crimsons. By night, skaters transformed to dancers, swaying through the old ballroom, adrift on a radiant tide. Someone had pleaded for fancy dress but, surprising them, Janet demurred. 'Please, no. ... And Della thought she heard 'never again'. The ballroom swaggered with tints and gestures, easy clips of grace. Long dresses fringed with ivory, with scarlet, gowns tasselled with gold, silks and flounces crinkled as if by starlight, young waistcoats dappled as golden plovers, merged with the racy quips and bland retorts of thirties' songs, the melodious scatter of 42nd Street and Lullaby of Broadway. Lady Clavering ogled her peke, for which personal popularity carried no priority. Lady Clegg, jewelled head and shoulders protruding as if from a pearly tent, announced that her son had disproved the Gulf Stream. Mr Blow-me-Tight, rural dean, opined that Christmas was more than a professional occasion. Glasses shone yellow, shone red, as, obedient to the band, dancers surged and drooped, swayed and spun. Lights rested on bare shoulders, shirt-fronts, bottles, ice-cubes packed with crystallized jonquils.

'Jeeves informed me that one motive for sixteenth-century dancing was to discover whether one's woman smelt of bad meat. Apply that to the girl by the window, marketing all-purpose bits of herself.'

Bayard moved away. Prince of the ice, he was in demand, would dance for a few minutes, not exceptionally well, then murmur something friendly and desist, joining no group but standing with an empty glass until another girl claimed him, his long-nosed attention to the muscians that of the know-all.

Janet Kirkland, slender in cloth of gold, the diamond spray in her hair suggesting small buds tight yet flashing, danced continually, Roger scarcely at all, but he made the rounds of swarming rooms like, Della thought, the commander of a crack regiment, then spoilt it by remembering Martin Montag starring as middle-period Mountbatten. He knew all Christian names, occupations, promotions, was ready to advise about builders, riding schools, offers of employment and, no doubt, conjugal relations.

Host and hostess danced together, once, very precise, in courtly, perfected accord, finally standing for an instant, smiling, his hand on her back, her head on his shoulder, to receive a basket of red and white roses

Clavering summoned Graham to the bar. 'Very proper music this, priceless din, not that vile skiffle that makes me so huffy. You know about the Duke of Windsor when Ambrose took his orchestra to Paris? No one danced, not a soul. The

Frog smarties resented a British band. But the Duke saved the situation. He'd often danced to Ambrose in pre-war London and wasn't going to let him down. So he and Wallis stepped on to the floor, just like Roger and Janet tonight, and at once everyone followed, dancing till breakfast. A fine man, with his flair he could have prevented the war if they'd given him half a bloody chance. I can't help feeling Winston's treated him shabbily. Jealous, wouldn't you say?'

'Of course not, Bertie, utter rubbish. That chap was a mischievous, self-important ass whose German sympathies made him forget that water might very well turn out to be wet.'

'Your chaff, of course. You always loved to gruff and grumble. But you may be right, you may be right.'

Graham danced with Janet, with Lady Clegg, counting the thuds, with all available girls, several times with Della, again in silky green barely covering her small breasts, twisted silver torque at her neck. After many drinks he was tireless, outsize, the Viking, ruffled, possessive, like a slaver, Della said. She too was roused, green and black, eyes enlarged, lit from music, scents, flesh, the brilliant swirl of couples. Strange sister, she was always close, always far; as the saxophone wailed, the piano jittered, she was clasping him as if from memory, hearing none of his remarks.

The music ceased, she recognized him, squeezed his hand, was recalled by Geralds and Ronnies.

Both had been astonished, then gratified, by Bayard's earlier performance. So easily derided, he had at last revealed excellence, like the schoolchildren in *Twelfth Night*.

Overheated, champagne in hand, Graham stepped unsteadily from saxophones, gossip, flirtation, to the terrace, to breathe sharp, windless air. The blaze of the tree enchanted the frosty grass, was forgotten by the dancers but probably affected them, stirring appetites, receiving unspoken dues, its sashes and badges of light outmatching the naked stars. Braced to outlast the night he stood still. Tunes slid into each other, dancers' shadows entwined on the coloured bricks and glass. A smeared hunk of moon was reflected on the lake. Glancing back, he saw Roger bringing drinks into the library, where old men sat with the local member. He felt far from the mirth and colour. There would be no wild riding, the dance was too decorous, too refined, they were all stranded in backwaters, and glad of it. Feelings were too muffled, music too polite, décor too perfect.

He grinned at the tree, imagining Roger in fireman's helmet, Bryce doing a strip, Bayard introducing his adders, the rural dean found in a position vilely compromising.

The cold closed in. His glass was empty. He returned, had a fit of coughing. Sounds, hues, were strident, garrulous, overheated, but a dance was starting. 'Hey,' he reached for the nearest girl, pretty Laura, perky Laura, boring Laura, 'come on ... our dance.'

She stared, startled under the trim fringe. He groped unsteadily, she dodged, cried out, indignant, bewildered. He had torn her dress. The band played on but the nearest dancers slowed, then halted. An older man, pinkish jowled, turned sharply on Graham, who struck out at him but, in ruffian disarray, ineffectively, felling not this hippo Galahad but himself. His legs buckled, the heat sunk over him, he stumbled into darkness, out for the count.

When he revived, Janet was kneeling over him, supporting his head; the band noisier, the dancers intermittent phantoms resolutely unconcerned. Friendly hands raised him, voices murmured pleasantly, the floor swayed and stairs were strewn with traps, though, with Janet's hand under his arm, he gained his room. She kissed him as she always did, promising to return. A golden shimmer lingered, after the door closed.

Next morning he apologized for his harlequinade.

'But my dear fellow,' Roger made it sound as if he himself had been at fault, 'I can't tell you how often I've felt like doing the same. Furthermore, you refrained from vomiting. If you allow me to say so, if not the highest praise, it's very considerable.'

Inwardly he must have been furious, always angered by plans leaving the track.

On their last night Bayard, in Chinese-style robe splayed with lotus and hermits, sat late in Graham's room, still with its rows of Buchan and Henty, Walpole and Haggard, where he had once talked, talked, about divorces, illegitimacy, Ramsay Mac, departing in mid-sentence, not to know that in clumsier dreams he would be rescued from a runaway horse, Dr Fu

Manchu, the Sign of Four, and periodically revived with a kiss.

'Roger's wine commands respect. So, of course, does Roger. He's got his name and crest on the bottle, handing you your share as if adding a clause to a decidedly one-sided contract. Though he's not exactly a god, or perhaps not a god all the time. These sessions at his feet leave me both sleepy and sleepless. The isle is full of noises. In my work, I sometimes hear the hour at hand when the looting starts and the sahibs begin to run.'

'It's never quite clear what your work is.'

'Well, I look in on my youth club. I've bits of knowledge available to certain quarters, which anyone of my age is likely to have picked up. You might relate me to an office boy, in the League. You and Della are specialists, I'm the handyman. Fingers in pies. Notions without ideas, like Mr Maugham.'

The narrow head, with its lack of expression, the light, unconcerned voice, were determined to leave no imprint, seemed absorbed only in the flimsy, dangling Chinese sleeves and small bed-lamp which left most of the room in shadow.

'You've been talking politics?'

'Roger and I share a dislike of theory and a need to keep an eye on passing events, though after that we diverge. He's something of a Roman censor, I have a little in common with a tribune. We bounce through our times as if spun by a patient spin-bowler. He has reasoned affection for our old friends, Vested Interests. They endow his plans for Britain, concrete, unutopian, unromantic as real estate, rather stealthy, like a bank account. Though you notice how he continues to go public? Those Third Programme talks, that monologue on *The Brains Trust*, I rather pitied the other three, particularly the Jesuit, stuffed full as an egg with good talk that was barely allowed an airing. Mention to Roger that goats wrecked classical agriculture, as I've good reason to know, and he'll tell you who bred the goats, in that sublime manner that makes you forget to demand evidence. And, ah yes, the Burlegh Civil Rights Lecture. A hornets' nest, that one.'

Seated outside the lamplight, he was now a dimmed, prosecuting figure, very rigorously controlled. 'Such as he, Graham, are always immune from the popular vote. They survive upheavals. After disasters, like the defeated generals, they make splendid come-backs. They enjoy their jobs. So of course did Himmler and, one presumes, Beria.'

'I take it you've quarrelled.'

'Of course not. What an idea!' He bent slightly forward, a Scarlet Pimpernel examining his sleeve for an imaginary fall of dust, his superior, charmless smile refined to a flicker by those ill-defined five centuries of experience. 'Roger's brains are very useful checkpoints. He's got an immense store of political facts which I can pass on to appropriate quarters, as soon or later you'll be reading about. Probably sooner. He was saying, and saying rather well, that Britain exists as a Great Power mainly by bluff and humbug. Pretending that Dunkirk, the loss of India, were all-time moral victories. Every schoolteacher is instructed to denounce a Mr Astor for making millions, rotting harmless Bengalis by selling them rum. Lost days! Times when I imagined that holding master classes meant seducing women. Talking of that, did you notice the other night, before you put on your comic turn, that Roger was wearing make-up and Janet wasn't?'

'How do you know that?'

'By correct siting and sighting, as always.' As if he were embarrassed by a show of cleverness, his voice minutely shed monotony, went more confidential. 'I can tell you something we hadn't realised. Janet is very rich. Not just nicely provided for, like Rockefellers and Kennedys, but in grand measure. Roger inherited this place, and barely that. Actually, it was owned by banks.'

Della had related their Bayard to the Delphi oracle, about which it was clear that Apollo replied on expertly organized advance information. Bayard might not be Apollo, but at least the bookmaker who privately knows that the favourite has been nobbled. His revelation, doubtless true, meant that tiny incidents, remembered but scarcely noticed, might now assume different, perhaps unpleasant significance.

'When Roger plays a shot, it's not always to score a point or contribute to the common good, but to score off his partner. He sets traps for the young. So watch out.'

'You mean...'

'Of course I mean.' Now the sneering Chinese refugee with favours to bestow. 'He don't regard you as a one-man awkward squad. You'd fit well into his entourage. The more discriminating call it his claque. He doesn't want experts and the usual channels, he's master of short-cuts and off-beat solutions and junior partners. He regards governments as colleges of untrained physicians, and says of Parliament that you can judge a household by its rubbish-bin. Well, one can't quarrel with that. And he speaks from the inside, after all. We're not yet ready to use it, but have proof that the Air Ministry and his own Foreign Office sabotaged, as impossible, direct orders from Churchill to bomb Auschwitz, which the Yanks actually did. The FO buried the orders under memoranda deploring exaggerated and hysterical rumours. This was even after the *Daily Telegraph* had printed the facts of the Final Solution. My own feelings . . .' – Bayard's feelings if any, were neutralized by his voice – 'induce a suspicion that Roger's stately departure from the Foreign Office, which became him so well and won so many plaudits, was timed very shrewdly, to dodge some uncompromising questions.'

Hearing this in Roger's home, with Roger and Janet sleeping a few yards away, was worrying, carried reproaches of disloyalty, even treachery, though also some soiled allure. Bayard was waiting, as if about to deliver information conclusive, final, damning.

He said, 'I can tell you that the Air Vice Marshal had something very sticky to say.'

'Which air vice marshal?'

'He's got a placid wife, like a turbot, of whom he's deeply ashamed, however useful she may be for target practice.'

Their converse, as intimate as it would ever be, weakly subsided in a solemn joke. One thought of Bayard on the morrow, not writing a thank-you letter to Janet, but, while composing a story about a Professor of Darts, awaiting her to telephone her thanks to him for coming.

2

Masts of *Eastern Queen*, tea-clipper, soared, sails were furled along riggings, the gilded mermaid gleamed under the bowsprit, bare-breasted to abash storms. Obsolete words revived: brigantine, jib-boom, lanyard, dead-eyes, letters of marque. Wide, dirty water slopped on the narrow beach, slow drab ships steamed past, cranes swung over air grey and jagged, squeezed between the desolate towers hunched above Victorian sheds, wharves, warehouses. Behind him, countering, yet in its day dependent on sea and ship, ranged the glistening, symmetrical palace, with its crescents and domes, squares and pillars, statues and huge windows.

Graham relished contrasts: squalor and splendour, collapse and recovery. He enjoyed masts, they sparked off signals from Moluccas, Indies, the Spanish Main and Golden Man: chance, possibility, challenge – the beyond. Always, when publicly alone, he waited the strangers who so often, attracted by some trick in his appearance, that of a carelessly dressed navvy with money, would stop to beg, confide, occasionally threaten, and now as he moved from the long, towering ship and the sedate neoclassical pile, two youths slouched from an archway. They addressed him familiarly, looking for a caff, perhaps more. Their shaven, spotty heads, faces pinched, scarred, bloodless, their derelict jeans, suggested jobless matadors. Each called himself Dave. In a tea-room incongruously dainty, he recognized a gathering, knocking excitement, a sensation of beckoning from frontiers, offshoot from the mast and prow. Involvement with the brutal, famished and impoverished rivalled Della's drives towards satyr and maenad.

The Daves, inconcisely, claimed to be ex-convicts, he suspected blackmailers, though they demanded nothing save details, preferably gross, of 'college life'. The raw, pale eyes emitted the pathos of intelligent illiterates shrinking at teacher's praise or blame, jealous of younger brothers, despising but envying the affluent, the orderly, and women. 'We don't screw, we hammer them.' But they sounded already defeated.

The thought of Miriam's face if she found them sprawling amongst her valuables deterred him from inviting them home. Instead, he took them to a pub where, with puritan glances at his Scotch, they affronted the barman by demanding milk, though accepting lime-juice. Their heads were spectral, but the show of aggression was puny.

He continued to see them. They avoided the flat but the phone might ring. 'Dave here.' He sat with them in parks, listened to suspect accounts of violence, once drove them to a Berkshire village where they left him to explore the church and enjoy a thought of Bertie Clavering in his riverside mansion close by, of the latest dinner at Montpelier Square, last night's dancing at L'Atelier with Miriam, both enjoying the lavish settings and grumbling at the bill.

Rejoining him, the Daves' small, impudent winks noosed him as sleeping partner. One was bruised about the mouth, the other carried a bulging sack which he stored in the boot. Conceivably they had indeed visited the Claverings.

He never saw them again. A rare postcard arrived, from Dawlish, Brighton, Rhyl, 'Love from Dave', in childish writing, followed by a single cross. They remained shadowy, a little menacing, figures of a bad dream which nevertheless gave curious pleasure.

After abandoning his classes, Graham heard from Sheila that not Kelly but the Revd Martin Emery had betrayed that tactless, dressing-room kiss. Emery himself was presently counter-attacking a book on the death of God with a proposition that the death of churches would entail divine resurrection.

Sheila's letters faltered, then ceased. Former pupils visited. With one he explored the Pennines, with another drove to Malaga. He heard of Jim, reckoned a future England footballer, who had let his hand go septic, then lost it, and of Bridget, promising historian, found poisoned in a side-chapel of Lincoln Cathedral. Fate-tales in action.

That hushed-up business in Austria too had dulled, staling like a love affair. He had been no lethal assassin, but, within confused orders, abrupt and bewildering confrontations, had fired into a crowd, mostly in German uniforms. The Allies had doubtless, after all, known their business, which, though mysterious, had foundered, evoking no mention in the multitudinous war books now appearing. Only a rare dream chucked up a face bleeding like a beetroot, a child with abnormally thin legs kneeling as if spiked beside a prone woman: or wails from trucks, the swinging rifles, his own vengeful spurt of pleasure.

Roger had introduced him to a merchant bank, where, after a year's training, he was offered substantial promotion but, bored, then left for Cambridge, as research assistant to an historian. This he enjoyed, discovering a false premise and many factual errors in the first draft, tracing a missing section of the Crediton MSS, and recalling Olyney's dissertation on Boniface of Savoy, manifestly improving what Bayard, without being asked, termed a goodish, unnecessary book by an academic prig.

The work allowed more sunlit adventures in Corsica, Sicily, Greece, with Sue, with Miriam, with his pupils Eric and Polly with whom, Viking astray from fiords, he got meshed in a tavern brawl against German tourists suspected of complicity in a Waffen SS massacre. Twice he proposed a vacation with Della. Each time, some triviality prevented it, and, needing occasions more exacting, neither was really regretful.

Back in London he allowed serious intentions to be obstructed by random beds after too many parties. Girls stood on turntables, girls with drooling eyes who sucked their hair, girls who on all occasions wondered who they were, girls ruthless for independence or shrinking from it, girls demanding privileges they seldom earned, beautiful girls forthright and intelligent, who yet allowed ugly grunters and guitarists to run through them like acid. More serious was a venturesome combat with a married woman of violet, open eyes and rancid dishonesty. They had months of anger and fun. Once, worsted by her husband, in tearful despair she had appealed to Graham by phone. He rushed to the pub in such haste that he left most of his money behind, and she, like royalty, carried no cash. Distressed, wet-eyed, she begged for champagne cocktails, then announced that she was starving, must have salmon trout. Hating to admit it, he knew he had reached his last coins. Then the door swung open and Bayard entered, as he might a dubious museum. Bayard who hated pubs, abhorred lunch, and had never met the woman. 'Just the people I'm looking for. I've reserved a table upstairs.' At the lunch, salmon trout was presented, without having been ordered.

The love affair ended on the husband's terms and Graham, resentful, but for Janet's few but determined words, would have volunteered for service in Korea, in Malaya. He had no job, loathed all girls in sight. Managerial Roger, perhaps displeased from the banking experiment, made no sign. Doubtless Bayard, clown-about-town, could place him in Saratoga's secretariat, as petty gagster, few duties and no pay, periodic honours from governments imaginary or in permanent exile, and honorary citizenship of the occupied Baltic states in which Bayard and Roger still shared unfailing concern, probably for different reasons.

Sexual indifference evaporated and he was soon sharing Miriam's flat. She was a science graduate, spectacled, slightly mannish, ambitious, described by Della as compact in mind and body, intelligent, fluent, and, like a Bergman film, going on slightly too long, demurely adding, in the childhood language she and Graham occasionally used without always knowing it, that the lady was nasty. Actually, Miriam suited him, pushing nothing to extremes, speaking of passion as an illness, convalescence as rather thrilling. They joked of their liaison of convenience and its built-in obsolescence, though when she left him, to lecture at Nottingham, confer at Manchester, he missed her intolerably, at unexpected corners of the day and in the infinite recesses of night. The best girls, she said, were loners, though at this her voice lost some of its ribaldry. A trip south together had been successful: they sailed between islands, drank copiously on sunset quays, explored the fallen castle and stark headland, said nothing very much, spent money which only she at the moment possessed. She did not forget to remind him.

London too had castles, caverns, inlets, thickets. He remained welcome, a tousled, Nordic Sugar Ray who, a girl said, was always wondering whether to hug you or knock you flat. A rebel angel, another said, at odds with a hurricane.

At partisan coffee bars ardent mouths yearned to devour the century, grimaced over acupuncture, herbal paradise, Sartre, Brecht, American criminality, the death of language, Theatre of Cruelty, while beneath lurked something further, the fear of rape, or the Hogarthian face, transfixed by horror, flaring from a Pimlico window. They merged into daubed, racialist slogans, a giant Fascist poster, *He is coming*, even the occasional Crystal Knot, always so meticulously outlined.

Impervious to Miriam's annoyance, Della would ring, very late, very early. He must take her to Egham. Why? Not his business. Did he want to see *Smiles of a Summer Night?*' No. Nonsense, of course he did. More often, she remained with those muscle-bound Picts, Lords of the Dolerous Blow, Daves. To imagine her within their claws, under them, jealously hurt, but she was no little girl lost, she knew life's tricks and exploited them. Like himself, she looked backwards. The Dragon House existed most fully in her poems, where a girl long strove to open a warped casement. Finally, on a hot, stiflingly dry day, she succeeded, and saw a cobbled yard, naked stone boy, drenched with rain.

Her poems were published frequently in *The London Forum* and smaller journals – though about her book she was strangely reticent. Presumably Allweather had accepted them, and he had indeed published a leader on her: 'How well she realizes the mean between making a point and seeing the point. To achieve this, her verbs appear mischievously haphazard, colliding at angles superficially eccentric, adjectives in places apparently grotesque, yet, on reflection, apt. They assist instants of startling perception, drawn like crossbows.'

Graham grinned sceptically, tracing certain lines and images to sources he himself had revealed: a North London memorial to British redcoats massacred by Russians by a Persian river, a modernist sculpture, barely visible, high over a fashionable street, the small Russian prince jittering on the gallows while people laughed. Reading, he also had to admit how little he had really seen.

He wished that Miriam could like, even love, Della, and was occasionally enticed by thoughts of the three of them in bed together. But now Miriam was again away, in America, sought by laboratories and seminars. Meanwhile, he had passed thirty, was adrift in very little. The old men at the Gridiron had not selected him to be the next prime minister but three.

Dangers menaced, more insidious than random bad behaviour and a girl too many. Through smudged trees and halflights filtered a dream of his being trapped in a burning hospital, choked in swirling, toxic smoke, fighting to escape but continually repulsed by an invisible hand.

3

Roger Kirkland's movements were easily charted. His day was public. National Parks, Censorship, Ethnic Studies, Astral Science Trust Fund, Royal Literary Fund, each had their known committee day, together with his interests in much-publicized commercial houses. A caricaturist depicted him juggling with a dozen caps but perplexed at missing that of the England rugby fifteen.

The Montpelier Square door was opened by a slim girl, a stranger, in tailored, carefully patched jeans and MCC blazer too large for her. Kirkland, in dinner-jacket, was descending the curved, grandiose stairway, the patrician acting with insufficient conviction the role of very ordinary man. Roger Optimus Maximus, already speaking in kind, in the tongue of respected, palsied Judd.

'Grahamus! Gaudeamus igitur. Just the stimulus I need. Get changed in a jiffy and we can snatch a drink before dinner.'

The girl had disappeared. Usually so polite to underlings, Roger had not introduced her. Graham, who kept evening clothes here, soon rejoined him. They dined alone, waiting on themselves from dishes passed through a hatch by unseen hands, possibly the girl's, certainly not Janet's. The atmosphere was one of amiable restraint, with a hint of expectancy, suggesting that the real talk would begin later, following the rich flow of wine. 'I'd like your opinion of this claret. You may pronounce it slightly too young.' The invitation flattered, though Bayard had once observed that the wines so amply produced were often Roger's defence against bores.

Sounds of cars and planes, agitations, salvationists, mythmakers, were extinguished by these thick blue and gold panels: threats of change repelled by heavy silver, ornate mouldings, crusted with leaves, birds, lions, by the tall Froquentin goblets, gold-rimmed on stems so thin that drinking was a serious, considered event. Here Dick Hannay could have awaited Sandy, here councillors collected to preserve footholds, sacrifice a reputation, risk others' lives, though violence, even emphatic contradiction, was as unimaginable as Roger falling into baby talk or imitating Stan Laurel.

The girl must be somewhere about her business, whatever her business was, or conceivably waiting for it to begin. Janet was not mentioned.

They returned to the private study – the orderly room, Bayard called it. Flowers, usually prominent, were absent. Jacobean church chairs and Flemish carpets incongruously matched high metal filing cabinets, harsh, though the light was intimate. Managerial, very black, very white, Roger sat over liqueurs, legs crossed, well balanced. 'I've always been intrigued by the Gospel injunction to befriend the Mammon of Unrighteousness. Posterity may have accepted it too greedily. Yet what does it mean? One has, surely, to imagine its tone of voice. Ironical, sarcastic, short-tempered, or resignedly conceding a place for worldly wisdom? Or angry comedian wit, close to despair.'

Feste, abandoned to wind and rain.

'Someone', Roger reflected, 'akin to our Bayard.' And they both smiled, thinking of Bayard masquerading as a joking saviour. He had once, though not recently, mentioned encountering Christ on some steps, and offering reasonable advice.

'You know', Roger sounded very deliberately offhand, 'that, on the whole, I'm disinclined to boast. Public matters don't extract our most appealing selves, and we've all got enough to stir the conscience. Last year I refused a safe seat. You know only too well that I can't get absorbed in old ladies' blocked sinks, in junkies' falling hair, or some youngster's opinion of his probation officer. I wish my neighbour well, I can scarcely love him. Janet, I dare say, can, and indeed does.' He did not make it seem the highest praise. 'Yet I enjoy having my small say. I dislike being ordered about. I've reasons by now for speaking a little further. Attend to your glass, of course. Well then...' – he smiled as though tolerant of his own grievous failings – 'I've always sought to be in the know, to get some inkling of the real goings on behind the headlines and smoke-screen. Not for my bank balance, of course, not really for status, which I've had for years. I really don't need to demand a Chase Manhattan signature or Mansion House pomp. No, but I do want the satisfaction Della gets when completing a poem, if poems are ever completed.... If not, it may explain that dark frown we sometimes see on her. The satisfaction that Bayard gets from, well, Bayard! The question is, however, where is your own satisfaction?'

The grey, level gaze belied the careless expression, and he allowed no time for a reply, had one been available. 'Be patient, Graham, while I ramble. The real Iron Curtain is what divides the ignorant and the knowledgeable. The latter, for instance, understand very well that the Great Powers' secret police services and their auxiliaries comprise more than the population of Scandinavia or Benelux. They include squads ununiformed but armed, virtually independent. Also spies, assassins, censors, railroads, secret airports, armed banks, protected estates and townships. They have private foreign ministries manufacturing war or revolution here, suppressing others there. Ike had personally to stop the military and their industrial confederates from using the Bomb in Indo-China. The CIA is more likely to listen to you and me than to Congress, let alone the White House. Such procedures derive from Nazi Germany, pre-war Japan, even tsarist Russia. Now, frankly...' – his smile was suddenly luminous – 'and, when anyone begins "frankly", look out for hanky-panky, but you can trust me when I say that some of us knew very early of the Katyn murders and I strongly advised against revealing them. Yet over fifteen thousand Polish officers massacred! Not to be sneezed at, even by the Left, which, of course, does just that.'

He gave an actor's pained, extended shrug. One sensed that the keen eyes had never gazed fully at the sun. Reluctantly, indistinctly, came a memory of Bayard mentioning a Foreign Office memorandum of 1944, leaked after the war, containing 'the disproportionate waste of time allowed to these wailing Jews'.

A very small protest was immediately punctured, Kirkland's voice much in keeping with the finely chiselled glass before him.

'I'm going to show you, quite illegally, at the risk of the Tower, a confidential British diplomatic dispatch to the exiled Poles in London. Note the date. May 1947.'

A thin, carboned sheet, offered with friendly gravity, accepted warily.

In the broad pit their comrades lay packed closely round the edges, head to feet like sardines in a tin, but, in the middle of the grave disposed less orderly. Up and down upon the bodies the executioner stamped, hauling the dead bodies about. When it was all over, the butchers seemed to have turned their hands to one of the most innocent occupations: smoothing the clods and planting little conifers all over what had been a shambles.

'Right, Graham, now glance at this, from the same quarter.'

In handling the public side of the Katyn affair we have been constrained by the urgent need for cordial relations with the Soviet Government to appear to appraise the evidence with more hesitation than we should do in forming a common sense judgement on events occurring in normal times or in the ordinary course of our private lives: we have been obliged to distort the normal and healthy operation of our intellectual and moral judgements. We have been obliged to restrain the Poles from putting their case clearly before the public, to discourage any attempt by the public and the press to probe the ugly story to the bottom. We have in fact, perforce, used the good name of England, like the murderers, to cover up a massacre; and in view of the immense importance of Allied unity and of the heroic resistance of Russia to Germany, few will think that any other course would have been wise or right.

The study's light seemed momentarily a glare from the square metal sheets of the filing cabinets.

'Roger, you really knew of this at the time?'

Bayard's Crystal Knot pals would have put it differently.

'Only HM and the Cabinet, probably not all of them, knew more. You can see the trickiness at Nuremberg, having to sit alongside Russians. Indeed, squaring up to Goering, those small, hard, blue Henry VIII eyes, I felt some sympathy at his objection to being judged by murderers. When Ribbentrop told Molotov in Moscow he could believe he was amongst old comrades, he said more than he probably intended. Still,' savouring the bottle, he handed it over, 'politics is never a clean structure of new bricks. Even an education act can induce superstition as readily as does illiteracy. You may think I'm sounding parsonical.'

He continued, each sentence pat as a footstep, but his listener had strayed. In this mood, this intimacy, Roger had again served the opportunity to expose, then exorcize, that cruel week of bloodshed and deportations in a far-off Austrian summer. If no longer a matter of urgency, it remained a question of interest. But he muffed it.

A familiar tennis syndrome is when a competitor, far in the lead, knows that he will eventually lose, and does so. Graham's reactions usually raced like fire-engines, but tonight they were clogged, blunted, divided. To win against Roger – he was convinced that his questions would involve that – was as unthinkable as parricide. He wavered. Yet discord sustains movement, and it overtook him with a more pronounced urge to protest, not malicious but impish, urchin, a younger-brother snook, not to be displayed. How, in 1940, would a Kirkland have acted had Hitler occupied London?

The metallic gleam subsided. Smiles ran in and out of Roger's face. He moved to a cabinet, returning with a sheaf of papers. 'Here's Mussolini's Foreign Minister on Munich: "The British Ambassador has submitted for our approval the outline of a speech that Chamberlain will make in the House of Commons, in order that we may suggest changes of meaning." That's as gross an interference with our affairs as the Pope deposing Elizabeth. Secret history encircles the world. This room is stuffed with it, a threat to any reputation you can name, a rehabilitation to precious few. The obliteration of the Crimean Tartars, FDR's dying condition, Winston's stroke, Woodrow Wilson's physical incapacity, all concealed from the public. Four years ago in this chair, I heard from the AED of a heavy-water reactor exploding on the Chalk River, Ontario, deliberately kept secret. More serious was the damaged Windscale reactor in Cumberland sending a radioactive cloud over eastern and southern England. We must in due course expect cancer cases in Australia traceable to the British atomic tests in the desert in 1954. Quite recently, some Ural cities were devastated by a gigantic waste silo explosion. Here we must concede that Bayard's synthetic Tom Paines and Zolas, in so blithely ignoring the Official Secrets Act, may be gaining some importance. High-ups are leaking stuff to them, often insignificant but occasionally dynamite. I've some sympathy with them. At home, I've never found it easy to stomach the motives and stability of some of our wealthy Etonians and Wykhamists, charming, talented, working so assiduously to destroy private education, the Empire, muttering "property" with a straight face, and ordaining vile housing estates, horrible architecture, new towns, racial mixtures, conveniently far from their own residences.'

'You consider the Saratoga League fairly widespread?'

Roger's smiles were effaced by a fixed, professional surface from which the eyes gazed as if at an official report.

'There's a largish group of resolute cosmopolitans, founded I don't know when or by whom, most of them probably operating from abroad. We suspect Lisbon and New York, as yet inadequately co-ordinated. The claims of historical lineage are pretty dotty. Where Bayard fits in is rather nebulous, save in the teasing, gadding role he's always enjoyed. He was ever a joiner of esoteric cliques rather than causes. When he was small, a newspaper ran a children's racket, Wilfred's League of Gugnuncs. Bayard hastened to enrol, and was thus entitled to wear a blue tin badge, and, when passing another child similarly enlustred, had to indulge in some idiotic manual dumb-show, then intone, "Ikk Ikk Pa Boo", evoking the impressive response, "Goo Goo Pa Nunk". I fear the excitement went permanently to his head.'

Della would be amused by this. Bayard had arrived somewhat mysteriously at the Dragon House before either of them, establishing with Roger his favoured status obviously not seriously impaired by gadding.

'I fear nothing from fiery zealots and libertarians, but from those I call the If Onlies – exorbitant in babble and self-esteem. *If only* people were nicer, life would be nice, changes too easily into Rousseau's belief that beautiful people are ever corrupted by police, foremen, managers – that hoary catchword, The System. They jibbed at Nuremberg, but were blankly ignorant of the Kellog Pact. They prefer Henry James to Orwell. They imagine that if you blind a cat, you're entitled to seek indemnity not only from the owner but from the cat, that by ejecting an armed burglar you've infringed his rights and jeopardized your own. They prefer quiet nuance to hard fact. In the Army you must have noted that though officers could be crude, stupid, mechanical, you scarcely concluded that they were unnecessary, that chaos and mutiny were preferable.'

The trained advocate, Roger leaned forward in his customary way, awaiting rejoinder, or cross-examination, but Graham, choked with words, queerly at bay, had nothing to say, while knowing that silence was capitulation.

'Well then, we'll agree that neither of us would enjoy life to the full on a ship in which, in crisis, decisions were subject to majority vote. I loathe the messianic. I don't want the Perfect State, I want better government. Most of us can labour only in our own field, though sometimes I'm tempted to assume that my own is larger than it really is.' Now leaning back, he had not relaxed but was somewhat brooding, with an eye on the jury. 'You remember Frazer's priest of Nemi, taking office only by butchering his predecessor, knowing his own fate would be identical? Now, why should he have wanted the job? Tell me, and you tell me the difference between Churchills and Bevins, and the If Onlies. The former had solemn convictions, at whatever cost. The rest, well, Balzac says, doesn't he, something like this . . .' – Roger's quotations, delivered so deprecatingly, were always accurate: '"Is not music, even the music of opera, for tender and poetic souls, for suffering and wounded hearts, a text which they developed at the bidding of things remembered?" At Oxford that sentence compelled me to realize that most political and moral judgements spring not from reasoned evidence but from music, vulgar tunes and big bangs, leaving the devotee at the mercy of memories, sensualities, the fragmented and sentimental. Castro, for instance, inhales the claptrap of youth without a thought in its head but living in a sort of anthem. Like Lenin, he holds his election, reverses the demands of the majority vote, then forbids future elections.'

Far from vulgar, he had moved back, almost into shadow,

head and shoulders like a powerful etching. 'There's work ahead which Della, for all her perceptions, can't envisage, and which Bayard sees clearly, while drawing conclusions sadly at variance with my own. This arrogant old country of ours grousing for rights it no longer earns, fed from loans from those it despises, needs its strong young men. You need a desk here, in our little cabinet. You, my dear chap, are one of us.'

4

No prince abolishes winter, green knights no longer ride with transforming glance and healing blow, but the initiate survives tortuous trials, learning from messages on leaves or dust. Life gives the onus of learning the insignia of clouds, passing safe through forests, evading the witch who dances in a circle or gibbers beneath gingerbread roof. Riddles are solved through alert waiting, clues still abound for the treasure hidden in the garden, for the spaces between words. They are discovered in libraries, heard on radio, are whispered from faces not always seen.

'You will', the magician promised, 'be as beautiful as the day.' The day was raining, nevertheless her own face survived. The mirror, mirror on the wall denied that she was the fairest in the land yet added that the dark princess could still win a prize. The golden apple was collared by those serious about the future. Faith, wrote Musil, should never be more than an hour old. Already she had seen aspirants gasping, faltering, tripping not others but themselves. Alec's second novel had destroyed him, Jane had quailed, instead of flaying critics who told her in bad prose how to write, Basil had stumbled headlong into politics and, before the overdose, Judy dried up in marriage.

Dragons and unicorns derive from those we know but, more unmistakably, from those we do not. They can be challenged, set to maul each other: even the curse can be deflected into an image, a confrontation, test, like the surfer manipulating his wave. Each day bristled with pain and omens. A white stick tapped the pavement, it implied seven years' bad luck, but forced her to imagine the rounded coldness warning the blind of a pillar-box. A blind crow, mobbed by starlings, froze the blood which, melting, released a quatrain. Chalked on the road: *Do not Look. Jump over your Fear*. London was hung with the finely inexplicable, the hints of grotesque lives: *Bridegroom was Wife*; *Import of Umbilical cords from Iceland*.

She must be the tree spirit, awaiting not release, but the first dim promontories that assemble into words, then analogies insufficiently obvious to destroy themselves. The doorless rooms of the Dragon House had been unfailing teachers, leaving so many vistas, colours, shapes to be completed. Tiny grails persisted against all odds, flowers clinging to the perilous, crumbling cliff. In a Japanese death cell an English soldier kept sane by concentrating on an imaginary rose, building it, petal by petal, minutely examining each curl, cavity, ridge, perfecting it, until, in that squalid hole, his fellow prisoner was puzzled by a sudden smell of rose. Her father once returned to Egypt, unannounced, and awaiting him at Port Said was his former Sudanese servant who had travelled two hundred miles to greet him.

London, under a sky cleared too ruthlessly of gods, had small, skinny pockets of nastiness. In a powder-room Della saw steel ladies locked in grey trouser-suits standing motionless, as if wondering if she wore anything underneath. The ugly, the charmless, shards of life, were dreaming of smart air hostesses flying to new lives. They sank to James Dean, to Elvis, reached for the unspeakable or marshland hopelessness, and, in Antarctics, mumbled of immigrants and conspirators, while beautiful faces passed with small, private smiles, perhaps seeing, amongst shuffling crowds, the fox move, the lover stripping, the gift lying in the golden field, a favourite number gleaming on a cloud.

She herself needed no acid to convulse the mind. Skiers dropped from a royal monument and raced down the Mall; camels, transformed to gondolas, drifted through Piccadilly; green swans perched on branches wild and black as Medusa's locks. Slim Byrons and pert ladies floated above cornfields alongside Bayswater. Leopards stared without past or future, but elephants were always looking backwards, sometimes carrying the bones of their dead.

Della enjoyed afternoons alone with Janet, usually in a tearoom. Janet herself was looking tired, though her personal complaints remained oblique.

'Cowslips are getting rarer. I planted some in that hot summer of 1948, but almost at once they withered. Now, I can scarcely believe it, after all this time, at exactly the same spot, I've found, just imagine it, cowslips! I told Graham. He always loved digging beds for me, even weeding, and I could never get myself to show him how many of my favourite plants he had uprooted.'

'He probably stamped out the cowslips.'

They often discussed Graham who, though always in motion, seemed not to develop, still sojourning with seal women who granted him bed and board providing he broke no taboo, though he always did. Barbara, with violet unending blink and dying voice; streamlined Hazel who rated T. S. Eliot great fun; talkative, donnish Miriam who could calculate the degrees of energy beneath each poem. Someone had said that Graham could be a blue-eyed Fascist but never a red. Despite his gladiatoral attitudes he needed assent and popularity like income, though had apparently swiped at a youth for demanding income for the Guy. Of his joining Roger's staff, Janet had said nothing. When she mentioned Roger, it was as always: affectionate, concerned, often admiring. Where she was now living in London was uncertain.

Bayard the celibate also disdained to develop, relying on ribald affrontery, never very comic and forced on friend and stranger alike. 'As you must have read, it's generations since I saw Central Asia.' 'Why is it', he once inquired, 'that so many of your guests always turn out to be Russians?' No Russian had ever been present, but the host, a celebrated art historian, went crimson. As for Bayard, he was a sort of abbé, not exactly within the church.

Roger had found Della a flat on North London heights, from where synagogues, homes, steeples, tennis clubs, a dome, a turret, swelled into a speckled mass of quail's egg blue, Devonshire red, Merlin green, slanting on hills beneath her. A huge sky looped the capital. Bluebells survived from woods almost vanished. No stinking centaur would befoul this suburban pastoral, a fastness where she could repulse some who attracted her but who had no feeling for those who shape the light and who punished her for her success.

Clothes for tonight must be chosen judiciously. The choice of caskets. The notch on the beanstalk. Back from the typist, neatly bound, were her thirty-nine poems, eighteen unpublished. She fingered silken green with golden tinges, mused over blue sheen, contemplated her jewel box.

Rick Allweather, celebrating the fortieth birthday of *The London Forum*, had been interviewed everywhere, behaving with bustling panache. Mauriac, Frost, Eliot, had wired congratulations, the *TLS* produced a three-page leader alight with established names, some established rather too firmly, the Arts Council awarded a Grant Extraordinary. A reception was being offered him tonight.

Now frowning over a patch of terrain that promised difficulties, she picked up a long, black, polished hair, and held it to the light. Quivering like a dowser's rod, it refrained from foretelling snow but shook out a tiny spark that at once expired, becoming part of the mind like the Schubert notes emitted from the downstairs piano. Had song, she welcomed the brief distraction, preceded speech, Schubert himself tweaking some buried life that continued to scatter husks just beyond reach? Some spoilsport air vice marshal would say, Certainly not.

The frown remained, she moved away to caress the book again. Though no contract had yet been signed, Rick had spoken of autumn publication, possibility of an American offer. She would be, he enthused, his only hard-cover author under thirty.

Rick was the giant, slowly merging into the massif. Lichened, craggy, a landmark, sometimes clouded, sometimes flagrant with volcanic energies. He had opened her the glass door in the rock-face but would not live for ever, despite trumpets now blaring.

Young Rex Elsen, the new poetry editor at MacEntee & Holbrook, was excited by the vistas he was creating now that he had hoofed out mouldy old Vickery. His American connections were strong, *The Bookseller* had acclaimed his new distribution project, his firm was backed by a powerful Midlands car grouping. Elsen had traced in her work a geometry of mazes and criss-crosses, spirals and circles within the mythology of forest trails, labyrinths, alchemical stages, hunters and treasure-seekers. She was, he wrote, a true thief of fire. Her 'Land's End' glimmered like starlight.

Two hours later, faces turned at her entrance. Smiles of recognition, affectionate pecks. Rex Elsen, sharp-nosed, grainy, freshly laundered skin under crisp hair, lifted his glass. The lark ascending. Then he was engulfed by editors, TV executives, bossy directors, scowling hopefuls in open-necked shirts, Mr Readymoney glistening, Olive Product complaining of disrespect by paperback houses, Martin Montag in good shape, though out of uniform, publicity hounds in wide Hockney designed ties, novelists, poets, a thick group swirling around the hewn, bulky Allweathers in their changeless tweeds. Rick's great, bald head was lowered, periodically jerking up as if struggling against sleep at a concert. He had quickly noticed her, had waved with palpable relief. But now a *TLS* editor called for silence, to introduce their old friend, verily a standard-bearer who throughout had demanded high standards, a true man for all weathers. During the war, he, together with *Horizon* and *New Writing*, had, by sustaining literature and the critical canon, won a battle for Western culture, nay, civilization itself. Only last year, in Belgrade for PEN, he had been the true voice of Britain while politicians fumbled and statesmen betrayed their states.

Mottled, laborious, Rick took his ovation like an ageing actor-manager, breathing heavily, but still challenging. Old Rick! Nods were exchanged. The dank wine and perfunctory sandwiches were due not to parsimony but to expensive, lifelong struggles to sell the public wares very solid though perhaps by now over-traditional in an era of New Wave, New Novel, concrete verse. His opening words were slurred. The small, boar's eyes grumbled. Stella, loyal adjutant, nudged him, he slowed, was more distinct, but affronted.

'It wasn't the treatment I'd expected. That wretched little Jack-in-office crouching there at taxpayer's expense! I told him to his foul, neutered face that I could show letters from Ezra himself. And, my God, Ezra's facetiousness rattled the teeth but he didn't use his nimble footwork to stamp on others' talent. He respected my belief that good writing is more than self-protection. It's texture, emanations, shadows, enduring as moorland stones. Readers must belong to it, work it like a wireless. He can get Mozart, he can get that howling of cats entitled pop.'

Overgrown, accusing, he implied that most of them preferred pop. Their soothing gestures, appreciative smiles, irked him, though he seemed unaware of embarrassment fidgeting behind them. Stella brought her hands together, doubtless in a plea for Mozart.

'It was in my presence that Scott described America as a willingness of the heart. I urged him to write it down, he was sober enough to do so, without showing much gratitude. But, returning to the coal-face, most stuff submitted me hasn't much craft, very little heart. Middling things. Cold as a nun's lips. And their begetters expect me to change their nappies and tuck them up in bed.'

He suddenly stared down at Della, saluting the good comrade, the reliable, the true talent, then resumed, growling at enemies.

'I can claim that even before Cyril I acclaimed poor, gifted Denton. I was certainly the first to encourage Alicia, though when she collared the Via Femina I wasn't invited to the beano. I had to warn Edith that her adjectives could heat a liner. I tried to drag de la Mare into the twentieth century but his wits were made of moonlight. Some would say moonshine. Public honours are dished out for much less than this. The luxury editors of trivialities. All those specious grants and interviews for those who don't deliver the goods. Well, most friendship is feigning, the fellow who wrote that knew his oats, and he didn't hail from Cambridge. A new book used to make me scent battle. Norman Douglas, D.H.L., even Virginia ... but now I read my eyes down to the stumps and all they see are young pirates with stolen typewriters and pansy voices who consider – I don't say they imagine, they've as much imagination as a fossil has spunk – they consider that novelty of technique can disguise paucity of matter. Where are the wits of yesteryear?'

Evidently elsewhere. A slight shuffling had started, then a murmur, a cough, but the ruined, glowering, moistened face, that of a threatened sun-god trapped in bad light, was undeterred, the voice rasping, punishing.

'I tried to build two generations into a fortress, I've preferred walking to sprinting, and have lived to witness total unrestraint fobbed off as experiment. A feeble misunderstanding of Joyce. God Almighty couldn't stand it and nor can I. Toadying to juniors passes for dynamic editorial policy. Well, old Chesterfield declared that a gentleman is he who knows how to play the trumpet, but doesn't. I'm surrounded by an unholy blast of self-trumpeters, drowning out the dedicated scribblers. Grub Street had its own glory, but now we see writers as an endangered species, like tigers, indeed whales, at the blunt end of a bad bargain, while the chosen few fatten in dishonest hothouses at public cost.'

His head jutted forward against dissent which did not come. Listeners stared into glasses, flowers, at their own feet until a voice, less friendly than it appeared, murmured, 'Dear Rick, we are all your pupils.'

The tension slackened. Facing them, beleaguered, Rick Allweather again drew breath, but at once, cutting him off like a thermostat, congratulations bounded up at him. He looked astonished, then stricken, a little lost, one hand wandering as his audience dissolved into over-loud groups, leaving him only with Stella, no sun-god but a bombed lighthouse.

Della had involuntarily moved towards him but Rex Elsen was at her side, whispering, bending closer for her reply.

5

Bayard's flat, uncurtained, with spyhole in most doors, was impersonal as an hotel cruet, sparsely functional as his own face. Very clean, spinsterish tidy, never a coin or button loose on the bare polished floors with their circles of light, thin spars of shadow. All five rooms had desk and telephone, none a bed, there was no kitchen and the tiny bathroom contained two baths. Everywhere the fittings might have been incompetently delivered by mail order. In this, the largest and coldest room, several hundred discs were meticulously ranged, Albinoni to Webern, but without a record-player. Long bookcases, more glass than wood, were empty and a thickly gilded frame displayed only the white wall behind it. Opposite hung an enlarged photograph of the Turin millionaire lately arraigned for financing Red terror squads. Coloured pencils on the white desk might have symbolized flowers or toys, for the desk itself was empty save for a purple telephone, the very drawers were missing, suggesting three grinning, toothless mouths. Over the door was an abstract drawing of thin, wavy lines piercing an irregular circle apparently representing the Crystal Knot. A low, black table held a small glass, a large glass, a chipped flask of wine, a single book. The small glass was for her, assiduously replenished though with an air of apology, the other he would pick up, contemplate with collector's pleasure, but keep dry. In all, an improvement on her last visit, when he provided barley-water in more than sufficient quantity.

As always, he sat very upright, very still. The telephone rang at intervals so regular that Della imagined a personage in another room paid to call him. Invariably he uttered only 'yes', sometimes allowing the other no time to speak.

'Now, Della, that gipsy Graham's installed in Roger's barracks, rebuilding the country, he's had to remove a few rings from his ears, and get a new dinner-jacket. The old one could have been used as a rug, and I dare say it was.'

She had been gazing at the solitary book, an interim biography of Bing Crosby. She moved to pick it up, but he smoothly removed it beyond reach. 'Not a first-class work, which may surprise you, and the author misspells my name. And I've had a journeyman day. After committee, a woman stopped me to outline in very considerable detail a play she wanted to write. I gathered the actual writing was to be left to me. She did not leave me merry as a grig. Only you can tell me what a grig actually is.'

She did not think so. Instead, her laughter rippled out like a pennant, her green eyes lightened. Sir Herbert Clavering, for outstanding public service, had been promoted to the House of Lords. Bayard was solemn.

'I'll tell you how Bertie started that public service. He gives us the usual patter about character, hard work, rectitude, but in fact, when scarcely out of Varsity – his name for the Exeter Polytechnic – he'd read *The Times* very carefully, and attended every illustrious memorial service. He'd met none of the corpses but gradually their live counterparts got used to his presence, even his voice, and eventually began inviting him to share the bakemeats. At one of these shows he met his wife, actually at the service for her first husband. That's something you can tell your children, all of them.'

'I'm only going to have one.'

'My dear girl, you don't have to, just to please me. And you dislike children.'

'I've never said that.'

'Words were never necessary. But what shall we call her?'

'I shall have a son. He'll dazzle.'

'The right school I've found is more important than the right name. And I dare say he won't be named Rick.'

Even when joking, Bayard had goblin malice round eye and lip, a Gothic menace. Her laughter dried. 'I'll call him Andrew. Not Andy, at any time. But why mention Rick?'

Bayard's voice was polar in its chill. 'Because I know why you've come here, I know what you're not anxious to tell me, I know what's in that bag you've carefully left outside, and I know where you're taking it.'

She left the room, returned, and defiantly lobbed him a thin, square package. He fingered it as he might a guitar. 'Of course. Your book. All your own work. Written, I dare say, whilst inspecting five rows of water-colours, as presented in the Sea Scouts' Hall, West Wittering. One of Rick's ancestors incurred a disparaging footnote in Gibbon. Rick himself may bear umbrage at your defection.'

The room was more naked, Bayard, with the window behind him, blank as enamel, appallingly tall, uncannily motionless. Outside, the darting bird, the spring leaf, invited escape.

'Bayard, you know Rick's out. Out of touch with reviewers and advertisers, out of money and sometimes out of what's left of his wits.' This was more vehement than she had intended, and she now changed too rapidly to little-girl appeal. 'So you think I've behaved badly!'

'I would not have done it myself.'

The mild words had a damning ring from Mordred at his silkiest, dedicated to mischief yet confronting accusers with pleas difficult to refute, and for whom innuendo was more lethal than fresh air, cutthroat conflict.

Graham she had often kissed, but never Bayard. To do so would be to contact the freezing or the scalding. Yet she needed his approval. Deprived, she was near tears, while, in his chattiest manner, he reminisced about a lady of whom Talleyrand said that, to avoid the scandal of flirtation, she always surrendered at once.

6

Lord Clavering tapped the other's grey waistcoat as he might a barometer. 'If you ask me, the real villain was Dulles.'

None, with experience, ever asked Clavering anything, and Kirkland did not do so now. 'The real doubt was Anthony. The spoiled star in search of a quality role. He screamed like an alarm bell ... didn't we understand that he wanted Nasser destroyed, and that he didn't give a damn for anarchy and chaos in the Middle East!'

Escorted by friends, clients, supplicants, courtiers, he paused, one hand on Clavering's arm. The Montpelier Square lawn was dappled with the bare-armed, ribboned, flowered, the sedate and morning-coated; champagne glasses twinkled in May light, thin gold through the elms. Jonathans and Nigels, Harriets and Petras, Excellencies and Right Honourables.

Clavering, ruddy, white-whiskered, was bland as a travelogue. 'Well, crisis clears the air. We can see our friends, we can see our foes. Poor old Ike. Chattering about world indignation and the moral course. He's senile, and his only course is the golf-course. The Generalissimo! Terrified of "All Africa", "All

Asia". Collections of gollywogs and ex-houseboys!'

Graham was nearby, amongst Roger's personal assistants, nicknamed behind his back the Imperial Guard. Never off-duty, he supervised waiters, joked, introduced, rescued, refilled, listened, unseen notebook at the ready.

After the autumn Suez near-riots, all was peaceful as a deck-chair. Rustling dresses, perfected cravats, scented dollish girls with the sexual mystery of bridesmaids, sweetly polite to high-coloured buffalo gentlemen, and nodding, cow-faced ladies of antique lineage inherited, claimed or bought. Yells of 'Wogs Out', 'Eden Out', had long rotted.

Roger had opposed Suez, stating that the Canal was advantageous but not essential. With London rocked by demonstrations, ticker-tapes, editorials, a Crystal Knot article daily exposed enormities: the killing of forty-seven adults and children at Kajr Kassem, the French shooting and drowning of unarmed Manzala fishermen, machine-gunning an Egyptian officer for refusing to sweep his prison floor, Egyptians left legless in the desert; gougings, scorched genitals, civilians hanged from telegraph-poles, gnawed by dogs, jerked by electricity, napalmed in hospitals while, in Hungary, Russians were shooting, hanging, betraying safe-conducts. 'Scandalous,' Martin Montag told his press conference. 'No country in Europe more appreciated my work.'

Della was here, now by the flowers, now under the trees, in yellow coat, green scarf, black trousers, her gestures like rapid stitching. Bayard had not come, presumably judging the world from a Stockholm bar or reading-room in Hull, and citing some Dark Age interview. Janet, in tiny brown-feathered cap, brown trouser-suit, was more guest than hostess, unobtrusively confining herself to old friends, the Claverings, the Cleggs, though her demeanour remained that of a woman still desirable, enjoying rights that it would not have occurred to her to question. Gentle, she also rode well to hounds. She had only once referred to her position with Roger, saying that she knew he was doing very well, though adding, as if her thoughts were elsewhere, 'But, Graham, what do you really want?'

She was staying with London relations, perhaps because of Sarah, the MCC girl, only glimpsed leaving a room, flitting down a passage, not actually seen for many weeks, and of whom nobody spoke.

This afternoon, one had always to watch Roger, hub of the gathering, tirelessly dispensing smiles, like invitations to those he delighted to honour, though one could detect beneath the smile, hand grasp, expansive gesture, a signal, impatient, abrasive, dismissive. One must be alert for a particular gleam, a scarcely perceptible wink, the summons for relief, at this instant from Lord Clavering.

'Graham, dear chap, what a very happy occasion! You can tell me all that's going to happen. Central Africa, isn't it? Kith and kin, how easy it is to mock!'

Bertie Clavering had never mocked, would not know how to, though receiving unawares much mockery. He had made kith and kin sound like comics. 'Yet for me they are those whose religion I understand, whose values I share, whose company I relish. And we'll see them kicked into kingdom-come.' He chuckled, selecting a sandwich. 'How delightful to see so many of the young! I like to call them our new aristocracy. Despising the past, I dare say very rightly. Out they go, overseas, Nepal, India, Thailand, to clear up the mess we made. Our young Liverpool singers, magnificent types – swinging, I believe it's called. They may well be showing us what Christianity's all about. New Elizabethans, eh! Frustration's the danger. Audacity, audacity, and again audacity. One knows instinctively that a young Englishman wrote that. Mind, Graham, frustration's not your ticket. With Roger behind you, you'll scale the heights. You love to hit the ball out of sight, straight down the line to all corners of the earth. I hear your name, I hear your name. And I'm looking forward to Della's book, though I must confess I don't get on best with the modern stuff. Old Tennyson's good enough for me. After many a summer dies the sun. Just so.'

He waddled away. Graham smiled. He was fly enough not to be lulled by bright façades, calm, patrician voices. Partisanships, cross-currents, flowed unimpeded by coiffure and couture, herbaceous outfits and elaborate hats, well-tailored greetings, and the radiant aftermath of a royal celebration. Roger's movements, Janet's reticence, would be noted by sharpshooters and bookmakers, the resentful, thrusting, and those who, meek or shrewd, inherit by biding their time. This reception, trained on Roger's will, was not very different from an 'art-designed' party to which Miriam had taken him, where the host, a social Cosgrave, imperiously rearranged groups and individuals to suit his arbitrary colour whims – 'Will that girl in red kindly move alongside the yellow screen.' He was once disposed to order a woman to discard her skirt, its pink upsetting the general scheme.

A general, an actress passed, very polite, small pivots of the high circuit of reserved rooms, the right quarters, private boxes for opera, for Test Match, Glyndebourne nights, parties in Mr Speaker's great apartments, breakfasts with the latest TV ringmaster, in country houses and millionaire restaurants. What did he really want? For the moment, little more. He was breathing the secrets of men and power. From across a Gridiron table, or in a famous garden, a dispirited aspirant, a relegated minister, would speak as if to a palace marshal. 'Graham, I know Roger's so frightfully busy, but I wonder if you could possibly....'

Offhandedly, Miriam reminded him that he was shedding old friends. Deterred by his engaged phone, his absences and reputed grandeur, former pupils were ceasing to call. People seemed to be existing only in the immediate: like tennis players, waiters, Commons orators, fixed into position but evaporating when out of sight.

He was not yet included in Roger's inner cabinet, the property and financial experts, technological savants, political insiders, and sensed that the colour of his official sash had not yet been decided. He provided minor social and topical data, helped map the Kirkland programmes, drove Roger to airports, accompanied him to dinners, theatres, particular parties, played tennis and squash with him, the older man's even-tempered determination usually outlasting his own wayward energy, which had a brilliance vulnerable to anger, recklessness and fits of irresolution. Older associates treated him politely but without warmth, as a favourite denied exceptional skills. He did not care. Roger was generous financially, remained exciting, oiled and timed to precision, easily adjusting to all demands and opportunities, still buying streetcorners, watching the fashions in neighbourhood values, the rise of a laboratory, experimental hospital, aircraft consortium, media enterprise. To Roger he owed membership of the Gridiron, White's, Beefsteak, Pratt's, small outposts of information, influence and good times.

Miriam could be caustic, like Bayard, largely avoiding Montpelier Square. 'You're too whole-hearted, lovey. At supper-time, do you ever calculate the length of your spoon?' Behind her glasses, she was severe. 'You're a historian, though a rum one. No method. But you know as well as anyone that autocracy is subject to helplessness. Can be broken from unexpected quarters, sometimes from its own retainers.' Then laughed, before he had time to.

Returning to duty, Lady Samler's car, Dr Landeer's briefcase, he was not laughing. The taunting reminder of Miriam, whose body he needed, whose judgements he respected, minutely discoloured the shimmer, the iridescence around him on the fresh grass, the tinkle of glasses, tiny witticisms, delights. At a touch, he turned brusquely, but was at once kissing Janet.

They watched Della, ballerina between poised figures. She was merry, talking very fast, hair tossed back, face alight.

'Is she happy?' Janet's smile contained worry.

He could not answer, meeting Della only in her circus mood, tuned to the clatter, disrespect, punkish clothes of her own slice of London. Had he asked, she would have told him, but he respected independence. Indeed, Miriam declared, respected it too much. As a boy, he had rejoiced in secrets.

'She's nervous about the book. It's sad when we can't help.'

He was too often surprised at what Janet realized at a glance, though years were teaching how a hesitation, unguarded look, a silence, can transform cherished assumptions. At dinner, Lady Clegg had suddenly whispered, 'He never took me dancing', the words wrenched out by some quietly inexpert wrong, her ridged, painted face a splodge of lost beauty, filling with holes.

His misgivings resumed later, in a taxi with Miriam. She flipped him with her bag. 'Of course she's nervous. You, my darling bear, wouldn't know a real poem if you met it head-on in a deserted ballroom, but anyone can see her stuff's not much good. Her butch pals of God knows how many sexes must be holding not their breath but their sides, behind her back, and not at the sight of her pretty little bum.'

He rushed into the quarrel he invariably lost.

On publication day MacEntee & Holbrook gave a launch at which the Allweathers, though invited, did not appear, though perhaps represented by a Miss Verity, who had forgotten to shave. The gathering was more than literary, dividing obsequiously as the Kirklands arrived, all points ashine, on their way to Covent Garden, Roger agreeably waving away a covey of journalists. Bayard stepped in later, much as if he were feeling a draught. On the walls, on the piled volumes, Della's slight, cocky face championed her own cause, while she herself, summer princess, kissed, embraced, signed copies, received tipsy congratulations from those doubtless with half-completed reviews in their pockets.

I'm building up, Astaire had sung, for an awful let-down. Della had craved publication, caught the hard ball slung very high, then discovered that it was spiked. Reviewers, Miriam asserted, had got her measure. Almost unanimous, their bombardment mounted, so that within a week she vanished into leper's compound, refusing all company.

Anonymously, but rumoured from Rick Allweather, or at his behest, last salvo of an expiring command, the *TLS* condemned a young person who, on evidence, had read too much Marianne Moore, misread too much Emily Dickinson, ending in the lower depths, sub-Sitwell. Other reviewers skidded in eagerness to assent, ravens converging on quarry. 'A hired, prefabricated style presented as if wastelands and cantos were still news.... Quick responses but on an ornate plane of pure sensation untrammelled by thought or abiding purpose.... In an era of maximum publicity for minimal quality, such writers speed towards nowhere with ever-increasing sound and fury.'

One sensed that vengeful, unpublished Catos, usually bespattering public library books or correspondence columns and feeling themselves authors, had emerged to pelt her.

Olive Product, in *The London Forum*, gave considered verdict: 'There are experienced artists, too obvious to name, who, like fifteenth-century armourers, perfect their craft at the instant when it becomes professionally obsolete, and they have nothing further to express. The present case is sadder, for we are forced to consider a versifier hitherto over-praised by her friends or by kindly seniors, now revealed as a talent woefully inadequate, with too little to impart, in a space granted too generously.'

Miriam's tactful silence, though welcome, infuriated.

BOOK THREE

*

Primitives treat things and animals as people, and experience feed-back from them. We treat people as things or animals and attempt to manipulate them. The disparity between humans and this attitude is what, in my opinion, the revolution is all about, but it is also necessarily about – or affects – everything down to our experience of separate and individual identity.

Alex Comfort

This fellow is wise enough to play the fool;
And to that well craves a kind of wit:
He must observe their mood on whom he jests,
The quality of persons, and the time.

Shakespeare, Twelfth Night

I didn't want to harm the man. I thought he was a very nice gentleman. Soft spoken. I thought so right up to the moment I cut his throat.

Truman Capote

1

Imagine cold blue when it meets the sun above the Alpes-Maritimes, then subsides into warm, frantic clashes of colour, cars already moving towards it, winding up steep, coastal roads, leaving the baked, corrupt mileage of soaring hotels – balconies, bright shutters, slave labour in smart gloves. Blue weather was slotted in daily, blue casual waves slopped on to sand as if cautious of dislodging the summer content, scarcely noticed by tourists at play by pools, at rainbow tables, on pretty boulevards under the plane trees. The summer sea was weak, its storms had only the mock-ferocity of an heraldic lion, guiltless of the occasional stranger found washed up under a cliff with papers missing.

The eye lifted to the old Arab fort on the hill, to spire, turret, snow-peak, to tall rectangular apartment blocks, which, in baffling pride, Le Corbusier had styled Machines for Habitation. Like giant hi-fi sets, they were replacing villas in the prolonged, post-war boom, the property explosion of gaudy façades, swirling balustrades, strips of glass set between purple oblongs of bougainvillaea, soft red bands of arbutus, which must underlie Della's poem *Screens*, in which sun-bemused people crawled like insects, protected by high luminous screens, always about to topple and disclose the jagged rock, a full, roaring tide, a beast with bloodied horn.

Vestigial lives survived at second hand; in the Bronze Age Ligurian cemetery, a hill gashed by Hercules, the Roman fountain sparkling at Barjols where Marius swept off Germanic invaders. Here Phocaeans, Celts, Visigoths, Franks had fought and settled, their swords, shields, cauldrons, stacked in local museums, antique when Norman belaboured Saracen, and Barbary pirates savaged the coast.

Names spoke: Avenue Masséna, Rue Verdun, Place des

Maquis. A broken castle displayed a medieval profile to distant Cannes: the bandstand, filling with pop-groups, flaunted the gilded crowns, flamboyant dome, fretted ironwork of the Second Empire.

Graham remained in a hurry, for lost frontiers and the unique encounter, for caves, deep waters and olive groves, for cave and high path. These lands held the unseen but inescapable, sometimes accusing. Young men were missing, they had flopped into the Aisne, been sucked into whirlpools of horror at Verdun, exchanged death and torture on mountains with Germans and Italians, or been executed in the Place, by SS, by Resistance Purifiers. Few Jews had returned, having been dug out by Laval for Himmler, Speer, Herr Saukel, and the death factories of I.G. Farben. Today, in recompense, many Germans were about, striding, loud, cancelling history.

Della demanded the stillness of heat and sand, would doze by shuffling waters or sit with wine, staring at the Alps, hard and spiked at noon, crumbling by sundown. Inattentive to lively streets and historical details she would watch, as if unzipping the air, a cactus, rose, pastel door. Twice she repeated Enright's line, 'Statues too tired to talk'. Intent as a robin, she pored over an elderly Swedish couple, all pearls and shirt-front who, as if meeting for the first time, would swap ornate compliments, but regularly upset the cutlery in manic rage. She might see crocodile waves, nightmare toad-kings, breathing lighthouses. Art, she had said, could derive from memories slightly askew. Watching the small sea-ripples she had murmured 'Blunted scythes'. At once he responded, 'Sedgemoor', but the word, long dead, fell without echo.

She had once come to Oxford. Together they had seen a youth punting, reflected in green, sunlit water which the pole scattered into golden chips that at once regathered. She had held his arm, as though the bright fragments were solid enough to pluck and throw, though her subsequent poem, 'The Punt', described a canal, darkened, swollen, and an oarsman not quite dead. Verse, as so often, excluding strangers, non-members. Now, the dirty bars, cabbage-patch cafés, dance-halls, cinemas, abounding in her later work, extracted only her indifference. She would interrupt with urchin grin. 'Graham darling, you never stop. And you always forget the eunuchs.' As though he had betrayed the horrible. She had described with verve and queer comparisons a daub of Poseidon impaling a boy lover in an underground temple a few kilos away, adding an obscene local tradition, but was irritated when he suggested they visit it. That D.H. Lawrence had died in these hills concerned her less than *Vive Sagan* chalked on a wall, at which she swore coarsely. She refused to inspect towering Giacometti statues, and a walled village with wooden Catalan Christ of the Black Plague. A registry office designed by Cocteau she pronounced not worth seeing. How did she know? She only stared back contemptuously. She did condescend to mention Matisse, Bonnard, Dufy, but as if in minor good manners designed to avoid gratuitous offence. Instead, she ordered he drive her to a casino, a new restaurant, where no Phoenician handed the wine list, no Norman peered between sagging figures, though, at the tables, where she always won small sums and he lost large ones, she surreptitiously drew certain faces, much enlarging them, landscaped with enamelled cheeks and ringed, dying-down eyes. Really, she must hanker for a Californian sky, a New York apartment high above river and avenue, free of time and space. She would utter Florida, Cape Cod, the Village, even Hollywood, and, several times, Pulitzer, as once as a child she had 'Tomorrow ... let's....'

Through long warm days and flashy nights she would open a book only to close it at once, professing clinical concern for his own habit of reading. Cool jazz, cool wines, were reviving her more. Visibly, she was at last recovering sensation, unfreezing in new suns. Familiar ribaldry reappeared, taunting them both not for disasters but for bad luck self-induced.

Driving to Grasse for a cosmetic with name lewd or grotesquely silly, she had crossly dismissed Troubadour verse as repetitive and tedious, annoyed that he should refer to it, then, seeing a blue and green mirage on the tarmac, in another, fresher voice, spoke of the Grail. 'At the start, it wasn't very holy. Maybe a pot of blood and a head floating on it. Then it grew, like a vicar or blinded rabbit in dreams. The Church didn't like it at all. Chrétien, remember, saw it as dangerous, slippery enchantment.'

They rounded a corner perched over dry, freckled plains, above the flat sea, then she added, as if he needed convincing, 'In the States, the trash-can is the new Grail.'

An immaculate summer was hoisted. For Graham, brazen limbs cooking on beaches were intolerably boring, but he was excited by yachts riding far out, white and gold nudges on the dense blue, innocuous, or trimmed for the audacious get-away, stacked with weaponry, drugs, kidnapped millionaires, sad pretenders and pretentious opera stars. Masts, masts, while, nearer, each noon under the same feathery palm, the red-hooded horse-carriage lingered until dusk, no one emerging. What did it conceal? Onassis counting his millions, a Ripper, a ruined Duce no longer astonishing? Perhaps nothing. Adventure remained just beyond reach. He ventured into morose, twisted alleys, casbah-like *pissoir* airs, under narrow windows hung with drying sheets, banners of the poor. An old woman, cracked like dirty porcelain, cajoled a monkey; shabby girls, with bare pretty legs and inquisitive eyes, had queer, repellent allure, passing as if on film in an endless quiver of sick light and glistening shadow. Back-street tensions, never defined, were more devious than sex, induced by cripples, squalor, expectations of violence, though but a few yards away were shining American automobiles, café Iturbis with flying fingers, flower-markets in pillared arcades.

He climbed dusty tracks, pulling away from the garish rind of hotel and esplanade, to failing, half-abandoned villages and stealthy churches where Italian voices clashed with Provençal, and red-shirted youths, pidgin Garibaldis, watched him suspiciously, fingering their belts. He wandered headlands, drank rough wine in taverns, on old quays under torn awnings, on benches of small, leafy squares, and, as so often, people, usually young, always disappointing, offered him drinks, showed photographs, confided lives which like those moaned or gasped at seances, were glumly trivial, while small boats drifted in from twilight, lovers tangled in grass and the sun sank into the sea.

They imagined him a rich drop-out, a fake beatnik, idle artist. When he reported them to Della, they staged a double act of inquisitive foreigners.

'I invite your sympathy. In your country ... Shakespeare and Lord Byron ... Miss Sayers ... Dr Rowse ...'

'Mr Profumo, Miss Keeler ... all very well, yes? Mr Vassall's taste in boys! You get in on the act, yes? Your Foreign Office, the bad joke of the century.'

They relished hotels, the sham castles, each a springboard for secrets, like the opening of a novel. Della at last took the lead, laughing in mock-shock at five shoes left outside a bedroom, envisaging twin boys or girls riding the deformed. Short stories sat at each table, people's mystery intensified. Girls clamoured from a tree at 3 a.m., a dead snake lay on a carpet woven with classical serpents, an itinerant revivalist, Miss Christina Meditation, was terrified by an empty room, widows like cold hot-water bottles grazed in lounges, with cats and boiled legs, and, in corridors, people passed with demeanours of grandeur; and a tired lady insisted on *Poisson mélancolique*. They were always listening.

'Absolutely unforgettable...'

'Yes ... unforgettable.'

But the face was puzzled, or suffering from airlock. A Chinese lady spoke continually as if on a disc played slightly too fast: 'Lovely, lovely, I adore it ... very comfy. My father wanted a boy.' Nothing, Della said, was hackneyed, she was glad of such minute episodes: an exchange of glances, a furtive gesture, clamoured louder than cannonades at El Alamein. She loved the half-opened door, the barely seen, the inexplicable, the overheard like erratic sounds of a radio with fading batteries. She saw life from the margins, unaware of some political procession, some thundering Jaurès.

'But, Della, you must have noticed ... you're incredible.'

'Yes, I'd make a rotten detective.'

She was glad of it.

He was very alert for danger-light, new soundings in her mood and caprice, but by now all was well. Daily they breakfasted on some dainty balcony, mists towards Italy concealing brightness to come, long silver waves cutting into shores still hazel, or piling against short, barbaric cliffs not yet tamed by high-rises, resurfaced by hoardings, while, farther back, terraced, vine-hung slopes tilted towards meadows. Very soon, a white peak would thrust into brilliant azures, a mule-track point skywards.

Sunset and olives, caves, sunswept sails, shimmer of dune and mimosa, cypress and oleanders were poetic props seemingly alien to her, also the fig tree writhing over a well older than Lionheart, with its frieze of dolphins and demigods. She looked not for dolphin and rockshine but for movie stars, spectacular tax-evaders, troublesome artists, spectacular cars whose gadgets created new words, new vistas, for the multiple gargoyles stuck on the ordered day. 'Yesterday, that American gentleman ... well...,' she grimaced, 'the Chicago gent, said that he himself wasn't, like his lady wife, stir-crazy, he liked to stay in one piece in one place. The Greek chauffeur was very impressed.'

Beneath, early tennis players darted on tight red and green courts, and from the adjoining balcony a voice repeated, 'Precious must drink his milk like a good little boy. My little lambkin.'

They had pitied Precious and, when finally seeing him, elderly, bearded, heaped in a wheeled chair, pitied him more.

'Algerian riff-raff!' In green, trailing dressing-gown she gestured at Chasseurs Alpin marching down Avenue Kléber, eyed by sullen *blousons noirs*, black leathered Teds with heavy cycles, flick-knives, urgency for heroin.

Newspapers they avoided, letters were news. Della had one from Janet, and two cards had arrived from Bayard, posted on the same day. Della's, stamped in Wolverhampton, was French, with a view of La Porte des Oudaias, Graham's in Cardiff, depicting a chapel inscribed *1882, to the glory of God and his wife Ethel*. From Grenoble they had sent him their own card, showing Le Col de Bayard.

She tossed them aside. 'Why does he bother? He doesn't care for any of us, except Janet. Yet he doesn't quite let us go. We're his fidget string. He skates across life as he did that day on the ice, intent on himself alone, like Crookback. He smokes out wrongs, but is loveless, perhaps from spite. I'm sure the Air Vice Marshal is a puritan fad.' Her eyes went large, lively, under hair fussed by a warming breeze. 'Yet he's part of life, like an uncertain climate. Once, at Rick's, a pompous man intoned,

> "Oh, no man knows
> Through what wild centuries
> Roves back the rose."

And Bayard butted in, announced that he knew perfectly well,

it would take some time but he'd tell him. And he did.'
'He wants Haydn symphonies played at his funeral.'
'Wow! How many?'
'All of them.'
This silenced them. Graham still thought of Bayard with irritated affection which came like a *non sequitur*. Bayard inhabited space apparently protected, never saw death walking towards him while he chatted to Pompey and offered Simon Peter a cigar.

In a Cannes foyer someone had dropped a blank piece of paper embossed with the Crystal Knot. In a casino garden a Dutchman submerged them in brandy when they admitted having met Bayard. 'A man of charm, a man of originality.' And he was puzzled by their sniggers when he added. 'You might say, a man of the future.'

Neither did say it, though Graham reflected that, at the Gridiron, the Saratoga League was now mentioned with annoyance but not contempt.

Sunlight was filtering through alpine mists. Della began in Merry Widow guttural, 'You might even say...', then ceased, looked down, sighed. 'Oh, honey, the tennis, the little ships, it's like holidays before the war with Roger and Janet. Can any of the wonder-working saints here cure nostalgia.'

'They're probably out of practice. Too much confusion since the Revolution. Reds and Whites have always been sloshing each other. The Resistance was very vicious, not only to the Krauts. Above Menton there's a pretty nasty plaque. The splendours of Paris never meant very much down here. The Albigensions...'

'You know so much!' She was caustic, glad to know very little.

'I'm a magnet, picking up all sorts. Yesterday some cut-price professor let me pay for his drinks, and in return informed me that we're near five rivers, all drawn from the tears of Mary Magdalene, who lived back there on the Carmargue, a red-light Annie who'd seen further light. She lived as a hermit, handling her chastity like a snowflake.'

'It may be true.' She affected to consider it very seriously. 'But she couldn't have liked it much.'

He noticed that she had not opened Janet's letter. In profile she looked less decided, even vulnerable, her sharp, decided eyes hidden. She remained abstruse mingling of lover and sister, neither role quite fulfilled. Kissing, they never embraced, his own desires were usually those of curiosity, disinclined to impair the balance between them, perfected for so long by generosities of sharing, bound by common memories. His occasional madcap impulses usually faltered, in some short circuit of spirit while, in her poems at least, sexual love was an afterthought, automatic as unfastening a tie, or, more appropriately, a belt. Certain poems minutely described children, seen only as problems.

Beach crowds were regathering, eruptions of colour, like those embalmed in recollections of the thirties, happily, preposterously sunk in deck-chairs, lounging at picnics, in summers steaming headlong for war.

Hours later he found her, drink in hand, glossed in black jacket, black trousers, green tie, green cap, matching her eyes, square diamond between her breasts. Happily she had discarded the dirty bowler with mirror inside it, the expensive, ink-blotched tartan skirt, the overlong coat with bootlaces trailing from the sleeve.

Leaning from a window, her floppy eyelashes longer, she did not greet him. They stood together, silent, as a sunlit cloud dissolved into vast, flamy bubbles. Above red tiles a sparkling Coca-Cola sign spoiled the nearward sky. Shutters were opening, windows glittered sharply, garden umbrellas seemed swollen, untrustworthy sweets. New sounds were starting as the sun burned the horizon and light blue dusk ambled shorewards. Small orchestras, radios, hum at the bars as the heat lowered.

She said quietly, more to herself than to Graham, 'Picasso ... Pablo Picasso. Clean and hard and dry as a pebble.' Then, as if at last fully recognizing him, 'Well, did you wrestle with giants and Algerians down in your badlands? Not forgetting, of course, the stray Mary Magdalene!'

'Something better. A down-and-out, looking like a runaway friar, told me that at Menton, after their row with God, Adam and Eve planted the very first lemon tree. And in a market I met the chap from Antibes, who so admires your legs, very properly so. He told me he's a Mormon, and whenever he swears he has to go and wash his mouth out.'

'I did notice when he didn't like the coffee he muttered something, hurried out, I assumed for brandy, and came back wiping his lips.'

They were at one with the brilliant sunset, the rising evening life, and, touching glasses, chanted another childhood refrain: 'And the Pig got up and slowly walked away.'

He had understood her choice of clothes. 'We'll drive out for dinner. What about Oliver Hardy's place above Vence. Providing he keeps in the kitchen there's enough room. Just.'

'Oh, do let's.'

They drove through pine forest, up the winding Grande Corniche. Scarps and hamlets had darkened, a few lights lingered on the sea. Farther up, she indicated a layby. 'Stop a minute.'

They sat in silence. Somewhere a water-mill turned, a bird squawked. The cap further shadowed her face. He awaited a declaration, confession, plea, felt sudden excitement, but she said nothing. Now the waves could be heard, hoarse upon stones.

'You OK?'

'Oh yes.' But she seemed groping for what was unlikely to come. She was never flirtatious, always purposeful, grabbing without much thought, scarcely any conscience, like a football manager or, he admitted, himself. Or else she was in dire retreat, curling away from life. She touched his hand, a bird's flutter. 'Right, I'm hungry.'

In the fake Moorish entrance the outsize manager greeted them as though they were Mr President's intimates, kissing Della's hand, slapping Graham's shoulder as if swiping a wasp. Moorish lamps glimmered through imitation grilles. A few hotel acquaintances stepped towards them, the English couple about whom voices speculated, the dark, captious, cat-eyed girl, the restless, untidy man with corsair expression and eye for drink.

Talk was formal. Cuba, rumours of fighting on Indian frontiers, orgiastic explosions in a hippie community farther south. 'What chance of joining them?' Della said. 'Golly, these decorations are a moral assault!'

Everyone paused, and, from behind a pillar a voice, thickly accented, continued some argument. 'He was eighteen, slowly bleeding to death on the Wall. The East German police stood watching.'

Della at once left them, making for the terrace, where their table was ready. Far below, phosphorescent water spread from dark, bare cliffs and, along the curved sea-line, small towns were winking like regalia. Pallid moths circled the table lamps which flipped unnatural tints over terracotta vases, sham-Pompeian busts, the coarse roses, and made Della herself taller, sterner, the night huntress.

At tables around them, bottles were emptying, and a German announced that fish, being grilled to the most delicate brown, might prove just tolerable. Graham winced, Della giggled, and they relaxed, talking with bandaged foils. She praised his fingernails, he complimented her exquisite manners, feeling heady, above the world, following small, lit ships edging towards the low moon, a white wave moving like a muscle.

Della's mouth was critical. 'That moonlight ... a veil becoming a plough. Not delicate any more.'

He spoke of a trip to Norway, not naming his companion: the empty fiords, cumbersome mountains, motionless forests that had bred legend and obsession, little fires on shores, the weekly steamer.

She brightened. 'A steamer, on old, old water. It used to be called Beauty.' She affected a shudder, a puckish smile slanted to the green, the black. 'Pale water, very calm, strewn with tiny suns. Schnapps and cakes in a small harbour, old Ibsen's Sea Lady about to show up, travellers waiting for nothing very much, and the steamer waiting too. It makes the provincial a haven of glamour.'

She had once written a poem, hitherto obscure, in which a foreign-cut ship, flying no flag, possibly armed, anchors in a bay, starting wild rumours like a flock of birds. When he spoke of it she clenched one hand. 'Rotted, worn out.' But he knew she was pleased.

Over the mullet she at last mentioned Janet's letter. 'She says nothing of Roger. Sometimes I've seen her standing near him as if waiting to be introduced. But she loves him.'

She said with subdued vehemence, 'I used to watch Roger and Bayard and was jealous, and angry. I probably still am. Roger was always caring, but Bayard, even when he condescended to listen, somehow offered presents with empty hands.

He once said, as if he hated him, that Roger was both judge and coroner.'

Her head, arms, hands, went despondent, heavier. Her eyes, avoiding his, were as if watching goldfish. 'Neither of them are fathers. Bayard's a monk, you and I are promiscuous as turtles, but....' She did not finish, and at once feigned interest in a nearby couple arguing about Franco's Spain, leaving him to reflect not on Bayard but Roger.

Before they left England a political weekly had denounced a wartime agreement with Russia, allegedly emanating from 'The Kirkland Memorandum'. That same week, on TV, Roger had perhaps over-contemptuously dismissed an anti-Bomb demonstration as childish breast-beating. 'When two heroes meet, only one of them armed, history at least hints that he will give the other more than a friendly wink.'

A pianist was playing, scattering notes like fireflies, and as she still did not speak, he remembered the boy dying on the Wall, then the little Russian prince jerking on the rope, while a crowd applauded. On the Eastern Front, men had sawn through frosted feet for boots of the dead.

To awaken her, he leaned over and lightly kissed her cheek. She grinned, brimming with new play, new occasion for new laughs. 'Don't you ever shave?'

'Seldom. But will our relationship survive these excitements?'

'Have we a relationship?'

'You've got charm, of a sort.'

'And I'm the one that doesn't gobble.'

2

In boyhood, Graham would mutter 'the edge of the field' and see bright, safe pasture ending in marsh, quickset, fierce nettle, a frontier beyond which awaited the bull, the weir, the idiot dwarf. Thenceforward he was aware of frontiers. The renegade Russians he had seen spitted, shot, abducted, had been dragged over a frontier unsensational as electronics and as powerful.

His present work held promise of crossing another frontier into Roger's territory of power complexes, secret webs of information concerning the subterfuges of authority, a hinterland of technological espionage and theft, industrial deals, alliances and betrayals beyond party and sect. Roger himself was vice-chairman – a position he now almost always preferred – of 'the Mafia', semi-official, virtually autonomous committee of experts with hot lines to certan interests within Cabinet, higher Civil Service, and police, providing specialized information, advice, warnings often unknown to the responsible department and in contradiction of official policy. With the Government threatened by pending scandals, Roger's own Imperial Guard was kept busy. Listening to club disputes, Graham had frequently to bank down temptation to rout, clinch, crush, by some spectacular revelation. As if reporting the latest score from Lord's, Roger would casually refer to the pirating of a shipload of uranium for Israel, the crash of an American B21 off Spain with four neutralized hydrogen bombs, and British bombers awaiting the signal during the Cuban missile crisis. The Mafia, apparently, was suggesting outlines of international agreement to resist unflinchingly and absolutely all hijackers' demands, in whatever circumstances, at whatever cost, even the life of Queen or President. To each his chance, his nod from fortune, his responsibility for the public good against the anarchic, criminal and bloody-minded.

Much of this was not writ large but sensed, less from formal concourse at polished tables, meticulously prepared data, courteous amendments and quiet resolutions, than from awareness of a note concealed in a cigar-case, a director lingering over waste paper, a glance intercepted in a passage, though one was not yet a full officer of the Guard. This status, relatively junior, was still tolerable, indeed more, crowded with journeys, social occasions, interesting research into personal backgrounds, political factions, bastions of unrest on Tyneside, Merseyside, Clydeside, half-forgotten intrigues, together with companionship, if not yet full intimacy with Roger himself. Roger's expansive gratitude for small services, minor trouble, his request for opinions, his apparent need to consult, enthralled, as always.

Slitting envelopes, lifting receivers, dictating to machines, tending word scramblers, accepting this, rejecting that, Roger, with confidential smile and sudden warmth, was ageless. You passed him invitations, prospectuses, appeals, sometimes threats, and usually he replied good-humouredly, though perhaps from disdain. Yes, the Left's mistrust was amply earned. Assailed for élitism, oligarchism, the Mr Fixer syndrome, he smiled with cutting amiability and cited miners' refusal to work with refugees, London dockers' rejection of blacks, the unions' loathing of women in office. He was unfailingly courteous, though the glint of his eyes, teeth, even hair, reflected the knives, steel rims, mechanisms on his desk, on his walls. It was said that Sir Roger Kirkland was always delighted at your arrival, and delighted even more at your departure.

Maybe, but with Uncle Roger one had shared lifelong talks, occasions, attitudes. Neither had joined the prolonged applause when bandits grabbed millions from a train, coshing the driver into senility, or when cycle-chain maniacs smashed an elderly actress on a sea-front: neither professed personal guilt for the death of Marilyn Monroe.

'Oh, heavens,' Roger feigned impatience, 'only yesterday that white-haired novelist who still whispers that he's really a teenager was telling me that D. H. Lawrence and Henry Miller knew how to think, and that the future lies with black boys and flower children. There's too much youth, tiptoeing through the tulips, eyes awash for jittery, screaming Elvis ... how quickly Castro, Kennedy, Guevara, Mao, are going to crumble, like Stalin. Meanwhile, youth's in the chariot, spitting at past and future, craving to be thrashed painlessly. Now, that nice Miriam of yours....'

Miriam distrusted Roger and seldom consented to meet him, while agreeing that young lives were cheap in a barbituric era. She restrained one's zest for experiment. No more than Roger was she tempted by parties where a Della mixed with cybernetic girlies in battery-powered tunics, hair smeared with fish-fry oil, revering collages made from food wrappings, and, fuelled by heroin, lying hand in hand to watch a billiard-table melt into purple fog and re-emerge as a liner; later, in bed, fixing a machine to record the love gasps.

Roger's cycle of efficiency, planning, co-ordination, could not wholly exclude intrusions from below. Graham was always convinced that, once met, people remained linked, that coincidences never occurred. Devon villagers, Bryce, a school lover, slender and violet-eyed, Army pals, Cosgrave, bar acquaintances were always in the wings; vanishing for years, Bayard is only out of sight. Thus, in the park, a jeaned, scarved, youngish, balding man spoke from a bench as if renewing a claim. 'Graham ... you won't remember me....'

He did, with no surprise. The radiant college boxer, Antonio, from the play. *Denied me my own purse.* The line seemed fulfilled rather too literally.

They sat together, formal Londoners strolling past through the blur of daffodils, the sweetness of cut grass. Graham inspected him. Nothing boyish survived in the warped face, bent shoulders, trembling hands. Lord Clavering would not have acclaimed a new aristocrat.

'Well, what are you up to?'

'Nothing. By choice. Sartre is bloody right. We're what we choose to be.' The trained, VI Form voice did not fit the shabbiness, the slurred features. The eyes in the ravaged head looked contemptuously at Graham's new coat, thick, shining brogues, the hands tried to stiffen and clench. 'Fucking Tristan and Isolde, no heart for anyone but themselves.'

Attempting to sound peremptory, the words were already defeatist, like an appeal pinned up in a boarding-house bathroom. 'You gave us too many books. You told us too much, trying to trap us in your own sodding world. Carving us in your own image. It can do harm. We called you the Viking. I suppose you still think yourself that. But the world's moved on. A very long way past you.'

At once, he himself was moving on, slightly limping,

resentment piled on the lowered head, rigid arms. Graham knew that he should follow, offer drink, money, time to listen, but jarred, did not until too late, with Antonio back in nowhere, without altogether disappearing. His accusation lingered, delivered like a warrant, expecting answers.

Was it believable that people were what they chose to be? Führer and Duce, the objectors, had made stupendous bids to prove it, but had been toppled by their own nature, by rooted fantasies.

Suddenly physical strength, promising career, hung on him like a rotten overcoat. He had inherited images of certainty, inviolate as a closed shop, reliable courts of appeal: Janet amongst her flowers, Roger, always confident, in hand-made shirt and club tie, crossing a lawn to dispense, if not justice, at least fair play, the Dragon House too secure to need guarding. Now, cracks were appearing without warning, unless he had been too busy, too loyal to notice. But, wretchedly, the Kirklands seemed informally separated. Janet had intimated that the Dragon House might be let.

He, Graham, had naggings, murmurs that he himself was obstructed by the best of possible backers who was, nevertheless, too concerned elsewhere. This tested his feudal allegiance. Questions began, not yet quite expressible, certainly not to Roger himself, whose elder-brother camaraderie, reserves of patience and feeling, imposed their own terms. With him, as with certain male royalty, one did not initiate conversations of consequence.

Meanwhile, Graham shirked consulting Miriam, knowing that she hated Roger's self-proclaimed lack of politics which so contemptuously rejected the party system; she shrugged at unquestioned loyalty, absolute love. Her help, her strength, might later be needed. Meanwhile he worked hard, spoke to no one, certainly not Della, shocked by her book's fiasco, and, not always realizing it, inspected Roger more closely.

At ease with all ranks, Roger might be experimenting with too many. Cocktails with regional planners, small-town Mussolinis, upstart financiers, controversial architects, property millionaires continued in gaudy suites, despite several enforced disappearances, but with few scientists, fewer ministers, and additions which even Guard and Mafia might question. Captioned 'Men above the Law' was a newspaper picture of Roger, in rare fatigue, even strain, at an Earls Court boxing arena, propped between two East End protection terrorists whose attire could have been filched from opera, and who were later sentenced for murder. People claimed to have seen him in bingo-lands and pot-house areas, once with a noisy songster on hire to all sexes available.

From such expeditions Graham was excluded, they remained perforce unmentioned, unmentionable, until one day he had to pass Roger an invitation from a prostitutes' club farther west. Whatever his thoughts, Roger gave a laugh of superb assurance. 'All of us have periodically to take fresh soundings. Some of us must seek allies and buddies in unlikely quarters.'

He did not remove Graham's misgivings, the laugh sounded a gambler's, the entire sequence was as unreal as a juke-box at the Gridiron, Roger's cheque hitting the ceiling, Roger himself cadging drinks from the Daves. Very soon afterwards he believed that Roger was confiding less, seeing less of him, on prolonged, unexplained absences. Resented by his associates as a personal favourite, he could talk to none, even had he wished to.

Della had never envisaged flaws in Roger and did not do so now, and was concerned only with his estrangement from Janet, of whom he often spoke, but as if about a figure long liked and admired but on some schedule not at the moment of foremost importance. Still called Lady Kirkland, she was living alone, entertaining considerably, referring to Roger as if he were upstairs and about to join them. She was known to give money to the CND and Conservationists.

Only solemn Bayard was wholly constant, though the Saratoga League might be proving of more than nuisance value. In the clubs, in Fleet Street, it was often discussed, as it issued pamphlets still stocked only in small shops in obscure streets, though dispatched to all prominent editors, politicians, media-men. Cuba and the Notting Hill race riots it ignored, but was credited for exposing a French minister's stake in an African cartel to which he awarded a government contract: in eleven countries it published a killer's brief given to a CIA agent, a suspect Moscow–Bonn contrivance in Poland, a

Jamaican murder plot, a proposed multimegaton test. In all this, Bayard disclaimed any function save that of 'very private public relations'.

From the start, Bayard had been consistent. One remembered him suspiciously examining the coins at the church collection, relating bizarre tales of the Kirklands' guests, strolling down currents of equivocal untruths, pledged to convictions he enjoyed keeping undisclosed, as though he were a deliberately contrived counter-Roger, whistling irreverently at what was now being called the Establishment, giving facetious praise to politicians he disliked and very probably loathed, and demanding a spittoon, an ear-trumpet, kedgeree, on inappropriate occasions. And, locked within Graham and Della was that glass day when, neither languid nor strenuous, he had streamed through the skaters as of right, a perfector.

Della's book had been a gift from the Greeks, King Midas's gold. Its reception must have been the first knock-out shock of her life. Usually agile, often vicious in repartee, she had said little, seen few, sought the solitude from which she had hitherto recoiled. She had once grabbed newspapers, for mention of herself, now she shied from them, her nerve bruised. Her Boleyn face sagged, and Janet worried about her dejection and loss of weight. 'She was always very brave.'

Young Mr Elsen was undismayed. No one wilted beneath a parcel of hired, crappy hacks. There must be a second book. He was kind, he was assertive, he was practical, but her recovery was slow.

'They're saying that the world's worn out. Top-heavy with cars, fake reputations, sex diseases, lack of spare parts, lack of decency. I've got the lot, except the cars. So why write?'

'None of it matters. It scrubs clean a few more pages for you. So get on with it.'

'There's a new girl around, poet of course. A gut-stopper, called Strawberry Ice or something. Adored by the great public which, if it must choose between good poets and a spitting cobra, chooses the cobra.'

'Well, do better. You spit better than most.'

Once more, her work began circulating in mayfly journals, was read aloud in pubs, jazz cellars, on radio. The announcement of her new book coincided with obituaries for Rick Allweather. The best concluded that as a writer he was negligible, as a critic, worse, but as booster of talent, in his day, long past, he had been fearless at crashing the traffic-lights. For his memorial service, Ezra Pound, T. S. Eliot, Robert Frost were said, erroneously, to be coming.

'Big church,' Bayard reported, 'few mourners. It was the same when Laughton died in Hollywood. Rick was what used to be called a game chicken. Della should have gone, she always called him her first publisher. Had she known her real publisher she'd have thrown mud at the coffin. Aiming badly, of course. Her place in the English ladies' cricket eleven is by no means assured.'

'But Allweather put her on the map.'

'You're the weightiest of all in our time but you're always a bit behind the times, an orphan of the storm who doesn't stray far enough from the farm. Rick no more put Della on the map than Thomas Cook put Corsica on it. He was only her printer.'

'But who did?'

Bayard was very, very patient. 'Roger, of course. He paid the costs, somewhat above the odds, because of Stella's new studio. The wise man doesn't tell her.'

'But how do you know all this?'

This elicited the thin, familiar, infuriating look of wry, slightly aggrieved astonishment. 'It was my idea, naturally. My part in swinging London. I dare say Janet said a few quiet words. Not for art's sake but for Della's sake. She doesn't keep her short of cash. No one does.'

Allweather's death revived Della. She reappeared at parties, with the circus men and pallid, listless girls, leaving Graham to Miriam. Their jokiness remained, Miriam had her life, he had his; always disagreeing, they could make truce with a laugh, affectionate shrug, gift. Her severity dissolved in bed, though here too she could teach. *Here. There. Wait. Your turn.* He was better for it.

Returning one early evening he decided they should dine out, extravagantly. The day had been tedious, Roger failing to keep their squash appointment.

'Miriam?'

Time's favourite cliché, romance at plus minus. The hollow air, silence, the letter in a flat otherwise empty, all else removed.

He had so often been astounded by the obvious or missed it

altogether. Ordered to cover a papal enthronement, he would have dispatched a piece colourful enough but two days late, through tardiness in locating the Vatican, distracted by random adventures, inconsequent beckonings. When his house burned, he would realize he had forgotten to renew the insurance.

Miriam had given the landlords notice two months previously, the lease expiring at today's noon. Wretchedly, bemusedly, he searched for signs, intimations, for recollections of his own grossness, of quarrels and anger, but found nothing exceptional.

'People could give you love but not what you seem to prefer, humiliation or hate. You are cruelly stupid, you enjoy crushing. You never hear what I say, and would refuse to understand if you did. You will never be satisfied with your share of the bed, your half of the world. I was a useful way of making your sandwich last a bit longer.'

Still no incident, change of voice, stillness surfaced to explain. She had been, as ever, competent, decided, planning her week, talking politics, gossiping, often sardonic, with no sign of need or distress. But his assets were evidently liabilities, she was not one to stage a dramatic return, was one more girl at the end of a well-trodden path, not always identified in the old diaries.

Mauled by errors, lost chances, falsified witness, he was not a man of the future with omniscient Air Vice Marshal within call.

Della's second book, launched unostentatiously, seemed an uncharacteristic bid for fashion. Geometrical pattern was replaced by description: mainly of lugubrious bordellos, winter bed-sitters, seedy cafés and lodging-houses, areas far from Della herself. Unwaveringly fastidious, she wanted Dragon Houses.

Critics were not appeased. 'Mr Auden's dictum that one cannot review a bad book without showing off need not here be seriously tested.... A running lack of ideas.... She sets up townscapes of no purpose, underpopulated, underemployed, with a vagueness inexcusable for one old enough to know better, though evidently to age is not to develop.... One senses an author hungry, perhaps starving, for recognition, with simultaneous doubts about whether she deserves it.'

They saw each other daily, enduring long, tense silences, unable to communicate, unable to remain alone, and exchanging insufficient sympathy. She thought him well rid of Miriam, he considered her poems shallow, false to herself.

Finally, though doggedly reluctant to confess failure, to seek help, he forced himself to address Roger, ostensibly for Della.

A curious gratification crossed Roger's face, then he was at once what he had always been, capable, incisive, shaming those stealthy doubts, their intimacy returning on a spring tide.

'Both of you need not rest but change, what old Arnold calls the stimulus of new ground. And you, Graham, have very much earned it, you've helped me again and again, sung marvellously well for your supper.' He was subtly delighted at the chance to provide, to rescue. 'Take her away, look after her. You may of course...' – his smile was courteously apologetic – 'find that she's looking after you.' He hesitated, then spoke more slowly. 'She may never write a good poem, but you may keep her from finding a bad man.' Reluctant to criticize, he was glad to be candid, familial. 'We haven't been happy about her. Her concern for animals doesn't entice her to possess any. She does claim, probably correctly, to have changed a feral literary gent into a weasel. The work may not have been arduous. And I no longer very seriously envisage her as a mother.'

Miriam faded, as if at the director's bidding, as they drove along the trail of ex-royalty, oil magnates, movie stars, Asian playboys, over-manned heiresses, halting at Miramers and Bristols, Hôtels d'Angleterre, Hôtels des États Unis. One establishment, discovered on an impulsive detour, particularly pleased them, embalmed in nineteenth-century hush, with creaking servitors wound up daily, towering furniture, each wardrobe, Della insisted, a minotaur's cavern, blackened Old Masters. Here she no longer shrank from tourists, particularly from the young. Henceforward, advancing into sun, she was thawing, the scars left her face, smiles began, and with Graham she shared the instant in a rehearsal when the play finds momentum. Holding hands, they bowed before a tooth, no less, of St James the Less, encountered a youth, totally sightless, who cleaned windows 'so that the sun would go blind if he saw them'. In an English cemetery, crammed with dogs and governesses, a Spanish gentleman formally instructed them that in a province 'distant, but not far from here', a vampire had been pursued, and almost captured. She laughed excitedly, as if infected by orange blossom.

On the coast they sped into carnival uproar, crowds pulled hither and yon as if by unseen hands. Here was the necessary dissolving of frontiers, routine, stability. Della showed childlike wonder at whirling, artificial birds, prancing hobby-horses, three-handed muleteers, the sword dancers and harlequins on canopied wagons drawn by dragon or pegasus. Huge, sexless masks paraded on poles, masks with huge teeth and tiny noses, with mouths on foreheads, arousing clattering applause and mirthless laughter from streets, windows, balconies, the last throw of Gallic head-hunters who had threatened Rome. Other memories jostled amongst the dwarfs and Cyclopses, the griffins and stags and swamping trumpet and drum-beat. That decrepit figure on scarecrow horse, in dirty white tunic, saucepan-lid breastplate, coal-scuttle helmet and huge, upturned moustaches, could it be the Kaiser, earliest nightmare of the very old? 'Look, look!' Della's grasp was very tight. Gigantic effigies of de Gaulle, Johnson, Khrushchev, Nasser, Ben Bella, James Dean. One absentee, Graham shouted at her, was the Air Vice Marshal, but she whipped back that this could not be proved. Look, look, an emerald float strung with balloons, like a chopped Neapolitan ice; a grotto of mermaids, a unicorn before a crimson, tasselled pavilion, glass lances embedded in a fierce sun, could it be the Crystal Knot? No! On the clear sky, a plane scrawled 'I love Bardot' in white foam. From a world reversed, a tom-tom, astrologial era of Illyrian sea coasts streamed cast-off survivors, the crazed quacks, raggle-taggle scaramouches, ribald columbines, pantaloons haunched and paunched, a buckled rope-dancer in a barrow, in whose hands the rope became a snake, then a large, squatting toad, then a menacing noose. Look. Scarlet, raucous somersaulters, Pans romping round a coarse, jewelled Virgin or Great Goddess rattling tambourines and bellowing insults; capering half-naked zanies, jazz-combos in sports cars, a huge, striding upturned chessboard, leopard men hung with claws, dwarfs again, on stilts, in steeple hats, earrings reaching the ground. Wheeled corsoes trundled by, glittering with local starlets and water-belles, waving within brazen torrents of music, catching bouquets. Confetti whirled, as if the air were being shattered by the tossing medley of tricornes, dominoes, capes, Punch noses, live cucumbers and radishes gesticulating with rabid obscenity, Merlins in feathered capes, imitation Beatles, creatures with heads between their thighs jiving with popular saints, Denis holding aloft his own head, Lucy displaying her eyes daubed on a reddened plate, Agatha with pumped-up breasts dangling from her neck.

Graham wanted to rush into the processions, join the dance but, knowing him, she pulled him away, back to the hotel balcony. He at once rang for drinks, while she stood, eyes still dilated, mouth a little open. 'They're so real....' She swallowed the whisky at a gulp, without knowing it. 'At cockcrow, you know...' – her laugh was unconvincing, little more than a gasp – 'they go back. Figures looming through frosted glass. Like the future too.'

She turned to look at him, extending her empty glass. She was serious. 'If you'd joined them, you wouldn't have returned. Ever.'

She did not expect a reply, was already back with the rowdy motley below. Carnival unzipped time, uncorked a half-history, letting fizz this circus communion of jeering misfits and defiant cast-offs, a sacrificial Bacchic deliverance, the tidal-flow of distorted traditions. The chilly, haughty SS, black and silver, had included druggists, forgers, astrologers, alchemists. A trap-door was opened, leading nowhere but, in a soiled plume, a cloak strewn with pearls and roses, an aigrette of devils' faces, a double-headed cock, touching the untended nerve, taunting the Roger world of cause and event, the signed and delivered, the solid.

It may have cut deeper. Afterwards, in a night still flamy and agitated, they agreed that within the pop and crackle of fireworks, the blare, the jangling, feverish bells, the drumming, had been sounds as if of gunshot, not quite believable, by no means incredible, if no more than wildcat greetings to Carnival King, enthroned in the Place, destroyed in fire before a hooting populace, a last, agonized scream, Graham suggested, as if from a crack in time.

'Maybe.' Her smile was mischievous.

3

'In the thirties...'

'No!' Her stamp was less petulant than it seemed. 'There weren't any thirties, don't you see? Time is mood, it can't be measured. And the little girl is always setting out for Grandma in the wood, the little boy always pulling out the plum. It's moments that stand out. Not minutes but moments, as Proust knew. So do I!'

Her gaze was disconsolate, as if the gently heaving sea, the tourist-blue poster waves should not only conceal masked swimmers, the octopus, algae, frogmen and nuclear submarine, but immediately present a shipwreck, pageant of mermen, an irrefutable moment.

'I remember on a nursery wall was a ship, under a perfectly round sun. Some suns can be rounder than others. Now, this morning, I was looking out to sea, very early, I was still quite naked, and I saw that ship, under the same sun. On the sea. And at last it began to move. Elsetimes – is there such a word? – I'd often thought of it, waiting for it to sail.' She was light, merry. 'You can see I don't want to translate *Anna Karenina* for computers!'

They continued to drive on, to other hotels, other bays. Against evidence, she insisted that the mountains were always moving closer, threatening the coast. 'There's always death from mountains. They're getting very large.' But she was laughing, back on another hotel terrace, amongst pots brimming with harsh blossom, and reverting to discussion of time. 'Whatever your history bug says, years were invented by priests. They wanted a world they could boss, trapping the rest of us with the glamour of dates and prophecies.'

In this mood she disliked interruption, and he was glad of

her recharged resolution, her joy of words.

'Once I left my bag in a post office. A lot of money was in it. I dashed back, quick as a ferret, but of course someone had swiped it. I was desolate. Only others find treasure, the golden guineas.' Her eyes glowed not with envy but pleasure in the existence of luck and guineas, the golden spur deep in the white stream, the Edward VII sovereign. 'A week later I went to a restaurant I'm absolutely certain I'd never heard of, it had chef's titbit of fried snakes' lips or something as horrible. And they all rushed at me, terribly excited, and handed me the bag, without even knowing my name. All the money was there. You won't believe it, of course, you always laugh at the spooky. But, at the *moment*, it was quite natural. Only when I was back in boring old minutes did it become incredible.'

He did not laugh. People had stepped into his life, and, without seeming wholly real, uttered something simple but fateful, then vanished, unexplained, yet not inexplicable. This cheerful jaunt with Della had *moments*. At a bar they met an American couple. The husband left them to inspect hollyhocks in the garden. When he did not return, they followed, finding him prone under the flowers, white suit soaked in blood, wallet, watch, ring intact, he himself remembering nothing, save that the hollyhocks had looked unnatural, uncannily still and powerful.

The décor changed little, the road a moving frieze of long cars, sickly in sunlight, pink and red roofs on hills, children running into the sea, where she would soon follow. Sometimes, on her departure, he wished to search her room, uncertain of what he expected to find but convinced that he would be surprised. This he never did, less from his having heard her lock the door on departure than from an uneasy thought that the door would open to his hand and he would find her within, without much friendliness and sceptical of his explanation.

Undoubtedly, however, she did lie on sand, swim, net the small, brilliant images of a seaside day, culled from the secret lives of rock-pool and foreshore, a grey-haired child on a breakwater cruelly ostracized, an ex-movie star in a beach café, huddled, despite the heat, in long furs. Once famous, he had been ruined by a studio scandal and now, still handsome, still talented, he had only this toy sea before him. 'I wanted to take his hands, hug him. He'd been so marvellous. People have no mercy....' But she ceased, perhaps arrested by a thought of Rick Allweather.

Once he saw her by chance in a *musée*, and knew that she was offended, always preferring to wander alone in such places.

Before she motioned him to leave her, they had stood together in front of a tapestry in which angular men in leaves and skins writhed, their hands like birds fleeing a tree, their bodies drenched in flame, surrounded by horrified, resplendent watchers and a naked girl.

Della was intent, like, he thought, an heiress reading the will. At dinner, as though repenting her aloofness, she asked him to decipher the story.

He was the teacher, had never forgotten the rows of faces trained on him alone, the sudden question, the gust of affection.

'At a ball, the French King and five courtiers, dressed as wild men and covered with pitch, began dancing. The King's brother, Orléan, was French to the life. Not his own life. He chucked a torch into the dancers and at once they were alight. The King, as kings do, had paused before a pretty girl and she pulled off her robe and, bare as an eel, quenched him. None could get near the others.'

She was disappointed. 'I imagined something quite different,' refusing to say what. She half-closed her eyes, drooping her hand, like an unwanted fan. 'I've heard that young storks, even when their elders die, still know exactly when to emigrate and where to go. It makes me happy.'

'Mark my words...'

'Have you noticed, love, that those three Grand Vizier words are always followed by something silly? Like at tennis, when you shout "Mine", and do a thoroughly stupid shot!'

In recompense for his intended remark, itself, in his own judgement, not irredeemably silly, she fondled his hand, briefly laid her dark head on his shoulder. 'Darling, in a Musil story, a promiscuous wife – horribly like me – says, "Within, one can be as holy as Apollo's horses, but, outside, only as official papers describe it." And that, she goes on, "is a mystery unfathomable to your institute". I wish I could say such things.'

'You should say things a bloody sight better.'

Light was melting, sea was losing weight, and flattening;

blue crushing silver. He began again. 'M. Achille was telling me that, actually, bulls are colour blind.'

'Must we keep meeting him? When he takes my hand, I expect him to smear it with mayonnaise. As it is, he kisses it like some old-hat matinée idol, and it feels like sticky flies.'

'He's not for the sensitive stomach. But as Roger says, we don't have to like our friends and very seldom do. Incidentally, he was telling me that the French Secret Service owes him eighty-five thousand francs.'

Her laugh was that she had used when executing a collage of skilfully arranged obscenities, to be dispatched to a literary critic. 'He told me it was three million. Also, that he'd sold a tax loss for a million.... Do you understand that?'

'Of course not.'

The greeny eyes suddenly flared. 'You're a bad judge between phonies and the real thing. I choose badly, but I choose deliberately. You, my poor dear, never know the difference. Your girls ... the last one's always the worst. Remember that cow always gazing up at you as if working out the various meanings of that terrible word "soul". Now you've landed us with M. Achille, M. Achille Unlimited, star of stage, screen and air. We don't know who he is, but at least I know what he is. A leaden butterfly. Too ingratiating, like pimp or pusher. He shoots out more discrepancies even than Bayard, and with sex into the bargain. When he looks at me or grimaces at a woman I want to pull the chain.'

'He knows something of the Saratoga League.'

Assuming their interest, M. Achille had produced from a pudgy brief-case a *Manchester Guardian* leader, heavily underlined, quoting a League pamphlet on a secret decision of the Genoa Conference on human rights, with some acknowledgement of the general accuracy of the Saratogan bulletins.

They mused further on M. Achille. His soft voice, foreign but indeterminate, they decided was Portuguese Levantine, in descent from a randy unicorn. He was oily without being urbane, his smoothness applied daily, like make-up. He might also, perhaps, have Albanian blood. After shaking hands with an Albanian, Bayard had said, count your fingers.

M. Achille ventured to believe that the unknown backers of the Saratoga League were entitled to consider themselves saints of the Orthodox Church. An engaging view of Bayard.

Discontent flickered across her face. The eyes, with their long lashes, darkened. 'I'm convinced he's following us.'

'But who wouldn't?'

At a previous hotel M. Achille had knelt to pick up Della's scarf, then introduced himself, his gestures guaranteeing exchanges of pleasure, and now, wherever they halted, he seemed awaiting them, on a promenade, in a restaurant or park. Where he slept was unknown, never in their own hotel, perhaps in no hotel but in beach-hut or brothel, subsisting on cheap biscuits, rare chocolates and erotic postcards.

Plumpish, baldish, shortish, youngish, sallow, in pink bow-tie, gold-rimmed, polaroid sunglasses, with rounded head, rounded shoulders, stumpy legs, a cigar, and the shallow smirk that accompanies too small a tip, he was Toad of Toad Hall. He had, without being told, praised Della for having published poetry, for being famous, then spoilt it by adding that he had himself begun as a poet, his manner suggesting some larger success, still a state secret. 'A very wretched little state,' Della grumbled later. 'The world's littered with them, though we're barely allowed to say so.'

Her dislike of him would not, however, impair this healing summer, though she too now wore dark glasses, a protection from his dirty teeth, stained yellow fingers, and, when occasionally displayed, his spaniel eyes.

'He's like a *patron* who sits down with his customers uninvited, grinning like a sliced melon, ordering double brandies for all and putting them on the bill. Take his photo, and what you'll see is a damp grub.'

'To be fair, he pays his round. Rather more.'

'You're so literal. You'd make terrible movies. But, of course, you love terrible movies. But I suppose you're after his watch!'

M. Achille's watch, the latest thing on earth, he assured them, contained a calendar and radio, and was not quite accurate.

That evening, their first here, M. Achille appeared in the swing-door, brief-case under arm, and in what they termed his white planter's duck suit. He sauntered towards them, and, after fluent preliminaries which implied they were reunited after years of hardship and loss, led them on to a patio, nodding condescendingly at the small statue now burnished by sunset. Already he was calling for wine, praising it immoderately, with untrustworthy details about its vintage.

Della had at once resumed her dark glasses, was ostentatiously more interested in the sea.

'The croupier here', M. Achille smiled as if at the sort of joke once restricted to men, 'does not have a steady hand.' His own hand, firmly enough, now clasped his stomach, as if, Della whispered when he went to buy his cigar, to prevent its theft, though only the cat's-meat man would wish even to imagine it. Seldom amiss to rudeness, she promptly left them on his return, but, after dinner, they again encountered him, a quiet ambush on Avenue Foch, M. Achille holding not his stomach but a broad, black, somewhat ecclesiastical hat, his fatty smile well primed.

'Do I intrude?'

'Plainly.'

'Pardon?' He bent towards the hand which she had not offered. 'Moment, moment. I know the best bar in this smelly little place. It's all on me. I'll pay.'

He was gently insistent, indicating the bar. It was undistinguished and almost empty. Most were still at dinner, in cinemas, returning from the hills. 'This is', M. Achille was proprietory behind the bottle, 'what I call spot-on', inducing Della to say that she herself couldn't find a name for it. He nodded, very satisfied. Graham nodded. In his careless way, he was well enough amused by M. Achille, as part of the foreign adventure, though no candidate for the Gridiron. The barman had greeted him with a vulgar familiarity that hinted at some previous transaction, probably commercial.

Ignoring the drink, Della crumpled into a sulky trance which M. Achille affected not to notice. While he talked, Graham, only half-listening, suspected that throughout there was always some plea, some demand, intention, and that for M. Achille nothing was casual, all was a ploy in his struggle to survive.

He drank Della's share of the drink, pleased with light forties' music relayed from beyond, pleased indeed with the absence of *moments*, now that Della had refused to create one. But very soon he sat up, with unexpected intentness.

'Up there,' M. Achille was saying, his cigar pointing over his shoulders, 'in the hills, very barren, that's what we must call Outside Territory. The villagers, poor stuff, ignore the last few centuries. They're bandits, ragamuffins, left-overs from the Resistance. Listen. A British family, very well connected, well spoken too, they knew the lordly owner of Syon House, disappeared. Stabbed behind a church. Children as well. Very shocking. Who did it? There you have me! Locals, Italians, who knows?'

'What about the police?'

'Ah! Well put. They do know, but it's not worth their while to tell. I should say it hasn't been made worth their while.'

Della too, though covertly, had begun giving him attention, and her frown at her empty glass made M. Achille signal agitatedly for another bottle. Had she too remembered the shots, imaginary or not, beneath carnival uproar, and the Grasse men exercising with wooden rifles on an isolated hill?

Moonish in subdued lights, M. Achille glimmered with disapproval, the dark glasses like huge pocks. He resumed with some importance, 'Italy wants the return of the Nice-Menton lateral. It won't happen, 1940 was her only chance. But to a certain type...' – he was more censorious, very prudish, contemplating his cigar as if willing to stub it on a certain type – 'the more impossible, the more urgent. You and Miss Della see it daily in Ireland. I see it in Trieste, the Tyrol, amongst the Basques. Even these dumps, Tende, Menton, have it, though tourists never know it. Always there are feuds. Arson, bombs, knives. Insurgents – very disgusting, not the thing at all, though,' he looked admiringly at Graham, 'you and I sometimes appreciate a bit of fist. Once, for all his bodyguard, some of us fixed Sinatra, you must have read of it. It was all over the best papers – New York, Düsseldorf ... night work. They called me the lucky owl.'

A fool can speak wisely. Lost provinces gleam more fiercely after surrender, people warm hands on loss, people love their defeated generals. These smart, Mediterranean pleasure-grounds, like the gleaming SS uniform, absorbed the ruthless: black marketers, drug-racketeers, torturers, parlour blackmailers, pimping extortioners. Faction smouldered. In 1945 Purifiers had gouged, castrated, buried alive. Nothing ceased at frontiers. Each month it was said, though by Bayard, a Russian task force landed in Sweden, to note defensive installations, check contacts.

With dramatic caution, M. Achille glanced around, wary of a shadowy potted palm, a tall curtain. 'In West Germany itself, when they first reached post-war full employment, jobs for the lot, the youth crime reached maximum. It shouldn't have done, but it did.' He spread his hands like a fisherman or bawd, 'Gross National Product! Gosh! In East Berlin, my cousin's stopped from leaving his own home. I'm old-fashioned myself, though you might not spot it, there's only one shoe worth wearing. Not long ago I was roughing it in Lisbon. The Hotel da Gama, a private suite. The service was rotten, though they showed me the largest diamond in the world. I get by, the old night owl. I watch the others go up, I watch them come down. Crash, boom. And I don't give a damn. One has duties.'

Della had begun to giggle, the drink was nearing reordering point, but the words had forced a recollection that, in his evidence to the MacCunn Report, Roger had queried the dire effect of unemployment on crime. The inevitable often fails to occur.

'Listen,' M. Achille, rapt with his audience, was dropping information like burrs. 'In France now, there's constant decrease in thefts of valuables, the wallets of the rich, treasures ... and plenty more of the trivial and worthless. For kicks, as the old saying goes.'

'You're envious!' Della, wholly recovered, gazed at the versatile bric-à-brac on M. Achille's watch, and spoke as if she had been leading the talk.

M. Achille was nervously eager. 'No. Not so. Never. Why, I was absolutely put out ... teenagers, expensive schools and all the rest, threw a plastic bomb into the flat of the Minister of Culture ... M. Malraux. M. André Malraux. It blinded a girl of four. Why? God may know, but we doubt it. Such insects! Real vultures! I beg you, Miss Della, believe me, I deeply disapprove, all the way. They've no interest in politics, no pity, they just want noise. A bang, a whirl-up, what we have to learn to call a gig.'

'So do I. And it's what I've always wanted to do to a minister of culture. Particularly Malraux.'

'Oh, Miss Della, Miss Della! No, no, no.' His yelps were virginal, the yellow finger indicted her, making her fumble for sunglasses, 'Your English humour I can only call impeccable.

I go Hee Hee Hee. But where, may I dare ask, is your sense of responsibility?'

'Where it always is.'

'But are we not all God's children?'

'Certainly not.'

M. Achille waved aside Graham's perfunctory offer to subsidize more drink. His roundish face had the brisk changes of light, bright yet flat, of a juke-box fulfilling needs from outside. 'My treat, I insist.' As if repeating a lesson, he said anxiously, 'Graham, I'll pay.' He was at once expansive, treasuring them both. 'I like to be on the high. Good friends, fine wine, the summer sea,' making them sound, Della softly reported, like a decrepit Cantonese restaurant.

They glimpsed M. Achille declaring that he had owned shares in the Mukden–Peking railway and knew all about China, though using chopsticks for his soup.

She was freakish with M. Achille, short temper alternating with shows of suspect amiability which he seemed to overvalue. When she brought herself to raise a glass to him, he rushed into too much gratitude. 'I can get you a fur coat. Very cheap. There are ways.'

'It would seem rather unnecessary.'

The last slants of sunlight were fiery on glasses, bottles, mirrors. Graham yawned. Instead of knife-edge escapades, punch-up occasions, the imperfections of travel had produced M. Achille, a pander breed, product of forged passports and unofficial visas. One had met many such. In small-budget films as the type so crooked that he deceives all but the scriptwriters; in big-band sagas losing Betty Grable, Betty Hutton, Alice Faye; fake connoisseur of wine, furniture, women; overmeticulous in dress and adjectives, masquerading as man of mystery, bowing from the waist, with toadying mother and imaginary father, a midget replica of the Mammon of Unrighteousness.

As if sensing this assessment, he dropped his pride, his petty, supervisory grandeur. Humble, tentative, his voice quivered with hopes. 'I have placed arrangements for a sea trip. For all of us. Start early, return late. We could have a go.'

Della's ill-wind rushed back. She left them so hurriedly that he stood up only when she had gone. Still smiling, he passed Graham her glass. 'It will be splendid. Absolutely so. You won't need a penny.' Reseated, he sighed, began polishing his glasses. His round eyes were tired, but very confidential. 'You're English, you can go anywhere, knock off whatever you want and tell all others to put a sock in it. Such a fine country, you manage things well. It's more than being in the black. Though as a cricketer,' he was weightily apologetic, 'I am no great shakes. Miss Della, I fear, considers me a flibbertigibbet, but I can rely on you to put things right. Shipshape, they say. Meanwhile, I speak to a gentleman, do you know that lady by the door? No? Ah! There's this feeling, every so often, wanting, I do not offend you, what I can only call rump steak.'

Back in the hotel, one had no need to mention rump steak, though he referred to Mr Flibbertigibbet. She was delighted. 'The lucky owl. Not exactly Black Rod. But it's you he admires. When you ask the time or repeat that joke about Castro, his face looks up and begs. You like him because he's servile. Like all schoolmasters, you enjoy being the big man. Roger must guard his job from you like a robber baron, which, I suppose, he is. Me, Achille only fancies, and mostly, can you imagine it, he thinks I expect it! His idea of good manners! He's unknowable to us because there's nothing to know. But for him, you're the gladiator who drives away terrors.'

'Terrors?'

'Sort of terrors.'

They exchanged a half-glance from long ago, when they had crouched from catapults, before she said, 'Don't you feel like going Hee Hee Hee? One has instincts.'

The sea was polished by sun not yet high, the breeze still cool. From the deck, the houses, trees, terraces were sharp-edged, Cubist, Della said. M. Achille was slap-happy to agree, adding that he had once offered Renoir's son a hand in an important project.

'Renoir was not a Cubist.'

'Indeed.'

As if on film perpetually rerun, small resorts glided by: theatrical piers, chartreuse pinnacles, cake-like roofs, pastel façades, new high-rises staining the hills, curved midget harbours, toy forts, yellow, scarlet and lavender gardens wedged between buildings, above yellow beaches. An occasional fishing-smack passed, or trawler carrying olives, coal, perhaps arms, their contrast with neat, bobbing pleasure-craft a reminder of other instincts beneath those of tennis, film, flower and music festivals, of flimsily clad tourists and their attendant porters, waiters, liftmen, strippers. Instincts of harpooners, gipsy horse-dealers, shabby priests, conspirators, of silent herdsmen, beggars, of vine-tenders and astrologers, their feelings for strangers concealed by the shrewd salute, muttered greeting, the open hand. A barnacled prow jutting above water warned that even this flaccid sea still had claws.

Graham's affection was constant for the simplicity of boats, the waves crumbling on rocks, for musty churches, old eyes watching the sea, pavement dances, processions, the huddled figure cursing, praying, lamenting. They were close to legend and might be the last, their children seeking Party membership, drugs, the beat of a sham America.

Confirming this, a radio exploded into 'Rock around the Clock'. Della glared, M. Achille shook his head, unctuously sorrowful. 'Tomorrow', a young American voice spoke, 'is only a half-truth.'

'Nice thinking. Electronics....'

The music quietened. M. Achille's salesman's patter resumed. 'That house, above the potty little trees, was owned by a Hungarian millionaire. He quarrelled with his *petite*, Mr Desmond, and gave him the message of the sack. But first painted and signed an order for twenty-seven thousand dollars. On Mr Desmond's buttocks. Legal tender. Perfectly.'

'Mark my words,' Della said.

'Pardon?'

A motor boat cut across, gulls rose. Distant sails touched the skyline like flamingos. 'There's plenty going on.' M. Achille was busy too. 'You don't have to tell me.'

Neither wanted to. Rounding a headland they distinguished Italy, blurred in heat-haze. The radio ceased in mid-song; on the higher deck, Germans, lords of the earth, had dislodged the self-absorbed Americans who seemed not to mind where they talked provided they did talk, and now clustered at a bar, demanding, but not getting, Sazerac. Youthful enough, the Germans were not boyish, though loudly jocular in shorts and bright jackets. Evidently they were war comrades, strategically familiar with this coast, where, Graham reflected, despite their self-satisfaction, they had failed. He was not eager to forget his fracas with their compatriots a few years back: prisoners of the dream.

They stood by baskets filled with fruit, sausages, wine. Their faces, browned, ridged, a few scarred, were staring at M. Achille as if scenting quarry. Graham they might have hailed as fellow conquistador, surviving sodden field and reeking bastion. Amongst the French families, with whom they exchanged no word, their assurance gleamed like a capped tooth in an ageing mouth. The expedition was already unpropitious. Further memories stormed back. On these waters he had once reached for a bottle, a rough Lancastrian tried to snatch it, 'That's reserved, mate', a short struggle, then the other buckled and fell, whispering 'Psychopath'. Near that hill a lout had thrashed a bleeding, overladen horse. In Menton, he had violently abused a youth fumbling with his car, before realizing that he was blind.

The Germans were speaking in low tones, and M. Achille, who had once claimed not to understand German, was listening intently, until they moved rather purposefully away, on to the seaward side.

Above the shore, Graham saw again the circular redoubt where Templars had piled treasure, acquired sinister repute, until summoned to Paris for an atrocious end.

M. Achille's hands were as if tying invisible parcels. 'Somewhere there, Miss Cora lived, the famous black number. A marquis, her richest lover, strewed her food with Cambodian garlic to keep her faithful, keep her just so. He was mistaken. He was a scientist, with ideas about birds, moths, and, I must say, slugs, which he passed on to Lord Walter Rothschild. Once he turned up at Cap Ferrat, at 3 a.m., with his portable shower-bath which opened like a tent, and demanding admittance to Mr Somerset Maugham. The good author, very industrious, failed to appreciate it. As for Miss Cora, she kept a different physician for each part of her luscious body, her framework. We always called her the Countess behind the Hedge. Not strictly the thing, wouldn't you say? Her daughters were the first Western ladies to enter the Eastern Zone. These little matters have significance. They make metaphysical balance, like dumplings contenting a wise man.'

He looked anxious. 'I do not lie, my friends, you could see me clean my lips.'

'I'd like coffee.'

He marched off to fetch it. 'I wonder, Graham, what Lord Rothschild would make of that.'

'He'd have examined the lips, then looked around for a sponge. He could probably have afforded one.'

Surprisingly, Della had not only consented to come but insisted. M. Achille, varnished in happiness, greeted them in yachting-cap jauntily askew, dark blue blazer, white flannels, the smoked glasses, binoculars hanging with price-tag still on them. They were relieved he was not in Bermuda shorts. 'I was', he informed them, 'once a sailor.'

'An admiral, of course!'

'No, Miss Della. Today, authority has departed from admirals.'

Aboard, he was constantly using the binoculars, mysteriously scrutinizing inlets, caves, landslips, mostly devoid of tourist charm.

Landing, they ascended a narrow, crooked street, its shelf markets aglow with cheeses, lemons, melons, peppers, tomatoes. M. Achille, who appeared to have been here before, led them to tables amongst orange trees, Spanish broom, fleshy, hairy shrubs, bowls of flowers hanging above violet lamps. White, swallow-tailed butterflies wavered past. Within a ramshackle wooden house a girl was singing. Behind them, a pale green hill was strewn with white boulders. Tourists wandered, faces smeared with dark glasses, jazzy ties in full throat.

M. Achille clapped his hands, a bent waiter was wrinkled as a map. Della was contented, eyes softer. The heavy sunlight covered them, a golden network shimmering beneath leaves. Down in the port, the light was harsher. Three small figures disputed round a bollard. Gazing at Della, dark head tilted, legs crossed, Graham wanted to be alone with her, to lead her away from this place, and from M. Achille's busy tone, ordering de Bellet '74, which the café had not heard of. Eventually, a *vin de table* was produced which he sniffed with proprietory relish. 'That's the full flavour.' The flavour was rough, barely drinkable, but he was unperturbed. 'Now we toast the occasion. A blow-out. Beauty too is here. Alpine rose time. Myrtle trees, you know their meaning?' He hurried on, in case they told him, 'Trees of death.' He chuckled unconvincingly, the flat, blank face swerving aside. 'I may never be able to leave. I pledge my word I'd remain for ever if you wonderful people would do so too.'

'People should lead their own lives...?'

'Of course, Miss Della. You are always right.'

'Yes.'

One of the Germans passed the gate, the oldest, Graham reckoned, his face like a chipped air-brick. Canned Chopin began, tinnily, dogged by a slight echo. Della glowered at it. 'A doll, trying to clear its throat. Horrid.' Even M. Achille forebore to relate it to alpine rose time.

Afterwards, exploring the small town, they reached a shaded, arcaded place, once a forum, with Gothic statue, blazing marigolds, a *parfumerie*, people at coloured tables. 'Moment.' M. Achille doffed his cap, dropped the cigar, smiled uneasily. 'Moment. I'll be back at once.' And stepped aside into an arch of shadows.

Glad, lightly kissing, they waited a polite space, then hastened away, to the old church, the spectacle of a wedding party gathering at the Marie, then to watch sun-sprites glistening on the small park lake. He had taken her hand, she squeezed his, they were at last together, humming an old favourite, 'On Sunday in the Park'. They kissed again, strolled on, until, turning a street-corner, were stopped as if by snipers.

Watched cautiously, mostly by locals, the Germans, outsize, tensed, were grouped around a table. A girl in a doorway was softly weeping. Then one German beckoned to a figure lurking in the café doorway, and a boy of perhaps fifteen, jeaned, in red singlet, emerged, reluctantly, but with some grace, slightly on his toes, hands before him as if protecting or pleading. A few words were said, seemingly orders, for he jumped on to the table, in feline perfection. The foreigners made a tableau, ringing the slight figure above them, who waited without bravado, but in resignation or fear, and, Della thought, in some beauty. The scene suggested a mock-auction, the detritus of Carnival.

The onlookers stirred, muttered, but remained as if enchanted, unable to intervene. Before they hushed again a cautious but judicious voice said at Graham's shoulder, 'We can't expect blood.' M. Achille was back.

The quivering, oppressive sunlight stilled on the boy, no word came from those in doorways, at windows, under trees. Expectancy neared the intolerable. Della leaned against Graham, though both were infected by the soundless paralysis. In such extreme, she might have sought even M. Achille, himself standing a little apart, a figure professionally astute, like a bookmaker. Then the boy's eyes moved, bright, feverish, desperate, until, as if at a producer's command, the scene broke. Commotion rose from the café, glass was smashed, hubbub swelled from the street and, closing like a rugger scrum, the Germans pulled down their plaything, hustled him inside, slammed the door. One sensed them, fantastically, plunging out again through the back, bearing the victim like an effigy now gaunt and hollow, in regular formation making for the heights, for the cliff-edge.

At once, the townsfolk, trippers, were shrugging, smiling, moving away. 'I do not', Della curtly addressed M. Achille, 'want to be told what that was about', then tugged at Graham. 'Come away. You can do nothing there. You'd make a mess of it, for me to clear up.'

M. Achille hastily agreed that that was the ticket.

On the homeward voyage the Germans were missing. The boat swished through air stained with sunset. Passengers were quiet from a hot, cheerful day, spread drowsily on benches or, like the Americans, slumped at the bar. Even M. Achille was subdued, only the cigar showing his wakefulness. He had not explained his earlier absence, though he was now carrying a small bag that he had not had at the start.

Della sat, head bowed and listless. Beside her, Graham angrily wished that they were alone, marvellously renewing their holiday. The boat, the day itself, imprisoned him, he dreaded a wearisome dinner under M. Achille's presidency, and wondered how many recent incidents Della had registered as *moments*. Della, who had once, though not lately, ended a letter with 'tons of love'.

He wanted to touch her, but could not bring himself to, then was aware of a changed atmosphere. A bell rang, a light shone, stirs and little cries were beginning. Mist was rolling towards them, wet dark bulges and nooses smudging out sun and coast, the immediate air changing from bruised violet to thickening grey. The last scraps of light flickered on masts, then vanished, rain hissed, pelting the decks, Della awoke, rushing for shelter under a narrow strip jutting from the engine-house. They forgot M. Achille as, tensed, they saw, or seemed to see, out of a thunderclap, electric green sheeted before them, dry despite the rain.

The storm dropped away as swiftly as it had come. Clear blue and green covered the sea, the land revived, a sharp sun minted wave and metal anew.

Graham was happy, arm in arm with Della to join the drinkers. She was beautiful, lit from within, storm spirit, bidden, undisputedly his.

4

A generous reminder of slow arts of stripping, of miracle revelations, surges of passion renewed to order, wordless explosions, mindless words, the primal, the instinctive, neither conquest nor submission, dream nor waking, brutal nor friendly, soft nor hard, but exquisite comminglings of all: a lavish prolonging of curves, exaggeration of points, the liquid, the molten, superb pain, virtuosities of turning, mouthing, clasping, of exacting and fulfilling, thrusts into burning crevices, fairground pullings and dainty, enthralling beckons, bawdy whispers and reckless cries, every square inch an adventure playground, shamanistic ascents and downfalls, nakedness evoking new grooves, fiefs, mysteries?

Not so. Della had lolled bare-breasted, murmuring her desire to have been Countess behind the Hedge, and he himself, undressed rather than naked, found his explorations more joky than lustful. Their laughter, at first muffled, became disconcertingly candid. She was not the metallic huntress disinclined to hunt, rather the actress absently fulfilling her part in an over-long run. Their drama ended in ironic strokings, a torn sheet, a blur of absurd cul-de-sacs, rueful amusement as though once more the pig had slowly walked away, the life between them long completed.

'Oh dear,' she was fondling not him but her own hand, 'it must be my fault. When you tried to lug me on to the bed I could only remember being silly in a school drama festival. I had only to cross the stage, open a deck-chair, then stroll off. But it seemed to take hours. I jammed my fingers in it, tried to open it inside-out, upside-down, it knocked me over, tried to chase me into a corner. A furious mistress had to pull us both off, everyone yelling "Encore".'

Though neither admitted it, waiters' greetings, strangers' bonhomie, children with streetwise, bandit charm, bar chatter, were palling. Summer's leaves were tiring but sunlight still blistered, evoking desires for wistful, pale blues and browns of English autumn. Yet Graham remained uncertain of her expectations, the extent of her cure, whether she yet had courage to resume work. He sensed she would not be the first to suggest departure.

His misgivings about Roger had receded, had perhaps derived from a brief flagging of his self-esteem. He was happy at prospects of resuming their excursions, the calls and telegrams, sensations of conflict, plot, momentum, the moves he could suggest, the hints of advancements. The daze of blue, the sea or sky usually faltered earlier than they were doing now, but his need for London, for the Mammon of Unrighteousness, so commended from on high, increased.

Nevertheless, they lingered within sight of Italy. The blue was deeper, the mountains, Della insisted, closing in rapidly, together with new gossip, new laughs. 'Lotus is good.' She was artificially dreamy, buying scarves, coats, bizarre adornments, unlikely to be worn save in the deepest of London's cavernous alternatives.

They were stranded, she observed, in the hour of youth, not to be wasted by eyes trained to scalpel spurious romance, whirligig Bacchanals. Montségur, emblem of lost causes, was to be renamed Mont Elvis. Bob Dylan was expected, the royal suite at Cap Martin was reserved for Warhol's troupe, and private movies: *Trash, Norma's Bed, Flesh*. Miss Strawberry Ice might descend from a sunlit cloud to read manifestos. The Cannes Film Festival accoladed a teenage masterpiece, dismissed by Orson Welles as an imaginative structure insufficiently imagined. Youth swarmed naked on beaches, violently robed elsewhere. Youth drug-punctured, red-neck, flamboyant, youth with hair styled like tricornes, wattle-roofs, September stubble, steeples: hair from which the face peered like a caged bird, hair like a pagoda, like a comet. One envisaged acid kids dreaming of Byzantine orgies lit with candles stacked on backs of tortoises swimming in scarlet, crystal tanks.

Simultaneously, unknown youngsters were said to have occupied a hill village, clubbing away the elderly, knifing a rich peasant. Indifferent children of the earth, Della brooded.

Night noises outbid the cackle of hookers in a tree. Off the Bay de Carousel a yacht had blazed to the waterline, youngsters jiving on a deck, slanting, slanting, had laughed and shrieked as they repulsed rescuers with gunfire in mantic rejoicing, their beautiful bodies, flower images, their silver cords all smashed and still, weeks later, washed up on a millionaire beach, on which medalled, besashed notables were shown on TV screens handling charred breasts and buttocks, a hairless skull, gashed sirloin, two fingers petrified on a crucifix hung with Monroe, a hand clutching against all odds a locked box of needles.

Admitted by a hotel manager in the licensed inaudibility of current Hollywood stars, a lift failed, imprisoning an elderly tycoon and a girl. Retrieved after several days, the tycoon was relatively cheerful, his dead companion in a condition totally censored, his identity undisclosed.

Devoted as a Gridiron servitor, chatty Mr Toad, night owl, flibbertigibbet, still paying court, added the dissonance that exorcizes the facile from a divertimento. They rinsed out opportunities of fleeing him, by midnight flit, by fantasies of masks, false accents, borrowed phrases, 'I'll pay ... the Earl of Warwick...', yet never very seriously, Della indeed at times defending him as a carnival teddy, seasonal grotesque, a notion of drifting improbabilities in times menaced by the standardized and ruthless.

'Della, he'd love you to call him Baby.'
'He'd love it even better if he was beaten even sillier by you.'
'Did you know he'd a nine-year-old sister in a cabinet.'
'What?'
'Her picture, in some glassed cupboard, in that imaginary home of his. The Château, Schloss, or merely the Colosseum.'

'He told that American colonel that Frank piled too much on his own plate.'

'Frank?'

'FDR. One doesn't actually think of him as Frank.'

'One doesn't actually think of him very often.'

'But you know what Toad calls us?'

'Heartless, of course.'

'No. The grandees!'

'I'm only dry eyes.'

Yet, as so often, she changed course, pushing away coffee cups and planting her chin on her hands, her face a little pinched, between black flaps, eyes dry but widening.

'Graham, do you remember ... before the war, the men – Roger, Sir Hartley, Bertie and the others – talking about a Russian, Suvorov? I imagined a giant, Cyclops, all stinking armpits, horrible pelt, cock like a broomstick, and that glaring, pathological eye. Bearded like the pard, absolutely brutal. Yet sad too. Goaded by the hunters, then blinded. I never quite forgot him. But tell me now, who was he?'

Suvorov. Old legends stirred, half-secrets, wartime heroics: then classroom faces absorbing tales of a hero of Stalingrad where the war itself strained to its limit, then started to crack.

'A non-person today. But a tearaway Errol Flynn, probably unique among tsarist generals in smashing a German army corps in 1915. Not, as Roger thought – I should say, forgot – a descendant of the Suvorov who defeated the French revolutionary armies, but of Cossack peasant stock. In 1918 he joined the Reds, was pally with Trotsky, did well in the civil war, but got mucked up by Stalin and damned nearly got shot in the Tukhachevsky purge. They gaoled him, but when Stalin let in Hitler he got his command back. He quickly became something of a hero again, perhaps at Leningrad, certainly at Stalingrad. I seem to remember that he finally overdid the attack, and got captured. Along with several million others. After that, the trail gets cold. But ... yes, there's a curious tale, I don't quite understand it, about him bobbing up at the end of the war and chasing an SS army out of Czechoslovakia, or some bit of it. There may be more, but I don't know it. I've never heard of him since, he probably borrowed Stalin's braces and forgot to return them. Never very sensible. He wasn't quite of our age. Cavalry charges, lost endeavours, busy resurrections and the rest. But why think of him?'

'Somehow, I don't know, it's important. I've told you I'd never quite forgotten him. A dream figure, like Bryce's brother being shot – of course he wasn't, though I always think of him with a black hood over his head – but this morning, I heard his name, or something very like it, in the town. People were talking, they weren't French, perhaps Polish, at the time I wasn't really listening, not knowing the language. But suddenly, there it was, "Suvorov", hanging with air all around it.'

She said no more, and when, maladroitly, he began again, she tersely motioned him to desist, for the remainder of the evening lingering quiet but watchful, slightly fretting, like a child after a dream irredeemably private. She left very early for bed.

Beneath his obsequiousness M. Achille had altered. His bounce had gone, the planter's suit was unpressed, cigars were dropped half-smoked, he was older, more restless, could be envisaged striving to climb the steps of a single-decker bus or, going sick, dying in a locked room, croaking 'I will pay' to the last. One no longer expected his letter of introduction to Dr Albert Schweitzer, or his recollections of lending cash to Dr Adenauer. He had several times stated that he was Virgo, very interior, very complex, but that Saturn could invite disaster.

'I would like another little expedition. Another perfect day.' Neither replied, his dejection spread. 'We should go into Italy.'

'Why?'

Della was discouraging, he smiled bravely and soon departed. Yet, though nothing definite followed, the trip, the perfect day, somehow seemed agreed. 'You're on,' M. Achille said finally, as if granting a favour, his spirit reviving. 'This is not the best cognac, it is the worst. In Italy, we will make more of a splash.'

'We'll be arrested, of course,' Della sighed later, 'but you'd enjoy that. What do you think he's trying to fix? Heroin, jewels, the Queen's telephone number? Probably a woman, but when he mentions sex you don't hear the words, only see the leer that goes with them.'

'He wants a head in a casket. The Grail you know about.'

'Well, you can share it. You love go-getting. Getting on with the show. Well, let the circus leave town.' The green eyes saddened. 'I suppose it's time to go. These places stale. But it may not be real departure, only another arrival. Would you say he's got a passport?'

'Far too many.'

M. Achille polished the car, inspected the engine, angrily told a garage hand that he didn't know one quack about engineering, bought petrol. On leaving he was in black suit, the broad black hat, with several brief-cases and – Graham and Della swapped winks – a rounded, plastic box. Beside him was a girl, very tall, very thin, with indeterminate eyes, sharp chin, bleached hair and chin. His introduction was inaudible.

'Would it be possible', his anxiety was unmistakable, 'for me to drive? I know an unusual route. Beautiful views.'

His manner did not promise any lingering over views. Graham shrugged, already bored, and, resigned to show-off carmanship, pushed with Della into the back. The girl said something in some harsh tongue, assertive, even threatening, no victim of sex-traffic. 'His keeper,' Della whispered.

M. Achille did not head for nearby Menton on the coastal road, the obvious frontier-post, but drove inland, into the hills, Outside Territory, past a Saracen tower, up towards the blue. Sunlight was scattered on a stony peak. At intervals the sea swung into view, flat and empty. The road wound above sheer drops, M. Achille driving fast but with smooth, precise timing, until, rounding another crag, he had abruptly to brake, halted by a wide, black machine like a police van with anonymous sidings. Several young men in silky, townee suits were already approaching.

They gave neat, polite bows to the girl, opened doors, shook hands with M. Achille, offering him a cigar, a light, bowed again to Della and Graham, who had remained seated.

M. Achille's face lowered to them, moist, very pale, streaked like a cracked plane. 'Moment. Just wait, please. For a very little.'

Puzzled, then angry, Graham pulled open his door and was stepping out, when Della urgently pulled him back. 'Keep still. Keep absolutely still.' As if a snake lay in the car. 'Don't wreck it.'

One of the newcomers moved over. 'Sir, excuse me,' his

accent perhaps Dutch. He deftly removed the car key, shaking his head over it, implying that it needed oil, repair, replacement. His smile was pleasant, complimenting Della for her womanhood, respectful to Graham's reddened face. Talking amongst themselves, the others were affectionately taking M. Achille's arms. His head was bowed, as though the neck had lost muscle. The girl had already clambered into the car. All was informal, casual, suggesting a picnic ahead.

M. Achille's head lifted, he straightened, raising one hand warning them to remain in the car. Shaking aside his escort, he came a little nearer, sunlight breaking on the dark glasses, the cigar glowing well. 'My friends.' He had unexpected dignity, his mouth grave. 'My very good friends.' Then the small group, like a slide removed from a magic lantern, had gone, smoothed out of the air as the car reversed from sight.

'We abandoned him.' Graham was horribly ashamed, but she seized his arm, face stinging and vehement.

'Don't talk crazy. It was sordid. Sordid and stupid.'

That evening she wept, hopelessly, inconsolably, alone in her room, while he sat drinking. He had wanted to chase the van, spread mayhem, hurl the young men, puny enough, to rocks far below, but was left the most ludicrous of them all.

Outside, the town was darker, quieter, as though the mountains had finally reached it, thrusting one vast foot into the sea. No one would miss M. Achille. He was, despite a cosmopolitan horde of relatives, not a family man.

BOOK FOUR

*

In October 1944 Churchill and Eden flew to Moscow to confer with Stalin. It was at this meeting that Eden, without argument or objection, hastened to promise Stalin the return of all his subjects, whether willing or not....

Of the few who were aware of what was happening, a majority strongly opposed what they regarded as unjustifiable and unnecessary inhumanity. On the British side, moving protests, extending on occasion even to ignoring unpalatable orders, came from distinguished figures such as Lord Selborne, Sir James Grigg, Field-Marshal Alexander and General Montgomery. Amongst Americans the objection was almost universal, opposition being led by diplomats such as Joseph C. Grew, Robert Murphy and Alexander Kirk, and soldiers like Eisenhower and Bedell Smith.

Nikolai Tolstoy

A President typically says he wants to get rid of somebody and obviously he and everybody else would much rather get rid of him in a rather nice way.... If the emphasis is on getting rid of him by whatever means have to be used – this I would have taken as an authorization. There is a difference between assassination and killing. Political assassination is a very sophisticated subject.... I did not have any serious doubts about assassination plots as long as they were never disclosed or suspected.

Richard Bissell, of the CIA, 1959–62

1

'I suppose I didn't know, when I was pregnant, that one's supposed to keep off the booze. Daddy Freud, of course, would explain this, in his usual way. No comfort. I drank myself stupid half the time. My fault if there's brain damage. I felt like a squirrel setting up a winter larder but gobbling too early.'

'Darling, there's nothing wrong at all. He's beautiful, filled with a lovely life.'

Janet stroked the sleeping child, her hair, eyes, ochred suit, glowing with the soft, pale gold roses behind her.

They had finished tea. This room was safe anchorage from small, choppy days. Niches, very fresh and white, shone with porcelain, books, photographs. Bayard at twelve gazed from beneath a naval cap, already inquiring, inquisatorial, sceptical: Roger in tails, all features in perfect balance, before a Palace garden party: Graham, grinning, in ugly battledress: Della herself, small and shy, hair very black, limbs very white, a cat in her arms which no one remembered. Roger had banned cats. Above the photographs, warm in firelight, in candlelight, were the fens and cottages, windmills, meadows, the slow rivers and great trees, great skies, of the old East Anglian water-colourists. Much had come from the Dragon House boudoir – the place 'where ladies retire to sulk', Janet had once explained, laughing, where she had read aloud and mended wounds and listened. A blue perfume burner, the ormolu vase, perched on golden dragons, the ovalled walnut chairs, a Ladik prayer-rug of interlocking crimsons, burgundy reds, indigo blues, bronze yellows, that had once concealed spiteful elves, the Dire Fish, the rings of Prince Broken Promise, and others who gave life a bad name. The teapot, embossed with kingfishers and acanthus leaves, joined a time when waves could become flowered meadows or mineral coverlet, and bridges lead to the unlovable, sometimes to the unspeakable.

'You're too good to us, Janet, and I'm an impostor, it's becoming professional. It's you whom he'll call mother!'

Smiling, Janet looked younger than her years, the brown, massed hair very clear, unfretted with grey. Yet sentimentality would glance off her as easily as reproach. Her demands were unknowable, they would not be tepid. Her brown, contained eyes were neither dreamy nor demure, her sympathies were not smug, and her smile could reveal irony, which yet did not attempt to score points. Anti-Kirkland factions gibed that she laid up treasure in heaven but, despite reports that Roger had withdrawn his favour, her invitations continued undeterred, and few refused them. Like a planet, she had her own orbit, her personal name.

Still fondling the baby Andrew, she spoke of Graham. 'I always saw him as a redhead though of course he was not. Now he was fiery, now he was stricken to the heart. I still imagine him trying to shoot an apple off his son's head.'

'He's not going to try on mine. He'd certainly miss.'

'That fair hair made him look angelic.'

'Not much else did. His temper was foul.'

'He would get so angry with Bayard, yet he so much wanted his praise. I always see him standing alone in dust and dirt, glaring at other boys, desperate to make friends with them, until they ran away in terror. He seemed to be daring himself to attempt some sort of loss. At school he was forbidden to join in the hymns he loved, because he was so loud and dreadfully out of tune.'

'In the old days he'd have been hanged young for nicking what he didn't really want. A sheep, a grandfather clock, even a grandfather. He'd make a good end, showing off madly to the drunken multitude.'

'He always demands his own terms.'

'And they're often too high.'

Both paused, in separate degrees of silence. Outside, dusk was already seeping through gardens, swathing the trees, while Della watched, not Andrew, but Janet's slim, jewelled hand.

'Several times I've had the same dream. I'm driving a bus. It's very long, very narrow, my hands are on the wheel but simultaneously I'm sitting a long way back, behind passengers who are always at a distance, however close I try to get to them. I can only see their backs, but, as I say, I'm also driving them, in front. I stop for petrol at a weird building. It's garage, motel, betting-shop, supermarket, flop-house all in one. I wander about, searching for a petrol pump. A man is paying out money to another man, who departs, followed by a third. There's a sudden squall, a quarrel, something looming. Blood squirts from a neck. Now I'm lost in a muddle of alleys, ladders, evil doorways. A girl, smudged, almost faceless, runs past, at a woman's cry. Her skirt lifts, her loins are red. Then, in panic, I realize the bus has gone, I'm lost, and wake up, shivery. Can the bus be my work, which I can't control? Or Andrew, whom I'm not giving enough love?'

Janet was able to respond without actually saying anything, and, somehow agreeing, Della said more calmly, 'Yes, really, it's that I don't seem, at the moment, able to feel. As though I've lost something infinitely precious, which can't be far away, but has got covered up by the muddled and disjointed and in back-streets. My work's gone mouldy.'

'But I see your name everywhere.'

'In the wrong places, and with pretty nasty remarks trailing after it. I'm not in the proper circuit any more. A wretched Pauline Henry burst out at me, not for writing that her play was mindless, but for calling her "Miss". The cow might have preferred "It". I believe she hit a man for opening a door for her. I'd have shut it in her face. No one speaks of my new poems,' her eyes darkened, rank not with grievance but self-irritation, 'and I must confess that they're not really new. Mostly old, dead stuff, or imitations, which I'd hidden away and should have burnt, cleanly, wisely. And I'm now relying on them, like stupid pills. The pathology of words!'

Andrew stirred in his cot, she did not notice, though Janet quickly glanced down. Briefly, Della seemed the older, her hair drier, her face lined with discontents: in jeans and tired green coat and skirt, she looked dependent, even importunate, amongst the fire-struck colours, the freshness of leaf and petal, and the grave, intent woman who, seldom initiating talk, induced talk in others.

'I've got a horror, it's immature, of going for long without appearing in print. I've not learnt to wait, the role of patience, withholding. Like a lunatic seeking identity. Like an actress, when "resting", shoves into drugs, gin, movie-houses.'

'Darling, you don't...'

'No, no, of course not. I've still got bits of my own imagination, I don't need to pay crooks for grey wits and second-hand sog. But, Christ, I seem to have been baptized too late. I suppose I really was baptized?'

'Darling, I don't think you ever were. Does it mean anything to you now?'

Della tilted her head like a blackbird. 'It might. At present, I'm a bit like Graham, who doesn't know it, in having a religious temperament, rather a pagan one in my case, without your belief. An impersonal god is believable, just. Jesus, well, I see him not as a super-star in a dreary musical, certainly not a god, high praise on general divine form, but a furious man, old before his time, scalding with anger, apt to lose hope. All too human. Very believable. I've read some stuff, trendy but interesting, by that charlatan Emery, whom Graham knew. But you ... we never know what you really think.'

'It's generous of anybody to think I've any thoughts at all, and I dare say I haven't. But I like to think of you happy again. When you were little, every night you used to say "What's going to happen tomorrow?" You had a tone of wondering, eyes full of wonder. So eager for the new day.'

'For another chance. It was all so simple, simple as a cowbell.' Then, more to herself, 'Where is that girl now?'

She shook her head, over the wilfully mislaid. 'A professor said that in the Middle Ages there was no boredom. It's difficult to believe, but maybe. Someone else claims that boredom has no history. Perhaps. But it has more power than any old king or blazing dictator. It spreads out like bog gas, it becomes crusades, rattle-headed monsters in arenas and rallies and pin-tables, treks to the underworld looking for green folk. Its silence shrieks, like hunger, it doesn't even cast a shadow, it doesn't need to, it's complete already. Roger's never been bored in his life, he's strong, perhaps Graham too. I don't know about Bayard, he may be bored all the time, weaving fantasies to keep himself high and dry. You just look into yourself and are already in the best chapter of your favourite book. But is it a novel, short stories, poetry.... You won't tell us, you're a deceiver without being a fraud.'

They smiled together, and, involuntarily, Della laughed. After Andrew had been taken upstairs, they resumed. The candles had sickened but Janet did not replace them: shadows constricted some of the room, enlarged the rest, placed small scattered tints against cushiony blacks, reaching out into the obscure garden, dwindling to small circles round flames, the voices ebbing, in keeping with an hour not gloomy but hushed.

'Roger says. . . .'

When Janet spoke of him, it was still as if all was unchanged and he was about to enter from the next room, though none could know where and how often they now met. She said, not confidingly, but matter-of-fact, 'We have decided to let or sell the Dragon House.'

'Oh no! You can't.'

'Roger never goes there. We are on different journeys but there may be a place, even a home, where we can arrive together, if not quite simultaneously.'

She nodded the thought away, as if dismissing a joke appropriate but weak, then rose, switching on lights, drawing curtains, and at once the room was defined, familiar, normal. Janet seemed very neutral. 'He shows no strain at all. He's wonderfully fit, certainly not bored.'

Student riots had convulsed European and American cities, against the established, the academic, against authority, mechanical, rational, impersonal. An American poet howled, 'There's nothing to be learnt from history any more, we're in science fiction now. We're back to magic. Fuck for Peace.' A mass-murderer had identified the Beatles with the Book of Revelation. In processions, swirling charges, headlong disarray, texts, flaunted from Sartre, Marcuse, Fanon, justified conflagration, dissolution, the wild, impassioned, and fleeting. Supported by the cheques of rich daddies, communards denounced pollution from positions of squalor, gates were smashed, colleges occupied, files rifled. Tremendous slogans strove to smash the Brandts, Johnsons, de Gaulles, the old men, the entrenched officialdom with barbed papers and defensive eyes: *If you destroy the Word you destroy the System*; *When in Doubt, Burn*. A leader declaimed, 'We've combined Youth, Sex, Music, Drugs and Rebellion, with Treason, and that's a combination hard to beat.'

In London, Sir Roger Kirkland was especially denounced, pickets attempting to barricade Montpelier Square. A governor of a university college, he was accused of regarding students as bedding plants, to be grown to order by stereotyped and thin-blooded process. On TV he had maintained that too many demanded higher education as right not as earned privilege, were shying from genuine scholarship, preferred linguistic laziness to thought, dreaded facts, precedents, debates, examinations, anything likely to disperse not ideas but quotes, facile and borrowed. He contemptuously cited a newspaper article which recommended bad grammar and inaccurate spelling, as witness to live, demotic speech liberated from fusty restrictions, then, with his cool smile, quoted a critical assertion that clarity was the death of language, and, following a yelling, demented assault on the American Embassy, with mounted police crashing to the pavement and a rumour of bayonets unsheathed within the building itself, he declared in a radio forum that the Left had been wrong on every serious issue since 1792. He was said to have advocated, in Downing Street, conscription, to emasculate hooliganism and sloth, grants to encourage repatriation of black immigrants, and had certainly dominated an official report on ethnic abilities which allegedly foretold the necessity of total revision of education presumptions, syllabus and standards. It had never been published, the succeeding Labour administration was believed to have suppressed it, fuelling immoderate racialist jeers, accusations, threats.

Della was embracing Janet. 'It's awful how much I leave with you. Andrew, my complaints and affectations! You should be more hard-hitting, you more than any of us.'

Four o'clock had gone, the sweetshop hour. In huge skeleton fans, the trees merged blackly into failing, porridge sky. Statues, residue of Empire, ravaged by uncertain lights, offered a bearded face, a grim horse's head, the winter thrall recalling her mother's death: 'I'm frightened', wrenched from a mouth so seldom relaxing, and she herself, daughter unfaithful, unable to bring herself to enter the ambulance for a last kiss.

Now she had her own motherhood, a gift to herself that approached the sardonic.

She hurried. On the corner of a silent street, pig-tailed,

mauvish figures stood under a lamp, one with a cracker-box pearl necklace, all huddled as if in ambush, in motionless state, worse than gesture or sneer, though, fiercely aloof, she strode by, up the hill to safety, where locks and chains gave comfort more immediate than climbing plants, glass maquettes and tables, the cold, northern woodwork and striped walls, the Kandinskys and Légers.

The messages from beyond were ceasing, like the radio taps on a sinking liner. Or she noted leaves on rainy pavements, so less substantial than the skies and trees outlined within the stone. A reviewer had derided her as ceasing to develop. New theories bemused. 'Language', Barthes asserted, 'is, quite simply, Fascistic . . . every form of classifcation is oppressive.' She needed more than ever Roger's respect for solid achievement, his mastery of debate, ability to deal out the assured, sometimes unanswerable, his incessant support at her most abject.

Now the Dragon House was to go, woodland powers, benign or eldritch would be dispossessed, her old home be transformed to the righteously impeccable, to Borstal or asylum, trade-union hospital, tourists' haven, where citizens would gorge themselves back to life, or swill each other into death, but scarcely glance at the vistas and spirals, the crossing paths, statues, trees and courtyard which had sent her early imagination out to work. Doors would block the gracious arches, those entries into pictures and stories.

Stories still came, but too often refined from dreams and swiftly lapsing, as if she had gagged herself. In one, M. Achille referred to his cousins the Habsburgs, but no epic would come from that. In dreams, she was on journeys abruptly abandoned, leaving her alone on a mountain, in a brothel, in a medieval Highgate lane that did not exist. A voice trickled over her. 'I have ordered you my very best doctors. They will dedicate themselves to you alone.'

'And then?'

'Why . . . I shall behead you.'

Or, nightly, a tiger roamed a market square, very tense, very beautiful, surviving in a poisoned world. The people treasured him, gave him food. Joints of lamb, then live pigs. But he began wanting more, sniffing at children, nosing virgins. In crisis, the people then assembled and, beneath subtle evasions, reasoned casuistry, purring compassion, the single issue was gradually exposed, not what, but who?

Hunters were at hand, God help her. The history of art, Bayard said, is not a roll-call of nice people.

At best, the weeks smouldered. MacEntee & Holbrook had ditched her, affable Mr Elsen with his New York connections had backed into advertising, while soft voices confided that she had been published for her skills not on paper but in bed. She had misread signals, the treasure lay beneath moongrass and violets of a thirteenth month. From the expedition with Graham little seemed to have come, though one could never be certain. There was much more she hoped to forget, or transform. A few lines had started from a bronzed Celtic mask. Holed, impassive, cruelly human, it suggested unearthly song, the twisted face of Dionysos, victims strung from a branch, life dropping from them to the vines. Graham had been glad of girls laughing on swings at vintage time. A poem should show feelers from this, but had not yet done so.

Sadness, loneliness, stalked bright cities. Sexual freedoms into which Graham plunged so rampantly and which, apparently effortlessly, Bayard ignored, or, if threatened by feelings, consulted the Air Vice Marshal, were not blossoming into all-purpose happiness. Many Pills became many grievances, everyone resenting all privileges save their own.

At school, with older girls, she had been taken to a hospital vault to see diseased bits of people, purple, leprous white, jagged, punctured, crusted, hanging in jars. A lesson against immorality. Sometimes, amongst feasts and music, she saw those jars and the girls' faces, starred like cracked windows.

The room was warming, lights glowed, whisky shone. Inevitable cycles of pain must await transmutation as they had always done. Nerve-ends were now moribund, now brilliant. Moments solidified into conflict, into union, into events, into blood: a purple patch behind the air hardened into a face, softened into promise of the marvellous new. Scaffolding within can be resolute ascent or mere safeguard against collapse. She must keep at concert pitch. A tiny fault in the window, a barely transparent whorl, like a thumb-mark, suggested a fixed presence neither inside nor outside, a wily Merlin with his packet of illusions. She herself was an autumn tree, shedding leaves, stripping not for love or vanity, but for the dead season, before renewal. She had the son she had deliberately sought, promptly received, from the handsome cipher now, unaware of paternity, safely back in Sydney. But Andrew was an investment, babies bored her. Janet, while no earth goddess, had always desired them, and was happy. The future would serve them both.

She drank, suddenly glad. From the window she gazed down at flashing lights, brilliant panes, the black voids of heath and woods, St Paul's floodlit dome on the reddish skyline and, nearer, the cavernous railway station with its temptations to wander, very late, down empty platforms alongside carriages slumped in unearthly lights under gallows ironwork and red, unblinking eyes, a few loiterers drifting past like figures in a bad dream who move without touching ground.

Swiftly she forgot herself, puzzled by Graham, Captain Cartridge, matador, legionnaire with a flourish, but surely, like herself, momentarily stalled at vivid crossways, surely not to be long content as one of Roger's heavies. They were no longer in aspiring youth. His bright hair and eyes were frayed, lines were starting across his rough, soiled skin. She had seen him angry, challenging, rudely impatient with party games and crossword puzzles at which he was grotesquely inexpert, but never had he been, as he now was, heavily morose, like the perpetual Irishman leaving a betting-shop. Could he have quarrelled with Roger? He had become unusually taciturn, over more than his war service, war valour, about which his modesty was out of character. He might be goading himself by feeling that, far from winning battles, he had yet to fight them. She had surely saved their lives from guns or knives on that hot mountain road, but for this he only blamed her, claiming responsibility, too loudly, for the fate, probably gruesome, of Mr Toad. Fast going, Mr Toad had said, like a horse on fire.

Could he be resenting Andrew? Surely not, though people could be outraged at the forfeiture of imaginary rights they had never actually claimed. Or disapproving of some of her girl-friends, usually so much younger than herself? Unlikely, not impossible. But he himself was amateur in the warfare of bodies, though his sex energy appeared index-linked, and fuelled on the national grid. His affairs always ended foolishly. His sexual offensives, grandly conducted at the start, dwindled to manoeuvres for self-defeat. He lacked the shrewd patience of seducer or artist, his girls were schoolboy crazes, like conkers, or his absurd pride in the Gridiron Club. Confusing orgasm with true, true love, he had remained curiously stationary, a collector desiring fine volumes but never reading them. He cherished lost loves as he did Offenbach's jolly tunes and fierce climaxes, even the war wounds he had missed. He fell readily into love as a jousting preparation for falling out of it. Incapable of long-distance planning, he would marry some militant impossible in an outburst of bad manners.

She loved him for what he never realized: not for his runaway grin and generous tastes, certainly not for a thick cock and strong arms – to give one's life for a Graham would be easy, but bed trivialized him – nor for his university learning and ease in high places, but for his voice, richly assertive, ruefully self-mocking, with the impetuosity she was losing. He could be a trudging St George in an age of animal rights, she herself a chessboard queen moved by incompetent hands. Loving each other just off-centre, they needed the Grand Telegram, the splendid reprieve which always arrived. It had arrived last month, not, as so often, in a hamper or call from Roger. At one of her own parties she had been overcome by self-doubt in one of those long, perceptive moments always in her gift. A hunting lioness selects a victim from a herd of gazelles: the rest understand, drift away from the doomed one, continuing their placid grazing. She had felt herself prey thus marked. No one here wished her well, all were secretly gibing, criticizing, and she overheard talk of another party awaiting them that evening, to which she alone was uninvited. Angry, wretched, she then realized that the party itself was askew. Altering it like an adverb, Bayard had entered, pausing to salute them en route to Leeds, to Lisbon. She had told him of no party but here he was, unemotional, studiously polite, salvaging the evening, gathering people around him like a maypole, winning neither laughs nor full-hearted friendliness but some ill-defined curiosity, reluctant interest, as, primly dressed, unsmiling, he listened with suspect curiosity and, as if recollecting matters of no very general importance, recommended the operas of Meyerbeer, reproached governments for facetiousness, adjudged that the Arts Council had lately accepted goodish advice, denied any responsibility for the Warsaw Palace of Culture, foretold the next Director of the

National Gallery, then paused to sneeze. The sneeze was no vulgar explosion bespattering all comers. In advance warning, his long face and nose quivered, the token brows collected over the close, indeterminate eyes, assisting a frown, his left hand gestured in minor apology, his right extracting a purple handkerchief, then hastily replaced it by a blue one with further regrets from the left. This second handkerchief he accepted, then hesitated, his face again intimating forthcoming eruption, until, as if in sad but irrevocable decision, he released his sneeze, very soft, barely audible, almost musical.

2

Graham was unconcerned with Andrew, babies were irritants like hay fever or bridge. Della unabashedly felt likewise and as often as possible surrendered to Janet this noisy product of one more idle, uncouth love. Of Della herself he saw little, but Janet reported her religious interests, doubtless fleeting, more fanciful than reverent, aroused by Emery.

Now principal of a theological college, Emery had grabbed headlines by his treatise exploring Jesus' remark recorded in an apocryphal gospel lately discovered in Egypt. 'The Kingdom will not come merely by sitting around and hoping.... It is spread throughout the world and people simply do not see it.' With pulpit lordliness, Emery concluded that the visible but unreal world, acceptable only as metaphor, is always disintegrating into evil, redeemable by the individual behaving as if he could cure it. The Kingdom is not of this world, the resource of the lazy, indifferent, self-deceiving, of which the Devil is literally prince, not consistently evil but spewing out values merely relative against the absolute demands of Christ. In leaving the world for the Kingdom is Resurrection, posing the impossible, not for practical results, though these may follow.

He too was interested. Expounding this too freely he was briefly known as Brother Graham. He lacked disciples. The Daves had long dropped into some hole, flummoxed by the sniff, the puncture or, like an Achille, had been split by a machete or washed up on a hard shore.

Personal kingdoms were not yet at hand in the visible world of Montpelier Square. Much of the sixties' property stampede had subsided, more millionaires, civic leaders, architects had collapsed into prison, exile, suicide but, with habitual finesse, Roger still occupied arcane regions where a Graham could follow only at a distance. Paid well, still courted in clubs, ministerial outposts, fashionable maisons, he remained underemployed, his rackets, road-maps, dinner-jackets his effective tools. He had a courtesy title in the select cabinet of Guards, had tournament rank, but purely as a stand-in for the champions, while, from behind closed doors, at the live end of electric currents, a council faction was crushed or appeased, a new shopping centre eliminated the hopes of small-holders; alpine offices, to be kept empty for years, soared above towns, hitherto finely proportioned. A celebrity resigned, a strike collapsed, auditors fattened, take-overs multiplied. Talk abounded about a Channel tunnel, American and Japanese join-ups, piers into infinity.

Hints still emerged, though now more guardedly, of half-lit subcultures and alternative livings, a frontier where brightly publicized interests merged with protection rackets and hit-squads. Roger had invested in the new minicabs whose intrusions into established territories erupted in violence, sometimes bloodshed. He continued to acquire bombed buildings, abandoned docks, desolate streets, despite anger from tenants, squatters, the very old. Titled front men processioned through Montpelier Square, then abruptly fled to the Bahamas or Switzerland, Mafia personages appeared in honours lists.

Still shunted on sidelines, Graham watched with resentful misgivings. Backed by the smooth Guards, Roger must guess him unreliable. Insulting and unfair, but the chance to prove it lagged. Unlikely to overreach himself, Roger was conceivably capable of error, like Emery's God endlessly experimenting for the zest of it. He was more elusive, though unobstructively or slyly. The arm round the shoulder, the summons to dinner and squash, the talk of a trip to Bahrain, a holiday in Florida remained, but the confidences, the demands for advice, could now be seen as trivial, the chucking of largesse to a poor relation whose fealty was both satisfying and unnecessary. Ill at ease in the new computer-room where younger men were brisk and knowing, but still allowed to handle Roger's social mail, he occasionally encountered a new type of letter, hand delivered, with curious markings, stamped *Very Personal*, their lightness suggesting codes. He was becoming impatient, imagining that Guards' greetings were now too loud, their voices too obviously secretive. The politicians he was meeting were mostly decayed; exposed as intellectual slovens, masters of no very definite discipline. Occasionally he envied the Daves, footloose, work-shy, improvising life in twilit ranges. More often, he did not.

Roger was increasingly, sometimes needlessly, unrestrained, in publicly baiting what he called the trendy connection, lacerating it with statistics about genetic inheritance, censorship and capital punishment in Cuba, in Eastern Europe, agricultural incompetence in Black Africa, the advantages of the Common Market. Sometimes his disclosures seemed indebted to those of the Saratoga League journalists, Bayard presumably amongst them, who entered the same donjon from opposite doors, though remaining at one in condemning the post-war extermination of professional classes in the Red-occupied Baltic states, and wartime Russo-German collaboration against Ukrainian Jews. In 1939 Stalin had toasted Himmler as guardian of order. Once, Roger entertained alone two retired Army officers and an ex-Nato American general, whose faces subsequently decorated the liberal press together with leaked proposals to enlist 'loyal, level-headed men' as mobile task force against unsocial elements. These vanished in derision and, though Roger's name was not mentioned, Aerosol Man dabbed his wall with obscene, libertarian war-cries.

Perhaps he too needed risk, even pain, and, climbing high, giddily awaited what Della called the Grand Telegram. She herself, fellow castaway certainly needed it, a fat vulgar wallop of success. But he glowered most at himself. His bed housed no Miriam, old friends were warnings, on free transfer not to a Kingdom but to cosy homesteads where, with feminist wives and expensive children, they became domestic pets or angry freebooters raising bats for applause long ceased. Your trouble, Della was quick with unnecessary information, is that a wife of yours must be available for instant beating, wild reconciliation, but rebellion is now heard on the campus.

Grand Telegrams can sprint from the unexpected. As winter crumbled, wavering lights of the Kingdom were blanked out, with need to stand four-square with Guards as telephones sounded, huge mail torrented, voices jabbed like mad birds. Well-printed, anonymous Saratogan pamphlets regularly circulated from West Berlin, Rome, Lisbon, Brussels, sometimes from Paris, Montreal, New York, surreptitiously reaching Eastern Europe where they were proscribed. In London they were no longer restricted to obscure bookshops: in clubs, public libraries, homes, they nibbled at official cover-ups, ministerial *non sequiturs*, UN procrastination and timidity. Never apocalyptic, they had glacial sting. At Montpelier Square they were received but perhaps unread.

Pamphlet No. 37 was on Graham's desk, amongst the usual invitations, minutes, digests. He glanced at it cursorily, as he might at a rose catalogue, recommendations for bed-sitter cuisine, offer of instant salvation, then, quickly sensing trouble, realized that here was more than tired scandal – a grey patch on sunlight, a slither in the bedroom.

It began with assertation, now familiar, that Nazi gassings though described in a London newspaper in 1942, were officially ignored by the Allies for almost a year. Continuing, it suggested that in protecting Jewish minorities, the weaker the country the more generous and courageous the response, Denmark, Bulgaria, even Franco Spain risking more, achieving greater and more imaginative success than had Downing Street or White House. As if in flippant afterthought, it cited the Prince of midget Lichtenstein withstanding the victorious Allies' demands for assistance against groups anti-Stalin, anti-Tito, a matter to be examined more fully in a subsequent pamphlet.

Against protocol, Graham hurried uninvited to the orderly room. Roger was alone, leisurely examining documents.

'My dear fellow, how good of you to look in!'

Yet, handing over the booklet, Graham felt he was displeased, turning the pages too quickly, as though, unwilling to admit it, he already knew them. Then, very deliberately, he dropped them into a waste-paper cage.

'Yes, Graham.' There sounded a half-disgusted question. He sighed, released a donnish smile, superior. 'It has the middle-class insignia of those fire-raisers who, wouldn't you say, model themselves on Camille Desmoulins. Having stormed Whitehall and the Palace, they will be the very first to be disposed of by those they so intemperately encourage. They get their sexual movements by screaming slogans. It might perhaps be better to get them through sex.'

'This stuff isn't exactly revolutionary.'

'It so seldom is. For years, poor King Louis had few intellectual adherents more wordily loyal than the future Jacobin terrorists.'

In the silence he was suddenly cold, the smile reduced by bleak airs. Neither spoke of Bayard, and indeed a glance from Bayard would dismiss revolution, like war, like the Kingdom, to second-rate entertainment, ill-considered and nondescript.

Not quite convinced, risking *lèse-majesté*, Graham borrowed all available Saratogan publications. Mostly translated from German and French, they shared a tone, laconic, often ironic, making bizarre play with Vatican investments in the Pill, union and Russian investments in South Africa, extravagant shortcomings of statesmen. The death of a UN diplomat in a Lagos hotel was linked, unconvincingly, to manoeuvres of an oil consortium, a British Cabinet minister was accused of improper building involvements, the Shah was warned against American promises. The League claimed credit for the arrest of Tenner, a German officer who, in 1943, while eating almonds, had ordered the shooting of every Greek male in Kalávrita, the killers singing throughout, then demanded, unsuccessfully, the burning of the women and children in the locked school. Earlier, he had publicly sworn on his honour that no villager was in danger. Dying, a boy had asked what his crime was.

Roger's gleaming cabinets hoarded the alien and far-reaching. Another pamphlet queried the affability of a scientist, once foremost in Albert Speer's industrial front, now managing an Argentinian plutonium plant and promising a nuclear weapon very soon. Inconclusive references to emergent post-Resistance killings outside Grasse might have led towards Mr Toad, the night owl, but the trail then slackened and expired.

He remained restless, ready to catch Grand Telegrams on his shield, but uneasy, as he had been when pink fingernails blacked in the night.

Another Katyn. Cossack Hero Betrayed. Goering's Revenge for Nuremberg. We Cannot Afford to Be Sentimental – Eden.

On a May Sunday, national newspapers reproduced large slices of Saratoga's Pamphlet No. 38, some with a quotation from *Tass* of Moscow, that the grandchildren of the criminal Suvorov, executed in 1946, were to be tried for extortionate speculation. Suvorov's career was detailed with a uniformity suggesting a handout hastily supplied by Saratoga and news agencies. A tsarist cavalry general, awarded a decoration by George V for gallantry in the Allied cause in 1916, had finally joined the Reds during the civil war and been prominent in defeating Kolchak's Whites before Moscow. His ferocity against the Kronstadt mutineers was commended in telegrams, now reproduced, from Lenin and Bukharin. He slung armies against Poles, Romanians, French, repulsed German-backed Cossack nationalists with atrocious losses and, against orders, gave the losers choice between transferring to him or immediate execution. During the twenties his portrait had hung alongside the ikons of Voroshilov and Budënny, then he vanished in the Stalinist purges.

On Monday, Pamphlet No. 38 expanded the story, without comment.

At the German invasion in 1940 Suvorov was disinterred, fought valiantly with Timoshenko on the Central Front, then blazed his name anew at Stalingrad. In 1943, at fifty, Hero of the Soviet Union, in personal command of a small counter-offensive, he recklessly disobeyed Stalin's direct orders for a strategic retreat, continued his advance and, outspeeding his tanks, lost communication and was captured by German-led Whites – Cossacks, Crimean Tartars, Georgians, Balts, Armenians, Turks, Ukrainians, volunteers who hysterically prostrated themselves, belaurelling him as prince, ever victorious, one of themselves.

Months later he was back, under Hitler's Special Operations Executive, commissioned to recruit White prisoners of war, displaced persons, slave-workers, as auxiliary to a larger army led by another Russian turncoat, Andrei Vlasov. His glamour was star-struck; covered by a brief Wehrmacht recovery, he swept ten thousand men into a bedraggled Russian town, was hailed as liberator, held it six weeks against thunderous odds. In April 1945, with the Nazis collapsing, he again changed sides, sending a battalion to help enter Prague and himself, by an extraordinary forced march, defeating fifteen thousand Waffen SS, delivering thousands to American prison camps.

At the end, relying on a British general's safe conduct and on King George's medal, General Alexis Suvorov, still in German uniform, swaggered, all smiles, into the British encampment with his staff and family. At once the Foreign Office indignantly cancelled the safe conduct and, too late, the prisoners, disarmed, were removed at gunpoint into open carts for what the British general, game to the last, called honourable captivity.

Saratoga had scooped a klaxon tale that hustled through all Britain, though reporters, converging on the League's dreary Maida Vale office, met only a locked door, from behind which a woman's voice monotonously repeated that a senior Air Force officer had forbidden interviews.

Henceforward the League placidly withdrew, abdicating on behalf of the newspapers, a bombardment of explosive facts that shattered all-party assumptions.

Over five million Soviet nationals and Balts had been captured by Germans, some three million dying of wounds, overwork, starvation, execution. Of the rest, a million, as fervid volunteers, conscripts or from hopeless necessity, fought Stalin's armies. In defeat, together with thousands of royalist Serbs, these Whites, men, women and children, begged against repatriation to Russia and Yugoslavia, already promised by their Allied rulers. 'We don't want them here,' the British Foreign Secretary had minuted.

In Russia, as in Japan, surrender itself was cowardice or treason, forfeiting legal rights. In Schleswig-Holstein, Carinthia, North Italy, thousands were hunted down by Allied troops with arms and promises. A Scottish officer had to dispose of eight pregnant girls, moaning in their own blood, having stabbed each other. He could only recommend their men to do likewise. Survivors were eventually dispatched to Russia and Yugoslavia, for execution, imprisonment, internal exile. Some thirty thousand had been temporarily landed in Britain, while the Foreign Office secretly conferred with Washington and military representatives from Russia. Amongst them was Suvorov, demanding recognition as a Geneva-protected prisoner of war, then audience with the King, then open trial before judge, jury, the press. Summarily returned to Russia, he and his two sons were publicly hanged in Kiev for treason, sabotage, espionage. With the war long over, public opinion at once embraced him as the romantic Cossack, fiery particle in a sterile, mechanized order sacrificed for expediency, appeasing the Great Stalin, who, several weeklies began insisting, had salvaged Western democracy at its last gasp.

Politics was momentarily stunned. Like anti-Semitism, religion, and capital punishment, personal courage revoked party lines. Commons disputes, in this furore, seemed those of dogs over a maggot. Questions were shot to experts, alive and dead, old heroes were cross-examined, half-dead party veterans revived, though certain officials, youthful in 1945, now of international importance, pleaded the Official Secrets Act and said nothing. The Foreign Office slid the shutters down, but a leading article stated that, deploring the possibility of parliamentary questions, it had connived at the concealment of the whole matter. The Army had been asked to request coroners to divulge no suicides – 'We do not want trouble' – and exclude the press. Now, an independent's request for a Commons debate was rejected by the Speaker, and initial Labour howls against Tories and Whitehall were stifled by revelations that Bevin and Attlee had continued the Churchill–Eden policy. 'We must', Bevin declared, 'make a difference between traitors and refugees.' In some forty thousand tons of print, unpleasant voices released shocking truths, the generous and sincere could only mumble, the bland remained righteous. 'We obeyed orders.' Anger swept the nation, high-pitched, as if in sexual rave.

Graham's own dusty memories rushed back on the tide. A lurid glow had sliced the blue sky and revealed not angels but

Panzer material, Corsican in savagery, Cretan in implacability ... refuting the politeness of diplomacy, conference and the last glimmer of the wartime Grand Alliance. He read on, then jumped up, incredulity bursting into new vistas. As though a child's spade had dug too deep, striking the mine that had lain unexploded for years within holiday sands. In mild throw-away, Pamphlet No. 38 on its final page disclosed that Suvorov had been interviewed in London by Sir Roger Kirkland, who had signed what had been long unofficially styled the Kirkland Memorandum.

On the Wednesday, an extract from this document, illegally smuggled to Fleet Street, was slammed on to front pages. 'It really does not concern us whether Stalin treats his hundreds of thousands of deserters honourably and with justice, as under British common law, or whether, as we can presume, he stands them against whatever wall is handy.' Anger from all quarters coalesced into another headline: 'The Cruel Young Men in the Foreign Office.'

The air now crowded with poisoned feathers, poisoned beaks. Words closed over like hoods for those lined against the handy wall. Insult blew Hurricane Cato, one could choke on a bracket, on italics. An historian compared the Anglo-American dealings with Stalin at Tehran and Yalta with the deal between Emperor Theodosius the Younger and Attila, by which any Hun renegade was returned unconditionally. Another tolled descriptions of nineteenth-century British genocide in Tasmania, in Newfoundland. A tabloid caricaturist scrawled naked women imploring vodka cooled from a chip of Lord Kirkland of Suvorovgrad's heart. Roger was reviled as though he were Dracula's dentist; was lampooned in 'Blue Chip Man', a song of profiteering meddlers. Turning from the investiture of a hallooing, drug-crazed pop group as honorary doctors of law, a TV satirist gibed at a past home secretary as a Kirkland in human shape, and a columnist averred that Sir Roger, throughout a career shrewdly planned, had been modest only in self-criticism, but had now lost the ladder which he had so industriously climbed. Headlined 'A Political Albino', a smart feature outlined his triumph at Nuremberg, over Nazis who had themselves pleaded obedience to orders. A Midwest senator from the Truman administration broadcast that, had Suvorov surrendered to Eisenhower, he would yet be alive.

Throughout that enflamed, pillaging week, Roger was out of town. Graham awaited his return, impatient, lonely, sickened by the periodic breast-beatings the country so enjoyed: Suez, Versailles, Wilde, bombs of conscience that could resound like boasts. That Roger, so measured, so unanswerable, could be aligned with Katyn and Belsen slaughterhouses was abrupt and horrifying, the mad screech of brakes zigzagging through dreams, pinching the nerve, tripping the heart.

Stations of the past were being blown. Gazing into himself he saw a wolf in a cage too fragile, grey with complicity, nearly two decades ago, with tragedy in Carinthia. Trained to rely on HQs and seasoned institutions, on Kirklands and Claverings, he had not roused mutiny, flung down gauntlets, but had advanced with the herd he despised, conventional in spirit as he had been in upbringing. He could not approach Janet or Della. King's Regulations had offered him the exceptional, a veritable *moment*, not a month pegged by ludicrous images dragged from self-disgust. He could have been Jack Cade running a filthy tongue into the sky and shaking whole counties, Hamlet vengeful amongst suspect shadows and putrid reality. The exception in a thousand. Cagney fisticuffs, Bogart menace, the crafty violence of Edward G. Today he was nothing, loud but obsolete as a bombard. Grails deceived too often, like girls' beds, like nights of good cheer. People queued for their own execution. He was like Roger himself, encrusted with the snow that ended *Twelfth Night*, obliterating mirth, tenderness, ornate behaviour. Was soused, trying to fill his pen with coffee, was anguished beyond precedent, was friendless, despicable, had exasperated the century and, on a knife-line of ignominy, had let slip the world.

Recovering, contriving a grin, he rang Della. No reply. Then Bayard, Bayard the unreachable, holding press conference in Dieppe, being modelled for unofficial stamps, planning to replace the National Gallery. But no. Bayard answered at once, inviting him to meet him at an address in murky West Kensington, perhaps the property of a lanky, highly spectacled Sandra or degenerate Nick.

Neither greeted him in the wide, poorly lit basement, an imitation bank hung with pallid announcements of deposit accounts, a heavy clock, a metal calendar, two leathery upright chairs separated by a narrow dun-coloured table. No boudoir for a sugar-plum fairy, with Bayard emerging from behind the grilled counter in dark blue office suit, prim white collar, vague tie, cheap striped socks. 'Life goes on.' He was neither listless nor involved. 'It's sometimes uncertain why. At the moment, visibility moderate, with fog patches. You've just missed Rydstrom, special correspondent, though offering nothing very special. When drink flows, he flows with it. One of those Swedes whose handshake squashes you flat and who leaves you to clean up the mess. He demanded damages for some piece we'd done, but caved in when I mentioned Section 603E of the Companies Act. Well, you've arrived on time.'

His sigh was despondent, repulsing. Intimacy with Feste was not paradox but contradiction. What preposterous jape had required this fake counting-house?

Too manneredly, Bayard enacted the kindly host. 'There's a quote I remember from Spinoza, not my usual reading for leisure, that whoever imagines he acts from his own free will is dreaming with his eyes open. This applies rather too pointedly to Uncle Roger, who's always had difficulty in recognizing himself as part of the human race, doesn't always recognize the race itself. But none of these fellows are as grand as they suppose. The men on the bridge, steering towards fair havens, giving commands, are yet actually on tides far from their own making and liable to upsets. This Russian shindy....'

Swept by his own tides, Graham was at once alongside Roger, dispatching rockets, loyally seeking life jackets and escape. 'You've known about all this, you've known for a long time. You've been waiting.'

The badly spaced eyes turned on him, expressionless as headlamps, in keeping not with bank or office, but with the precincts of a kerbside cashier serving only those who shy from regular channels. The voice had tipster's fluency. 'It's seldom a question of forgiving those who know not what they do, but of nudging those who know only too well. Actually, though, I had almost nothing to do with this Gale Force Eight, which may of course fall slowly into intermittent light drizzle. At most I checked a few notes, was neither the judge nor foreman of the jury. Only Honest Joe, the poor man's friend.'

'But in your hugger-mugger way you've always disliked

Roger, perhaps hated him. None of us know why. Still, I want whatever you know about this business. I got my own feet muddied there.'

'Even granted your own theatrical tastes, you couldn't have done very much.'

Exactly. Bayard's tiny, drooping smile knew all. 'It's all true, of course. Djilas, who by now has seen enough to make him change his tune, has declared that Tito, our vaunted ally, gratefully accepted our gift of thirty thousand repatriates, and shot the lot, without benefit of trial. We ignored the Geneva hand-out: that captives in battle should be accepted as legitimate prisoners of war, whatever their uniforms. Many whom we shoved back to Odessa were in no uniforms at all, some weren't even Soviet nationals. Ninety of their officers accepted in good faith an invitation to an imaginary conference and found themselves in horse-boxes, moving east. A girl in Suvorov's troupe had a Latvian passport. She pleaded that Latvia was an internationally acknowledged independent state, acknowledged by Lenin himself, though pouched by Stalin's lot. Nobody cared to listen. She was shipped off with all the others. Bang bang, dig dig. Including some fellow Balts and Poles whom the Reds hadn't yet demanded. Plenty of children. The psychical research technicians may have processed their comments.'

The bony nonentity funny man, so seldom funny, was turning terrible, bloodlessly, thinly inquisitorial in this barren room, his tone slouching, never quite monotonous, now quickened by puritan, unwelcome reminiscences. A rope trickster, following no rules, he had always been impossible to master.

'Children, we remember from the September Massacres, fight for life in ways that adults often do not. They dodge, they struggle, they beat against walls, without need to preserve dignity. They don't kneel, fold hands, bow heads, assume detached silence and refer to Montaigne or Oliver Wendell Holmes. So they get ripped from unusual angles, writhe in peculiar ways. Those photographs ... Korea, Vietnam ... tell the same story.'

A girl, freckled, red-haired, about nine, had chucked herself at the British bayonets. Another, younger, had smiled, unhesitatingly stretched out a hand as if for a toy. Her scream, years later, reached Carnival.

Bayard had resumed his dry granite poise, Keaton without style, the bank manager examining a client's importunity without favour or sympathy, his lack of interest studied to an exact degree. Suddenly it was the life outside that waxed mysterious, the young with stripy, flaked Red Indian heads, editors fanning hysteria, children's peculiar ways.

'How difficult it is', Bayard's cool flip made it easy, 'to talk of governments without sounding like Third World complaint or Deirdre of the Sorrows! Yet one has to go on.' He did so with muted yet evident pleasure. 'You yourself recall, after the Glencoe Massacre, when English and Scots hirelings were commanded to murder all MacDonalds under seventy, that the Scottish parliament ordained that, even if given direct orders, a soldier must not infringe the laws of nature. One can follow the drift, more closely than Roger, in his pleasant sanctuary in the Foreign Office, though, like the French, he's usually preferred logic to charity in matters of policy.'

'He should have sabotaged the orders? On his own?'

'Others did. George Patton, not the best of company, seldom permitted into the best company, let several thousand Russians escape. Sir Andrew Thorne, Alex of Tunis, turned blind eyes, ignored orders, from Whitehall, snubbed Stalin's menials. Ike, some politicos ... Acheson, Harrison ... forced the State Department's hand.' Hardness, even enmity touched Bayard's eye, as if childhood quarrels had been nourished, protected, for unnatural harvest. 'In general,' the spurt of feeling had flashed by so quickly that it left only doubt, 'civilians usually surpass the military in simple nastiness, simple brutality. Our own were like a fine lady of whom Talleyrand remarked – I can still hear that low, honey-spun voice – that she had all the virtues and only one defect. Being insufferable.'

Bayard valued the unexpected. At long last, after so many years, he laughed, a sound hitherto unimaginable, as if through closed lips, thin and sharp like wood splitting under a slow axe. Not loud, but, from the quiet, unmoving body, startling, as if Venus de Milo had belched.

'Whitehall, twelve lords aleaping, licked Stalin's boots and lost a few front teeth. Even before Yalta, the Foreign Secretary, quite illegally, allowed Stalin almost twenty thousand so-called Soviet citizens. If you mention Roger, he's always followed to the letter some medieval pope's directive, that cunning and deception are needful in politics, for, in certain circumstances, deceit is only prudent. He also remembers the old Czech saying, "One need only look into the windows of the Good God", which he seems to interpret as let others do the dirty work, then trust to luck. The luck seems running out. Faster than Concorde. We're dealing with men of principles, very bad ones.'

The stuffy place was dingier, with sensations of curtains closing. The grille, very possibly cardboard, was yet a reminder of prison examinations, glum secrets. A sort of two minutes' silence ensued, time dragging feet like an old lag or a defaulter; Bayard very upright, arms folded, no Gugnunc, not yet a warder, but a dead-pan surveyor, noting defective joints, skeins of dry rot, suspect plaster under fresh varnish, new paint. As if engrossed in the wall opposite he said that the present clamour would not affect the price of bread. 'For myself, to quote an old friend, I like to have about me such as sleep o' nights. Wouldn't you say that Janet found Roger rather too restless in the bed?'

3

'Graham, not for the first time, you merit the impertinence of my advising you to grow up and cease cultivating the looking-glass. Nothing is easier than thoroughly sincere passion. It can be menopause stuff.'

Through tall, ovalled windows, sunlight reduced the orderly room to a haphazard machine of blades, gleaming surfaces, sharp edges. A curved reading-lamp, gun-metal grey, seemed poised to strike, cabinets were miniature prisons, ball-points abnormally pointed, the wireless telephones worked as if by telekinesis. A Paolozzi maquette of roughed iron, a lump of bulging screws and painful angles, the face a knobbed, handless dial, formed a yellow, molten threat, balanced two new paintings: of a male surrealistically angular, open-mouthed in pain, trapped on a glinting, twisting fire-escape, and of sickly, towering colonnades with shadows of unseen people and animals thrusting between them on to wide, deserted steps.

'Roger, you never once considered...'

'I suffer from inability to make myself clear. Permit me to recapitulate. Since 1939, sixty million had become exiles, refugees, slave deportees. By 1945, under saturation bombing and broken frontiers, Europe was an inferno of smoking cities, footloose populations, a plaything for Himmler, the reincarnationist, fancying himself the German Fouché ruling with Allied support, the protector against Russia, and chiefly bothered by whether to greet Ike with handshake or bow! Goering, expecting to swagger into Allied HQ and be honoured as a fellow commander. A real world operating on false moves.'

Returning to London, systematically brisk, Kirkland had refused interviews, withheld statements, pushed through massed reporters with patrician calm, surrounded by his high-nosed young men. Crowds lingered, daubing insults, scrawling protests, waving placards. *Back to Odessa. Two Million Dead.* Twice, mounted police cleared the Square. Windows had been smashed, the front garden invaded, one thought of hill tribes descending to plunder a city gone soft, a place of badly locked coffers, vulnerable archives, awaiting the shots and tom-toms.

Within the house, the atmosphere was very deliberately normal, the talk leisurely, stylized though, in off-moments, the Guard seemed supers, on set but uncertain of production. Graham moved amongst them, undisputed but with little to do, seeking an interview with Roger who he sensed was avoiding it. When he secured it, it was with no violent, black-cap confrontation, but a courteous summons to produce an address book at his own convenience.

'Roger, I'd like to sort things out....'

Feeble, at odds with the rowdiness outside, the horses, the clubs, and he began again, too loud, in Viking greed for the spectacular instant, the knock-out. 'It sounds appalling, wicked. Why on earth...'

They were standing, the desk between them a loaded no-man's-land. In pale, finely creased suit, faintly dotted tie, Roger could have spent the week in some mandarin suite, some millionaire yacht on a blue, slack sea. His dark, cropped head glistened like the gadgets beneath it, the eyes, grey, filed, were forbearing, trained to prolonged sessions with those of small experience, trivial knowledge, insufficient willingness to learn.

'I scarcely claim infallibility, but do cool down, take that chair which, to do it justice, is no bed of nails and do me the favour of not offering me sackcloth but of exercising a modicum of common sense.'

Taking his own chair, carelessly crossing a leg, eyes unusually agile, he was the composed, omniscient housemaster, needing no cane, no appeal to higher authority, certain of quelling unruliness with a glance, certain too that the hot-eyed delinquent before him would, despite feelings foolishly, boyishly ruffled, accept the vaunted chair and obediently listen.

'Ah, that's better. To resume. In victory, Winston and FDR wanted a tripartite alliance with Russia. The business of Russian deserters and whatnot was very small beer. The press, of course, don't bother to mention that at Tehran, Eden, not my first choice for absolute perfection, did make a spirited, rather impressive plea for them but at once read danger signals in the Generalissimo, and desisted. After all, the SS had already shot 473,000 Russian prisoners of war. We thought, however crassly, that minor disputes should not endanger Russian goodwill. That we could not begin the peace by outraging the ally who had done so much to ensure it. What you all so ineptly overlook is that a quarter of a million Allied soldiers were then in Russian hands, rescued from German camps, a strong card in Stalin's hand, possibly a blackmailing one. It was more important to retrieve them than to coddle suspect Slavs.'

'But...'

'Hold on!' Roger's cocktail smile held all before it, his shrug was deprecatory. 'My own role had hitherto been confined almost exclusively to problems nearer home, if scarcely domestic. My history had rusted a bit, I'd forgotten that, west of Slav lands, the more strenuous the resistance to Russia, the more is achieved. But I did realize that we were facing not only triumphant Red legions but imminent European elections, calculated to produce a twelve million communist vote. Now I'm suffering self-righteous brickbats from many who have no right to be surprised or angry. Their accusation is perfectly straightforward and grotesquely wrong-headed. They clamour that, even before victory had been won, we should have risked Allied unity, on behalf of whom?'

'Thousands of men and women, whole families ... I saw them, ordinary people, half-starved, dazed, lost.'

'Far too ordinary. Displaced persons, plain traitors, derelicts tripped by misfortune, historical accident, bad bets, led by a few crackpot idealists, some hopeless muddlers, and some desperate crooks. Good God, we had eleven Balts in uniforms of Himmler's execution units. We understood, earlier, I think, than the Americans, that unpleasantness would be necessary. And recollect that in May '45 no one was certain that the Russian advance would halt, even when Berlin fell. We were beginning to fix gun emplacements, in case they failed to stop.'

'Meanwhile, there were damnable mistakes. Disgusting cruelties. Ordinary rankers faced with hangmen's choices.'

'Mistakes, no. Tactical errors, yes. In trusting Stalin and Molotov as far as we actually did. But it was a risk that had to be taken, we'd have been crucified by Labour and the Liberals if we had not. To have questioned Uncle Joe's good faith would have wrecked the coalition. I could tell you plenty of undercover activities deemed permissible or inevitable. We arrested a major in Political Intelligence, caught red-handed with Middle Eastern secrets he'd stolen for the British Communists. It was hushed up, and when I met him again he was doing very nicely in the Control Commission in Germany. Today you'd call it appeasement, but then it was diplomatic tact. As for the mistakes ... I myself was certainly not mistaken about Suvorov, any more than I was about that pernicious humbug Gandhi, who treated his own family with what one would call hypocritical cruelty. The truth, when I care to reveal it, will not enthrall our mindless fishers of men. I had two hours with General Suvorov, who expected to find tears in my eyes, and my humble self kneeling before him. I can see him now ...' – Roger unexpectedly swivelled in a half-circle – 'boarhound face and fangs, ragged hands generally adrift in stolen goods and ladies' bellies. He offered me Czech money, stolen by the sackful, swore he possessed a stupendous secret he could reveal only to HM. Suvorov, the fighting warrior, growling some drivel about Antichrist. Ah, yes!'

His smile switched from contempt for Suvorov to concern

for the wayward foster son before him, a need, even anxiety, to convince, together with ability to produce the unanswerable.

'I had no sympathy with him either as loser or champion, though I knew that Winston did. Suvorov was convinced that could he reach the PM, he'd be safe. Winston was troubled, in his romantic way, but fortunately was so busy with bigger affairs that we headed him off. Also he trusted Tito's advice. Eventually he left it to Eden, who concurred absolutely that so squalid a lecher wasn't worth the risk of endangering perhaps two generations of world peace. Stalin had scores to settle, and was determined to do so. Suvorov rode out of countless trashy novels, mostly written by ageing girls of both sexes. His own needs were for women, the occasional pretty-boy, drink, furs, jewels, hard cash and plenty of it, and the cards. He begged me to read selected, probably doctored passages from his memoirs – bits of astrology, special favours from Uranus – gambling, erroneously, on my ignorance of Russian. I saw plenty I wasn't intended to. The battles read well enough. When sober, he was a better commander than Budënny, more rousing than Voroshilov. A Prince Rupert without the intelligence and steadfastness. But a sot, scared of Stalin from the start. The thirties' break-up is obscure but he knew in 1943 that a single lapse would cost him his neck, and that too obvious success would also ruin him. So he arranged his own capture by fellow Slavs, after a secret deal with Erich von Manstein, and collected his motley division with no other thought than to prolong his own existence. But he could divulge nothing to warrant my recommendation for special consideration, and when he began threatening me, like a bear with a cardboard pistol, I called a halt. He would have to go. Tito wanted him for war crimes anyway. Even the SS had queried his gratuitous, unstrategic cruelties, not least against Polack Jews.'

'But all those others! The safe conducts, traps, deceptions. More or less decent men forced into crime. You saw nothing of it. Fucking hell, Roger, you can't lump it all together as small beer.'

'Remind me why I cannot.'

Roger was leaning forward in familiar consultant's pose, awaiting the brilliant refutation, the inspired evidence which he knew would not come. A vulgar hint of a sneer, hitherto unimaginable, lurked within his ease, his comfort. Irritated by the dainty tie, the luxury trimmings, Graham remembered

James II, marble faced and scornful, as Monmouth pleaded for life. He too was scornful, rough as Suvorov's pelt. 'Reasons of policy, blind obedience to orders! It stinks. Winston was claiming that the war was against just that. He could be a show-off, but he wasn't a methodical killer and moral street arab.'

Well-bred affront flitted across Roger's supple skin and lost itself farther off. 'Winston liked things in black and white. He would certainly have agreed with old Samuel Johnson that in political regulation the good can never be complete, it can only be predominate. The sentence, unfortunately for contemporary understanding, contains several words of more than one syllable. Johnson also said, "Grief has its time." Just so. That solves one problem.' A lawyer's creased smile admitted, though, that it might create another. Years back, Roger had read aloud from Boswell, by the study fire, giving breadth and majesty to life, though could an appeal to Johnson now hint at sudden unease?

There was no real sign of it. Roger was already sitting back, one hand open on the desk as if expecting an invisible flunkey to serve him whisky. 'Good heavens, outside these very windows, what do you see? Invincible ignorance, minuscule talents, tenderfoot brains, raging against Fascism which they can't even spell, let alone accurately define, simultaneously lamenting this ruffian in Fascist pay. Moral humbug and political imbecility. Trimmers all. Tinder for cant.'

Graham's silence was taken as an invitation to continue. Roger, saviour of society, silver-laced apostle of reason, honorary associate of Dr Johnson.

'Public opinion, such as it is, raises Cain at the behest of hired boobies, ranting on brimming bank balances, and foul-mouthed expatriates, the acne brigade – swiping at those of us who saved their hides twenty years ago. Look at them! Squealing, squelching lady mud-strippers from Brighton! That white bishop who keeps telling us he'd rejoice to import ten million blacks to enliven our weary old land, restock the genes bank. His black brother in God who informed me that, freed from white brutality, Africa would evince ability, honesty, unadulterated compassion hitherto unprecedented. That rich Socialist windbag who manages to utter "Comrades" with a straight face and whose resemblance to a sheep almost impounds copyright. The immaculate highbrows who once recommended us, from California, to discountenance Hitler's bombs by meditation and deep breathing. It's all like photographing ghosts. They hate the EEC as a source of wealth, and pray in curious dialects for Britain to wobble itself into becoming a potty little country, tongue out for international cheques, to be promptly given to gun-toting regimes in the Southern Hemisphere. A man adds up not to his waffle but to his achievements, and these gymnasts are less than memorable. Today they pelt me with incoherent rubbish, tomorrow they'll bawl hallelujahs to some anti-British fanatic, one more Suvorov who'll one day shoot them in the balls, assuming of course that they have any. The sort who revered that phoney ass Stroheim, fraudulent as his own *von*. In that demagogic prayer meeting in the House, the noisiest corresponded exactly to Tom Mosley's description of Baldwin, that every time he ran away he proved afresh the honesty of his convictions.'

Roger never needed new intakes of breath, the words rolled out on ball-bearings, he reached the tape without having to get there. His voice remained even, almost neutral, marshalling sentences into formations of rigorous correctitude, his hand refusing Graham permission to speak.

'What emerges is not the unreality of the mass mind but its preference for unreality. All that blather it inflicted on us about Swinging London! Yet what in God was it? Eleven streets, hideously amplified row from lunatic bards, some over-priced boutiques, night-haunts and drug-stands, considerable hearsay, some advertising gimmicks, and addicts of what is misleadingly called adult cinema.'

Withholding the knock-out in pleasure at prolonging the contest, he invited blows that fell short, scarcely needed parrying, and with feints playful yet fooling. That he had not named Bayard could be threat, magnanimity, or part of another shrug. Graham, obdurate, unconvinced, remained the novice, red-faced, top-heavy, tapped off course by the professional.

Roger Kirkland was patient. 'In your invaluable sojourn in these more or less salubrious quarters, you must have noticed one fact. The underlying problem is not wholly political, managerial, scientific, nor those of moral undertakers bleating for the ideal, with excruciating silliness, when they should be working honestly, just for something better, not filling us with the ritual screams of girls enjoying abduction on Chios. It's that we're breeding too many bodies for a world that can't use them. The bodies themselves know it, and are starting to turn ugly. Ugly to themselves, to each other, to us. Mongols! What you once dreamed of as Picts. And I myself have never denied that reverence for life includes reverence for my own life. I don't love my enemies, I'm inclined to respect strangers. Perhaps a better translation of a question-begging line.'

The opening, cheaply, disdainfully allowed, still begged a retort. 'You're side-stepping. The ugly have grubbed up ugliness, vilely kowtowing to Russian gangsters. The best of reasons bloody quickly show themselves the worst of reasons. Usually some smooth, grammatical stuff about the good of democracy and the lesser evil. A whacking great moral overdraft.'

But he heard himself bluster, had trembled in voice and nerve, with sandpaper prickling of skin, a creepy, crippling fear of breaking trust, a parricide, the crushing of an earlier, wonderful day.

Roger's second sigh suggested the first-class offered steerage fare. The sharp edges enclosing him were keener, aiming outwards: the anorexic writhed on his zigzag steel, the shadows jabbed brutally from the soundless columns. Roger's tone was bladed.

'One can say a good deal about rudeness, there's seldom much to say to it.' An older, alien voice, the Nuremberg intonation, mapping cruel possibilities. Gleaming on polished wood, a silver paper-knife could be envisaged slitting envelopes as if they were throats. The bleak tape-recorder, square and squat, a mouth with a hideously trim mouthline, might secrete abject confessions and pleas.

'There's always a tendency, fashionable amongst professional non-combatants, to ridicule self-defence. You yourself enjoy a scrap, would be perfectly at ease in the seamier parts of Cambodia or the Congo, but you toss out rather too glibly undefined notions of justice, fair play, and all else which is so admirable a part of your make-up and which you've been given a position to afford. But, when the dust lays, where do we find you? Preaching with the bread-loving multitude against easy targets, those guys who keep the wheels turning and the locks oiled, hoisting any available charlatan into some god betrayed by the smug intolerable, and lavishly dying for universal salvation. Just so. You've convinced yourself that the badly made is preferable to the well-made, that muddle is better than solutions.'

'Solutions!' He recovered, saw straighter, Roger's dry face, caustic eyes and lip, bones hard beneath fine pallor, hair like the judge's black cap. 'The worst word you could have chosen. God, Roger, a great, fucking blunder! Final Solutions!'

Agitated, accusing, in coarse pullover and corduroys like a navvy strayed amongst the Guards chatting without in club-land uniforms, tapping papers with slow, manicured fingers, he had urchin need to hurl ink over that parlour suit, Turnbull tie, that fibreglass immunity. But the more vehemently he spoke, the less he was heard. He was too much himself. With the grand volley within reach he could falter: an easy overhead smash could bang the ball out of court. Raw, Viking strength gave its usual gibber and fell away, needing Bayard's charmless impassivity. Softened, outraged by loves, his will was an empty holster when the saloon turns nasty. He groped inexpertly as the grey eyes slightly enlarged, considering him in mature affection grievously tried.

'Graham.' He was indeed Uncle Roger, Janet's Lancelot, Dragon House seneschal, at the candle-lit table proposing expeditions, or handling notebooks and telephones while the children read, explored maps, exchanged delights. Yet, throughout, the face had been Venetian, in quiet powers exercised without appeal and reaching into the deadly. So interrupt, shove rudely through the persuasive and diplomatic, keep in the bitter ring.

'Janet and Della will stand by you, Roger, through hell and high water, and a long way beyond, and I dare say you'll count on me in a crisis. But not Bayard. You've always admired him, looked first for his applause. But you're not going to get it. To him you're unforgivable, and I'm beginning to see why you always have been.'

Self-fouled, sinking after a last, breathless, jiving flurry, he awaited the stinging riposte, the flailing hand, the count. They did not come. Incredulous, he could see the Venetian diplomat's glance slipping, a spirit, hitherto royal warranted, striving against cold, seeking escape from features abruptly pinched, already too small, the eyes bruised from a desperate blow landed without proper aim. Goggling at his own fortune, the clown fells the giant, a horse-shoe unwittingly stored in his glove.

Shrinking further, Kirkland was unboned, holding the desk for support, only externals left secure, the dark hair, pale lapels, but with sunlight now seeking lines and torments of a stricken face, the eyes half-closed. All crumpled, very quiet, the shock of inaudible reversals.

The desk hardware glittered, ruthlessly extinguishing its master, and Graham found himself already departing, pushing through the inquisitive into violet, heated afternoon, seeking a cool layby.

An oath was cracked, no matter by whom. He would not return. The city itself was treacherous; canals were too dark, too deep, bridges deceived as they did in Della's poems. Soon he would weep, not for private loss – he might have gained – but for that sight of Roger, unimagined, unimaginable, hunched without warning in agony.

Later, alone in a pub, hoping for a girl, preferring the whisky, he wondered whether Roger had a future. Extraordinary question, yet which demanded an answer. Momentarily the pub receded, he was in a cinema, with the sounds wavering, the actors starting to blur, the screen blotched by technical disease, crazy fragments, chips of disorder, before burnings uncurl from one corner and claps jeer from the dark.

4

Defections Start. Kirkland's Trusty Quits. A Friendship Shattered. The brightly tabbed trusty lost temper with reporters, refused a press conference, berated Della for her letter accusing him of disloyalty. Let her learn to wash nappies, teach her son the

ABC, meddle only with literature and produce some herself. From Janet nothing, itself a declaration of grief. She must have suffered during vilification and threats, as the dark prince of Suvorovgrad stalked through human rights in boots of intricate design, with spurs of sharpness above average. Simultaneously, he was Uncle Roger, all pomp lost, flattened in dust like an Achille, Janet kneeling beside him, Niobe all tears.

Actually, Roger Kirkland issued an uncompromising account of Suvorov, referred to small, overlooked strictures by major historians unanswerably supporting his case, then, without publicity, left for New York, not by Concorde but on a sumptuous Italian liner, one of the last of the breed, to complete some microtechnological project known by arcane capital letters. Mr Fixer, the inquests declared, who had fixed too much. An ego spun so keenly that it threw out images of power giddy, perhaps illusionary, inviting retribution though, Graham thought sourly, the sight of Roger breaking at touch, like a meringue, was no longer believable.

He would wait before relenting, allowing himself to talk reasonably to Della and detail her errors. Janet, very probably, was ordering new outfits and packing her bags.

Without pennants or outriders, Graham drove into the country, his vows swinging between the fiery and sullen, biting his nails, disinclined to shave, opting for no future and very little past. Expectations, the fresh blues of a missal, had bluffed him into no more than tutoring Roger's self-esteem. Others had ridden to Samarkand, planted flags on the moon, invented a country, scribbled doggerels that enchanted the millions, produced world-splitting pamphlets, but he himself might at best have kept wicket with average success for Cumberland 2nd XI during a dank summer.

No more ante-rooms, smiles ample and famous, no more booming welcomes and murmured requests. His last London encounter, perhaps the very last, was with Bertie Clavering, rubicund with low-cost good cheer, as the Gridiron ticker-tape spelled out Roger's departure.

'His ability to think ahead, make the right moves, is little short of uncanny. But I fear me I'm wrong. It *is* uncanny. In America, not exactly a council flat bathroom, he will have space to rethink his objectives, establish new bases, redirect his forces. Mind you, Graham, dear lad, it's been a most useful fuss about very little. Politics, of course, fattens on short memories.'

The matter lingered for a few weeks; Kirkland's communiqué now attracted him to sections of the Stalinist Left as if he were qualified to govern Albania. Then, as if at backroom signals, he fell from news, replaced by Middle East massacre, beauty competition misbehaviour, Test Match ill-feeling, his name liable to become musty as Saxe-Coburg-Gotha.

No so General Alexis Suvorov. He sprang up live and tormented, at nod from a new witness, Miss Nowhere, who gatecrashed the court, demurely requesting attention. In Della's *The Hunt*, quasi-narrative poem, thirty-five pages cheaply published by a private press, Suvorov was unmistakable though unnamed, very oblique, in scores of insets, continually recycled, protean, both hunter and hunted, dying on the rope, last seen transformed to a vandalized tree. The poem eschewed chronology and historical fact, was a scatter of contrasts, now violent, now reflective, dominated by avatars barbaric, reckless, on the move at whatever cost, betrayed, victorious, sole survivor, a threat to the order of desk and paper; with manic savagery, extravagant largesse, a gambler's joking despair, comet brilliance.

An early *TLS* review hoisted the book like a TM levitationist. MacEntee & Holbrook reissued it with D'Aubeny illustrations and design, and it sold lavishly, particularly amongst those who seldom read verse, buying it only for plain girls at Christmas. A feminist group made Della Woman of the Year. Briskly, critics revoked former verdicts. 'She has rescued her craft from cliques and restored it to society.... Distillation of Time and events, etherialization of chance and fate.... Explores metaphysics less of barbarity than of barbarism, echoing the minstrelsy of the chain-gang, the death-house, the war-cry of the steppes, with an unflinching gaze at man in nature, an appraisal, unstated but clear as a monastic bell, of a noted historical figure, archetypal, menacingly indistinct, as if bowed under rain: grandiose, ruthless, Graves-like in purposeful independence, yet withal pitiful.... The perennial glamour of bandit and brigand ... hypnotic short-cuts into distant horizons, attempts to ride clear of the earth ... Audenesque concern for small fêtes of existence ... prophetic, bardic, each phrase a small voyage of discovery....'

Pocketing the book, Graham wandered roads bluish after storm, tramped winding hills and muddy riversides, pausing at the furrow clean in damp brown earth, glad of the woodman's track, the publican's greeting; reading, brooding, seeking patterns amongst 'Suvorov's' flamboyant excursions. He was excited, perplexed, occasionally astonished. Some titbits emerged from long ago: the executioner on duty, in dinner-jacket and white gloves, wartime partisans bound face to face in evil marriage and left staked in tidal marsh, the black and white Templar banner honking in the wind over a blanched field. In Della's pages, old friends appeared in new guises. He could probably see himself in the toping porter assiduously opening doors at the wrong time, and blindly selling the general his own hat. Bryce filtered through, spectral and deformed, from a burnt village, where Janet, as a shepherdess, had walked through autumn hues. A secret agent with eyes centuries' old in tired suspicion, expert skater, morose skier, intensified his solitude into vengeful art. An hotel manager avoided sunlight, like a troll. A brief-case, unfinished cigar, glasses like circles of black paste, lay on darkly stained concrete. 'The uneasy grin of bearers of ill news.' Shots rang through jubilant carnival, the pied pipers, capering antics, absurd doctors. A telephone rang, rang, no one willing to answer, though locked in the wire was an appeal to be allowed to pay. A French boy, dandelion in mouth, hung crucified on a high, lustred Christmas tree. Della's cherished stage props were unmistakable, a chorus to her life. The naked boy holding a fish, the one-eyed poacher in broad hat, the self-satisfied unicorn, the grinning satyr with ridged, lolling cock. Then more from himself. A raving Duke of Burgundy galloping into a church asmoke with corpses, Danton, exhausted, reflecting on woods and fields, Ludendorff, vain, ambitious, superstitious, at last learning to fear mud. Such passages became the child Della and he might once have had.

Tents darkened against bloodshot sundown, lances scraped the sky, masks hung like severed heads: balloon in hand a child fleeing tusk-helmed pursuers was stranded in a river choked with plastic rubbish. A description of an aftermath of defeat must derive from the terror of pigs in a slaughterhouse which, Billy Fisher claimed, causes chemical change, protecting the carcase from infections damaging to pork lovers.

Many incidents, profiles, details, evoked with the clarity of moonlight, related to rooms and vistas, incomplete, glimpsed through arches. And throughout the rider sped, dreadnought, under mauled skies, through angry gales, through plague, falling cities, starvation valley where Asiatics had mouths but no faces, through death-camps over 'tinned children', towards a barren shore where Mycenaean Apollo, Light of the World, surrendered to the crudely carved Scythian Great Goddess, clotted with blood. Saddle-bags thick with jewels, the rider lusted, terrorized, fought, yet, taunted by omens, was at the mercy of astrologers and buffoons. His father had strengthened a bridge with blood of a stabbed girl, he himself, defying life as angrily as he did death, ever victorious, ever defeated, flouting laws and frontiers, had once thought people were jars and shrunk from spirits six inches above the floor. He died in the starry hat of a carnival king, pelted by those who would never forget him.

Della's fly-over technique compressed eras to moments, Rome to mayfly afternoon: buds formed, burst, blossomed, very slowly, while centuries collapsed. 'Suicide of a Hotel Lift'. Despite global village and space-age clobber, people still nourished the wilful, the passionate: lakes froze, leaves browned, animals struggled for secret life. Suvorov was free, he was darkly fettered, one of the defeated generals, whom Roger had once declared, people loved. Or another Antonio, left howling when all others left for the moon.

5

'Didn't Ryle believe it, in his earlier days?'
'Far too often.'
'But Freud himself thought...'
'When did he not?'
'Also Wittgenstein.'
'More fool he.'

The Pratt-Durlingham Award dinner, for *The Hunt*, buzzed, fizzed, lit by chandeliers, sparkling firmaments erroneously associated with mid-eighteenth century Heinrich Wilhelm Stiegel. Walls shimmered with thick, crimson mock-damask. In the chair was Doctor of Literature, the Noble Lord, Lord Clavering. Radiating from high table, guests duelled between flowers, electric candles, bowls of massed fruit.

'The dear girl's going up in the world. She's fluked a very nice little prize.'

'Nice enough, considering the talent in question.'

'Amendment. Very questionable. Talent, mind, can be little more than a flair for timing. Like patriotism. Well, we'll wait and see, probably not for very long.'

In a silver gown of Janet's, seated between Bertie and a junior minister, Della was laughing, strewn with chips of excitement, radiant compliments, but aware of the watchful juries looming through crimson haze, grimacing as if flyblown. Amongst the serried faces was Ingrid's, wan as damp linen, streaked with hippie loathing, for the Booker Prize exhibits, Sunday paper darlings, the aces of *Vogue* and colour supplements, art gallery frillies, lords and ladies of paperback trillions. Old Rick would have grabbed all drink within range but remained loudly undeceived. If she had drunk less, she would have been wary of Rick's ghost hovering within the unforgiving instant.

Each success, a poem, a love, was temptation to believe that oracles were unambiguous, escapes were guaranteed, beauty never seen spitting. A story began while the minister joked and Bertie shuffled his notes. Listen. Look. A sad man in a train sees a woman naked in a cottage. Next time, he sees her again, leaves at the next station, tramps fields by a lisping river. She opens the door, still naked, young, one hand flat and useless. 'I'm from the train.' But she shakes her head. 'You're not expected. Others have come. They are always sad.'

Voices were shrilling like Hungarian violins, from Olives and Verities long out of the race. Their embraces had the subfusc quality of usurers' pleasure, a War Office's regret at atrocious casualties. Meretricious as a Christmas tree in a Chinese tea-house. Names plugged into celebrity, personalities with high running costs, had swarmed to honour her, but the real great were elsewhere, solitary at work, imbibing the vast night, leaving her to parasites whose visions had lost heartbeat, dwindled to jottings, false starts, flirtations with words. Versailles courtiers, scents and paint covering stink, ruined mouths bespeaking worse. *The Hunt* would give them no kiss of life. Muriel, screeching fire-engine; Stefan unpublished for years, once an Allweather recruit, now stranded between rebuffs he so deservedly earned; Myra, much divorced, shaped and sounding like a double-bass, boss of a marriage guidance clinic; Edie, waspish with bangles, needing fame and children, but resigned to cats; Basil, declaiming that he put himself only in the second rank along with Updike, Bellow, White, Lessing, but that he could at least have taught Virginia Woolf a thing or two. Screened by ferns, Martin Montag, chat-show automaton, stardom gone, tommy-gun, maps, swagger-stick laid aside, was swaying and laughing in red shantung shirt, frizzy collar, buttons like black florins. They would wear nakedness like a shroud, always sad. Lewis, nature columnist, listening to no one, was writing on his menu card, 'As I tramp these Wiltshire downs perceiving the kestrels....'

Bertie was leaning towards her, very earnest, ancient eyes screwed up as if over a map, heads and shoulders were a vague drizzle, waiters moved forward with coffee, with brandy, the noise a rising, tuneless scherzo, or a quilt of sound continuously held up, let fall. On their way out, her thoughts caught at those who were not here. Janet had not been reached, Bayard had accepted but had not come, Graham had not replied. What Janet called his natural manners were too often no manners at all, displayed like a chef's hat amongst toppers. He was staging new acts, Graham the angry Grand Master, Graham the Renouncer, in keeping with the unchanging boy whom Janet had thought red-headed and who had once eaten a pencil.

Not defiantly but as a matter of course she had insisted on an invitation to Roger, not knowing he had departed without farewells, for the first time failing her. But he would return, bringing her the red, red rose, once more driving her to suppers, theatres, walks in small, closed parks. He was no robber baron skewered by peasants, he was Merlin enamoured by magic occasionally faulty. They said he had made a pact with the Devil, but who did not? The Devil himself was God's need for dissonance, to break monotony of purity and success.

Bayard's sardonic catalogues of human failings misunderstood love and predicaments, cut people like cakes, equal shares of the uneatable for those he did not like.

She quickly began talking, her drift to Roger would have read like an obituary. After Bertie's speech, she must utter the few gracious words from the throne. She grinned into herself. Should she tell them that, by treating Suvorov like Achille, Roger had offered her the chance of a masterpiece and should now at last be applauded with all generosity possible? It would not tinkle the chandeliers and split the ceiling, and anyway poems were not delivered ready-made in caskets. *Suvorov*. A moment, a word, casually falling into her in childhood, becoming wedged, building up a little dream, a little pain, stories, living in dark humous, growing, finally blundering into light, hung with underground spoils. Ingrid would understand, not always caring to do so, though she was capable of love.

People were clapping, the little minister refilled her glass, smiled, perhaps wondering who she was, and Bertie Clavering rose, head like a peach-stone, eyes in fissured skin just alive. Jokes and laughter subsided, the waiters stood to attention, bottles still raised, all was like a fate-tale transformation, the palace arrested for a year and a day.

This might be insufficient. Bertie was slow as a tap dripping at regular intervals.

'I am no deep thinker....' The gentle pressure on the words implied membership of an exclusive club. 'But I appreciate excellence. A moonshot, a Mr Kennedy, a book. It is said that English has lost grammarye. It is not for me to pronounce, but I must declare that I see no such loss in the work for which we are now gathered together in delight. I am proud to say that I knew the author as a small, wide-eyed child, watching us, believe it or not, as though we were all mad. Now, to cut a long story short....'

He did not do so, he would go on and on, with anecdotes and comparisons, deft allusions and methodically constructed jokes, listeners restless, praying for exhaustion, explosion, or acute loss of memory, until the waiters, not contracted for overtime, would induce measured, finalizing applause, leaving space, barely sufficient, for Della, dark, silver, illuminated, still seeing tableaux of Kirklands and three children, and envisaging Graham writing an obituary of his best friend with so much confidence and pride that he could not throttle eagerness to see it in print.

BOOK FIVE

*

We are often told that the present is an age of cynicism and despair, of crumbling values and the dissolution of the fixed standards and landmarks of Western civilization. But this is neither true nor even plausible. So far from showing the loose texture of a collapsing order, the world is today stiff with rigid rules and codes and ardent, irrational religions. So far from evincing the toleration which springs from cynical disregard of the ancient sanctions, it treats heterodoxy as the supreme danger.

Isaiah Berlin

I was asked how I would react if I were handed a gun and President Amin were sitting opposite me. The only reply I could give was that I would hand the gun to the President and say, 'I think this is your weapon. It is not mine. My weapon is love.'

Bishop Festa Kivemgeri

I happen to believe that the long and glorious Christian tradition of speaking about the immortality of the soul is only a period in the Judaeo-Christian tradition, and that period may now be coming to an end ... the whole world which comes to us through the Bible, the Old Testament and New, is not interested in the immortality of the soul ... it is very clear that Abraham, Isaac and Jacob ... believing that the only immortality ... is in the germ plasm, or, as they called it 'the loins'....

'The dust returns to the earth, whence it came, and the spirit returns to God who gave it.' Here the spirit is not the individual's little identity, but the life-giving power of God, the *ruach*, the wind which is withdrawn and so man disintegrates into dust ... the New Testament speaks constantly about resurrection, as against immortality ... the question is not: What is going to happen to little me? Am I to survive with my own identity or not? The question is whether God's justice will win out ... how God can win ... does crime pay? Will evil win? ... Will God ultimately come through somehow....? The Lord's Prayer does not have a single word about little me.

Revd Dr Krister Stendahl

1

'Graham, you live in a picture postcard.' Mr Backwater.

The cottage, beamed, tough and damp, was a legacy from Sheila, spinster of some distant parish. Lady Clavering then bequeathed him furniture, embarrassing in ugly bulk. He gave it to some earthquake relief committee which sold it for fifty thousand pounds. The widower and his messmates uttered reproaches.

Here, no laser spliced the sky, warning away Martians. Allotments were unprotected by radar. The cottage, far from Picts and dragons, was in a loosely wooded Hertfordshire valley above a stream that in summer periodically vanished. One expected Samanthas and Jamies with Frisbees, transistors, cassettes, chatter about workshops, macrobiotics, but also with rag dolls and hobby-horses. Touching a Roman road, the village was rated in Domesday with a forest for fifty pigs, a weir yielding forty eels. It still had them, a pale green region, where prayers had volleyed to St Uncumber who gutted unwanted husbands; once bruised by rebels and mercenaries and, in Civil War, stiffly Puritan, its tombstones still advertising Mr Lamentation Lamprey, Mr Humiliation Scratcher, Mr Mephisbosheth Caudle, Mrs Tabitha Renunciation Graft. Structuring a landscape apt to become flaccid, pylons stalked between old market towns with post-war coating of standardized high streets: sizzling take-aways, transient, wispy boutiques, shining marts of computer and hi-fi, raw brick pubs pulsing with juke-box classics, draped with paper roses, plastic harvest dollies, phoney horse-brasses.

Sunlight was smoothing the lawn after dew. The day would glitter, repelling the body's slow warnings and pert complaints, the sudden aches, angry starts of pain, breathlessness, the relapse into the hard, dry and cracked, like stale boot polish, also the hovering melancholy like that following the dismantling of festival decorations. Graham's face lowered over the mail was chipped and stained under his streaked grey hair.

The postman's knock invigorated, letters always came, welcome as spring. Invitations to dinner, tennis, proposals to visit, requests to become patron, vice-president, hon. sec. Letters from the renegade docker who had stolen, wept, stolen again, and now promised to return soon. Notes from the vicar, to Graham as churchwarden, wanting half a jiffy to discuss, evade, lament. Youngish, energetic, the vicar, unusual amongst his craft, had theological inclinations. 'I say, your friend Dr Emery does us proud.'

Gusty championship of Emery's claim that the resurrection symbolized psychic change, the gasp of illumination, alarmed congregations. Jesus, he continued, purposefully indifferent, would neither commend nor denounce bombs and wars. The Kingdom was all. Whoever has faith in Me has passed from death to life. A man, Thomas More said, may lose his head and come to no harm.

In *The Hunt*, God had been a hard core of brilliance, a fierce kink in a circle of light, but usually mistaken for a head-hunting, gun-toting corps commander. Conceivably, one contained some apprehension of divinity, barely developed, with unsteady powers, liable to fail, occasionally felt, like the quiver of trees on a still day. With no word for God in their language, the Basques endowed marvellous possibilities.

As governors of a church school, the two men had tussled against a vehement majority over the vacant headship. One candidate, ultimately winning, was Marxist, gifted teacher, loved by children, humorous. The other was a solemn lay preacher, purified in CND, with two posts lost by his classroom futility, the children pelting him with torn-up books.

'Brother Graham,' old friends chuckled, repeating Della's complaint that he had lost his fun. Here, all called him Graham, enjoying the blue-eyed jogger, one for the fast lane, the free-loading bachelor, demanding untrustworthy respect, carrying an air of defiance like a castle heavily defended in a landscape peaceful for generations. That he possessed no TV was perplexing, perhaps snobbish, perhaps immature. His townee friends could be top-grade, more often they were outcasts. He carried unexplained clout. His nails were often bitten, his temper flammable. He gathered hearsay like dust: he had known the hangman, had absconded in Dublin with the takings of a theatrical troupe, had been court-martialled for assault, drink, gambling debts. His sexual habits doubled the servant problem, Mrs Elmes said; Dora Development, he called her, reaching almost from wall to wall, wide as a goal. 'All honour to him,' her husband said.

At cricket, despite age, he remained the hitter with bragging swipes, low scores, and spectacular risks when least needed.

'Graham, you're a trouble-maker,' the Colonel was envious, 'but we need you at our little gatherings. We lock up our daughters, of course.' But his standard bark disparaged his own daughter, her bedroom eyes and defensive hands.

Trees were glassy, sunlit. He must tackle grass, hedge, a broken tile, but with ear cocked for news beyond honeysuckled wall and roseate borders. Agitation seethed against a proposed airport, atomic dangers, the sale of a church to Muslims, badger-baiting sadists from Stevenage and Ware, communard happy-baggers professing organic life style, graduates of oil-crisis living, stealing vegetables, driving stolen cars not by maps but by the sun, squatting in weekenders' pads. 'Man, you should try the glue, it makes you touch bits of the night.' He had joined the vain fight to retain a popular but privately maintained cottage hospital.

Full employment was finished. New crafts, new play must follow. A carpentry club had failed, a self-publishing unit might succeed. Bob and Mary had vanished overnight, replaced by Ugandan Asians. Dissent was blaring against a newcomer who refused to mow or weed, so as to help butterflies, birds, wild flowers, menaced by pesticides in the sedate, treasured plots around him. His stormy acreage blotched the village neatness but attracted Graham, whose own gardening had deserved reputation for knockabout, misdirected energy. His ditches, deepened for frogs, seldom bore water, the frogs shrugged and departed. Birds ignored his offerings, his box hedges refused to grow, a projected maze remained ankle-high, seeds too often remained inert, herbaceous set-pieces seldom performed, his prunings were too slapdash, the roses lolling, drowsy, top-heavy.

He remained undeterred, absorbed. Roger Kirkland had

owned marvellously finished woods, fields, gardens, but had scarcely noticed them.

'Always out of step, our Graham,' the Colonel grumbled contentedly. 'When the dear old fellow thinks he's punishing himself, he's only annoying the rest of us.' His wife sighed, she remembered days of the Great House, where servants warmed the newspapers before breakfast.

The morning climbed. He cut and sawed and dug, then, bored, dropped the trowel where he would be least likely to find it, went indoors to read, prepare a lunch he might not eat, fix a cup of Dandelion Coffee Compound. Frequently, the telephone rang, but this morning he did not answer, dropping the drawbridge, in control of events.

Imagination still drifted south and east, to sapphire waters, sack-coloured hills, broken columns: to dome and pinnacle, to junk, China Seas ... Silk Road, Bukhara, Lands of the Golden Horde. But few masts had survived chopping, he had sailed no great distance, met no star-crossed collision, no Grail had split the soul. He had filled no bellies in Campuchia, had pulled up no sinking boat people. Spirit could tumble like the hopes that had soared with the fall of Berlin, with the UN, with the British flags one by one thrown from Africa. Perhaps he had lingered too long in this valley, easy to overlook, though with humane reminders, like Norway. He might have to settle for the Kingdom where first was last, riches were dust, and all was demanded.

Meanwhile, Isolde had not trodden the threshold. Insufficiently priapic with a Della, immoderate with a Countess behind the Hedge, side-stepping the left-overs nudged towards him by seasoned, lean-to mommas, bored by the virginal, he roamed for the love he would not whole-heartedly welcome.

Bayard, to whom countryside was an irritating gap between towns of unsurpassed excellence – Hull, Watford, Birmingham – never came, but ex-pupils were returning: bald teachers, service officers, resting actresses, nurses, spreading out their lives like cards from a fairish hand. Strangers still accosted him, vaguely familiar, not always credible, with queer tales, suspect secrets, more often with nothing very much and usually reluctant to depart.

Ancient pools, timbers, airs, induced curious stirrings. An electricity inspector knocked on a door, heard bolts, rattles, a key, but doors remained closed, and neighbours breaking in found the place empty.

Late afternoon he enjoyed, drinking amongst surviving flowers, watching bright flying tips circle a butterfly tree, sunlight passing from roof to roof between leaves, a long flurry of tiny speckled clouds like a paper-chase. Yesterday he had seen a childhood name amongst the Deaths: Rosamund Lloyd, who had read Blake, the poet, not the admiral, to hollyhocks, till they surged above the wall. The father, Bayard said, hoovered the lawn when royalty was around.

At the garden table he made notes for his WEA current affairs lecture, where unemployed youth, glad to gibe at war dead and revere gossip columnists, parasites of the commonweal, sat with those who had learnt to be afraid of mud and, with heads bowed over vile wounds, had heard Herbert Henry Asquith declare with barman joviality that the Great War had cleansed and purged the world. An American computer, of course, had now proved that the Great War never happened.

Current affairs. Nothing wholly died, all remained more or less current. Pictish wildness persisted beneath Rome and Saxondom, reluctantly surrendering to London – to bandits in court dress, dry parchments, to wealth encased in nine hundred and ninety year leases – but never quite perishing. Today tribes once more shaved heads and arms, detached from imperial England with its flags, battlefields, prefects, and its superb achievement of legal, indeed paid opposition, which Roger in his hauteur deplored, and Bayard indicted for employing Bertie Clavering.

Nothing was inevitable, texts deceived, more torture existed today than yesterday, advance could be flight, the tribes might again shrink, baffled by another Rome, with government departments, nuclear bases, civil defence fortresses, police barracks all fiefed to war-lords of invincible technology and drumhead powers of search, arrest, punishment, and the issue of internal passports, while specialized interests sealed off coalfaces and the nation was lit by the flares of dying oilfields.

After the lecture – Iran, President Carter's worries, Ireland, Gulf dilemmas – he joined most of his audience in the shadowy beer garden under wreaths and fringes of elms lofty but threatened. He drank too fast, argued too strenuously, opposing the baker's faith in unilateral nuclear disarmament, which the

Russian leader was calling unadulterated madness. He was happy, resting mug in hand, dated as a coracle, almost geriatric, amongst friends of proved, though not unlimited, trustworthiness. Sometimes, at the owl's hoot, arguments paused, giving the bird its due. Tall shades floated above, quiet as hang-gliders.

A gruff voice spoke over his shoulder before its owner refilled his mug. 'Mr Graham, you're brave when you tell me that a bull has five legs, you've got tall words, but clever talk can be thick as soap at the end of Monday's wash.'

On summer nights, never quite sober, he perforce totted up reminders of a past now liable to mistranslation. Bayard, getting no laughs when he claimed that Kathleen Long was short, Miss Jessie Matthews warbling about the light of the silv'ry moon.

2

Papers had been kept: memoranda, conference records, witness from newspapers, autographed confidential letters, covert appeals. After leaving Montpelier Square, shaking off those whom within seconds he was cursing for befouling even more regularly than Lady Clavering's cavalier dogs, Graham found that his flat had been ransacked, all papers stolen.

Furious outrage unexpectedly cooled into relief. Like the dictator gloating above burnt books, ravaged libraries, he envisaged a new start, unencumbered by lumber and the dead. He was free of Roger, who had always been both player and referee. The clubs, the polished surfaces gleaming with Lafite and Latour, with notebooks and ball-points, were corrals for time-servers and go-getters in a rigged contest. Faces slipped into the tusked, the snouted, fanged, scouring and tearing softened lives.

One must always move on, like a city collecting at crossroads or river mouth, ascending with possession of spurious relics, grandiloquent legends, inserts of marvellous gods, declining with shifts of trade, new horizons, but perhaps with possibilities of revival. The magnetic pull of the Dragon House itself must weaken: old homes were everywhere academies for shop stewards, topless barmaids, abortionists, nostalgia lost as a hurdy-gurdy or Mr Blow-me-Tight's swanee whistle.

Roger remained in America, cultivating the Mammon of Unrighteousness. In Britain he was a statue, some faded industrialist or regicide, a Mosley of tarnished brilliance enveloped in thickening dust. He had resigned from no club, occasionally recorded for international media, had twice successfully sued for libel.

Back in London, Janet spoke of him as she had always done: the City occasionally rumoured his impending return, planning a coup: North Sea oil, solar panels.

General Suvorov, a footnote, was buried beneath new arraignments, triumphs, mysteries. His name had failed to join those which, in stark shorthand, reddened the glow of an incredible planet. Certainties, majority verdicts, cracked as those who accused or defended him, got entangled in perjury, illegal bank transactions, the murder of an informer. Graham, in country exile, sometimes pondering the accuracy of his own memories, saw little more than shapes falling as if over tripwires in a western. History was at the beck and call of failing intelligence, rumour, fraud, partisans. The Holocaust itself had been queried, impugned as invention of Jewish editors, Leftish conspiracy.

The Hunt must rely on its own merits, without support from Suvorov. Though the affair might have slightly stunted a few reputations, minutely warped the long, patched British chronicle, educationalists were now debating the value of history itself, some demanding the obliteration of trashy pasts, the lighting out for fresh territory.

But no. We may forget the past, the past does not forget us. In his garden, hidden by albertine and delphinium, Graham swivelled for sight of the world, telling himself a fate-tale. Once upon a time, long ago, in sunny Rome, a vain people had been chilled by a new and ominous sound: Emperor Aurelian's builders erecting a defensive wall round the city which for centuries had never imagined needing it. Now, on wide rainbow patios, in high-rise palaces, almost beyond card-vote acclaim and stadium frenzy, sophisticates must crave such a wall, strong against tumult and encirclement, fuse lines of a time-bomb planted years before, by a phalanx not yet numbered.

History had pulled rank, closed doors, debarring him from the party, beleaguering him in agony of peace. Beyond hedge and church tower was ghoulish comedy, haggard carnival frolic, a floundering from underworlds to the moon. 'I am not mad, Sir Topas: I say to you, this house is dark.' Wind-up strangers, abbots of unreason, moved in and out of fables, following the white, cynical stag of enchantment.

Whatever had breathed life into dust might have started something too big for it, leaving the hurly-burly to grotesque establishments. Prague had invented a machine for detecting homosexuals. Cities with fallen centres paid builders not to work. Dark with Hanoverian vengefulness, two thousand strikers out-Heroded Herod, valiantly grappling with a single scab. In a nearby church a joker, Bayard perhaps in his clerical outfit, had preached in favour of Zeus, and no one noticed. KGB buskers spent millions on astrological research, the US Navy placed dolphins on its payroll, the Shah fled, his resplendent army unused. A Vietnam draft dodger had faced the court successively in Red Indian body paint, Santa Claus robes, Vietcong flag, brandishing a toy pistol at the indifferent judge. A composer copyrighted four minutes, twenty-three seconds, of utter silence. At a Bologna art exhibition a goat was disembowelled to electronic music. Comedians tortured goldfish, and jeered at audiences as Cruise-missile sheep. Quiet as surfers, police patrolled school corridors. Quietly, acid rain drenched great forests, condemning them all. Data banks of a giant computer were reported wrecked by a mental process which softened metal. A cheerful lyricist sung a long, slippery night at Chappaquiddick, despite a rhyming difficulty. Interviewed by the Saratoga League, now unquestioned, famous authors boasted that they had secured parole for a bank-robbing murderer in tribute to the literary power of his letters. Released, he stabbed to death a waiter who had asked him not to use the staff toilets. 'You can see the spot. It's a target between the second and third button.' The foremost writer explained that culture was worth a modicum of risk: he was prepared to gamble with certain social elements, to foster talent. Later, the victim was himself revealed as a writer.

It's foolish, jabbered the song of yester-year, but it's fun. He had missed the party, was sheltered from all but the patter of news, heard through the thirties' radio set, its frontage cut like a fretwork sunset.

3

Latterly, Della had apparently written little more than tart reviews of those younger than herself. *The Hunt* had pulled in money, a niche in an Honours List, but seemed to have flashed from a sky now emptied. Greying, her gamin charm was discontented, a little dusty. She was usually seen with that sly elf, Ingrid, composer, whose music sounded like the slow stacking of plates of unequal weight. From her tired face sometimes stared the child on a birthday of disappointments.

A day might come when, at a Kirkland memorial service, an elderly woman would join him, not immediately recognizable as Ms Della, old comrade-in-arms. Graham wondered about her dreams. He knew from Janet that she wrote often to Roger: about scandal, money, grievance, or the silent purr of falling leaves? It might never be known.

To reach her now, Graham needed the visits from Andrew. He had her young eyes, soft, light, captious, her slightly pouting lips, slender neck. It's such a little neck, Anne Boleyn had whispered, on a grim morning, in some film, then screeched with laughter. So had the audience. It was as though she had surrendered him her beauty to avoid anything further. On his holidays from ill-chosen boarding-schools, she gladly exhibited him at publishers' receptions, riverside parties, private views, ignoring his boredom, but then dispatched him to Janet or himself. Andrew spoke little of her, or of anything. He was unaccountably jealous, quarrelsome, sulky, lacking Della's quick moods and mischief. One could envisage him stealing, though he probably had not yet done so. Yet in Hertfordshire he had started to thaw, to enjoy training for books, games, the countryside.

Look. Look.

White sapling, Grecian runner. One could imagine holding him very close, sharing a couch, a goblet, in sardonic consummation of old, confused imaginings of Della.

'Darling, it's bad news.'

Absent for so long, her voice over the wire was hard, angry, beneath agitation. Her tears had often been weapons.

'It's Bayard. He's dead.'

With small scores to settle, life had revoked its pledge of immortality and exacted a disproportionate penalty. One joker less paced the carnival. Over an empty coffee-cup and untouched sandwiches, Bayard had been alone in a late-night café asprawl with taxi-drivers, theatre couples, drifters. Two stocking-masked hoods had glided in, at knife-point demanding rings, watches, credit cards, money. Bayard alone refused, rather sadly opening one hand, closing it, then, with his usual teaspoonful of smile, returning to his sandwiches. Dying silently, almost instantaneously, he had been wearing no watch, his wallet contained only a pound note and a newspaper clipping, his pockets some obsolete sixpences. Those many centuries of his extinguished in a trice.

'When I told Professor Antrim, he only said, "I always thought he greatly admired me." About *Bayard*!'

The Times' gaunt obituary, giving no dates or birthplace, mentioned that, if scarcely prominent, he had been considerable, a contributor to information agencies, notably the Saratoga League, itself of marked international standing. He had owed much to the guidance and assistance of Sir Roger Kirkland.

On a warm afternoon, at the scattering of ashes at the Maurice Carpenter Memorial Garden, Bayard's claims, Della observed, came home to roost. The lawn was crowded. A few personal friends – two poker champions, a Beethoven specialist, a rock singer, some unknowns and, amongst them, timid yet resolute, a pale girl on crutches – were outnumbered by others who filled a *Times* column inches longer than the obituary. Seen in deep focus were sober, formal delegates from youth clubs, galleries, an orchestra, from associations for prison reform, civil liberties, rights of international political detainees: from embassies and goodwill committees, from Baltic governments-in-exile. Amongst them were jeans, leather jackets, wooden beads, cheap bracelets belonging to young blacks, whites, browns: boys coiffered in dyed fluffs or thick bushes, girls with huge eyes, parched faces, shredded bodies, drawn here by who knows what feelings, memories of curious confidences. Bayard, Della had said, would never have backed the Holy Innocents with hard cash, but these were assured, firmly conversing with chieftains and chamberlains: log-cabin democracy, they were grave, interested, friendly.

One senses, Graham said, his arm in Janet's, several Bayards, each with his followers. She watched them with reserved affection.

They heard no ninety hours of Haydn, no music whatsoever, not even the Joe Loss Band, no address. He was leaving as anonymously as he had come, and, as swallows fled through rings of light, the ashes were scattered – one of them, in Bayard trickery, casual benediction, alighting on a white, feathered hat. In short silence, all stood, bowed, separate as towers, then again were strolling, talking, in pairings unlikely but pleased.

Stories, seldom authenticated, were repeated, embellished, invented, playthings of the overheard and misheard, of air and sunlight, of Bayard himself. Once again, the tale of Bayard and the putty-faced Soviet official arguing about a toboggan, Bayard in dog-collar marrying Swedish couples, Bayard at a picnic, mistaken for a chauffeur, requested to withdraw and dine behind the cars, pleasantly complying, taking with him two of the best wines, before being hailed and embraced by the Indian High Commissioner. Reports of him arranging succour for Jewish children, Arab children, lecturing a British royal on the five unexpected virtues of Romanian republicanism, and addressing an English Nazi as Rabbi, then, concerned, offering a thermometer. Bayard, pleading for Frisbees at the Olympics.

Graham felt Della's hand slip into his, quiet as a mouse. He still saw Bayard as Feste, insolent as a dictator and as vulnerable, dependent on others' applause and whims, his laughter only will without gaiety. Making an art of loitering, he was solitary on crowded pavements, at parties; however quick his jokes and repartee, he rejected the Antonios who needed his love. Bayard, excessively public, abnormally private, the skater cutting brilliant corners, squaring circles. And the mutely complaining schoolboy in uniform of not quite regulation cut, murmuring 'Ikk Ikk Pa Boo' as if slipping Suvorov the password.

He had gone. Roger was far distant. Not so Lord Clavering, now kissing Della, kissing Janet, very bent, over an ivory stick, yet perhaps likely to outlive them. Last year, he had buried the two fellows.

'Bertie, who's the chap in uniform?'

The rheumy eyes blinked in surprise, the eyebrows lifted rather testily. 'Air Vice Marshal Hugo, of course. Sir Roderick Hugo. Where would the Battle of Britain have been without him?'

Della and Graham afterwards sat with Janet, at home with the dragon vases, the parchment screen painted by herself, the porcelain hen in which Bayard had once disclosed she kept babies, the floating hues of kingfisher and acanthus, the portrait of Roger presiding with the pliant, composed humour of total authority.

Janet, compact, secure, had been silent. When at last she spoke, she was unusually dispassionate, surprising them by beginning not with Bayard but Roger himself, quietly, as though from the dull silver frame he might be listening, while preparing an illustrious day of return, slaying any available suitors.

'Roger would have felt more deeply than any of us. He could, you know. There was once a picnic, on the shore. He risked his life in a dangerous current for a child's toy. I found it hard to forgive, and the boy took it as a matter of course. Strangely, he was later drowned, when Ida and Douglas sent him to Montreal to escape the bombs.'

She had a subdued insistence, though smiling as if grateful for their presence. At her next words, Della glanced involuntarily at the empty hen. 'That we could never have children hurt him. Often it brought us closer.' She looked up, not defensively but with touch of radiance beneath clear skin, brown trim eyes. 'We have truer understanding than most. Now more than ever before.'

Della, slightly puffy, hair tired, her beige trouser-suit too youthful, looked slightly impatiently at Graham, as if already knowing that Janet's next words would take him unawares. His perceptions had never been delicate.

'Roger needed women. To overcome what I could never quite realize, and what he found impossible to reveal. So we shared it without naming it. There was a girl from his Oxford days. She died two years ago, not very happily. He knew her before me. She worked for a decorator. Later she was quite famous, with her own design business. He was very frank about her. They met, not often, until he went away. It seemed strange. She had so much that he hates – incessant talk – yet he could never quite let her go, always returning in relief, a sense of escape.'

At last she hesitated, picking at her cuff. 'I was less generous than perhaps I should have been, but I just refused to marry him while she remained. When the baby came she very gladly surrendered him to us. Her own idea. I never met her, probably I should have done, though I might then have understood less. Towards the end, she did write me one letter, rather bravely, asking me not to reply. She didn't mention the child.'

'Bayard!'

Graham's astonishment fetched further scorn from Della. Anyone, Bayard would have said, of course realized that.

Unsensationally, without sentimentality, sanctified possessions stationed around her, in quiet evening, Janet was changing into an old woman, her long velvets hanging too loose, her face faintly lined, hands slightly shaking as though rings had become painful. But her voice was steady, even decided.

'Bayard and Roger did care for each other, Roger too possessively, though he tried to hide it. But there was a clash of beings. Roger, in this alone, was ordinary, sometimes less than ordinary. He wanted more from him, more even than what you both gave him so lovingly. For such a man, it was very weak, diminishing, and very mistaken. Gaps opened between them. Very long, very cold. Yet, years later, Bayard came to him, in that odd way of his, sincere though it was, I think affectionate.

Roger could not see the affection, only the dissent, the rebellion. Bayard advised him, he begged him to publish that interview with General Suvorov, before the papers got hold of it. He had not procured the story for the League, he couldn't stop it, he believed it should be known, but insisted that Roger be given his chance.'

She gave herself time to consider proper words. Clocks, birds, even leaves, were closer, the flowers glowed on parchment.

'Roger was offended. No, he was furious. He refused to discuss it, he wouldn't listen even to me. He was', her smile was sad, 'what I can only call a chump. Bayard too, you might find it difficult to credit, could be angry, hurt, behind his Chinese manner. He disliked himself, he disliked his own face. I think he wanted to be beautiful, to convince people that he was. There were those, we saw some of them this afternoon, whom he did, but could never have believed it. His feelings were buttoned so tight that he really only enjoyed people he didn't much like or had never met. He idolized Mr Wallenberg, never stopped trying to find out more about him, and help. Years before, he dreaded returning to school, we hated sending him. He envied you both, my darlings, for being so admired and popular. People always forgave you both, however you behaved. So he courted aloofness. Some thought him unpleasant, even not quite right-headed. He encouraged this, calling himself a kind of politburo. Roger would call it negative irony. But I believe it was ... manly.' Her little gesture was apologetic.

Della's face was hidden, shaded by plants.

'Bayard knew about his parents?'

'We never told him, Graham, but yes, he knew, with resentment – even, I think, fear. He never once spoke to his mother, but in that queer knowledge of children realized her existence. But he said nothing. Yet to me he would talk, I promise you that. He revealed things. In Warsaw he visited the Jewish Museum. The curator asked his opinion of some paintings. You know he knew something about art. They were of tanks, petrol bombs, he thought them terrible and was about to say so when he realized what they were. They had been done by fighters in the Ghetto, as records. Some by those with hardly an hour to live. There was so much else.'

But she restrained herself, as if rebuking a tendency to ramble, lose self-possession. She had spoken hurriedly, even awkwardly, but now resumed her normal calm, in place, even enthroned, beneath dense, winking lustres. 'During the war, Roger, without telling him, got him into Intelligence. He was sent to Alexandria, and stayed on afterwards. He liked Egyptians when not very many did.'

Afterwards, seeking coherence, Graham's feelings wavered like a faulty compass. He wanted to go back with Della and swap loose ends but, on the pavement, she hailed a taxi and, as he moved to accompany her, she gently restrained him, lifted her face for a kiss, her eyes dry but lifeless, then silently she hurried off.

4

In country fastness the internee is warned by Rick Allweather who had read with delight a book he no longer realized he himself had written and which should now be addressed as Text. Later, someone, Della perhaps, had published a story of an artist, once important, so entertaining a young couple with memories of John, Wyndham Lewis, Epstein, that they invited him to their seaside cottage. Transported, his stories palled, he stayed too long and, sousing him with brandy, they walked him, befuddled and toppling, through sea mist to the cliff-edge where mist was densest, leaving him facing the sea three feet from death.

Graham watched the young, defiantly awaiting their yawns. The Allweather story recalled a caliph, lord of lords, thrown beneath resplendent carpets and kicked to death.

Summer sauntered towards autumn, sending him headlong into a plan to forest five acres of scrub, attracting stupendous wild life, providing panoramas of green growth, russet bloom, and his own luxuriant pride of possession. Often remembering

Bayard, he missed him no more than he did Sheila. Explanations had stripped him of last tags of strangeness. His death had not impaired the Saratoga League, itself now reproached, before his imprisonment, by a French ex-minister for remorselessly, wilfully purveying stale news. A number of his fellows were also fearing exposure of collaboration with invaders, forty years back. Obscure witnesses were emerging, protected by the League's unexplained wealth with words very quiet, still timid, but fateful as the single hair dropped by a murderer. Staid papers continued to quote pamphlets stamped with the Crystal Knot. Catholic monsignors, still living, had ordered extermination of Orthodox Serbs. US Intelligence had co-opted Gestapo criminals in France, Germany, Austria, now, ageing but assiduous, organizing Latin-American cocaine traffic, private armies, and murder squads for export. Evidence was printed, of terrorism in Belfast, West Berlin, Rome, joining hands with brothers in Damascus, Beirut, Israel. The League was currently accusing the Argentinian Naval School of Mechanics of being a concentration camp using systematic torture.

History, Bayard had insisted in his tepid way, can hinge on some nonentity, passed without a glance yet who inexorably emerges at the exact moment, with a muttered proposal that topples the uniformed colossus so easily that posterity remains perplexed by the tardiness.

Heavily embossed, assured as carillon, the gilt-bordered card invited him to the London wedding of Roger and Janet. He told himself not to go. Anger can be sustained only by the obsessive, but Kirkland's handshake would resemble too closely a squeeze from Richard Nixon: to meet his eye would require glasses as thick as M. Achille's. Feelings for Roger immaculate, Roger full of grace, do not melt into slap-happy commonplaces, a Kirkland is god or nothing. Touched by aura, one can implore forgiveness for what has not been committed.

Nevertheless, on the wedding day, he was amongst a heavy, restless crowd, its mood like the flashy gyrations of a fruit machine, throwing masks, oranges, whorls of colour against a dark screen, outside the Grecian-style Westminster church, the afternoon rainy, as if smudged by charcoal, the dome damply hazed, the pillars glistening from lights within.

Expectancy was sharp, like the effect of a snake's imprint on sand, faces tensed, some surely master-minded by trained zealots and hired by the hour. Some had candid, youthful fervour, others, Bayard's killers perhaps, amongst them, had curdled from resentment, failure, fanaticism. Many were familiar: polytechnic student leaders, Black Power organizers, Christian software, Oxbridge theorists: spies and beatniks, picket-line bruisers, skinheads: caps and hoods, badges, posters waving a tumultuous *anti*, against Stalinism, racism, élitism, and ALL OTHERS. Pigtails, manes, clumps of hair tangled in wind and shaking as if something rustled inside. Here was stuff of riot, arson, the landlord screaming in his burning pub, shields clanging, the horses. On all sides, Suvorov's task force, spreading like frayed carpet with the pile worn off. Police were ranked, still informally, like extras, beneath the high church steps, keeping the road free for opulent cars and dignified arrivals.

Graham stood tall, silent, hands deep in his coat, flanked by a reefer in soiled windjammer and a bright-eyed, red-scarfed girl, a Friend of Nature, angered by blood sports, smoking, meat-eating, fishing, doubtless outraged by rudeness to a walnut. They ignored him. He was glad, he was aggrieved, but was soon intent on the guests now gathering thickly, shaking hands before moving up, meticulous in blacks and whites, an Aurelian brigade, Della and Andrew among them, ascending leisurely, imperturbably pausing to talk, disregarding the rain, the sodden, bitter crowd with its whistles and cries, its flanks now pressing against the police. A walkie-talkie blathered hoarsely, then cut off.

Stepping from a Rolls, on Lord Clavering's arm, several friends escorting her, Janet posed quietly for photographers, provoking no uproar. Her long brown coat carried no fur to anger the red-scarfed girl, and in low-brimmed hat she was not immediately recognizable, though, on the last step, with courtesy, not bravado, she sent down a smile, a brief, unfinished wave. She was forgotten as, almost at once, alone, on foot, as if from nowhere, Roger arrived, surrounded by several police whom he appeared not to notice. He carried his tall hat as if to allow no mistake of identity.

At a distance, in bad light, the head, carriage, step were unchanged, those of an obdurate pretender, making bid for a throne on terms unchanged for generations, and, careless of marksmen, coldly respecting strangers. Not for him the cloth cap, jeans torn at the knee, brass earrings of mock-Aztec design.

After momentary stillness, boos, catcalls, began, then, grinding on the wind, a vast lynching chant, 'Get him!' Several men and women darted forward led by a youth, coned, tawny head like a torch, the police swinging in long, single formation in front of the cars, linking arms, showing no weapon. The attackers paused, hesitated, stepped back, inciting a pounding 'Out, Out, Out .... Smash the Fuzz!', familiar throughout British streets.

Almost at the doors, Roger paused, looked down, a connoisseur savouring the enmity, Della's Burgundian Duke about to be spliced by rebel pikes and left naked on the ice though, for a blood sacrifice he looked decidedly spruce, with the blandness, usually insolent, not of a duke but of a Treasury witness.

Graham noticed, disgustedly, the hysteria of the anti-blood sports faction. The girl's screams seemed blown through her thick hair.

The police were holding firm, the swaying uproar sunk into a low rumble of disappointment during which a large, pink Best Man, one of the Old Guard, stepped out, greeted Roger with hands raised high, and they stepped together into the hushed church. After brief uncertainty, the crowd remained, the police slackened, chatting amongst themselves, several accepting cigarettes from the mass before them, though the atmosphere at best was that of truce.

Graham too remained, though the rain was faster, colder. Was this marriage one more of Roger's cards, finely timed, the coup, or his declaration of love?

Within minutes, beneath the low dirge of some action song, farther off, the tidal menace was regathering, in harsh groundswell. He saw no knife, stone, catapult, but large bags, clenched hands, bulging pockets, still foretold battle, indignant, full-fronted, until, in abrupt tableau, lit from the church now radiant, Roger and Janet Kirkland were poised hand in hand in the porch, from which a spurt of confetti danced crazily about them in winterset comedy.

Elbowing forward, Graham saw that both were frail, papery: seen closer, Roger seemed the weaker, his earlier manifestation surely from prodigious effort of will. Stooping a little, he was grey, his face sallow, the upper half lighter, the eyes still as wood. 'His eye do show his days are almost done.' Not quite that, but mouth and skin had slackened, the smile rough edged, as if left unfinished by a bored jobman. Thin rather than slim, he looked smaller, stripped of robes too ornate or cumbersome, a decayed ballet-star. The eye moved to Janet, the first to stir, in the huge, almost total silence, guiding him into the rain.

The rush of hunting calls and obscenities, as they began descent, unleased the militia, which, in irregular battalions, surged forward in vindictive gala, one hand aloft with a bottle, another with apples, again halted by the metallic band of police who themselves appeared larger, the nonchalant, expensive rampart of cars flamboyantly challenging. Undeterred by callous struggle and fury, quite alone, the Kirklands continued, very slowly, calmly, still holding hands, watched in freeze-frame above by the sedate Bourbons, and, from below, by those waiting within the punch-up.

Four ... three ... two ... one ... zero. As bodies twisted and yelled around him, Graham was instinctively braced for the rescue, the leap from the scrum, billed like any Beast from Castle Della, but, at the first bulky elemental quiver, he was intercepted not by nuclear missile but by the harlequin who roams above crowds.

The Kirklands had almost reached their car, the first rioters were grappling with police amid a clash of glass, a hoarse, daft voice sung out above fists and passions, 'Hey lady ... your bike's ready', and, following, a bulging African face, eyes and teeth sparkling, grinned mightily above the storm, flickered, then evaporated. But his outburst had stunned the warriors around him, rowdy laughter split the attack and, while others still struggled and shouted, the Kirklands were driving off, Roger at the wheel. As the car left the police cordons, he slightly increased speed. In slow, precarious suction the crowd parted, despite a woman's voice yelling for assault and, as the car turned the corner, allowed it a few cheers, reluctant, sardonic but not unfriendly, then dissolving into ragtime cheerfulness, carelessly deserting the angry, the dedicated, the vengeful. The demonstration languished, flapped a little at the centre, drooped, died.

Robbed of personal display, Graham was moved, was puzzled. What had really occurred? Pity for a couple of unexpected insignificance, sympathy for a true love somewhat desiccated, grudging respect for survivors? As the mobsters drifted away, the leaders doubtless with protests against cowardice, treachery, deception, he imagined some earlier melodrama when the messenger gallops to the scaffold waving the royal reprieve, leaving the huge, raucous concourse divided between decent pleasure at mercy and voyeur's disappointment.

The road was almost deserted, a few lingerers looked dishevelled, lost in quickening sleet. He remained, staring at the church, the last handshakes, the chauffeurs opening doors with fluent gestures perfected from old times, old privilege: still the musketeer in a time that had forgotten muskets.

The wedding reception would now be alight, held not in some service flat or hamburger joint with gratuities at customers' discretion. Miserable, petulant, self-satisfied, he yearned to be there, knowing that he was behaving badly to Janet. His refusal was wry tribute to what had been lost. Fucking obstinacy, Della would say, if she said anything, though, grabbing champagne, sweeping canapés into her bag, she might be young again, electronic, cruising, displaying Andrew, infuriating him with introductions to the famous, recovering voice in a world that she had once ridiculed as fit for Cleggs and Claverings.

Roger and Janet were now licensed to attend State functions together. Always the last to learn, Graham realized what Bayard had known instantly on the children's day before the war, why Roger had so grandly boycotted poor David's crowning. Roger would have enjoyed ruling Britain without the British, particularly the late arrivals, one of which had, a few minutes before, saved at least his bacon.

Graham suddenly grinned. Even he could anticipate old Bertie's speech. 'The very best that could have happened . . .', words he had mouthed so regularly through uneasy decades, and now, running not out of words but of life, the silly old chap was right. Walking through broken-backed afternoon towards his own car, learning to depart, he might at last be acquiring irony, though now only imagining his trees soaring like space-rangers.

There might occur a *son et lumière* which, spreading like bindweed, would present a dragon-born Black Knight, triumphing through excess of duty, and, in the nature of fate-tales, extending to some distant atoll – romance, the by-blow of distance – where devotees would build a temple of untidy proportions and unusual flourishes, gaped at by tourists, and by the lucky, spending their prize-money for, in a TV intellectual contest, giving the name of the composer of Grieg's piano concerto, and offering discreet salt to Roger Optimus Maximus.

5

'Where would you like to go, darling?'
'I don't mind.'
'But you usually know somewhere you'd enjoy.'
'There's the sea.'
Andrew was reluctant, greeny eyes under the black fringe dissatisfied. With the restaurant? With her?
Small Cypriot waiters crossed and recrossed in black diagonals under the high, pink ceiling. Their table had been laid for three and he watched the empty place as if in hope of relief. He had been embarrassed by young Hectors outside who had regarded her new furs darkly, ready to kill for compassion.
'Anyway, what will you start with? There's grapefruit, you like that. Soup, but it looks dreary. Avocado.'
'Whatever you like. Soup, perhaps.'
Reflected in mirrors, travestied on bottles, his triangular face, slightly too pale, had the distrustful remoteness which children with a future so often had, and which Miss Needham, ARA, must have seen on her.
She smiled, he nodded, cautiously polite, as if his own smile, should he allow her one, might fall on to the plate.

Several other parents, firm couples, or pretending to be, were lunching around them with neat boys, all anxious not to recognize each other though chattering eagerly, chirpily, boasting about games. The masters, apparently, were of low type.

She signalled for the wine she had already ordered. 'I thought you'd like to bring a friend, darling.'

He was silent. Had he no friends, or did he object to her being so at odds with these others, plain, tweedy, predictable? He scooped up the dim, packet soup with a relish he could scarcely feel. Perhaps, like the married, he stored lists of unkindness, unfairness, blindness, ready to produce them like some wily salesman, his thumb in a catalogue coloured too luridly.

Ray said . . . but she'd better not mention crew-cut, hustling Ray, sixties man. These dinky waiters were God's gift to Fascism.

'Would you like lemonade, darling?'

'I'd like some Coke. If it's not too much trouble.' Bolting a scrap of fish he remained defensive, choosing the cheapest dishes, in some internal tactic, unless he had acquired from Janet some scepticism useful in pretentious places. Did management here really believe that its *boudin de volaille* was much more than sausage suffocated by flour and water or that *tournedos poêle helde* had ever seen the north?

Pincushiony ladies would be scrutinizing her furs, calculating the value of her jewels, foraging for cosmetic secrets, murmuring questions to their spotty kids. By night they would swap spite with these florid, fattish men now recalling practical jokes and sporting feats. 'You won't believe this, Di, but old Rex and me. . . .'

It was pre-war talk of Mr Blow-me-Tight and Billy Fisher: their studies, where no one studied, would smell rankly of joggers. No fin in a waste of waters for Di and old Rex.

'Mummy, could we. . . .' The excited voice under the pillar emphasized Andrew's silence, then swerved back to jokes about masters. Most did seem both shabby hirelings – had Mr Cousins only one coat? – and petty kings. An appalling Mr Mackie had once appeared just before dinner with Ingrid, whom he regarded as though she wanted to steal his hat, and told some absurd story about Andrew possessing advanced musical gifts, so he should at once start on the viola. Andrew, who sulked whenever she put on a cassette, and said that Mr Mackie was not really a master and anyway had left at half-term.

'Darling, do sit up straight. You look like an old man.'

'Sorry.'

A single word could reproach, insult, suggest a hiding-place. He was more a Bayard, inscrutable, than a Graham. Earlier, he had muttered something about that awful adventure playground used only by Irish and West Indians – once, rather charmingly, he had asked whether all blacks were born at night – where the little brutes had tried to cadge from Ray a penny for the Guy, and when he gave them just that they hurled mud at him. Why should Andrew want to go there? He was showing signs in common with student activists who condemned fun as bourgeois deviation.

Refusing the salad, sensibly enough, he was eating apple tart, taking most of the cream, showing himself human, like the boring boys around them, so cheerfully munching. She smiled, but he was already looking, with impatience concealed too politely, at the window beyond which, beyond villas dully pastel, loomed the sea, where, of all places, he wanted to go. In November! Even the cinema, more or less derelict, would be better, but the school forbade it and, more important, the provincial circuits were interested only in cretins.

'Are you sure, darling,' she was absurdly nervous, as if before opening a newspaper wrapped around a review of her book, 'that you really want to go to the beach? It won't be comfortable.'

But the green-blue eyes at once rebuked her, through flat lack of expression.

The coffee had been drained from the nearest marsh, the waiters bowed them away, with elaborate insolence. Service charge was included but they still hovered for a solid tip. She ignored them. Too many today were frightened of menials, the traffic wardens, wine waiters, officials, who themselves yearned to howl out their throats for an iron master.

Autumn lay banked down by low, grey clouds, the wind was chilly, traffic leaving the sea road as people made for heated rooms while she must risk cold pebbles stretching towards cliffs already shapeless in weakening light. The beach desolate, the sea empty. Her spirit groaned. She could have been with Ingrid at Tangier, with the Kirklands in Cairo, or alone at some rich warm port with white terraces, red flowers, in Graham-like delight watching boats return as the first drinks flashed and plans were made for the evening. From this distance, their holiday together was green and innocent, a ball of pleasure tossed gently between them against distant revelry of carnival.

Andrew, walking beside her, was detached, he never took her arm, so seldom spoke. She had begun the day light with promises, hopes of finding him eager, affectionate – dazzling – but on meeting they were both unchanged. She was free only like the sharp kite flapping through skies but on an unbreakable string.

'Shall we walk faster, darling?'

She must keep warm. There were no shelters. At once, as though released, he moved ahead, down the steps to the shingle. His face would be stubborn, tight, still averted when she rejoined him, the silence a weapon barely sheathed until, indistinct in the wind, he at last spoke. 'I want the sand.'

The raw glass and steel of new hotels had receded into mist, here all was muted save for rapid water tongues, bright as they attacked the shore from huge, slowly thickening dimness. Despite grind of pebbles, the gulls' cries, frets of wind, she suddenly remembered London, and Dr Hassall's Psychic Parlour, the failed and unwanted awaiting him in trust, in fear, still lives breathing feebly from their own canvases.

The long, low rattle lay under the wind, sea perpetually clearing its throat. Soiled gulls swept monotonously over waves not steep but inexorably advancing, falling with bleak intensity on the narrow sand where Andrew now stood, looking outwards like Graham's beloved Ralegh, before, stooping for a wedge of driftwood, he began stirring the sand.

She was ignored, helpless, out of place and, turning, with some difficulty in high, thin shoes, reached a breakwater slimed green, crusted with tiny shells, there to huddle against wind. Over the invisible island, the sky suddenly gleamed, the last fragments of golden plates behind fast clouds. How smooth the phrases still ran, how seldom could much be extracted from them!

There had been a story about a magic fish, did he remember? He had long ceased demanding stories, her reading bored him as much as her cassettes, her friends, her love. An offer to help him with his sand project he would find as disagreeable as a croak from a rose. Small in the cold desert, he was kneeling, absorbed, digging pools, conduits, erecting dams. She was glad they were alone as she crouched, absurdly, against wind and tide, in Marcello furs, with Groz-Lepans jewels and bag. Nevertheless, she was not yet bored. The gulls, the blind, powerful sea, stirred cupfuls of memory, of self. The clues she had found throughout life, scattered by ironic magicians, often, like treasure, turned nasty. Dr Ramirez would remind her that magicians were within herself and she usually, very slightly, misread their signs, misheard their texts.

Unexpectedly, a jet sped by, low, its pale streamers becoming capes, bergs, islets, before being crushed by grey clouds.

Andrew had not looked up. One day, with this methodical, purposeful skill, he would arrange her funeral, glad to see her go, discontented to discover how many of her liquid assets belonged to Janet. Meanwhile, he had thoughts only for sand, building defences, against school, against her, against the adult life he had seen and must soon enter, where experts are always wrong, critics analysed words they cannot love, columnists leap to excuse the inexcusable, teachers are afraid to teach, and where terrorists have inalienable rights. Stefan ... Stephen had said that even that unlovely rogue Churchill had some rights of contempt.

The wind pierced. Shivering, she was trapped on the edge of the world under rotting wood on a day sprung untimely from blighted seeds. She must, as Mr Blow-me-Tight would say, pull herself together.

'Oh, laughter stemmed from the knowledge that the gods are not divine.' Tribute to Broch, she contrived, not laughter but a smile, recalling her belief in the son who dazzles.

'Andrew?' But the scathing wind blew her voice away, and at once she feared to disturb him, so supreme in his midget empery.

If this sea were to vanish, at archangel's command, or by Roger experimenting with gadgets, if it were pulled up and folded away, would he turn aside, interested, more or less, in the exposed detritus: barnacled tea-clippers, swollen fishermen, piles of surprised fish, treasure, perhaps those Jews whom Graham remembered, expelled by the Lord Edward and dumped on a sandbank by a cruel captain who bade them get succour from Moses?

The task of life, Wordsworth said, is to remember. She thought of words vanishing with their landscapes: barton, purl, dell, tussock, rill ... tryst, cohue ... then wondered what, massy as sand grains, lay behind Andrew's eyes so much her own. He had been taught that she was a widow, a word suspect in youthful imagination: asking nothing about his father he must have his own convictions, doubtless cynical. Already he must have accumulated something of the body's alarms, surges, ambushes – Maria and Estella pale and shy on the bed, Ray ordering them to love – realizing life's discrepancies. God from whom all blessings flow, they still sang, but within these were the mouthless beggar capering outside Santa Maria della Salute, his pain wheezing from a black-red hole in the throat, and Lisa, with her goodness to him and fine brain agonized by tumour, her hands uncontrollable, with fearful life of their own.

Feeling tears whipped from her by the wind, she wanted to call again 'Andrew', but flinched. Now, however, she was proud of him. Lordly in his own territory, he was making a world, it could be immeasurable. Solitary, unloving, he was armed for the century ahead. Already receiving punishment, he knew, justifiably, how to inflict it. Children cherished privacy, persistence, resilience, the glittering fruits upheld in fate-tales. He might easily outpace her, or end in a few years, ravaged by drugs into sobbing imbecility, driven to the railway track, the roof, the black tarn.

The waves were higher, faster, as horizons closed like pincers. Far out, spray jittered. Andrew's puny citadels were doomed, but he laboured on, fleeing the sickening lunch, wary lest she kiss him goodbye but primed for grievance if she did not.

Bugger Andrew! Could she be back in London early, Ray had promised ... though the promises of those younger than she were untrustworthy responses to prayer.

A gull hung, quite close, beaked and unpleasant. She put out her tongue, bugger you too, tightened her furs, scowled. Not yet the Old Hag of the Woods, she had place to quicken. *Moments* had shortened, they were fewer, but new starts still occurred, hiding-places, observation posts. She was freer than Graham who had wanted to reinvigorate the Empire and ride aloft, and, befuddled in pastoral beatitudes, was heading for firesides and dogs. She still sharpened herself. Speak of us, everything said, the clouds and pebbles, hotel faces, the spaces behind the air, tell our stories. *The Hunt* had drifted into her through innumerable clues, random or planted, and lately, dimly discernible, thin grey sketches on mist, like the dream that, on waking, leaves only a few ragged edges, was a skein of words within which glimmered a pattern, conceivably of Bayard, a Bayard who, in the muffled, interlocked scheme of existence, dangerous but thrilling, had received the blow intended for Graham and herself in French mountains.

All their stories – Bayard's, Janet's – could be written differently, from stances as yet unconsidered.

Beginnings. Buds half-opened, shining: words, images swelling, bursting into coherence, before, in print, losing lustre, eliminated like this sand swamped by waves, but instantly recovering.

'Andrew ... Andrew, it's time to go.'

He rose very obediently, as if having rehearsed it, then waited, slender, wind-ruffled, and, yes, rather beautiful.

'I'm sorry, darling....' Her compunction was real, lit by his walls and towers, already sodden. 'After all your hard work.'

'It's OK. I'll build another soon.' He looked past her, then stared, as if at last recognizing her and about to raise the cap as schoolboys would once have done, before he added, 'After you've gone. Graham will help.'